heartbroken

lisa unger

heartbroken

a novel

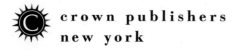
crown publishers
new york

Copyright © 2012 by Lisa Unger

All rights reserved. Published in the United States by Crown Publishers, an imprint of the Crown Publishing Group, a division of Random House, Inc., New York.
www.crownpublishing.com

CROWN and the Crown colophon are registered trademarks of Random House, Inc.

Library of Congress Cataloging-in-Publication Data
Unger, Lisa, 1970–
    Heartbroken : a novel / Lisa Unger. —1st ed.
        p. cm.
    1. Women—New York (State)—Adirondack Mountains Region—Fiction. I. Title.
    PS3621.N486H43 2012
    813'.6—dc23   2011050497

ISBN 978-0-307-46520-7
eISBN 978-0-307-46522-1

Printed in the United States of America

Jacket design: Nupoor Gordon
Jacket photographs: (*Island*) Bill Hinton Photography/Getty Images; (*Ocean*) © Adeeb Atwan/Dreamstime.com

10 9 8 7 6 5 4 3 2 1

First Edition

For Jeffrey,
because, really, who else?
Night and day, you are the one.
Still and always.

the journey there

In our desperate desire to recapture something that might never have been, one by one we've all crashed upon the rocks at Heart Island. And in doing so, we've ruined the very thing we all loved so much, made it something ugly and barren where no love can live, where nothing grows.

FROM THE JOURNAL OF CAROLINE LOVE HEART
(1940–2000)

p r o l o g u e

Birdie Burke stood on the edge of the rock and watched the first light of morning color the sky a dusty rose. As she perched on the cold, slippery stone shore, the lake water lapped at her toes. Other than the whisper of a light breeze through the trees, there was only the distant calling of a loon. She let her robe drop, and the cool air raised goose bumps on her flesh. No one could see her; the other islands were visible only from the north and south. Her husband had been asleep when she left him in the main house.

And even if anyone *could* see her, who wanted to look at the bathing-suited body of a seventy-five-year-old woman? Most people would avert their eyes in embarrassment, even though she was thin and fit. When fully clothed, she knew, she was very stylish. In fact, she still considered herself quite attractive. Even so, it seemed to Birdie that no one ever looked at her—not really.

Time had robbed her of the lushness of her body, her creamy skin, and the shine in her hair. And even though she didn't *feel* any different than she had when she was twenty, she was unrecognizable as the girl she was then. This was true for everyone, she knew. No one her age recognized the person she saw in the mirror. Most of her friends and acquaintances were engaged in a full-scale battle against the onset of old age, rallying teams of personal trainers, plastic surgeons, beauticians, aestheticians to hold back the clock. *How silly,* Birdie always thought. *If ever there's a battle you can't win, it's that one.* Not that she didn't take care of herself. Not that she didn't know about fighting losing battles.

The water was frigid as she inched in and then quickly submerged herself to her shoulders. Though she was well accustomed to the shock of the cold, her whole body seemed to seize in protest, her heart starting to race and her joints to ache. Then she began to move, placing one careful stroke after the next, her still-powerful legs pumping. Normally, she'd warm gradually, and the water would grow to feel bracing and crisp—refreshing.

But today was different. Maybe the water was just a few degrees too cold. Or maybe she was just old. She couldn't seem to get her rhythm. She hadn't gone far at all, and she was already thinking about turning back.

When she was younger, she'd effortlessly circle the perimeter once, maybe twice. She would enter, as she had today, to the west of the house at the only point that allowed for a safe plunge into the water. Then she'd swim out far enough to avoid being pushed back into the large, sharp rocks that surrounded most of the island. She used to relish the fresh water against her skin, the pleasure of her heart rate elevating, her lean, strong limbs pulling her past the dock, then around the east side, then another quarter turn back to where she began. The whole circle took her about half an hour when she was in good form.

She remembered the water being *warmer.* And the early morning was a stolen time, the time before the children woke and needed her. She used to wish it could last forever—the quiet, the freedom. Of course, now that it *could* last forever, now that she could pass an entire day without anyone needing a single thing of her, it wasn't nearly as pleasant as she'd imagined it would be. Birdie wondered why that so often seemed to be the case—once you had what you wanted, it was a shadow of what you'd dreamed it to be.

She'd made it to the dock, about a quarter of the way around, before she realized, frustrated, that she would need to go back. She couldn't manage the rest of the distance. Reluctantly, she turned around, swam to where she had left her robe in a soft pink pile, and stiffly climbed out. She was disappointed, even angry with herself, for not having what it took to complete the circle. She didn't like being reminded of her age. She was unbeatable once upon a time.

But maybe it was just as well; there was a lot to do. Everyone was coming on Sunday. There was so much required of her when guests were about to arrive. Her husband, Joe, was very little help; he fussed over details like the wine and the music, what games they should play. Meanwhile, all the heavy lifting—the shopping, the cooking, and the cleaning—were up to her. By sundown on the day after tomorrow, her children and grandchildren would be sitting at the long dining table for dinner. The blessed quiet of her island would be shattered. And the work would begin.

You do this to yourself, Birdie, her husband admonished regularly. *Why don't you just try to relax and enjoy? Everyone would be just as happy with hamburgers on the grill, baked potatoes in tinfoil, and a green salad.* Yes—everyone except Birdie.

She was so deep in thought that she didn't see him until she'd fastened her robe, slipped on her shoes, and turned around to head back to the main house. For a moment the shock of a figure standing at the edge of the trees didn't register.

Without her glasses on, she couldn't make him out. Who in the world could that be? Not her husband. The figure was tall but narrow, not powerful like Joe. One of the neighbors? No, it wasn't possible; she'd have heard the boat approach.

"Who's there?" she called.

But he stood motionless, possessing an almost ethereal quality. Birdie couldn't quite bring him into focus. Even though she felt a flutter of apprehension, she moved toward him. She was never one to move away from a threat. Always take it head-on; that was her philosophy.

"Identify yourself," she said. She didn't like the sound of her own voice. *Do you really have to be so goddamn imperious?* Her husband's other favorite admonishment. *You're not the queen, for Christ's sake.*

"You are *trespassing* on private land."

He didn't answer. What was she seeing? Was there anything there at all? Was it just a trick of light?

She picked up her pace. As she drew nearer, he seemed to disappear into the trees. She hadn't realized her vision was so poor. When she got to where he'd stood, there was no one there, no trace of anyone having been there. But someone *had* been there. She wasn't crazy or senile. She *had* seen someone. Hadn't she?

She walked over the rocky terrain that comprised the west side of the island and headed down toward the dock. Today, because there had been little rain for the past week, the rocks were fairly dry above the waterline, though somewhat treacherous. Birdie was sure-footed, having tramped over them at every stage in her life. Her feet belonged on those rocks, just as they had when she was a little girl, a teenager, a young woman. She moved quickly, her feet knowing which stone was loose and which was too pointy and which was a good, level place to step. When the rain fell and storms made the water choppy, this side of the island would become impassable—too slick, jagged, and treacherous by foot, waves knocking against the steep island face. There would be no way to traverse the perimeter except to get into the water and swim.

Rounding the bend, she saw the light gray dock against the steel blue of the water. A formation of Canada geese honked overhead, heading south already. The temperatures were growing colder without ever having seemed to warm.

Their old skiff bobbed in the water. Their cuddy boat, too, was fastened securely to the dock cleats, the cabin covered against the weather. But that was all—no other boat was docked there, as it would have to be if someone had come to call. There was no place else along the coastlines of the island where anyone could come ashore without badly damaging his boat.

Directly to the south was Cross Island. Only two years ago someone had built a house there. For most of Birdie's life, it had been empty. As children, she, her brother, and her sister used to row a small boat across the narrow channel, and explore. Though their mother always called them back, when she caught them, anxious and angry.

"Don't go there," she'd say. "It's not our island."

They'd come back, sullen and complaining quietly to one another. No one dared argue with Mother when she had that look on her face. She was rarely angry, almost never raised her voice. But there was a look. And when you saw it, you hushed and did as you were told.

Looking at Cross Island now, Birdie could just see the house that had been built there, its brown-shingled roof peeking through the trees, its windows glinting pink in the morning light. She didn't like it. It felt like an intrusion. Plus, the island itself held bad memories for her. Most often she ignored it, pretended it wasn't there, as she did with many of the things that pained her.

She glanced back the way she had come, then to the north, where she could see the main house. From the dock, a narrow gravel path led up to the main structure, then wound around it to the guesthouse. Beyond that cabin, the path wound on to the bunkhouse. She saw no one. No shadow followed her, no interloper. Toward the mainland, thunderheads darkened the sky.

The surrounding islands were occupied by private homes. Though the nearby island hotels and inns had shuttles from the mainland, there was no water taxi service. If you wanted to get to the private residences, you had to have your own boat.

There had been a rash of thefts in the area. Many of the homes stood uninhabited for most of the year. Undesirables from the mainland had grown wise, and they had been taking boats out, breaking in, stealing valuables, vandalizing—even spending a few days partying. Birdie had been angry when she heard the news. It was typical.

They were always waiting, angry and entitled, to take or destroy the things for which you'd worked so hard. There was always someone with less looking at you with envy and resentment, just waiting for your back to be turned so they could steal from you. Somehow they always seemed to get away with it.

About a week after she'd learned this, Birdie had gone into town and purchased a small handgun. She was often alone on the island. Joe didn't cherish his time here the way she did, and he went back to their apartment in the city when he tired of the solitude—or was it her company that tired him? After all, it wasn't his place. Heart Island hadn't been in *his* family for three generations. *He* hadn't spent every childhood summer here, as she had. She refused to be afraid in this place. And she pitied anyone who tried to take anything from her. She kept the revolver in its case, in a high kitchen cabinet. When she was alone at night, she moved it to her bedside table.

Birdie picked up her pace as she walked the rest of the perimeter of the three-acre island and ended at its highest point, Lookout Rock, as it had been named by the Heart children—Birdie, her sister, Caroline, and her brother, Gene. From this vantage point, she could see each of the structures, surrounded tightly by large rocks and trees.

The path was really the only way to get around the island now; it led from the bunkhouse to the guest cabin to the main house and then down to the dock, dimly lit by carefully spaced solar-powered ground lights. Once there had been only a single house, the one that was now the guest cabin. Then there was no path from the dock to the house, and everyone made his way up through the trees to the clearing. No one ever walked through the trees anymore, especially in the pitch-dark nights, preferring to keep to the path.

Up high and looking down, Birdie felt that maybe her eyes had been playing tricks on her, hard as it was to believe. But she didn't see a boat anywhere, run up ashore or tied off on a rock. There was no other way to get here. So logic dictated that she hadn't seen what she thought she had. Next time she'd bring her glasses or put in her contacts before the swim.

Her late sister, Caroline, would have claimed that Birdie had seen a ghost. Birdie's sister and Birdie's mother, Lana, had both believed that the island was home to otherworldly inhabitants. According to them, there was a man who walked the edge, and a woman who stood at Lookout Rock. And something else she couldn't remember. It was sheer silliness. Birdie had never seen anything remotely like that. Caroline hinted that it was because Birdie, as a pragmatist, as a cynic, wasn't worthy of a ghostly appearance. Even though Birdie couldn't explain what she had just seen, she wouldn't turn to the supernatural to do so. She was wondering about her vision, her sanity, maybe, but certainly *not* spirits.

Birdie walked the whole island and ended up back where she'd started. The stand of trees was just a blurry line of black. She stared a moment, willing a form to appear from something—a shadow, a swaying branch—so she could explain to herself what had happened. But no, there were just her old friends the pines, the birch trees, the sugar maples, and their eternal whispering.

Finally, she walked back up to the main cabin to start her breakfast. Her mood, which had been fine, had turned dark. She felt rattled in a way she shouldn't have, as though she'd gotten some terrible news or remembered something she had been trying to forget.

chapter one

The Blue Hen was bustling, and Emily had screwed up in at least three different ways since her shift began. She'd given one customer the wrong change. She'd given another the wrong order. And now, as some little kid ran out of the bathroom without looking, cutting her off as she moved down the narrow hallway from the kitchen to the dining area, she felt the tray of ice waters slipping from her hands. She'd stopped short to avoid a collision, but the glasses and the tray had not.

She watched the boy dart down the hallway, but everything else was in torturous slow motion. Four glass tumblers sailed through the air, water pluming, ice cubes suspended. The word "no" pulled and elongated in her mind. And then—the shattering crash. She backed away from the shimmering, slicing mess and stared at it. *Oh, God. Oh, no.* Why did some days start out bad and just get worse?

Angelo from the kitchen rushed out to help. He had a mop in one hand and a bucket in the other like some kind of diner rescue worker. Then Carol, the owner of the Blue Hen, came around the corner. "What happened?" she asked.

"I dropped it," said Emily. Obviously. She wasn't going to bother getting into it about the kid. And how the bathroom door shouldn't open outward into the hallway. Or how people needed to heed the sign that read: *Please open the door and exit slowly.* Carol looked at the mess and put a plump, beautifully manicured hand to her forehead.

Emily couldn't help but look at her rings—a big diamond engagement ring and a ruby "family" ring, as Carol had called it. They glittered like stars.

"Let Angelo get it. The order for your four-top is up. You fetch that, and I'll get more ice water," Carol said. Her tone was weary but not unkind. Carol was never that. "Try to pull yourself together, Emily. I don't know what you have on your mind today. But it is definitely *not* your work."

Emily nodded. "I'm sorry."

Carol looked at Emily over the rim of her glasses. She had a nice face, round and pink-cheeked, with pretty, darkly lashed blue eyes. Her body was short and soft—a mother's body. Carol was, in fact, a bit henlike, Emily thought, zaftig and proud, strutting about clucking. Emily wanted to put her head in Carol's lap and cry her a river.

"So, what is it, hon?" said Carol. "You need to talk?"

"No," said Emily. She tried for a smile. "I'm fine."

Angelo was already on his knees, picking up big shards of glass with calloused hands.

"I'm sorry, Angelo," said Emily.

He looked up at her with his dark puppy-dog eyes, big, devoted, and a little lovesick. "Don't worry about it," he said.

Angelo had a crush on Emily; she knew that. He gave her a wide grin, as though he liked being down on his knees for her. She felt a hot blush spread across her cheeks, and then she was chasing after Carol, who was talking to her. Carol had a fast, soft, but no-nonsense way of communicating. She didn't care if you participated, only that you appeared to be listening.

"When you get orders wrong, especially for someone like Barney, who comes here every single day at the same time for the same meal, it makes people feel like we don't know them, don't care about them. And if you work at T.G.I. Friday's or Chili's, maybe that doesn't matter so much. But here, at my restaurant, it matters—because it's precisely that kind of personal interaction that separates the chains from the independents. Also, when you give people the wrong change, it makes us seem either untrustworthy or incompetent. Do you understand that, Emily?" Emily knew this wasn't an invitation to chime in. Carol went on.

"Now, dropping things? Well, it happens. But it usually happens when we're not present. You're all flustered from a morning of mistakes. So I want you to take a few minutes, after you bring the food to your four-top, and go out back and take a break. I'll cover your tables. Then come on back in like it's a brand-new day, okay?"

Emily found herself nodding vigorously, then running the four-top order over to the family by the window. Pancakes for the girl, French toast for the boy, an egg-white scramble with broccoli for the mom, and a chili-cheese omelet with home fries and an extra side of bacon for the dad (boy, did he ever get a look from Mom over the menu when he ordered that). He looked like he could afford to take off a few, but not in an unhealthy, worrisome way. He was just a beefy guy who liked to eat. He probably had high cholesterol; that's why his wife had that kind of angry-worried look on her face when Emily placed the plate in front of him.

"Wow," the mom said. "That looks good." But what she meant was: *Oh, honey, are you really going to eat that?* At least that's what Emily thought. She was good at that, reading faces, body language. She felt like, a lot of the time, she knew what people were thinking even when they were saying something else altogether. She'd always been that way.

After she ran a bottle of ketchup over to the table, she went out back like Carol had asked her to. She sat on the bench where everyone went for a smoke break, and looked up into the sky. The day was warm and humid, clouds high and white. A light breeze made the leaves of the tall oaks that towered above the parking-lot fence dance and hiss. She took a deep breath, trying to shake it off, like Carol wanted.

Why do you want to go to that place and run around for that stupid cow?

That's what Dean had said to her this morning. He hadn't wanted her to go to work. He'd wanted her to stay with him. He didn't like Carol. Dean didn't seem to like anyone Emily liked. She wasn't sure what that said about him.

"You'll make more in a morning with me than you will in a week at the Fat Hen."

"The Blue Hen."

"Whatever," he said. He'd lit a cigarette even though he knew the smell made her sick in the morning. "You don't need to run around like that."

He didn't like the idea of her waitressing. His mother was a waitress, and Dean didn't like Emily to do anything that reminded him of his mother.

"It's low-class work," he said.

Emily didn't think any honest work was "low-class," whatever that meant coming from Dean. Carol treated her with respect. The customers, maybe because the Blue Hen was *not* the cheapest restaurant in town, were mostly polite. They tipped well. And usually, Emily was not half bad at the whole waitress thing. She liked talking to people, being friendly, and chitchatting about this and that with the regulars. Carol always made sure Emily had a meal before or after her shift and told everyone to help themselves to coffee and hot chocolate. The Blue Hen was the nicest place Emily had ever worked.

Dean was mad at her when she left. That was why she'd shown up to work all shaky and upset. Well, one of the reasons, anyway. She didn't like it when he was mad, but if she didn't go to work and bring in a regular paycheck, they didn't always make it week to week. Then she'd have to borrow from her mother—which she couldn't do right now. And that was a whole other set of problems.

It was true that Dean *could* make a lot of money. But he didn't always, and somehow it seemed to be gone as quickly as it came in. Then, of course, there were the times when Dean disappeared for days. Once for a week. She hadn't expected him to come back that time. She wasn't as happy as she thought she'd be when he finally did come home.

"Feeling better?"

Angelo had come to stand beside her. She looked up at him, and he smiled shyly, turned his eyes toward the sky. He was always sweet to her, and she felt an odd desire to slip her hand into his. He smelled like the lemon soap he used to clean the dishes.

"Thanks for cleaning up my mess," she said. She folded her hands in her lap.

"No problem."

She sensed that he was about to say more but changed his mind. He'd asked her out a couple of times. She told him she was living with someone. He'd given up asking, but he still smiled at her a lot, hopeful. She'd expected him to get angry or mean when she turned him down, but he didn't. He was just as kind to her as he always had been. For some reason, that made her think that he had a nice mom, someone who had taught him to respect women. She really liked that about Angelo.

"I think Carol's going to need you back inside," he said. "She has paperwork to do in the office."

"Okay," Emily said.

Carol kept the week's cash receipts in a safe behind the desk in her office. She did all the paperwork during the day on Friday. On Friday night after closing, she took the money to the bank's after-hours deposit slot. Emily had heard Carol's husband, Paul, complain about that. He thought they should take it every night on the way home, so there wasn't as much cash lying around. Carol had agreed. But as far as Emily could see, she hadn't started doing that.

Emily had noticed that Carol was a creature of habit, and everything had to be done the same way every day. She didn't like change. From setup to close up, everything—making the coffee, squeezing the orange juice, refilling the salt, pepper, and sugar dispensers, wiping down the counter and tables—was part of an exact ritual.

Emily liked that about Carol. She was predictable, reliable. There was no mystery to what she wanted, how she would react. It was such a comfort, because Emily seldom had any idea what was going to set Dean off. Or her mother. Emily never knew whether to expect kindness or cruelty from either of them. At the Blue Hen, there was only one rule. Work hard and be nice, and everything would go just fine. That should be the rule for life, too, Emily thought. But, of course, that wasn't how things went.

Once she was back inside the restaurant, it *did* feel like a new day. Emily let the rhythm of the place take her, and she was in the groove for the rest of her shift. No more mistakes. At the end of her shift, Carol made her a meat-loaf plate with mashed potatoes and gravy and a big helping of sautéed vegetables. Emily wouldn't have said she was hungry, but she finished every last bite and felt like she could have eaten more. She saw Carol looking at her, and then the other woman came to sit across from her in the booth.

The Blue Hen was in the lull between breakfast and lunch, a few customers lingering over their meals—a mom spoon-feeding oatmeal to a little boy, an old man reading a paper, a couple holding hands at the two-top by the window.

"How was it?" asked Carol. She tapped on Emily's empty plate.

Emily would have lifted it and licked the gravy clean if she'd been alone.

"Horrible," she said. "I'm sending it back."

Carol smiled at her and patted her hand. "You didn't have breakfast."

"No," said Emily. She thought of Dean sulking and smoking at the table over a cup of coffee. She'd left without eating rather than keep fighting. The cigarette smoke, his attitude, both toxic enough to drive her away.

"Everything all right with you, honey?" Carol asked.

"I'm fine," Emily said. "Really. I'm sorry about today. It won't happen again."

"Don't worry about it, kid." Carol leaned back, and Emily saw her eyes make a quick scan of the restaurant. If she saw anything out of place, she'd pop up, fix it, and hurry back. Apparently, everything met with her approval. "We all have bad days. How's school?"

"Good," Emily said. "Great."

Carol kept her eyes on Emily for another second, gave her another light pat on the hand, and then got up.

"Okay," she said. "Good."

Emily watched the older woman go, heading to the kitchen to make sure everything was ready for the lunch rush. She fought off the urge to call Carol back. She wanted to confess that she'd had to drop out of school, that it hadn't worked out and that she'd try to sign up for a class or two again in the fall when money wasn't so tight and Dean didn't need her help all the time. Emily's mother had stopped paying tuition because she didn't like Dean and hated that he and Emily were living together. And Emily wasn't making enough for rent, food, whatever else, *and* classes at the community college.

But she couldn't say all that, because Carol wasn't her mother or her friend. Carol was her boss. It was better to remember that, because she'd made the mistake before of getting too close to the people for whom she'd worked. It hurt a lot more when they had to let her go for whatever reason. And they looked so much more disappointed when she let them down, which she always seemed to do eventually.

"I can stay for the lunch shift, if you need me," Emily said. Though she could use the money, she tried not to look too hopeful.

Carol turned at the door, seeming to consider. "I have Blanche on the schedule. But thanks, honey." Then she made a sweeping motion with her hands and said, "You're young. Go enjoy yourself today."

Emily gathered her things from the back and left. Outside, there was a sudden light drizzle, even though the sky was blue in most places. A sun shower but no rainbow that Emily could see. Dean was supposed to pick her up, since she'd let him borrow her car and taken the bus to work this morning. But he wasn't there. Big surprise.

She waited for a while off to the side of the restaurant. She could have stayed under the awning to avoid getting wet. But she didn't want everyone to see her standing there waiting—again. Finally, after nearly twenty minutes, she headed for the bus stop.

On the bus, she used her cell phone to call her mother. Her mother wasn't speaking to her, but Emily left a message on the machine every day.

"Hi, Mom," she said. "I'm just getting off work, riding home on the bus. Dean had a job interview today, so he took my car. I was just wondering if you wanted to come over for dinner on Sunday. The house is looking really nice. I'd like you to see it." She paused, hoping her mother would pick up. "Okay, well. I love you. Call me."

Emily had thought that at some point, her mother would have to bail on the silent treatment. But so far, no. Their last fight had been a screaming match, or maybe it had just been Emily screaming.

"There's something wrong with that boy," her mother had said. She'd been sitting at the kitchen table, smoking a cigarette. Whenever Emily thought about her mother, Martha, that's where she thought of her: at that table, elbows on the vinyl, staring off at who knows what, smoking. That was why she hated the smell of cigarette smoke so much.

"Living with him is the worst thing you can do. He's going to hurt you bad. And don't you *dare* get pregnant. That will be the end of your life."

Then Martha told Emily that she wasn't going to pay for school unless Dean found his own place. Emily didn't understand that. If her mother was so sure Dean was going to ruin her life, why did she want to take away Emily's chance for an education, which her mother always said was the key to success? "I won't have that money going to him."

It was true that last semester Emily *had* dropped a class and then given the tuition reimbursement to Dean. Yes, she had done that. Martha had found out about it because the bursar's office had sent her the receipt. Emily should have known they'd do that. But she'd never been good about thinking things through. Dean had needed that money; she still wasn't sure for what. But he'd seemed so desperate at the time. And it was a film class, an elective, not important at all to her degree in early childhood education.

Her last visit with her mother had ended with Emily screaming, *"He loves me!"* There was a part of her that had stood above it all, disbelieving the level of her own rage. Emily wasn't one who normally resorted to shrieking. But she felt like something was going to come bursting out of her chest.

"You're jealous because no one ever loved you like he loves me."

Her mother had just sat there, staring at the wallpaper, cigarette dangling between her fingers. She looked so old and tired, used up. It was Emily's worst nightmare to wind up at a kitchen table, looking like that—as if she'd been ground down by life and couldn't even be bothered to care.

The old lady sitting next to Emily on the bus patted her on the leg and handed her a tissue, which Emily took without thinking. Then she realized that she was crying.

"Thank you," she said, wiping her eyes.

"It's hard to be young," said the woman. She wore a neat blue raincoat and had silvery-white hair. There was the slightest tremor to her hands. "I remember. You want so much."

"Does it get easier?"

The other woman chuckled a little and put a dry, soft hand on Emily's. "Not really, dear."

Great, thought Emily. *That's just great.*

chapter two

How do things start? How does your life begin? How do you go from being a child shuttled from school to soccer to playdates to the mall, then on to college and your first job? How do you go from the first job, to your first date with your future spouse, to whatever it is you wind up doing with your life, to being a mom with two kids, paying bills on your laptop at the kitchen counter? Is it that one event or choice connects to another until the next thing you know, you're looking at the chain of your life? How do things start? Chelsea wondered, looking at her mother. How do they end?

"You are not wearing that."

Her mother hadn't even *looked* at her when Chelsea came down the stairs, hadn't even *glanced* up from her papers spread out across the kitchen island. How did her mom even know what Chelsea was wearing—a black mini and knee-high boots, a purple knit sweater that failed to cover her navel? But her mother knew. Though there was no anger or heat to her sentence, it was unwavering in its tone. No discussion. Chelsea understood on a cellular level that there would be no whining, weeping, or begging her way around that sentence.

"Fine," Chelsea said. Not a "fine" with attitude, just a regular "fine." She spun around and walked back up the stairs.

Chelsea didn't want to wear the sweater anyway. Not really. She didn't feel that great about her middle. It was fleshy, doughy. She'd just be folding her arms around her belly all afternoon, self-conscious.

Not like Lulu, whose body was OMG perfect; not an ounce of fat anywhere on that girl. She strutted around like a cat, every line of her in perfect symmetry with the universe, not one thing about her—skin, eyes, lips, perky breasts—flawed in any way. Next to her best friend since kindergarten, Chelsea felt like an oaf. She flipped through her closet inspecting and rejecting a denim shirt, a pink graphic T-shirt, a ruffled, flowery shirt her grandmother had sent but which Chelsea had never worn. What would Lulu be wearing?

Lulu never ate a thing—she was a size zero. On the other hand, Lulu was not smart. But no, that wasn't entirely fair. Though Chelsea was forever helping Lulu with her homework (sometimes doing it for her), and the girl could barely spell, Lulu *was* smart—in certain ways. Even if things like math and English seemed to elude her, she always seemed worldlier, more knowledgeable, than Chelsea did. Lulu just didn't care about school.

Lulu's other defining feature: She had a tongue like a blade. Didn't it seem like really thin, gorgeous people were always so mean? Where did they get that aura of entitlement? And didn't it seem like people always fawned over them even though they behaved badly? Why was that? More questions in what seemed to Chelsea an endless stream of questions that had no satisfactory answers. Too many.

Chelsea pulled her favorite soft lilac tunic top from its hanger and slid that on with her black mini instead. She felt more comfortable instantly, more relaxed. There was nothing special about the outfit—it was neither slutty, nor super-cool, nor dorky and lame. Therefore, it should call no attention to her whatsoever. Neither would her passably cute but not really pretty face, nor her straight, shoulder-length wheat-colored hair, nor her boyish body. And that was fine, really. That was just fine.

Her mother walked into the room and bent down to pick up the sweater that Chelsea had tossed carelessly to the floor.

"Where did you get this?" her mom asked. She held it up, and it looked impossibly small, like a doll's top. Chelsea was almost embarrassed for it, imagined it wilting under her mother's disapproving gaze.

"I borrowed it from Lulu."

"Hmm." Her mother folded the sweater and put it down on the bed, sat beside it. "You know . . . beauty isn't about flaunting your body."

"I know." Really. How could she not know this? They'd had this talk about a hundred times. *Beauty comes from within. It's about intelligence, confidence, knowing who you are.* Also: *You can't buy beauty.* Or: *True beauty doesn't come from a bottle.* Or: *Beauty doesn't come in one size or shape.* Yes, Chelsea recognized all these things as inherently true. Too bad the rest of the world was so slow to catch on.

"You're beautiful without even trying," her mother said. "Maybe Lulu feels like she has to dress in flirty clothes to get attention."

Chelsea gave her mother a look that she hoped adequately expressed her skepticism. "You're not going to tell me that Lulu is not *effortlessly* gorgeous."

Her mother smiled. It was that very certain kind of "patient mom" smile. For some reason, it always made Chelsea a little mad.

"There are different kinds of beauty," said Kate.

"There's not a boy alive who wouldn't want to be with her," said Chelsea. Did she sound jealous? She wasn't. Was she?

Kate raised her eyebrows. "What do you mean '*be with her*'?"

"You know," said Chelsea. She felt her cheeks flush. "Forget it."

She glanced at the sweater lying on her bed between them. It was garish and cheap-looking. After a couple of washes, it would be faded and pilled. It wouldn't last a season.

"Anyway," said her mom. "I like your outfit. It's—"

Chelsea lifted a palm. "Don't say cute."

"I was going to say pretty, hip—*stylish*. It's a lovely color for you."

Her mother stood and ran her fingers through Chelsea's hair, then planted a kiss on her forehead and headed out the door. Chelsea shoved the sweater in her bag. Maybe she'd change into it at the mall. Or maybe she'd just give it back to Lulu.

"Be ready in fifteen," her mother called from the stairs. "I have to get to your brother's practice this afternoon."

He's my half brother, she wanted to say but didn't. She wasn't supposed to say that. It made everyone angry and sad, including her. Anyway, she didn't even think of him that way. Brendan was her brother in every way, especially the annoying ways.

"Okay," she said instead.

She sat down at her computer and touched the mouse. The screen saver gave way to her Facebook page. She scrolled through the news feed. Stephanie was, according to her post, miserable studying for her summer-school calculus exam (how it was possible to *study* and be simultaneously posting on Facebook was another matter). *Boring,* Stephanie wrote. *Who needs calculus in the real world, anyway?* Chelsea wrote: *Hang in there, girl!*

Her friend Brian was *psyched* to be heading to soccer camp. Chelsea knew this not to be strictly true; Brian was always on the bench, always the last player called into the game. She wrote: *Knock 'em dead!* Josie was getting her nails done. *I swear these Chinese ladies are saying mean things about me.* Josie always thought people were saying mean things about her, probably because she was always saying mean things about everyone else. Chelsea didn't post anything.

Chelsea had 109 Facebook friends, and all of them always seemed to be doing something worth posting about. It made her anxious sometimes to see that feed, to know what everyone else was thinking or doing, whether they were worried or excited, depressed or in love.

There was a perpetual stream of information about her friends and acquaintances, people from school whose friend request she'd accepted because they'd requested it but whom she didn't think of as real friends, her cousins in Washington, even her step-grandmother. It always caused Chelsea to wonder about what she was doing, what she should write in her status to make herself seem part of it all. No matter what she posted, she felt as if she were always falling short somehow. *Once upon a time,* her dad, Sean—who hated Facebook—always said, *people used to talk. We didn't post our thoughts and feelings on some digital bulletin board for everyone to see. You knew what you were doing and what your intimates were doing. And guess what? That's all you need to know.*

It seemed as though Chelsea's parents were fighting for some ideal that didn't quite match the reality of things. They were always trying to talk her out of the way things really were in favor of the way things should be. It was exhausting sometimes. *Give up,* she wanted to tell them. *You lost. The world is crap, and no amount of communicating is going to change it.* But they were so earnest, so well meaning, how could she say that?

She had a new friend request. She clicked on the happy blue heads, and the little window popped up. Somebody named Adam McKee wanted to be her friend. She had no idea who he was, but he was *super* cute, with spiky black hair and dark, thick-lashed eyes.

She felt a little tingle of curiosity. Who was he? And why was he sending her a friend request? She clicked on his name to see what friends they had in common and where he went to school. He went to high school in Brighton, the next town over. They had one friend in common: Lulu. Figured. Lulu was friends with absolutely everyone, even though she had something terrible to say about most of them.

There wasn't any other info about Adam McKee that she could access without becoming his friend. She'd ask Lulu about him later. She didn't accept friendship from a guy she didn't know, even if he *was* smoking hot. She posted on her page: *Heading to the mall for shopping and smoothies with Lulu. Anyone care to join? Meet us at the food court!* It was lame but the best she could do at the moment.

"Chelsea, let's go!" her mother called from downstairs. Something had changed her mother's mood; she sounded tense. She'd been like this—normal one minute, short and edgy the next. Chelsea found things went better if she pretended not to notice. She was good at that.

How could it be three-thirty? How did the days pass in this hectic rush? There was a moment after Kate had returned from dropping the kids off at school or at their various summer camps when the light in the house was golden and the day seemed to stretch before her with the endless possibilities of what she could accomplish. And then before she knew it, it was eleven. And then it was two. By three she was in the car again to get them both and cart them around to their myriad activities.

She wasn't idle. She was never idle. And yet it never seemed like there was any progress made on any of the *bigger* things she had planned. Sure, the house was spotless, the laundry was always done, dinner was always prepared, the fridge was always stocked with what everyone liked and needed. She did all that. She took care of her family. It was just that she couldn't assign any real value to those tasks. They were baseline, the things that needed to be accomplished in order for her not to be a complete failure at the major role of her life. Not that she didn't accomplish things—she was active in the school, in the organic-produce co-op. In fact, this past year she'd accomplished a great deal. But it didn't seem like enough.

"Chelsea, let's go!" she called. She didn't mean to sound tense, though she knew she did.

A minute later, her daughter glided down the stairs. Kate felt a familiar twist as she looked at Chelsea, who had no idea how beautiful she was and was all the more beautiful for it. Sometimes when Kate looked at the swell of Chelsea's hips, the milk of her skin, the golden flax of her hair, she felt afraid. She wanted to wrap her daughter up in cloth and hide her from the world; she longed for burkas and nunneries and sumptuary laws. How could you ever protect anything so lovely? How could you keep the dirty hands of the world away from someone so desirable? You couldn't. That was the sad truth. All you could do was teach her to protect herself.

"What's wrong?" her daughter asked from the bottom of the stairs. "Why are you looking at me like that?"

"Nothing," Kate said. She forced a bright smile and touched her daughter's perfect cheek. "I'm not looking at you any particular way. We're late."

Chelsea drifted past Kate, wafting behind her the scents of talcum powder, shampoo, Ivory soap. They were the clean, innocent aromas of childhood. Something about that made Kate feel calmer. She followed her daughter out to the car.

"You know, I'm not thrilled about the whole mall thing," Kate said, fastening her seat belt.

"What's wrong with the mall?"

What was wrong with the mall? It was a bastion of mass consumerism, a pusher of junk food, the natural habitat of every pervert, predator, and abductor, and a preferred target of terrorists (according to the news). And wasn't there some recent newsmagazine show about how kids were having sex in the bathrooms? They were locating each other with some phone app and hooking up. She hoped that was an urban legend. She couldn't bring herself to ask Chelsea about it.

"It's just an inorganic way to spend a Friday afternoon," Kate said. "And we're leaving on Sunday. We need to start getting ready tonight."

The mere thought of it made her stomach clench. The trip. The dreaded trip. Its looming presence was pressing down on her, making her edgy and snappish with Sean and the kids.

"You know, Mom," said Chelsea. Her daughter was too wise, knew Kate too well, to be fooled by those lame reasons for not wanting Chelsea to hang out at the mall. "The incidence of stranger crime is at an all-time low. Mall abductions and murders are a statistical anomaly."

"You sound like Sean," said Kate. As ever, she was simultaneously proud of and irked by her daughter's intellect, which she suspected was vastly superior to her own. Although Kate remembered being smart, sharp, quick-witted when she was younger—vaguely.

"I need things for the trip anyway," said Chelsea, the pragmatist. "So it's not like I'm hanging out aimlessly."

"What do you need?"

"Fleece tops and a pair of Keens." She shrugged. "Outdoorsy stuff."

"You can use your card."

Kate and Sean had given Chelsea a credit card when she turned fifteen, one that attached to their own account. But there were strict rules for use, and purchases had to be approved ahead of time, except in emergencies. They'd never had a problem with Chelsea; she was her mother's daughter—a straight arrow. Brendan, their youngest, was another story. They wouldn't be so quick to get him his own card when he was old enough. He was sweet, but he was wily. And he had a rebel's heart.

The mall stood white and meticulously landscaped, like some smug monument to excess. Kate pulled up to the entrance and watched her daughter gather her things and undo the seat belt.

"I'll meet you back here at six," said Kate. "Do you have your phone?"

"Of course," said Chelsea, leaning in for a quick kiss. She opened the door and hopped out.

Kate rolled down the window. "Text me," she called after her daughter. Chelsea lifted an acknowledging hand but didn't turn around and then was swallowed by a huge revolving door.

Even though she hadn't thought about it in ages, Kate found herself remembering the tearful preschool drop-offs. Chelsea used to cling like a spider monkey to Kate, wailing, *Don't leave me, Mommy* (possibly the four most devastating words in the English language).

Mommy always comes back, sweetie. Try to have fun, Kate would soothe, while gently extracting herself from Chelsea's small but powerful arms. She'd leave feeling simultaneously sick with guilt and desperate for a few hours to herself.

Brendan, on the other hand, even as a toddler, would run off without a backward glance. He was the more secure kid, not a child who, like Chelsea, had suffered through a bitter and violent divorce. Brendan's world had always been solidly intact; Kate's marriage to his father, Sean, was loving and rock-solid. Chelsea, on the other hand, had been born into the misery of Kate's first marriage. Kate was sure it had imprinted on her somewhere, even though Chelsea thought of Sean as her dad, and most of her life had been happy and peaceful. But her father, Sebastian, remained a destabilizing influence even today. Kate tried to breathe through the guilt and anger that inevitably arose when she thought about these things. She tried to release it. What could she do? Life wasn't perfect—not for Chelsea, not for anyone.

She was pulling up to the soccer field when her phone rang. She thought: *What now?* She didn't have any reason to think that. The day had been relatively uneventful, except for the call from her exhusband, which was always guaranteed to put her in a crappy mood. That attitude—the *what now* attitude—belonged to Kate's mother, always beleaguered or put-upon by things like the ringing phone or the doorbell, as if she were *so* in demand that she couldn't possibly keep up. Kate shook it off, as she did anything within herself that reminded her of Birdie.

"Hello?" She forced herself to sound bright and open, hopeful.

"Hey." Her brother. There was something about his tone. She knew exactly why he was calling.

"Don't say it, Teddy," she said. No, not Teddy, which was what she'd called him all his life. Theo was what he called himself and had for over a decade. All his friends, his partner, his colleagues knew him as Theo. Only she and her parents still called him Teddy.

Kate saw Brendan waving at her from the soccer field. He seemed smaller than the other boys. She waved back to him, lifted a finger to say she'd be one minute.

"I'm sorry," her brother said. He issued a long breath. "I can't. I just can't do it this year."

"You have to," she said. "You promised me."

She could see the boys jogging onto the field. Brendan threw a quick, anxious glance at her and then took his position. She heard the shrill of a whistle, the low sound of a few parents cheering.

"Honey, I know," her brother said. "But I've just realized that I can't do this anymore." She could tell by his tone that he was not going to change his mind. He added, "I'm not like you."

"What does that mean?"

"You know," he said. He sounded weary and a little peevish. "You have Dad on your side. I don't even have that."

She felt a childish rush of tears, which she blinked back. Anger, disappointment, sadness were the all-too-familiar horsemen preceding any encounter with her family. They'd come early. And she had a feeling they were here to stay. She didn't say anything.

"Look, Kate," he said into the silence. "I'm too old for this. I'm not going to travel for a full day to trap myself on an island with people who abuse me. There has to be a time in your life when you just start staying no."

She started to push out a disdainful breath. *Abuse?* That was a little melodramatic, wasn't it? But that was her mother, too. Always arguing semantics to avoid the ugly truth.

"What about me and the kids?" she said. She wasn't above the pity play. "We miss you."

"We'll come to your place for Thanksgiving."

"Teddy, please don't make me do this alone." Okay, now she was begging.

"Try to understand," he said. "You don't have to do this, either."

She *did* have to do it. There were a thousand reasons why, all twisted around one another, a big tangle of hope and fear and obligation.

"I have to hang up now," she said. She sounded cold; she didn't mean to.

"Kate."

"Brendan's game is starting. And I happen to care about the promises I make to my family."

"Oh, please," he said. Now he was angry, too. "You sound just like her."

That was a low blow. It was unnecessary, and a reminder that as much as she loved her brother, there were serious challenges in their relationship. How could there not be? How could the children of Birdie and Joe Burke ever hope to be truly close? Where would they have learned those skills? Certainly not from their parents. Maybe it was better, after all, if he didn't go.

"Bye, Theo." She ended the call.

She sat a minute, rested her head on the steering wheel until she heard the referee's penalty whistle from the field. Then she climbed from the driver's seat and went around to the trunk to get the big cooler of water and the oranges she'd promised the coach she would bring. Promises were important. Why didn't anyone seem to remember that anymore?

chapter three

Chelsea wasn't supposed to talk to her biological father, Sebastian, without her mother present in the room. So when she saw his name and number on her caller ID, she pressed ignore. It had nothing to do with the custody agreement. It was just something Chelsea and her mom had decided on a couple of years ago.

When she was younger, after calls with her father, Chelsea would feel inconsolably sad for reasons she couldn't articulate. Maybe it was because *he* sounded so sad and so far away. Or because other times he was angry and said awful things about her mom. Often he made grand promises that she knew he had no way of keeping, as much as he might want to, like "Next year we're going to go to Disney World for a week—just you and me." Chelsea knew his custody agreement didn't allow for weeklong trips. Early on, he wasn't even allowed unsupervised visits. Worse than that, she wouldn't have wanted to go with him if she had been allowed.

Sometimes after his calls, when she was a little kid, she'd cry and cry in her mother's lap; it felt like she would never stop crying. When her mother was there, even if Kate couldn't hear her father's side of the conversation, Chelsea felt better, as if her life were a solid place, predictable and safe. When she hung up, if her mother was nearby, she didn't feel like the whole world was built on quicksand, a place where even the adults didn't know what was true. That was why they'd made the agreement.

But her father was different now; he was remarried, sort of. He claimed he was *spiritually* married, though apparently, he eschewed legal documentation. He was sober. He wasn't angry anymore, not in the ranting, raging way he used to be. Recently, he'd found success again as a writer. So he was happier.

A couple of years ago, he'd formally apologized to Chelsea and to her mother for all the pain he'd caused them while he was drinking. It was part of his twelve-step program. *Or part of his publicity tour,* her mother had offered. Because his first successful book in ten years was about how drinking had laid waste to his life and his career: *The Bottom of the Glass.* His marriage to Chelsea's mother was apparently cataloged in grisly, Technicolor detail. Kate had asked her not to read it until she was older, and Chelsea had agreed. She'd happily kept her promise. Frankly, she didn't want to know any more about her parents' train wreck of a marriage than she already did.

Since the apology, whatever his reasons had been for making it, her mother no longer visibly stiffened at the mention of Chelsea's father. In the last year, Chelsea had been allowed two weekends with Sebastian and Jessica, his second "wife" and also his literary agent (who was *fine,* really—even Kate said so). He'd been asking for another weekend. But Chelsea kept coming up with excuses, and her mother certainly wasn't forcing the issue.

Chelsea couldn't say why she didn't want to go. Her father and Jessica bent over backward to please her, showered her with gifts—an iPhone, clothes, a flat-screen television in her room at their house. They indulged her every whim. But there was something about the way her father looked at her, as though he wanted and expected something that she thought she should feel but didn't. It was something she knew he hadn't earned and couldn't buy. She felt bad about it. She loved him; she did. But it didn't feel like enough. The truth was that she would never be "home" when she was with her father. And they both knew it.

"You should be milking that action for all it's worth," Lulu said. "Make him buy you a car next year."

They had started talking about Sebastian in Forever 21. Chelsea didn't think Lulu had seen the call come in. But maybe she had. Or maybe she was just reading Chelsea's mind, like she always did.

"Yeah," Chelsea said. "Sweet idea."

She had no intention of asking her father for a car or anything else. Even the iPhone he'd given her had seemed to cause some pain at home. She thought maybe Sean had been planning to get her one for her birthday. Of course, nothing was ever said. Sean, her stepfather (though she didn't think of him that way), was the man she called Dad. And he would never dream of making her feel bad about her relationship with her real father or anything related to it.

"Seriously," said Lulu, as though she sensed that she hadn't made her point. "He's, like, loaded now. And he owes you."

"Why are we talking about this?"

Lulu shrugged. She held up a tiny tie-dyed tank. "What do you think of this?"

"It's cute," said Chelsea.

Chelsea wondered what it would be like to look perfect in absolutely anything. And to have no one telling you what you could and couldn't wear. Lulu looked at the top again and then put it back. Chelsea wouldn't have been surprised to see Lulu stick the shirt in her bag, even though there were no limits on what she could buy. Lulu had her own credit card, and her parents paid the bill, no questions asked. But she still regularly pocketed small items . . . a shirt, a lipstick, a stuffed animal from the Hallmark store. *Why?* Chelsea had asked her friend. *Why would you do that?* Lulu had looked at her somewhat blankly, as though she'd never considered the question. *I don't know.*

"I saw him on the *Today* show," said Lulu. Now she was looking at Chelsea pointedly over a rack of yoga pants. Rihanna was singing on the speakers. *I love the way you lie,* she crooned.

"Oh," said Chelsea.

She didn't like it when her father was on television. The man she saw on the screen was a bad facsimile of the man she knew, someone put on and false. People would inevitably mention that they'd seen him or that they'd seen his book in the store. They were impressed and communicated it by looking at Chelsea with something like awe and wonder—or sometimes, she thought, pity. Chelsea didn't like it one bit. Because they didn't know the whole story of who he was, just the one he had chosen to tell. Only she and her mother knew everything. And having a best-selling book or a national television appearance didn't make up for the other things, not even close. Not that she was mad or anything. Chelsea decided to change the subject.

"I got a friend request from a really cute guy today. Adam McKee? Do you know him?"

Lulu started walking toward the door. "Maybe," she said. "What does he look like?"

"Black spiky hair, brown eyes. Lives in Brighton."

Lulu offered an elaborate shrug, a mask of indifference. "I don't know," she said. "Show me?"

Was she being cagey? Chelsea wondered. It was so hard to tell with Lulu. As close as they were, there were times when Chelsea wasn't sure what her friend was up to. Lulu sometimes held back, at least for a while—like when she lost her virginity last year. Or when she tried pot for the first time. Chelsea hadn't done either.

"He's your friend on Facebook," Chelsea said.

"Honey," Lulu said, world-weary. They'd left Forever 21 and were strolling toward the food court. "I have five hundred friends. I can't keep track of them *all.*"

Chelsea took the phone out of her bag, pulled up the request, and held the device out to Lulu.

"He *is* cute," said Lulu, grabbing it from her. "He looks familiar."

"So you accept friend requests from people you don't know? You're not supposed to do that," Chelsea said.

Lulu launched a dramatic eye roll. She thought Chelsea was too nervous, too square. It was a long-running argument. "Isn't that the whole point of Facebook?" she said. "To make *friends*?"

"Hello," said Chelsea. "You've never heard of Internet predators? You know: Hey, I'm a sixteen-year-old hottie. Meet me at Starbucks! Then: Oops, my bad! I'm a thirty-year-old serial killer, let me give you a ride in the trunk of my car!"

"God, Chelsea," said Lulu. She pushed out a little laugh, put a hand on Chelsea's shoulder. "Chill out."

Lulu pressed the accept button and gave Chelsea a sly smile.

"Lulu!"

"You have a new friend!" said Lulu. "Ask him to meet us."

"No way."

Lulu took off with the phone. Before Chelsea could reach her, she saw her thumbs going.

"What are you *doing*?" Chelsea said once she'd caught up to Lulu in a plush seating area in the aisle between Coach and Tiffany.

Lulu sank onto a leather couch, put her feet up, then handed the phone back. "I told him to meet us at the food court, near Panda Express."

"You're kidding!" Chelsea was horrified—and thrilled. After all, wasn't she just lecturing her mother on the low incidence of stranger crime? "That's insane. How could you?"

"So call your mom," said Lulu. It was a dare. "Have her come get you. *I'll* wait for him."

Lulu and Chelsea had been friends since kindergarten. Chelsea was the smart one; Lulu was the pretty one. Chelsea was the careful one; Lulu was the wild one. Chelsea was conscientious and hardworking; Lulu skated by. These were their roles, and they both knew them well, especially when they were together. Usually, their friendship was an easy balancing act. Lulu tempted Chelsea to be a little bad; Chelsea pulled Lulu back from the edge. But lately, Lulu was going places that Chelsea didn't always feel comfortable following.

Chelsea *did* think about calling her mother. She had that feeling, which Kate always encouraged her to honor. *If you feel nervous, if something doesn't feel good or right, your instincts are telling you something. Make sure you listen.*

Chelsea snatched the phone back from Lulu, who gave her a wide smile. But the truth was, Chelsea didn't want to go. She *did* want to see Adam McKee in the flesh. And she didn't want him to see Lulu first.

"I'm hungry," said Chelsea. She stuffed the phone in her bag and looked at her friend.

Lulu stood up and wrapped her arms around Chelsea. She smelled of strawberries and cigarettes. "You love me," said Lulu.

"I do," said Chelsea. She gave Lulu a quick squeeze and released her.

They walked toward the food court. Chelsea told herself that she *had* posted about their mall visit, anyway. As soon as Lulu had accepted Adam's request, he'd have been able to see that was where she was going. Besides, what were the chances that he wasn't who he said he was? And if he was, what were the chances that he'd actually come? Brighton wasn't far, but it wasn't close, either.

"Don't worry, Chaz." That was Lulu's annoying nickname for Chelsea. "First serial killer we see? We're so out of there."

"Very funny," said Chelsea. She made this kind of mock-snorting laugh that they'd done since they were kids. "Really. You're a riot."

Lulu took Chelsea's hand and held it tight. Lulu had always been physical with Chelsea, very affectionate. Chelsea loved that about her friend. Lulu had a way of making her feel like the most important person in the world. There was a group of boys hanging out by the surf shop. Chelsea noticed that they all turned to look at Lulu. Lulu passed them by without a second glance.

———

Heartbroken

Dean Freeman watched the bus pull away, knowing that Emily was on it, that he had let her down again. Something about the way it lumbered off, spewing black smoke from its tailpipe, merging into traffic, made him ache. He didn't want Emily riding the bus. She deserved so much better. He was going to be the one to make sure she got it sooner or later.

He went inside the restaurant anyway. Carol looked up at him from the register as the little bell over the door announced his entry.

He didn't like the way she looked at him, as though he had done something wrong or was about to. It was the look of teachers and principals, truant officers, cops. Like they knew you, like they could see right through every lie you hadn't even thought of yet. Like they knew it all. People had been looking at Dean Freeman like that all his life. He couldn't wait for the day when he proved to them all that they didn't know shit about him, couldn't begin to guess who he was or what he had in him.

"Hey, Carol," he said. He put on his sweet face, the one he used for Emily's mom, potential employers, or anyone he needed to win over. "Is Emily still here?"

"Hi, Dean," Carol said. She took off her glasses and let them hang from the beaded chain around her neck. They rested on the cushion of her wide bosom, which—even though she was way old—he couldn't help staring at. "Her shift ended over an hour ago. She ate and left."

"Ah," he said. He pulled his face into a disappointed grimace. "I got hung up at a job interview. I'm late to pick her up."

Carol gave him a slow nod, a narrow up-and-down stare. Did she seem skeptical? What right did she have to doubt what he was saying to her even though it was, in fact, a lie? That was what he didn't like about her. She thought she was better than everyone, had that way about her that rich people always did.

"How did it go?" she asked.

"What?"

"The job interview," she said. She gave him a patient smile. He could never tell when people were mocking him.

"Um, good, you know," he said. "The business is hurting a bit right now because of the economy. But people still need contractors, right? I'm sure I'll find something soon."

"Well, if I hear of anything, I'll let you know," she said.

"That would be great," he said. "Thanks. Hey, mind if I use your restroom?"

He walked back down the narrow hallway, used the restroom, and on his way out took one last look at the place. The back outer door opened directly into the kitchen; it was always locked from the inside. The long wood-paneled hallway led to the office. He followed it and stood in the doorway. Paul was there, head in hand, tapping hard on a calculator.

"Hey, Paul," said Dean.

Paul looked up and gave Dean a smile—a real smile, not that fake shit Carol was always beaming on him. "Hey, Dean," he said. "How's it going?"

"No complaints. How's that ride?" asked Dean.

"Man," said Paul with an admiring shake of the head. "That baby's bad to the bone. I just love driving it."

Paul had one of those new Chargers, triple black. Dean had seen it parked in the lot on the way in. It was so sweet. Dean wondered if he'd ever have a car like that. He hoped he'd have one while he was still young, not an old man like Paul. He knew it was about forty grand, fully loaded. To Dean that seemed an impossible sum of money; he couldn't come up with what he needed right now, which was a fraction of that amount. He'd had to resist the urge to key that shining black paint.

"You still owe me that spin," said Dean. He scanned the room. He knew the safe was under the desk and that they rarely used it. He knew there wasn't a security camera. He could see the empty canvas bank envelope lying carelessly next to the computer. Just checking the details one more time.

"You're on, man," said Paul. "Take it easy."

Paul looked back down at his work. Dean felt like he'd been dismissed, and it made him a little angry. Who did these people think they were? He walked back through the restaurant and gave a quick wave to Carol as he exited.

Brad was waiting in the car, looking antsy and agitated. It had been his idea to scope the place out one more time, even though Dean had told him everything he needed to know.

"Where's your girl?" Brad asked as Dean climbed into the driver's seat. Emily's old Mustang looked cool enough on the outside, but it was a piece of garbage. The interior was a mess, even after he tried to fix it up a little bit with a leather repair kit. It smelled of cigarettes and fast food, mainly because he and Brad had been smoking and eating McDonald's in it a little while ago.

"She left," he said. "On her way home, I guess."

Dean thought again of that bus pulling away. He tried to keep the wave of emotion off his face. Brad was not the guy to whom you wanted to bare your soul. He was a junkyard dog; you didn't dare let him smell your fear or sadness or anything else soft inside you. If he got his teeth into you, you'd have to break his jaw to get free. Brad gave Dean a look that he couldn't read.

"That door unlocks from the inside only," Brad said. He reached to the dash and took Dean's last cigarette. He lit it with the last match. Brad always was a selfish piece of shit.

"You checked it out?" asked Dean. "What if someone saw you?" He was more offended than worried. Brad didn't trust his judgment. Never had.

"If your girl's not in," said Brad, "we have problems. We can't come in through the front, not unless you want things to get ugly."

"I don't," said Dean too quickly. He took a breath before he spoke again. "No one gets hurt."

Brad issued a sharp exhale of smoke. He regarded his cuticles as if he didn't know they were chewed to the quick, split and bleeding. "Then your girl better be on board to open that door."

"She is," said Dean. "Of course she is."

Emily had no idea what they were planning to do. Even Dean hadn't known he'd been planning it in the back of his mind when Brad showed up early this week. From his old Florida days, he owed Brad some money. Brad had told him that one day he'd show up to collect, not to worry until then. The time had come. Unfortunately, Dean was flat broke. Not that he wasn't always broke. Not that he wasn't *born* broke.

He was *trying* to get his act together, but it felt like everyone and everything conspired against him. For a while he'd been doing okay. He'd been working at Constance Construction, a successful local company that everyone with money called when they wanted houses built. He liked his boss, Ronny Constance, who'd given Dean a chance even though he had a record.

"I don't care who you were then," Ronny had said the day he hired Dean. "I only care about who you are now. Are you going to show up? Are you going to be careful? Are you going to do a good job? What do you say, Dean, are you?"

The only time Dean had ever been calm and happy in his whole damn life was when he was building something. In school, he'd been bouncing off the walls. Too much talking, not enough doing—he just couldn't listen while someone was up at a board rambling on about things that meant nothing to him. He couldn't stand to read; the letters seemed to swim and jump before his eyes. They got tangled up, made no sense. Shop class had saved him. When he had his hands on something, making it into something else, all the anxiety he'd had for as long as he could remember seemed to go still and silent.

If he'd finished high school, he liked to think, maybe he'd have had a business like Ronny's. But after his father died, Dean fell in with Brad and Brad's brothers. From there, things went from bad to worse. There was the armed robbery. Luckily, he'd been a juvenile, though he'd still done time in a detention center. They had classes, vocational training, all kinds of shit like that, which was great. But it was in there that he started taking pills. The place was lousy with drugs; anything you wanted you could get from other inmates, from guards. With the pills—mostly, Oxy was his thing—there was that easy quiet again. And it was a lot less work to take a pill than it was to build a bookshelf.

After juvey, he moved up north to get away from the old crew. His uncle gave him a room over the garage for a while, introduced him to Ronny. And then Dean met Emily. She was the prettiest, the sweetest girl he had ever known. For a while, his life had been perfect. He had a good job, he was totally clean and sober—he found he didn't need the pills when he was working with his hands. He had Emily, and he had started living in her cute little house.

That was the brief time when he thought he'd figured it all out. But that wasn't the way things worked for him. It wasn't the way things worked for anyone he'd ever known. Something always went wrong. That's what had happened to his dad. Just when he'd gotten clean—bam!—stage four lung cancer. Just when he'd stopped being a crazy, violent, scary motherfucker who beat the crap out of Dean and Dean's mom, some doctor told him he had three months to live. It turned out to be two.

It was Dean's temper that always screwed him up. The truth was, his memories of the fight with Ronny and what it had been about were fuzzy. He just lost it like that sometimes. It had something to do with a cabinet he'd installed. He'd put the door on wrong, maybe, a little thing. Ronny had laughed at him. If there was one thing he couldn't fucking stand, it was being laughed at. He felt the rise, the red swell he used to have when he was younger. After that, it was a literal blank in his memory. Ronny didn't press charges; Dean was lucky for that. But he lost the only good job he'd ever had.

From there it was one big downward spiral. He started doing stupid shit for money, which led to him starting with the pills again. Brad showing up? Well, Dean knew rock bottom when he saw it.

He pulled out into traffic, and in the rearview mirror, he saw the big blue hen on the restaurant sign. The sight of it got him to laughing, he couldn't have said why.

"What's so funny?" asked Brad.

"Nothing." The laughter dried up in Dean, and he started to feel a little sick. He always felt this way with Brad, a kind of wobble between edgy excitement and abysmal despair. Being with Emily gave Dean permission to connect with all the good parts of himself. Being with Brad connected him to everything that was rotten and black inside. Dean was worried that there was way more of the bad stuff, that it was sticky, like tar. If he dove into that place again, he wouldn't have what it took to claw his way back out. It would pull him all the way under, and this time he would take Emily with him.

"Maybe this is not such a good idea," said Dean.

Brad was quiet, just flicked the cigarette out the window. Then, "You have another way to get the money you owe me?"

Dean didn't need to say anything. They both knew the answer. As they pulled onto the highway, he heard that rattle in the engine. The car wasn't long for this world.

chapter four

When Emily got home, Dean wasn't there. But from the look of the place, she could tell that he'd been lying around most of the day. The television was on, tuned in now to *Oprah*. There was a pile of dishes in the sink. The microwave door was ajar. He hadn't taken the garbage out, like she'd asked, and it was starting to smell. Every light in the living room, bedroom, and bathroom was on. His underwear was on the floor. He didn't pay rent here (or anywhere else). Nor did he contribute to the utilities. But he seemed to feel very much at home. Emily supposed it was her fault. She didn't ask much of him. She'd found it was better not to ask too much from people.

When he'd first started staying at her place, she'd come home to find that he had dinner ready or that he'd brought her flowers. Every day she still hoped he'd done any of the small things he used to, like the laundry, or making sure there were no dishes in the sink. She couldn't remember the last time he'd been romantic or even considerate.

She set about tidying up. She really hated it when things were a mess; it made her think of her mother's house. Since Emily started renting the small one-bedroom cottage, she'd managed to get herself some cute pieces. Nothing expensive. She'd purchased a soft gray couch and a coordinating red and gray chair on sale at Pier 1. It had a rip in one cushion, so it was marked way down. She flipped the cushion over and forgot the tear was even there. Things didn't have to be perfect to be okay for Emily.

Dean brought her a beautiful rug that tied the pieces together. She didn't dare ask where it had come from. She'd refinished an old coffee table she found at a garage sale. Dean had installed some track lighting. She was proud of the living room. In the bedroom, she had a white platform bed and dresser from Target. She'd framed some pictures of her and Dean and hung them on the wall. She'd painted the walls a honey-beige. The little house was comfortable and clean. She liked it that way, and Dean knew that. He obviously didn't care.

"I'm working on something big," he'd said this morning. "Something huge."

How many times had she heard that? His first "big" idea had been buying and flipping houses right as the market crashed. Not that he had anywhere near the money for that venture. Next it was a Jet Ski rental company for a nearby lake, but he couldn't find the money to get the skis, or the permit, or the insurance he'd need. She didn't know what it would be this time; he wouldn't say. He hadn't said last time, when he'd taken the tuition reimbursement. Nothing, of course, ever came of that money. She had a bad feeling about this recent thing, whatever it was.

When she met Dean, he'd been working for a contractor, making a good living. He was great at that, building things, fixing things. He'd seemed hardworking, reliable. Truthfully, he was—when he was motivated, when he felt he was being justly rewarded. It was his temper that got him into trouble.

Emily heard a car in the driveway. She went to the window and watched Dean get out of her beat-up old Mustang. Another man got out of the passenger side. She hadn't seen him before. She had the odd urge to run to the door and lock it. She didn't do that. She was standing near the television, holding the clothes she'd collected from the floor in her arms, when the two of them walked in.

"I swung by the restaurant," said Dean when he saw her. He had a guilty look on his face. "They said you went home."

"You were late," she said.

"You should have waited." He had that edge to his voice. He got this way when certain kinds of people were around, as if he had to show everyone who was boss. She walked out of the room and put the wash in the white basket in the tiny laundry room. She didn't care if she was being rude. She took out the trash, came in, and started the dishes.

Then he was behind her. "I'm sorry," he whispered.

She didn't answer him. The television was louder in the other room. They'd turned to a game, and she could hear the tinny sound of a crowd cheering. She started the faucet to rinse the dishes before loading them into the dishwasher.

"Who is that?" she asked without turning around.

"Just someone I used to know."

She knew what the phrase meant. She spun around to look at him. "What does he want?"

He looked down at the floor. She noticed the half-moon scar around his eye where his father had hit him with a closed fist, cutting Dean with his ring. Dean had told her that he was twelve at the time. He smelled like cigarettes, though he'd sworn last week that he'd quit. They couldn't afford cigarettes right now.

"How did you do on tips today?" he asked.

She hugged her arms around her middle. She'd done pretty well. But she needed to pay the rent on Friday. "Not great," she lied. "How much do you need?"

"A couple hundred."

"I don't have it," she said. "I'm sorry."

She'd taken to stopping at the bank on her way home from work, not keeping a lot of cash on hand. She hadn't done that today because she didn't have the car, so she was carrying almost a hundred dollars in her purse.

He looked at her. "Then get dressed and come with me."

"No."

"Baby," he said. He wrapped his arms around her, placed his mouth to her ear. "Please."

He sounded desperate; she felt herself relenting. She knew he could sense it. "Wear the blue dress," he said. "It looks so pretty on you."

She walked away from him and went into the bedroom and closed the door, her heart pounding. Why was she so weak? She took the blue wrap dress from the closet and slipped it on. In the bathroom, she brushed her hair and put on a little lipstick. *Pretty enough,* she heard her mother say, *in a common way.* Emily grabbed the cute black patent-leather clutch and matching flats, other gifts from Dean that she knew he couldn't afford. She wanted to lie down on the bed and go to sleep. She looked over at the fluffy white comforter and soft pillows. She was tired after the breakfast shift, which started early and was always hectic. It would feel so nice to lie down. But she went to him, as she knew he wanted her to. He gave her a wide smile when she emerged; it seemed more victorious than loving.

"This is my girl, Emily," said Dean. "Em, this is my old friend Brad. We came up together in Florida."

Dean had done time in Florida, three years in juvenile detention for an armed robbery. He'd come north to escape that life, he'd told her. But Emily wondered if you could ever really escape where you came from. It didn't seem like you could.

She reached out for Brad's hand, and he shook it more gently than she would have expected. He had long blond hair that hung, uncombed and unwashed, around his shoulders and a goatee that needed trimming. He might have been handsome, but there was something mean about the set of his mouth, the narrowness of his eyes. He looked at her with naked desire, and she turned away, moved over to Dean. He draped a possessive arm around her.

"Pleased to meet you," Brad said. Was there something mocking about the way he said it?

———

Dean drove, with Brad riding shotgun and Emily in the backseat. Nobody said anything until they pulled off the main road into a development, following the paper signs to the open house.

"Look at these places," said Dean.

The houses were huge, each one grander than the last—brick and stone, some of them three stories high. When Emily first met Dean, she'd been working for a maid service. This was one of the neighborhoods where she had come to clean.

She couldn't believe the way people lived—with media rooms and gyms in their basements, master bedroom suites bigger than any of the homes she'd ever lived in, kitchens that looked like they belonged in a restaurant but so spotless she knew week to week that they hadn't been touched. The kids' rooms were what killed her, the closets stuffed with designer clothes, the computers, the iPods, the video game systems, the shelves of books, the mounds of toys.

"It's disgusting," said Dean. Brad grunted beside him.

Emily didn't think it was disgusting. Why was it disgusting to work hard and get wealthy and live well? Most of the people she'd cleaned for were nice enough. Sure, there was the occasional snob. Mostly, they were normal families, working too hard, too busy to clean.

When she was in those homes, it wasn't the wives she envied, with their manicured nails and stylish clothes; it was the children, the daughters especially. These were the loved children, the wanted ones. These were the girls who were cherished. Their parents told them that they were loved, and beautiful, and smart, that they could do anything they wanted to in this world. They believed it, so it was true. Emily would touch their clothes and hug their dolls, straighten their pillows with extra care. She wondered if it was like fairy dust, all that love. Maybe some of it would rub off on her.

When they pulled up to the open house, there were several other cars parked around. That was best, when there were other people there and the broker was busy answering questions and showing off the features of the house.

Dean stepped out and pulled the seat forward so that she could climb out.

"You look nice," she said. He'd changed into pressed chinos and a royal blue oxford with the red silk tie she'd bought him for Christmas. He closed the door, and they walked up the drive together.

"Thanks for this," he whispered. "You know how much I need you."

"What does he want, Dean?" she asked for the second time.

"I owe him some money."

"How much?" She felt a rush of disappointment and anger.

"Don't ask," he answered.

For a minute, before they got inside, she let herself sink into the moment. Both of them dressed in their best, her arm looped into his, she let herself imagine that they were a young professional couple, newly married, looking for their first home. He had a great job, making tons of money. He was a star at his company. She was expecting their first child, not sure whether she'd continue working once the kids started coming. She imagined that they were walking through the big wooden door with every expectation that this house, or one even better, could be theirs. She let herself be that woman. What did she do? She was a teacher. Yes, that was it. She didn't make as much as her husband did, but she loved her work. She loved molding young minds, giving them the knowledge they needed to succeed in the world. That was what Emily was studying in school, early childhood education. She'd go back. She would.

It was a triple-height foyer, which Emily just loved. High ceilings meant wealth; if you could afford all that space with nothing in it, you had money to burn. The staircase swept dramatically up the side of the wall to a landing. She could imagine herself gliding down in some fabulous party dress, Dean waiting for her at the door in a tuxedo. The floors were hardwood, solid beneath her feet. What impressed Emily most were the fresh white calla lilies in tall vases. Giant decorative bouquets like that cost a fortune and lasted about a week. Emily loved the look and aroma of fresh flowers, even though they reminded her of how nothing lovely and delicate can stay. If you could afford to surround yourself with flowers that someone else carted away and replaced every week, you had arrived at the good life.

Emily and Dean didn't need to talk or plan. They'd done this so many times. They would make sure the broker saw them; they would take the flyer and one of the little bottles of water. She'd coo over the double fireplace that could be seen from the kitchen and the open dining room. He would say he loved the floor plan but worried about the landing, with the baby and all. She'd marvel at how much natural light there was and wonder how they kept the skylights clean. He'd be disappointed that the pool didn't have an attached hot tub.

If the broker was an older person, she'd immediately sniff out that they didn't have any money, especially if she'd seen their car. Depending on her personality, she'd either ignore them or watch them closely. The younger ones were still naive and hopeful. Most of them probably didn't have that much money themselves and didn't yet know what it smelled like or looked like. This broker was young, probably not much older than Emily. And she looked nervous.

Dean held her up, asking things about the house. When was it built? Who was the developer? What were the private schools in the area? Emily drifted up the stairs. Most sellers knew to safeguard their valuables for an open house, so there wouldn't be jewelry lying around. Most homes like this had safes, and if not, at least things were locked up in boxes or drawers, though once she found a very expensive watch in a nightstand. And they knew to take down all their pictures so that potential buyers could envision themselves living in the home. Which was also good for Emily, because she didn't have to look at the faces of the people she was violating.

This four-bedroom house, she figured, would have three and a half baths. But it was only the master bath she was interested in. Root canals, migraines, back problems, sprains or breaks—most people had experienced some kind of malady for which a doctor would prescribe powerful painkillers. Most people didn't take any of it, or at least not all of it. But those bottles of OxyContin or Vicodin stayed in their medicine cabinets. Some people forgot about them, while others didn't know how to safely dispose of them; still others kept them, she guessed, for some just-in-case scenario, like an army of little orange soldiers with green caps at the ready to rescue them from sleepless nights, free-floating anxiety, or sudden toothaches.

When Emily worked for the cleaning service, she had ready access to medicine cabinets all day long. It was easy to see from week to week what was being used and what wasn't. She'd check the prescription dates, count the pills. She hadn't visited a home yet that didn't have something interesting . . . Ambien was popular for insomnia, Ativan for anxiety. Then, of course, there were Prozac, Ritalin, Zoloft, lithium. Those were trickier because people who had any of those medications usually took them regularly; they knew exactly how many pills were in each bottle. If they tried to refill before the time allotted by the doctor or insurance company, a red flag would go up. They'd know someone else had been taking the pills. Emily had learned that lesson the hard way.

She drifted around the bedroom, looking at the books on the shelves, moving into the bonus room, which this family was using as a cozy television sitting area. She could tell by the feel of the fabrics that the furniture was expensive.

There was another couple in the master bath, oohing and aahing over the steam shower and marble floors. Emily sank down on the love seat and looked out over the tops of the maple and sycamore trees, pretending to take in the view; this was where you'd come after the children went to bed. You'd bring your glass of wine and look outside, unwind. You'd talk to each other about your day—how the kids were wild, how the boss was a jerk.

When the other couple left, she went into the bathroom and shut the door. She'd have to be quick; she could hear other voices on the second floor. The master bedroom was one of the most important features of a house.

She didn't have to be cautious, like she'd had to be as a cleaning lady. Then she'd take only one or two pills from whatever she found, depending on how much was in the bottle. She'd carry little bags in her pocket, careful to keep everything separate and labeled. You got more money that way, Dean had taught her, when people knew what they were buying. The pain pills and the antidepressants had the highest value. The ADD drugs were good, too. Though Dean's dealer would take anything for the "cocktail parties." Someone would have a bowl of prescription drugs, and the people at the party would take whatever was in there without knowing exactly what they were ingesting. Mostly, it was kids. It was totally crazy. Emily didn't understand how anyone could take a pill without knowing what it was or what it could do.

She opened the cabinet and started rifling through. Cold medicine. She grabbed the Sudafed, because that could be used in making other drugs. There was always demand for it. There were Motrin, Tylenol, and a box of Imodium. None of that was any good. The top two shelves were all prescriptions. Jackpot. She didn't bother to look at what they were; she just put it all in her bag. They could sort it out in the car. There was no one in the room when she came back out. So she drifted down the stairs, where Dean was still talking to the broker.

"And it's well built, not like a lot of places," she was saying. "Some of these homes have paper-thin walls. You can hear everything from room to room. But not here."

"Oh, yes," said Dean. "I can see that. Very solid construction."

They made the loop of the whole house for show. Dean liked the office with its big oak desk and ergonomic chair. Emily loved the girl's room with the dollhouse and four-poster bed. The broker gave Dean her card and asked them to sign the sheet, provide an e-mail; she'd stay in touch about her other listings. Mr. and Mrs. Greg Glass, dneglass@hotmail.com. Emily liked it when he wrote that; it made her feel good, for some reason.

As they walked back out to the car, she almost told Dean the thing she'd wanted to tell him. But when she looked back, the broker was standing on the front stoop watching them. And when Emily looked ahead, Brad had rolled down the window. She saw his hand dangling out with a cigarette between the fingers. She had a strange feeling, a little rise of panic, that she couldn't move forward or move back. It wasn't the right moment for good news. Emily wondered if it ever would be.

chapter five

Dear Kate,

The weather has been cold here at Heart Island. The water never quite warmed this year. Be sure you bring the proper gear, not like last year. I wonder if Sean's kayaking skills have improved at all? Perhaps we can manage a day trip without someone needing to be hauled to shore.

I know Brendan and Chelsea complained about the lack of television reception; I am afraid that hasn't changed. Perhaps you'll want to bring a portable DVD player again to keep them entertained. Though I will say that cell phone reception has come to the island, so that should make Chelsea less sullen. It's very spotty, for reasons I can't explain. But at least it's something.

I'll be doing the final grocery shopping tomorrow. So if you have any special needs, let me know—or you'll be quite out of luck, since we're trying to avoid any unnecessary trips to the mainland. The menu for the last week will be written in stone unless you speak up now. Is Chelsea still a quasi-vegetarian? Does Brendan eat ANYTHING but macaroni and cheese? You know, it is impossible to be high-maintenance on Heart Island. I imagine, as the children get older, they'll understand that better. Though I'm still waiting for you and Theodore to come up to speed on this point—ha-ha!

Kate skimmed the rest of her mother's e-mail and fought the urge to lie down, the way she often (always?) felt after communications from her mother. The embedded insults softened with terms of endearment and the digs masquerading as jokes never failed to drain her of energy.

Your mother's an expert sniper, Sean had said. *You know you got hit; you just don't know where the shot came from. You can't do anything but lie there, bleeding out.*

The question was why Birdie always felt the need to aim and fire. If confronted, she'd say something like: "Oh, Kate, don't be so sensitive." It was a perfect double whammy, to hurt someone and then to act as if it were weakness on the part of the injured to cry out in pain. How could Kate have been angry with Theo for not wanting to go to the island anymore? The truth was, she wasn't angry with him. She was angry with herself.

"Are we going to go camping again this year?" Brendan asked.

Kate started a little. She was sitting in her office, at the desk with her back to the door, which was, she knew, very bad feng shui. If you kept your back to the door, allegedly, you were energetically turning away from new business and new opportunities. You were also allowing enemies to sneak up on you, according to the feng shui expert who'd written the article in one of the many magazines dedicated to simplifying life. It made an odd kind of sense to Kate, though she hadn't gotten around to rearranging the furniture. Why did the act of simplifying your life seem so complicated and require so much effort? Why was there never any time to do it?

"I don't know," Kate said. She closed the e-mail and swiveled to face Brendan.

Kate hated camping. It seemed silly to sleep outside in the woods when you could be sleeping inside in your bed. What was the point? To seem outdoorsy? Some people would give anything to be sleeping inside.

"We'll see about the weather," she said. She tried to keep her voice bright.

"What's wrong?" Brendan asked.

Both her children were delicately tied in to her moods; she could never hide anything from them. She was glad about that in some ways, because she didn't *want* to hide anything from them. Not the big stuff, anyway—she knew how toxic that was. On the other hand, they didn't need to know everything going on in her head every second, did they?

"It's nothing," she said.

"Lies," said her son. He flopped himself down on the couch next to her desk, put his feet up on the cushions. She could see, even from a distance, that his ankle was swollen. It was turning a deep purple around the bone.

Brendan was her little Tonka truck, sturdy and beefy, indestructible. The falls and accidents he'd had over his short life were legendary, but he seemed to get up and walk away, immediately game for the next adventure. Today he'd hurt his ankle during soccer. And now he was limping badly.

Instead of watching the rest of the game, they'd spent an hour at the urgent care center near their house. After he'd twisted his ankle, as she comforted him on the field and held the ice to it, she'd wondered—selfishly, guiltily—if this was reason enough to cancel the trip. But the doctor had said that nothing was broken or fractured; it was just a bad sprain.

"Where's your ice pack?" she asked.

"It's too cold."

She had to love the logic of her ten-year-old.

"It's *supposed* to be cold."

He gave her an earnest look. "I'm taking a break from it."

She got up and went into the living room, where he'd tossed the ice pack on the floor, and returned to her office. She placed it gently on his ankle. He didn't look up from his handheld game.

Sean had purchased the device for him recently, mainly because they felt like they had to, since Chelsea's father had given her an iPhone for no reason at all. This had been one of the major points of contention between Kate and her ex-husband recently: whether he could give Chelsea extravagant gifts without Kate and Sean's permission.

Even though they could, Kate and Sean made a conscious effort not to give the kids everything they wanted when they wanted it. Chelsea and Brendan each had a list, and they got what was on that list eventually—usually for birthdays, Christmas, or some school accomplishment, after saving for part of it themselves, or by earning it in some other way, and, of course, the random surprise. But because of her ex's sudden desire to win Chelsea over (now that he was sober and "confronting his past mistakes"), not to mention his titanic guilt complex, he was giving her things—like the iPhone, piles of clothes, designer bags.

"I have a right to buy my daughter gifts," he'd said to Kate during this afternoon's heated conversation. She was inadequate at the task of explaining why it was not okay to give Chelsea things that Kate would have made her wait for or earn. Or how it upset the balance of fairness between Chelsea and her brother. You couldn't explain the complex strategies of good and careful parenting to someone who'd never had a thought about anything or anyone but himself.

Close up, Brendan's ankle looked even worse than it had on the field. She put a tender hand on it and sat down next to him on the couch.

"Listen, bud," she said. "Maybe we should think about canceling the trip."

Brendan glanced up from his game with wide eyes. She pressed on.

"It's going to be hard for you there while you're injured." She was *such* a horrible mother. What a total cop-out to try to use Brendan's injury to get them out of this trip.

"It's fine!" he said. He sat up quickly. "It's not *that* bad."

He stood to prove his point, then tried to hide the resulting wince. He sat back down, deflated. She draped an arm around him and pulled him in close.

"I love it there," he said.

She felt a powerful twist of sadness. She loved it there, too. Something magical lived on Heart Island, something beautiful. It had been there long before her mother's family had ever owned it, and it would be there long after they were all gone. None of the awful things that had happened on the island, or because of it, could change that. It wasn't only the glorious air or the unspoiled lake water. It wasn't simply the rocky shore or the wind in the trees. It wasn't the musical quiet or even the clusters of butterflies. It was something Kate had never been able to explain or define, but it drew her there again and again, even though an equal number of things pushed her away. Theo had obviously given up on it. Kate couldn't do that. She wouldn't.

She looked at her watch. It was time to go get Chelsea. She told Brendan as much.

"Are you going to cancel?" he asked. "Because of me?"

He looked so sad sitting there, so disappointed.

"No," she said. She ruffled the soft mess of his hair. "You'll be all right."

She thought he'd smile in relief, but he frowned.

"Why don't you want to go?" he asked. He had wise hazel eyes that were green in a certain light, and the same sandy hair as his sister's (but his was a wild and untamable mass of curls). His nose and cheekbones were, to his eternal dismay, a riot of freckles.

"I do," she said. "It's complicated."

He shrugged, moving on. "Can I watch TV?"

She'd recently started allowing Brendan to stay at home alone while she ran a quick errand here and there. He was smart, reasonably trustworthy. And, she figured, how much trouble could he cause in under half an hour, especially if she told him he could watch television? She always had a low-grade feeling of unease when she left him.

"Yes, but order the pizza in about twenty minutes," she said. "Don't forget."

The odds were about fifty-fifty that he'd remember to do what she asked. She'd have Chelsea call and check when she got in the car. Tonight they'd all start packing. Tomorrow would be a frantic rush of last-minute errands and stuffing suitcases to the brim, arguing about what could come and what must stay. By Sunday morning, they'd be in the car, heading north. She tried to remember what it was like to be excited about a trip the way she was when she was younger, like Brendan. But she couldn't remember. All she really felt was dread.

It came to nothing. Chelsea was giddy at first, as she drank her strawberry banana smoothie, just wondering *if* he'd come, and if he'd be as cute as his picture. Sometimes it seemed like anticipation was the most fun of anything.

They waited, the scent of cinnamon rolls heavy in the air, getting excited every time they saw someone who *could* be Adam. In the seemingly endless stream of moms with kids and gangs of boys and girls all spending their Friday afternoon at the mall, no one approached them. There were a couple of boys with torn jeans and spiky hair that could have been the boy in the photo. But one had a tattoo, the other a pierced nose, and they didn't see anyone they were sure enough about to wave at. Slowly, the excited tingle diminished.

Lulu promised that she wouldn't flirt if he *did* show up. Anyway, Lulu had a sick crush on Conner Lange, who had been calling her the whole time. Lulu thought he was going to ask her to homecoming this fall. Lulu liked jocks, not alternative, punky boys. Chelsea did *not* like jocks; she did not understand the whole team-sports thing and why people were so collectively *into* it. She liked guys who were into art and music, who liked to read and understood poetry.

"Which is why you never like anyone," said Lulu. "Because no one cares about any of those things."

"Some guys do," said Chelsea. Didn't they? Her father did. Adam McKee looked like the type of guy who would.

"Maybe," said Lulu. "But they're all geeks. Or gay."

Chelsea didn't feel like arguing. Instead, they talked about how Lulu had to do better in algebra this year. Chelsea said she would help when she got back from her trip if Lulu promised to study harder and spend less time on Facebook.

"That island," said Lulu. She drank the rest of her water. God forbid she should have a smoothie. "You're going again."

"It's a family thing," said Chelsea. "We go every year."

"What am I supposed to do for the rest of the summer?" Lulu took aim with the bottle and landed it directly in the recycle bin.

"It's just a week until school starts," said Chelsea.

"I guess." Lulu looked a little sad, and Chelsea felt a tug of guilt. She'd never invited Lulu to the island, although Lulu had been on other trips with Chelsea's family. Heart Island was different somehow. For whatever reason, Chelsea couldn't imagine Lulu there.

Lulu didn't have many other friends. They both knew why; she was hot, and she was mean—not a good combination. Most girls hated her on sight. Chelsea had never asked herself why she wasn't intimidated by Lulu's beauty or why Lulu wasn't mean to her. She just didn't remember a time before she and Lulu were friends.

"It's getting late," said Chelsea. She took one last sweep of the huge food court, the giant beating heart of the mall. All the arteries led to this teeming center, mobbed with people eating all the food her mother hated. She looked from table to table. No Adam McKee. Chelsea was equal parts disappointed and relieved. "He's not coming."

Lulu glanced at the clock and nodded her agreement. "Oh well."

This would be the point when Lulu would normally say something mean about him, that he was a loser or that he was probably poor because he went to public school. But Lulu was strangely silent. Chelsea checked the Facebook app on her phone. He hadn't written on her wall or sent her a message. She shared that with Lulu, who was tapping away on her own phone and didn't seem to hear.

Chelsea said, "We should go."

She gathered up the bag containing the items she'd bought for the island—some cute fleece pullovers and a pair of Keen amphibious shoes. Lulu had complained about Chelsea's *seriously unsexy* purchases. But there was no one to be sexy for on Heart Island. That was one of the things she liked about it, the complete cessation of all pressure to be cool in any way.

Looking at her BlackBerry, Lulu frowned. Chelsea glanced at the clock; her mom would freak if they were late. She expected Kate to start calling any minute. "Are you coming?"

Lulu was spending the night since her own parents were planning an evening in the city to celebrate their anniversary. Even though the girls spent almost every weekend together, Lulu didn't seem especially psyched about it. Chelsea suspected that it had something to do with Conner Lange. She knew Lulu had been doing some sneaking out lately. And that wasn't going to happen at Chelsea's.

"Yeah," Lulu said. "Sorry." She had that tone, angry or sad but trying to hide it.

"What's wrong?" asked Chelsea.

"Nothing," she said. She picked up her stuff. "Just my parents being assholes."

Lulu's parents were practically ghosts. Her father managed a hedge fund; her mother was a plastic surgeon. They had lots of money but very little time, it seemed, for Lulu. Their family trips were to Europe or exotic tropical places like Fiji. Lulu rarely talked about those trips and never had any pictures to share.

Chelsea looped her arm through Lulu's, and Lulu dropped her head against Chelsea's shoulder as they left the mall. Who cared about Adam McKee or Conner Lange when they had each other?

Outside, Chelsea's mom was waiting in the idling Range Rover. Kate was staring up through the open sunroof. For a second, to Chelsea, Kate didn't look like herself. She seemed small and young, almost unfamiliar—a pretty blond woman in a big SUV waiting for something or someone. She looked sad and a little lost. For whatever reason, it caused Chelsea a flutter of anxiety. She used to ask her mother, *Where were you before I was born?* Her mother would tell her about growing up in New York City, going to college, or getting married. It always sounded like one of the bedtime stories Kate made up for her. Because how could her mother be anything or do anything without her? It hadn't seemed possible.

As she got closer, Chelsea could see that Kate was probably trying to meditate, to take a few calming breaths the way she'd taught Chelsea to do. Now Chelsea did that all the time, when she was freaking out, or overexcited, or trying to make a good feeling last. *I am breathing in,* she'd say to herself as she inhaled. *I am breathing out.* She didn't know why it relaxed her, made a moment seem to expand, but it did.

Chelsea opened the door, and her mother turned to her with a wide smile and was just her mom again—normal, happy as always to see her daughter. Both Lulu and Chelsea leaned in to kiss Kate. And then the car was filled with the three of them chattering. Both Lulu and Chelsea knew better than to tell Kate about Adam McKee, so they talked about everything else.

Chelsea was wondering what they'd have for dinner (probably pizza, since it was Friday, or Taco Bell, if Brendan got his way again), while her mom and Lulu were talking about Conner Lange.

Kate had seen Conner on the other field while watching Brendan practice before the spaz sprained his ankle. Kate agreed that he was *sooooo cute.*

"But is he smart? Is he a good guy?" Kate predictably wanted to know.

"Oh, yes," said Lulu, even though Chelsea knew Lulu couldn't care less about either of those things. "He is."

Chelsea felt her phone vibrate in her bag. She pulled it out and read the window that had popped up on her screen.

Adam McKee sent you a message. She didn't say anything as she opened up Facebook. *Can't make it to the mall,* he'd written. *But what are you doing tonight?*

She felt a jolt of excitement as she quickly stuck the phone in her pocket. She'd tell Lulu later, but she wanted to keep it to herself for a bit. She knew that as soon as she shared it with Lulu or her mother, it would be less special than it was right now, when it was her little secret. A cute guy wanted to know what she was doing tonight. Before anyone warned caution, or Lulu found something to make fun of on his page, Chelsea took a few minutes to enjoy it. *I am breathing in,* she thought. *I am breathing out.*

chapter six

Joe was half listening to the weather on the radio while answering e-mail on his phone—a habit that annoyed Birdie to no end. There was absolutely no reason not to get the weather from the computer. But there was something that appealed to Joe about listening to the weather forecast on the radio. He favored the foreign-language stations because he fancied himself a polyglot (which he wasn't; he had a middling knowledge of French, did better with Spanish). Meanwhile, whatever the language of the forecast, he wasn't really paying attention to it. So he frequently made serious misjudgments about when to take the boat out because he hadn't quite heard or understood the weather predictions. She would be forced to correct him in order to avoid disaster, which always got them into a screaming row. Birdie spoke fluent French and was quite capable with Spanish.

"How was your swim this morning?" he asked.

"Fine," she said.

"You weren't gone long," he said. She didn't answer.

"Sounds like the weather will be nice this weekend," he said into the silence.

The weather was *not* predicted to be nice. There were heavy thunderstorms in the forecast, as was evidenced by the gathering dark in the sky over the mainland. If he'd only look outside, he'd see that. Wasn't it Benjamin Franklin who said that people were divided into two groups: the weather-wise and otherwise?

When Birdie met Joe—a hundred years ago, it seemed—she

knew on sight that she would marry him. She was at a Christmas party, one that her friends had forced her to attend. They'd showed up at her door—Belle, Patty, and Joan—and lured her from bed with a bottle of champagne and a red party dress "borrowed" from Macy's. (They'd paid for it with credit. They would hide the tags, be extra-careful with their drinks, and return the dress on Monday.)

She didn't realize it at the time, but she had been depressed, hiding out in her tiny one-bedroom Manhattan apartment on Bank Street. Depression was a private monster she would battle over and over in her life, and this was her first real taste of it. She had suffered a humiliating split-up from her fiancé, and she was sure she'd never marry. A pall had settled over her life. It wasn't black but gray. A grayness that leached into every other color, draining her energy and spirit. She was consumed with gray thoughts. She knew she'd languish in the secretarial pool until the day she died. She was certain of it even though she was only twenty-three years old.

"Lying around here isn't going to make anything better," said Joanie.

"No, I'd wager it will only make things worse," agreed Belle.

They were all so pretty and fun—dressed up, hair pinned, lips red, skin white and flawless. Had they really been as beautiful as she remembered them? Or was it that they were all so young, so hopeful, with everything before them?

She allowed them to do her makeup, sweep her long blond hair into a stylish chignon. The dress—even in her doldrums, she had to admit it—was sensational.

"It's like someone poured you into it," said Patty. "Oh, Birdie. It's wonderful."

Whatever happened to friendship like that? That selfless, cheerful, loving camaraderie? Did it go the way of the bouffant, a silly style that people laughed about now? All Birdie's close female relationships had fallen away over the years. She wasn't quite sure why.

That easiness, that sweetness, when they were all on equal footing and just starting out, had turned bitter. Choices turned to consequences, opinions turned to judgments, and admiration turned to envy. Envy curdled everything, like lemon in milk.

And then they were on the chilly streets. Their coats were all awful, practical tweed and wool affairs worn two seasons too long because none of them could afford new. At the Stork Club, the coats were immediately shucked aside like embarrassing relatives from Brooklyn. Of course, they were *all* Brooklyn-born and -raised. But they thought of themselves as Manhattan girls now, leaving the outer boroughs far behind. They had educations and jobs, small apartments in the Village or on the Upper East Side. Men still paid for drinks and meals back then; a girl could live well on very little until she found a husband. For a certain set in 1960, New York City was a candy store.

What Birdie remembered most about that night was how everything sparkled—Christmas lights on the trees, sequins on the dresses, gloss on the lips, and bubbles in the champagne. A jazz quartet played hip renditions of classic carols. And then there was Joe, taller, bigger, than the other men. He didn't belong; she could see that. He played the game as well as everyone else, but there was something about him that stood apart and above. He had a way of squinting when he looked at people. He could have been amused or disgusted. It was hard to tell. Something about that excited her.

When his eyes fell on Birdie, there was something in his gaze that made her draw in a little gasp. Birdie had been beautiful then. She wouldn't have said so at the time, but she could see it in photographs of herself. She was slim and strong. The scarlet dress that night, her matching lips: Joe claimed that she cast a spell on him. He walked over to her, abandoning his conversation, as if drawn by a rope through the crowd. The men with whom he'd been talking turned to stare and then started laughing among themselves. She heard Joan, Patty, and Belle giggle and whisper and drift away. The band was playing a jaunty rendition of "Jingle Bells." In that moment, Birdie felt lighter, happier, than she had in weeks.

"You're too pretty to work at our company," Joe said as he approached her. In those days, it passed as charming.

What did she say to him? She didn't remember. All she remembered was the feeling she had when she looked into his face. He was strong. He was honorable. He would take care of her. She could see it all there in the square of his jaw, the wide knuckles, the thickness of his neck. She felt washed over by a sense of relief that left her lightheaded. He was the first safe place she had found, and she mistook it for love at first sight. Of course, that was before she knew the truth about love and marriage, about life.

"I've had a call from Teddy," said Joe. He poured her a cup of coffee, stirred in the perfect amount of half-and-half. He always knew how to make her coffee just right. "He's not coming." Joe tried to sound light, but she could tell he was angry.

He hadn't shaved, she noticed. When they were younger, she used to think he looked so sexy in the morning, before he was all combed and pressed. She hadn't had those kinds of thoughts about her husband in a very long time.

"Oh?" She felt something grow heavy and sad inside her. When she'd talked to Teddy last week, she'd had a feeling he might cancel. He'd hinted twice about work being hectic.

"Busy with work, can't get away," said Joe. "You'd think he had a real job, the way he carries on."

Teddy owned his own company, a consulting firm—whatever that meant.

"Oh, Joe. You know he has a real job," she said. "He's very successful."

Her husband issued an unkind grunt.

"What is it he does now?" she asked. Teddy had told her about his business. But Birdie honestly didn't understand what he was talking about—systems and infrastructures.

Joe shrugged, peering down at his phone. He was always staring at the thing as if whatever he saw there was much more interesting than anything going on around him. "Something with computers."

Birdie believed that Joe knew exactly what Teddy's company did. He simply, for some mean personal reason, pretended not to. Joe and Teddy had never really gotten along. Even when Teddy was small, Joe seemed to have trouble connecting with his son. As Teddy grew, the boy seemed so delicate, so frail—so *different* in every way from the thick and powerful Burke men. Teddy was slender and more careful, creative and quiet, like the men on Birdie's side of the family. Whatever early attempts Joe had made with Teddy—catch, ball games, fishing, golf—had generally ended with Teddy weeping in Birdie's lap. *Why do you have to be so hard, Joe?* Birdie had asked him a thousand times. Joe would rage: *What's wrong with that boy? He's like a china doll.*

Joe had worked as an aeronautical engineer for the entirety of his career. He understood meticulous design that led to the creation of a tangible object, preferably something made out of steel, something that defied the laws of nature. To her husband, if labor did not result in a physical product, no work had been done. Teddy couldn't show his father a solid result of his work, so Joe pretended not to get it. Was it coding or programming? Something like that. It had been lucrative for Teddy, she knew. He was successful. Of course, it wasn't really about Teddy's work, was it?

Kate had accomplished almost nothing, and Joe had only praise and words of affection for their daughter. *Oh, our Kate's so lovely, such a good mother, always stays in touch*—blah, blah, blah. Maybe because Kate was a girl, Joe had expected less from her and, unlike Birdie, wasn't disappointed or surprised when she never made anything of her life.

"It's just as well," said Birdie, though she didn't mean it. "He's always very distracted when he's here."

The truth was that he was always distracted, even when he wasn't here. That wasn't the right word. It was more that he was distant, disconnected. On the phone, he sounded like he was doing or thinking about something else, certainly not interested in anything Birdie had to say. When they were together, she found herself trying to catch his eye. He was forever looking away from her.

"He doesn't like the island, never has," said Joe.

"It's not for everyone."

She'd said that many times about a lot of different people. Not everyone had the constitution for this place, this lifestyle. It took some real grit to get by on Heart Island. Birdie had the fortitude for it, naturally. It was in her blood.

As if reading her mind, Joe said, "I think I'll go back to the city for a few days."

She drained her cup and put it in the sink. "Fine."

There was no point in arguing. She could say that Kate and her family were coming, that she needed his help with the cleaning, the shopping. Didn't he want to see his princess and her perfect progeny? It didn't seem to bother anyone but Birdie that each child had a different father. One of whom was a scandalous drunk, an adulterer, and a lousy writer. And Sean? What to say about him? He was not the type of man she'd have expected Kate to end up with. Once, Kate (Katherine Elizabeth Burke, a beautiful name, a regal one) might have had *anyone,* could have been *anything.* She'd had every privilege, a first-rate education. She'd thrown it away.

If Birdie made a fuss, Joe would stay out of obligation. But then there'd be some kind of fight, and he'd leave in anger. Joe Burke always got his way. You either gave it to him or he took it.

"I'll be back midweek to see Katie and the kids."

"And Sean."

"Well, yes, of course." There was that famous Joe Burke squint. "Him, too."

She thought about telling her husband what she had seen—a figure, a man on their island. But now she wasn't sure of it herself. What *had* she seen? Was there really someone there? Or was it some tricky combination of deteriorating eyesight and the wind? It would be silly to tell him, a play to any latent desire he might have to protect her. He might even mock her. He'd always thought she was an alarmist, too quickly frightened or overwrought. She didn't bother.

"I'll shower and bring you to the marina," she said. "I'll do the shopping for the rest of the week while I'm there." *See,* she thought. *I don't need you. I don't need anyone.*

"No rush," he said. He was staring at the new iPhone again, checking his e-mail. He was so proud of that thing, showing off photos of the kids, the amusing *apps* he had bought. She hated it for no reason she could name, often imagined the look of horror on his face if she were to snatch it from him and throw it out the window of their apartment, or a moving car, or into the drink. He didn't look up as she walked off to the bedroom. If he had, he might have seen that she was fighting back tears.

chapter seven

Emily was getting that feeling. It was a kind of swelling anxiety, a low-grade panic that made her say stupid things, that caused objects to slip from her hands.

The yield from the prescriptions she had lifted was low. The bottle of Adderall, a cocktail of amphetamines prescribed for ADD, and the bottle of Ativan, an anti-anxiety med, brought fifty dollars each, about five dollars a pill. The rest of the bottles contained only old antibiotics, which were worthless. What they really needed was OxyContin at twenty dollars or more a pill. In a perfect world, they would have hit the jackpot with the morphine ampoules prescribed to cancer patients. In the burbs, people would pay fifty or more for one of those. She'd seen the morphine only once. It was very rare.

She'd waited in the car while Dean and Brad took the meds up to the small split-level ranch where Dean's dealer lived. It looked like any of the other houses on the block, in a working-class neighborhood just like hers.

There were some untended shrubs along the walk, a welcome mat at the door, and a sticker in a window so the fire department knew where the kids were. There was a frog-shaped sandbox on the lawn, a tricycle tipped over in the driveway. If she didn't know who lived there, she wouldn't have guessed. There was a minivan in the driveway, two car seats in the back. But she noticed, on the street, a black slick of various oil and fluid stains from a parade of old beater cars. People parking to pick up or drop off drugs had left an indelible stain on the road.

Dean had forgotten to leave the car running, and she hadn't wanted to call after him to bring back the keys, so she could at least listen to the radio. She didn't want Brad to have an excuse to turn around. Every time her eyes fell on him, he was looking at her with an ugly grin.

It seemed like they were in there forever. She must have drifted off, because the sound of the closing door startled her. She saw them walking down the drive. She could tell by the look on Dean's face, the way his shoulders were hiked up and stiff, that he was not happy. Things had not gone well. None of them had said a word on the way home.

Now they were back at her place. Brad was sitting on her couch, feet up on her coffee table, a beer between his legs. He was watching one of those home-improvement shows, and he seemed very involved in it. Or maybe he was just high. She'd seen him pop one of the pills in his mouth when Dean wasn't looking. Who knew what else he'd taken. He had those bad teeth that meth heads had, yellowed, decaying. Meth mouth, they called it.

"Look, Em," Dean said. He had his hands on her shoulders, his voice a whisper. They were standing in the kitchen. He'd ordered a pizza and a liter bottle of Pepsi because Brad had said he was hungry. Why was Dean spending money when he seemed to need it so desperately? "The only way we're going to get rid of this guy is to give him some cash."

"How much did you get from the meds?" she asked.

"Two hundred." He'd had more medication to sell than the pills she'd lifted. She guessed he'd gotten them from the earlier open house, the one she'd refused to attend in order to go to work at the Blue Hen. "I gave him everything."

"Okay," she said. "You're going to have to tell me how much you owe him."

Dean looked up at the ceiling and then back at Emily, did this little shuffle from foot to foot that he did when he was stressed. "Two thousand."

She blew out a breath. "I don't have that. You know I don't."

"Who does?"

That was when it started, the feeling—as if she were standing on shore, watching a tidal wave wash in. As the crushing wall of water pushed toward her, she was not fast enough to run, not strong enough to hold it back.

"No one," she said.

He rolled his eyes at her. "Come on."

Did he mean her mother?

"She'll never give that to us," she said. "She won't even help me with my rent since you moved in. We're not even *speaking* right now."

"I'm not talking about your mother." He had these icy blue eyes, a powerful gaze that went right through her. When she met him, she thought he was the most beautiful man she'd ever seen. She also thought he was the sweetest, the most romantic. He was that still, somewhere inside. Wasn't he?

"Then who?" she said.

He ran his hand through her hair, then pushed back a strand that had fallen in front of her eyes. He'd be tender for a few minutes.

"They make that in a day at the Blue Hen," he said. "You said so yourself."

Oh, God, she thought. *Why* had she told him that?

"No," she said. "No, I can't ask her for that kind of money. Be serious."

"I wasn't talking about *asking.*"

She'd done things at his behest before. Things she hadn't wanted to do and violently regretted. She'd hurt people who trusted her, let others down in ways big and small. Since she'd met him a year and a half ago, she'd lost three jobs, dropped out of school, fallen out with her mother. All because she couldn't seem to say no to him. Why couldn't she? She wasn't afraid to be alone; in fact, she often preferred it. Was it love? Was this what love did to you? Did it cause you to betray yourself? She didn't think it should.

"I don't know what you're talking about, Dean."

She tried to move away from him, but he tightened his grip on her hair.

"Listen." It was more like a hiss through his teeth than a whisper. "You know what Brad served time for? After the armed robbery?"

She didn't answer; she wasn't expected to answer.

"Manslaughter," he said. "He beat someone so bad in a fight over money that the guy died three days later."

Emily could imagine Brad doing that.

"Emily, I'm scared," said Dean. "Doesn't he scare you? The way he's looking at you? Let's just give him what he wants so he'll go."

Emily didn't say anything. The words were all bottled up in her chest.

"She goes to the bank tonight after closing, right?" How did he know that? Emily hadn't told him that, had she? "They close at nine; it takes her an hour to finish up."

She looked at the clock on the microwave. It was just after eight. She didn't say anything; she couldn't.

"She'll have the whole week's worth of cash. It's one of those bank envelopes. The husband goes home; he doesn't stay with her."

Then she knew he'd been casing the Blue Hen, which she couldn't believe. Because he knew how much she liked it there, how much she liked Carol. And she wondered but couldn't bring herself to ask whether Dean owed Brad money after all. How long had he been thinking about this? Was Brad's showing up an opportunity for him to do something awful? Maybe he'd been planning already.

Her mind started racing, and through the hum of her anxiety, she examined her options. She could pretend she needed something from the car and then go to her mother's. Her mother would take her in; she'd call the police. Or maybe Emily could warn Carol. If she got the car away from them, they couldn't do much damage. But what would Brad do to Dean?

No, she couldn't face her mother. She couldn't admit it about Dean, about the kind of life she was living. She'd told her mother that Dean was on a job interview today. She'd been lying about him for months. Leaving messages about his job interviews, how she thought he might propose, how he'd brought her flowers. She had something else to tell her mother, too, but she was saving that for when all the lies she'd told about Dean turned out to be true.

"Don't hold your breath, sweetie," her mother had said during their big falling-out. "A guy like that will never do what you hope he'll do. And you'll keep on hoping until he drains you of that, too."

"You don't know him."

"Don't I?" she'd said. She'd given Emily a sad look of warning. That was when Emily had started screaming. She could still feel that shaky rage exploding from her.

Now Emily folded her arms across her belly. "Don't do this, Dean," she said. She hated herself for crying. But she couldn't stop the tears. "Please."

He bared his teeth at her. "I don't have any choice. And neither do you—unless you want him to kill me because I can't pay him back."

She felt the dry suck of fear in her throat. "I have eight hundred dollars in my checking account," she said. In her panic, her voice came out too loud. She lowered it. "That's it. It was for the rent, but you can have it."

Dean rubbed his eyes hard, something he did when he was stressed, getting himself worked up. "It's not *enough*."

"You said you gave him two hundred. That's a thousand."

"Half is not going to cut it."

She knew in her heart that he'd already decided; he'd worked out some deal with Brad. Dean was going to get a cut of the haul. Emily could see it all on his face. Still, she had to try.

"He can have my car," she said. "Between that and the cash, it's more than you owe him. It's fair."

Dean shook his head and backed away from her. "You're not *getting* it."

"I don't want your car," said Brad.

He was standing in the doorway to the kitchen. Emily looked into his eyes. They were blank, unreadable. That was the worst kind of person, the scariest—the one who'd learned to keep his feelings out of his eyes. Or who didn't feel anything at all. Emily had known people like that; they were the destroyers. They took things—everything you worked for, all your silly dreams—and smashed them beneath their boots for no reason at all.

"I'll get cash in the morning. You can take the car and the money and go," she said. "It's easy."

He gave her a smile, a laugh that sounded like a cough. "No. She'll have ten grand in that envelope."

"You're wrong," Emily said. She couldn't keep her voice from wobbling, but she wiped away her tears. "Not that much. Dean's exaggerating."

"Bullshit," said Dean. He tapped her hard on the arm, but she backed away from him.

Brad looked to Dean, then back at Emily, and apparently decided that she was a better source of information. "How much, then?" he said.

"I have no idea," she said. She offered an easy shrug. "People don't use cash that much anymore. It's all plastic these days. A couple hundred at most."

"She's lying," said Dean. He had that frantic little-boy tone he got when he was losing his temper. "She's *lying*. I've seen that envelope. It's *this* thick." He made a big U out of his thumb and forefinger, thrust it at Emily.

Brad rolled his head from side to side, and Emily heard a loud cracking in his neck. He glanced at the clock. It was eight-forty. "Let's go," he said.

Emily looked over at Dean, who was looking at the floor again. Once upon a time, she felt so safe with him, like nothing would ever go wrong in her life again. Those first few months when he was working hard, and she was, too, as well as going to school, it felt perfect. And she didn't even know he had a problem with pills. She would lie in bed with him, nestled in the crook of his arm, and she practically wanted to weep with relief that all men weren't monsters, like her mother had warned, and that her life was not a mess at all.

"I love you, Em," he'd whisper. "I'm going to take such good care of you."

She should have known better. She really should have known.

chapter eight

The girls were suspiciously quiet in Chelsea's room, and Brendan was lounging on the couch, watching television. When he was younger, Brendan would spend the whole evening torturing Chelsea and Lulu, trying to hang out with them, begging them to play games they refused to play, telling on them when they broke the rules. At some point, he'd given up and taken to ignoring them, though Kate had noticed him surreptitiously staring at Lulu all through dinner. He was playing it cool. But the girls didn't notice that, either. There were too many years between them; Brendan at ten barely ranked as a human being in the eyes of a sixteen-year-old, though Brendan and Chelsea were close enough when left to their own devices. Chelsea was very tender with him when her friends weren't around; Brendan looked at her with something akin to worship. They were good company for each other on the island. It was something they had in common, their love for that place, their endless desire to explore it.

Kate's suitcase was nearly full, and she still felt ill prepared for the trip. The problem was that her parents insisted that everyone change for dinner. She couldn't just bring the easy activewear that was appropriate for the island. She needed a suitable outfit for dinner every night, like everyone else. Except Sean, who absolutely refused to change for dinner, a ritual he found affected and ridiculous. Whereas Kate's first husband had kowtowed to her parents' many requirements and customs, Sean bucked them at every opportunity. He just didn't care what they thought. Their tremendous wealth failed to impress him or motivate his behavior—as it did with most—and he refused to be anything other than who he was. For this and so many things, Kate adored him.

Kate felt that when she visited them, which she did as little as was seemly, she owed them the respect of following their rules. She knew where they came from and why they felt the need to order their lives as they had. She didn't always *like* it, but she understood it. Both of them, for different reasons, needed control over their environment. And when you were in their orbit, they needed to control you as well. She'd grown to accept it and had learned to navigate it in a way that Theo never could and Sean didn't want to.

"Don't get yourself worked up." Her husband was lounging on the bed. She tried not to look at him, lest she be tempted to give up her task and join him.

"I'm not," she said.

"Your breathing is shallow." She could hear the smile in his voice.

Sean's suitcase was zipped and tucked neatly into the corner. They would be there for seven days, so he was taking seven outfits, eight changes of underwear (always good to have an extra), and eight pairs of socks. He knew exactly what he would wear every day. He had one pair of loafers and one pair of amphibious shoes. This time, just to keep everyone on their toes, he'd packed one pair of dress pants and a crisp white oxford shirt. One night he'd dress for dinner just to mess with her parents, who really didn't know what to do with him. He'd left extra space in his suitcase for the toiletries bag, which would never fit in Kate's suitcase. He'd packed for Brendan in the same way. Kate and Chelsea would be stuffing things into their suitcases up until they loaded them into the car. Even though they'd bring everything they could think of, they'd still feel like they didn't have enough.

"I saw the e-mail from your mother," said Sean.

"Please," she said.

"I wrote her back with all of our dietary restrictions and considerations."

She stopped and turned to face him. "What dietary considerations?"

Sean smiled his Cheshire-cat grin. In spite of the fact that she *was* getting herself all worked up, she smiled, too. How could she not smile at him? He was all mischief, just like their son. Though Sean had dark close-cropped hair, compared to Brendan's dirty-blond curls, and deep brown eyes to Brendan's faceted hazel, they were the image of each other: same sharp nose, same sweetness around the eyes, same fullness to the lips. Heartthrobs, both of them, her boys—but faithful and funny and full of caring. So unlike her father, her brother, or her ex. She thanked her lucky stars, or the fact that she had gotten smart and figured out a way to do better.

"You're mean," she said. She tossed a pair of socks at him, which he easily caught and threw back in one fluid motion. He was athletic, another way in which he was different from her first husband. Sebastian's physical prowess had been limited to pouring himself a drink and lighting a cigarette. His skills were cerebral, not all of them used for good.

"You love it," Sean said. She did. Kate abandoned the packing and lay down beside him. Her husband moved through the world with a centered, good-natured ease that Kate envied. She pressed her body against his and squeezed, hoping to soak up some of his inner calm. She took in the scent of him as he wrapped his arms around her.

"Don't worry. We'll just drink our way through it," he said.

"Stop."

There was a cocktail hour promptly at six, the point from which her parents proceeded to get properly soused on martinis, or whatever the cocktail of the evening happened to be. Wine was served throughout the three-course meal. By the time dessert was on the table, the mood would be dictated by her mother, whether she was happy or feeling bitter, whether she was angry with Dad or just had it in for someone at the table.

Luckily, only Kate seemed to suffer. Dad was in his own world, had learned long ago to tune Birdie out. Sean thought that everything about her parents' various dysfunctions was hilarious. And Chelsea and Brendan were too loved and praised to be vulnerable to any of the passive-aggressive attacks her mother might launch. So it was just Kate—and Theo, when he was around—who walked on eggshells, delicately tuned in to Mother's various ups and downs.

"We can cancel," he said. "Brendan's ankle is the perfect excuse."

"I can't disappoint the kids." That sounded lame, even to her own ears. It was a cop-out, because things were so much more complicated than that.

Sean draped his arm over her middle. "You know," he said. He paused a minute, as though picking his words carefully. "It's okay to disappoint people sometimes. It's okay for us to say no simply because we don't want to do something."

Intellectually, she knew that was true. It was just that when it came to her family, it didn't *feel* that way. "You don't want to go?" she asked.

He pushed himself up on his elbow and looked up at the ceiling, then back at her. "I don't know. Not really," he said. "I love the island. I know you and the kids do, too. But the price is high."

On the dresser, his cell started ringing. He didn't move to answer it. "You could use the disconnect," she said. She nodded toward the singing, vibrating device. Ten minutes couldn't pass without it emitting some kind of sound.

"I could use *a* disconnect," he said. "It doesn't necessarily have to be there."

Sean was constantly plugged in to the needs of clients, fielding calls on his listings, dealing with appraisers, mortgage brokers. He was good at blocking off family time, not one of those people who couldn't pry himself away from the laptop or BlackBerry. But with the economy and the real estate market in such chaos, he was working harder than ever and making far less that he once had. He needed a break.

"Really, we could go anywhere on Sunday," he said. He swept his arm wide. "Just get in the car and drive."

Freedom was something that, as a couple, they'd never really had. Chelsea was small when they met and married, and Brendan came a couple of years later. They had never slept away from the kids, and Kate didn't have any desire to do so. Suddenly, the thought of taking off in the car, even with the kids in tow, and going wherever they wanted to go filled Kate with a strange longing.

Of course, if they did that, the kids would sulk; her parents would be angry and disappointed. And Kate wasn't sure she could enjoy herself while everyone else was miserable. What did that say about her? She didn't know.

"Next year," she said. "Next year we'll go somewhere else, like Hawaii or Europe. Someplace amazing, just the four of us."

He gave her a skeptical look. "You promise?"

"I promise," she said. She meant it.

The more she thought about it, the better it felt. They'd tell the kids and her parents now. Everyone would have a year to get used to the idea that they were taking a break from the island. Theo was right; she didn't *have* to go every summer. It would be there even if she couldn't be. She felt lighter, more able to deal with the trip ahead, knowing that next year she wouldn't have to spend a week trapped in her parents' thrall. The timing, for other reasons, would be good for her not to be there.

She got up and went back to her packing, picking from a huge pile of stuff on the chair. A fleece pullover, a black sheath dress, a pair of sneakers, a pair of heels.

"Maybe we could even do Asia," said Sean. He grabbed his laptop off the nightstand. He would start researching right away, come up with the best possible and most expensive trips. Normally, she'd stop him, not let him get overexcited, make him scale back. This time she wasn't going to do that.

"Or one of those five-star African safaris," he said. "I think the kids are old enough to appreciate that."

"You know what, babe?" she said. "Anything you want."

"Nice," he said. "I *like* your attitude."

She was happy to see him excited. And suddenly, she felt better about the trip ahead. This year she *had* taken those boating classes. She'd done something else, too. Something huge. And it was going to change everything.

Once this trip was over, she was going to start to follow her brother's example. There was going to be a bit more distance and a little more of the word "no."

"You're not going to give him your phone number."

Lulu wasn't usually the cautious one. Chelsea peered over the laptop screen at her friend, who glanced up from the pink beanbag chair where she sat painting her toenails a garish pink.

"Why not?" Chelsea asked. She stretched out on her bed. Her foot had fallen asleep from sitting cross-legged with the computer on her lap.

"Because then it's—I don't know. Real. Like, you have to *talk* to him." She looked back to her toenails.

"So? Isn't that the point?" Hadn't Lulu said the same thing at the mall?

"Not really," Lulu said. "Keep it on *Fake*book, and it's safe. They can't get near you, not really. They just know what you *want* them to know."

"They can't get near you on the phone, either."

"Yeah, but that's the gateway to the real world," said Lulu. "Once they have your number, once they can talk to you, hear your voice, the next step is getting together."

Chelsea had been messaging back and forth with Adam, carefully coached by Lulu on how to be cool but not overeager, flirty but not too inviting. *And for crying out loud, don't sound so smart. Smart is not sexy.* Chelsea didn't like playing games with people. She just wanted to be herself and meet someone who was willing to be himself. She said as much.

"No one's *himself*," Lulu said. "Everyone's putting on a show. Especially guys."

"That's not true," said Chelsea. Was it true?

Lulu shrugged. "Honestly, Chaz, you're the only real person I know."

Chelsea didn't know what that meant. On the other hand, she didn't need to ask for an explanation. At Blair Academy, where they both went to school, many of the parents were mega-rich, like Lulu's. The kids wore uniforms, but the girls all carried designer bags and wore expensive shoes—everything was about what you had and what kind of car your parents would get you when you turned seventeen. A popular senior girl posted a video on YouTube of her parents surprising her with a Porsche for her birthday. Chelsea had shown her parents, hoping it would inspire them to buy her a sick ride.

"Wow," said Sean. He was speechless after that.

"Keep dreaming," said Kate. She walked off, laughing.

"Thanks, Mom," Chelsea called after her. "Thanks a lot."

Who went to Paris over break? And who was skiing in Vail? How much did your prom dress cost? And did you have the new iPhone 5? These were the things that mattered to the student population at Blair Academy. Somehow Chelsea seemed to float above it all, watching the competitions unfold. Not that she didn't like nice things or bug her parents for the things she wanted.

You don't seem stuck-up like the other girls at Blair. You're different. I can tell, Adam wrote to her.

How could he tell, she wondered, that she wasn't like the other girls? And was it true?

Chelsea heard Lulu's phone chime and looked over inquiringly. Lulu was always getting interesting communications . . . from exes, distant relatives, girls who thought Lulu wanted to steal their boyfriends. But Lulu didn't say anything. Then Chelsea got a message from Adam.

So do you want to get together tonight? She felt a little rush of excitement.

She read the message out loud to Lulu, who smiled for the first time all night. "So?" she said. "Are you up for it? I'll call Conner. We can double."

"Wait a minute," said Chelsea. "What about your whole gateway-to-the-real-world thing? If I get together with him, that's the *real* real world."

"Well," said Lulu, "if you really like him, let's do it."

Chelsea pushed out a small laugh. "Yeah, my parents will go for that. Sure."

"Who says they have to know?"

Lulu looked back at her phone and started tapping away. She was living in a fantasy world where she thought everybody's parents failed to notice their comings and goings. Chelsea wasn't even allowed to spend the night at Lulu's now that her mother realized that Lulu's parents were rarely home in the evening and the housekeeper/nanny went home at eight. Of course, that was three years ago. They were old enough to be home alone. But not, her mother contended, overnight.

"Scared?" Lulu asked when Chelsea didn't say anything.

It sounded like a dare. Lulu looked up quickly with a wicked smile and a wink that told Chelsea it was. Chelsea started to get the uncomfortable feeling she'd been getting around Lulu lately—when Lulu wanted something from Chelsea that she couldn't give.

They'd tried to sneak out recently, at Lulu's urging. Sean had caught them climbing out of Chelsea's window with one of the roll-away fire escape ladders they kept under Chelsea's bed. When they made it down (which was not easy and was more than a little scary), he was standing on the lawn. Weirdly, he was eating an ice pop; he seemed to be enjoying it and the whole scenario. He must have been in the kitchen and heard them unroll the ladder, which clanked loudly against the side of the house. They hadn't discussed the evening again, so Chelsea wasn't sure how he'd caught them. It hadn't been that long ago—a couple of weeks, maybe.

"Never going to happen, girls," he'd said. "Sorry."

He'd walked them back inside without fanfare or argument. If he'd told Chelsea's mom, it had never come up, which meant he probably hadn't told her. Because Mom would have blown a gasket. There would have been long, protracted conversations about honesty and trust, loss of privileges, possibly grounding. Sean didn't flip out like that. It wasn't his style. He acted like it was normal that they tried to get away with stuff, and it was his job to make sure they didn't.

"I can't," she said. "If he catches us again, he'll tell my mom."

Lulu rolled her eyes, looked disappointed.

"Just write: *Sorry, can't make it*," said Lulu. She sounded angry.

Chelsea was already typing a long explanation about how she'd like to but her parents were really strict, and anyway, she normally wouldn't meet up with someone she didn't know. She backspaced over it and did as Lulu had said, then closed the lid on the laptop.

Like that, he was gone. He didn't exist anymore. Lulu was right about not giving him her phone number; then he was part of the real world. She couldn't close him out. He wouldn't be just words on a screen.

There was a light knock on the door.

She took a quick scan of the room: Lulu's cigarettes were nowhere in sight. The television was on, tuned in to Lifetime, but with the sound down.

"Come in," said Chelsea.

Sean poked his head in. "How's it going in here?"

"Good," she said. "Just hanging out."

"Not up to anything, right?"

"Like what?" Lulu said. She opened her eyes wide.

Sean smiled. "Good. Great." He closed the door.

"He's hot," said Lulu.

"Ew," said Chelsea. It was not the first time Lulu had made a comment about Sean. It made her sick. "Stop it."

For a moment, there was only the sound of Lulu tapping on her phone. Chelsea watched her friend, the delicate curve of her neck, the slump of her shoulders. All at once she felt distant from Lulu, annoyed with her.

"You know," said Lulu, "have you ever heard of spyware?"

She was wearing a pink T-shirt of Chelsea's (it looked way better on Lulu); her hair was up in a careless knot; she was wearing an old pair of sweats that belonged to Brendan; and she looked perfect. Her skin was dewy, her green eyes bright and heavily lashed. She was a ten in borrowed clothes. When Lulu was crying, or throwing up, or sweating in gym class, she was still gorgeous. *God is so unfair in His distribution of beauty,* Chelsea's father had written in his first novel. For some reason, the sentence had stuck with her.

"Sure," said Chelsea.

"Are you sure your parents don't have that on your laptop?"

She considered it a moment. "No way," she said finally. "They'd never do that." Chelsea looked over at her computer; it sat slim and unassuming on her quilt.

"I was thinking of that night we snuck out," said Lulu. She came to sit on Chelsea's bed, snuggled up beside her. "We'd been e-mailing back and forth with Gwen about the party and where it was. We *told* her we were going to try to get out your window. And just now? That guy asked if you wanted to get together tonight."

Chelsea thought about this. She just couldn't see her mom doing that. Kate was so chronically honest about everything.

"Is that how it works?" Chelsea asked. "They can just watch what you're doing in real time?"

Lulu shrugged. "I don't know, actually."

"Do your parents have it on yours?"

"Please. My parents don't even watch what I'm doing when I'm in the same room with them. I swear I could light up a joint at the kitchen table and my mother would crack a window."

They weren't *that* bad. Lulu was prone to exaggeration. They were quite nice, actually, just distracted, into their work. And they'd recently been cracking down heavily, monitoring Lulu's comings and goings more carefully. In fact, Lulu's mom had called earlier to check that she was really here. This was a first.

"Maybe not your mom," Lulu said. "But Sean? I could see him doing it."

Sean's favorite line: "We trust you, Chelsea. It's the rest of the world we don't trust." He'd said it about a million times as they systematically said no to everything she wanted to do. *No, you can't ride to The Killers concert with your friends. We'll take you and pick you up. No, you can't go into the city alone with Lulu to go shopping. We'll come with you. No, you can't go to a party unless we talk to the parents who will be present.* Did they *ever* get tired of saying no?

"No way," said Chelsea again.

"I'm just saying," said Lulu. "I wouldn't put up with that from my parents. Especially if one of them wasn't even my real dad."

Chelsea felt her cheeks go hot in a rush of anger, along with something else—sadness, embarrassment. "He *is* my dad," she said. "In all the ways that count." Even though she meant it, the words felt hollow, as if she were just repeating what Kate and Sean had said a million times. It seemed like a thing you would say even if you didn't mean it, so it didn't hold any weight.

"God, Chelsea," said Lulu. She was sulking now. "Do you have to be so perfect all the time?"

Perfect? She was so far from perfect. She expected to look over and see Lulu laughing at her, like it was some kind of a joke. But she was staring off into space, grim-faced.

Chelsea didn't know what to say to Lulu when she got sullen like this, so she stayed quiet. Chelsea turned up the sound on the television and lay down next to her friend. After a while, Lulu draped her arm around Chelsea, and whatever angry feelings they'd had passed. And they were just as they had always been, best friends, closer than sisters could ever be.

Sean stood in the hallway for a second after softly closing Chelsea's door. He could hear Brendan playing a video game in his room, Kate down in the kitchen. He liked this time of night, the quiet hours after dinner and before bed. It seemed to him that this was the time in which life was lived, when the busy workday or school day was over and the family was under one roof. He cherished the chatter and laughter of dinner, help with homework or movie time, popcorn, bedtime for the kids. He looked forward to his time alone with Kate when they metabolized the day, analyzing, planning, discussing work, the kids, everything. He used to think there was more to life, that it was lived in parties and adventure, travel, girls, and nights out with the boys. But it wasn't. Everything he ever wanted or was seeking was right here, in this house, right now. He walked down the carpeted hallway and thought that it needed a coat of paint.

On the walls between bedrooms was a gallery of photographs of them and the kids and all their various activities and adventures— Brendan's killer soccer goal, Chelsea horseback riding, Sean and

Kate's wedding, the family beachcombing in Hawaii, Kate on the rocks at Heart Island. He especially loved an early photograph of him with Chelsea in which she sat on his shoulders, tiny arms wrapped around his head.

In Sean's memory, there was a discernible moment when Chelsea became *his*. She was four when Sean met Kate, and initially, Chelsea seemed like some alien life form, cute but strange and unpredictable. He'd never had to take care of another person; he'd never even had a pet. Kate was the first woman Sean had ever been serious about. He wasn't *totally* certain what to do with her other half.

Chelsea was a person, sure, he could see that, with a surprisingly bright mind and strong ideas already. She was also tiny and wild, in constant need of something, prone to wailing for no reason. She was fascinating and a bit annoying, adorable and kind of frightening. The kid was raw power; when she was unhappy, the world came to a grinding halt. It had been just Chelsea and Kate for a while. Chelsea's father had been living at the bottom of a bottle since well before she was born. And she didn't like to share her mother. In the beginning, Sean and the munchkin had what Kate liked to call an *emerging* relationship.

It happened the first time Kate left her in Sean's care. Sean and Kate had been a couple for over a year. He couldn't remember now what had been the reason for Kate's absence; he remembered only being touched that she trusted him and thinking that it heralded a new level in their relationship. His orders were clear. Chelsea could watch part of *The Little Mermaid* (no more than twenty minutes). Kate had left dinner—chicken, broccoli, and a side of mac and cheese. All he had to do was heat it up. After that, Sean could help Chelsea brush her teeth. Then three stories of Chelsea's choosing, then bed. Though Kate had written it all down for him, he knew the drill; he'd put the munchkin down before, albeit with Kate sitting in the next room.

After the third story, he tucked her in and gave her a kiss on the cheek, which she endured but didn't return.

"I love you, Chelsea." He meant it, man, he really did. He loved Kate. He loved Chelsea. He told the kid that every day. She never said it back. It didn't even matter.

"You're not my daddy, you know." She said it easily, just making sure they were clear on the point.

"No," he said. "I know."

"I already have a daddy." Driving it home.

"Yeah," he said. "I know, kiddo."

Her eyes got very wide, and then she took in a deep breath. The tears were what brought him to his knees. Literally, he sank to his knees beside her. Chelsea could scream her head off for any number of ridiculous reasons, and all he ever wanted to do was hide his head under a pillow until she stopped. The real tears came when she was in pain. He already knew that about her.

He put his hand on her forehead. "I don't have to be your dad to love you and take care of you, right?"

She nodded uncertainly. Still those big tears fell. Was there anything more heart-wrenching, more crushing, than a truly sad child? He didn't think so.

"We can have our own special thing going on." He tried for a goofy smile.

She seemed to consider that. He dabbed at her eyes with his sleeve. "Like, we could be friends?" she asked. She drew in another shuddering breath.

"Right. Like that." Keep it simple. If you could find a friend who would throw himself in front of a moving train for you, it would be *that* kind of friendship, he thought but obviously didn't say.

In that first year with Kate and Chelsea, something primal and unfamiliar had awakened within him, a powerful urge to protect and defend. Prior to showing them that house (the showing that had changed his life), Sean hardly had a thought in his head. He made a killing selling houses in a boom market, drank with his friends, had a steady stream of casual girlfriends. Yearly, he took outrageous adventure trips with his old college roommates—cage diving on the Great Barrier Reef, trekking the Inca Trail, zip-lining in Costa Rica, snowboarding in the Alps. The looming specter of forty didn't bother him in the least. Life was a party. Marriage and kids? Why? *When are you going to grow up, Sean?* his mom had wanted to know. Since he'd met Kate and Chelsea, she hadn't asked him that once.

"Okay," Chelsea said. "We can be friends."

It was settled. She gave a sniffle and a nod and dragged her arm across her eyes, wiping away the last of her tears. "Can I have some juice?" she asked

That silky blond hair and pink-cheeked cherub face: She ran him through. He was finished that night, in love with both of them forever. He wasn't her dad, no. But Chelsea was his in a way he couldn't explain and didn't need to.

Even when Brendan followed, Sean didn't love his own son any more powerfully. Parenthood wasn't about blood or biology, he found; it was about a joyful willingness to give yourself over, to subordinate your own needs for someone else's. When you loved your kids, you'd give up everything to keep them safe and make them happy, and you didn't care about the other things, the ones that went away. At least he didn't.

Kate would *not* be thrilled to learn that he had installed spyware on Chelsea's laptop. They'd discussed it in the past. And while she hadn't been totally against it, she'd expressed squeamishness. *It's kind of gross. I'd like to think they're talking to us.* Honestly, he wasn't too happy about it, either. He blamed his old friend Brian, who was admittedly a little crazy about protecting his twin daughters.

At first he'd thought Brian had officially gone off the parental edge, but then Sean was Googling about spyware, and the next thing he knew, he was installing it. Then he was keeping it from Kate. And *then* he actually *was* spying on Chelsea, catching her trying to sneak out of the house. He was not proud of himself, did not consider this a shining moment in his tenure as a parent. (Though stopping them on the lawn *was* pretty hilarious. He thought he'd handled that fairly well.) But who the *fuck* was Adam McKee?

Sean sat down at his desk again and looked at the screen. He could see Chelsea's Facebook conversation on the screen in front of him.

You're not like the other girls at Blair. You're different. Oh, puh-lease. What kind of a game was this kid running? If he was a kid at all. Sean had Googled him and couldn't find anything anywhere. Not cool. Although what could you find online about a high school student unless he was a jock written up in the newspaper, or had a record, or was a registered sex offender, or had a recent DUI? Maybe no news was good news.

"What are you doing?" Kate wandered into their shared office and laid herself on the sofa.

"Downloading porn." He switched off Chelsea's screen. She wasn't online anymore anyway, after telling Adam McFuckhead that she couldn't make it out tonight. Good girl. She was probably having flashbacks about his truly brilliant lawn interception.

"Ha, ha," said Kate. "I think I'm almost done packing."

He clicked back over to the adventure travel site he'd been surf-ing while spying on Chelsea. "How's Brendan's ankle?" he asked.

"It's pretty swollen," she said. "We'll make the call tomorrow."

Brendan's ankle seemed worse instead of better, the bruise at the bone flowering into a rich blue-black. Sean tried not to get his hopes up (awful as that was). Brendan had a legendary physical resilience, especially when he was motivated. And he loved Heart Island more than anyone. Except Birdie, of course, who, it seemed to Sean, loved *only* Heart Island.

"I have three possibilities so far for our big family trip next year," he said. *Where your intention goes, the energy flows.* One of Kate's favorite yoga-isms. He loved to watch her bend and flex her lithe body into impossible positions. Sean could barely touch his toes; he was that inflexible. It was fine, though—real men didn't contort.

"Tell me," she said. So he did.

chapter nine

The island loomed ahead, a great dark swell in the windy gray afternoon. It was waiting for her. It always seemed that way to Birdie on her approach. Even as a girl, she knew the place belonged to her. And one by one, they'd all gone away, leaving her alone with it.

Her sister was dead. She was long estranged from her older brother, Gene. *Take the goddamn rock, Birdie. You deserve each other.* In the bitter contest over their father's will, Gene had conceded Heart Island. Over time, she'd gotten almost everything else she'd wanted, too—her mother's jewelry, the art. People always underestimated her endurance. Her brother could have the classic cars, the music collection, the vintage instruments. His tastes were always so pedestrian.

The storm that threatened had never come. There was just a persistent drizzle and a strong chop that made the boat ride back from the mainland somewhat rough. A less nautical person might have found herself nauseated. Not Birdie. She docked the small boat with ease, tied her off, and proceeded to unload the groceries onto the dock.

"Take it easy on yourself, Birdie," Joe had said at the train station. "Take it easy on everyone."

She didn't know what to say to that. Was she not supposed to shop, prepare the menu, and create the itinerary for the week? Was she not supposed to pick up the clean sheets from the laundry and change all the bedding, scrub the bathrooms, put fresh flowers in the vases? She asked him as much, and she saw him shutting down, turning away.

"Okay," he said. He gave her a dismissive peck on the cheek and then stepped onto the train. She didn't wait to watch it pull away. She just got in the car and drove to the market. He was useless, anyway. All he did with his slovenly ways was create more work for her. In the city, they had help—twice-weekly cleaning, an occasional cook. Their laundry was picked up and delivered to the apartment. Here it was just her, doing everything. Why didn't anyone seem to care about that?

She unloaded the groceries and the laundry from the boat onto the dock, then started the trek with as much as she could carry to the main house. It would take two, maybe three trips to complete the job. She was still on the dock when she saw him again. This time he was standing on her porch.

Who was it?

Now, in the gray and with the wind howling, with Joe long gone, she didn't feel as brave. She stood frozen, her stomach bottomed out, her heart racing. He didn't move; neither did she. She couldn't see his face. He was nothing but a dark blur. She put down the groceries and started to back away.

As she did, she lost her footing and fell on her rump, saving herself with her elbows from falling all the way back and hitting her head on the hard wood. She heard him laughing. It sounded like a woman's laughter, a voice she recognized.

"Birdie!" Who was that? Another voice sounded small and far away.

She found she couldn't move as the form disappeared inside the house. She heard the familiar squeak and slam of the screen door. She wanted to call out, *Get out of my house!* But no words came.

"Birdie, are you all right?" The distant voice carried on the wind toward her.

She turned to see that it was the young man from the closest island to the south; he was waving extravagantly and yelling something that she couldn't quite hear.

He had told her that his office faced her dock. He could see them coming and going, he'd said. This had annoyed her. She'd rather not have known what he could and couldn't see, which was why she didn't socialize much in the area.

She found she couldn't answer him. A shooting pain traveled from her lower back down her right leg. Sciatica: the bane of her existence. She lay back as she saw the young man—what was his name?—get into his boat and race across the two-hundred-yard channel that separated them. Oh, John Cross, that was it—the publishing man who knew Kate's ex-husband somehow.

He tied off and bounded up the dock to her. She didn't remember what it was like to be that young and fit, with every confidence that you could manage any terrain before you.

"Birdie, what happened?" He bent down beside her. "Can you move?"

Shouldn't he be calling me Mrs. Burke? she thought. Wasn't that more respectful? These young people were so casual, so familiar, as if everyone were equal.

"Mr. Cross," she said, finding her voice. "There's someone on my island. I saw him earlier today and just now on the porch. Please, call the police."

He looked uncertainly at her and then around the island. "Are you sure?" he said. "Did you hit your head?"

"Young man," she said, "I did *not* hit my head, and I am quite sure of what I saw."

He gave her a deferential smile and helped her to her feet. "Of course," he said. "I'll call right away."

She stared at the house. The wet brown shingles glistened, the huge picture windows reflecting the trees from John Cross's island. She expected to see the man come to the glass.

John pulled a cell phone from the pocket of his Windbreaker

and called the authorities. Cell phone service was spotty at best in the area, but it seemed to work for John. When he'd completed the call, she told him, "He's in my house." She grabbed his wrist. "I saw him walk in the front door."

There it was again, that patient skepticism that the young reserved for the old. Suddenly, the children were in charge—the doctors, the lawyers, the neighbors were all shockingly young, thinking that they possessed some knowledge that you did not. *Suddenly,* your ways and ideas were dated, your memories were fuzzy, your opinions were silly and badly informed. John gazed up at the house. He had a large nose and a weak jaw. His blond hair looked as though it could use a wash.

"I'll go up," he said. He was not comfortable in the role of hero. A lover, not a fighter. Well, what could you expect from someone who worked in publishing?

"Don't," she said. "Wait for the police."

"I'll be fast," he said. He thought that she was afraid and that she didn't want him to leave her alone. And maybe she didn't. He was gone before she could stop him. Should she tell him that the gun was in a cabinet over the refrigerator? But he was quick, already on the porch steps. Then he moved through the door. "Hello?" she heard him call. "Is someone in there?"

He disappeared inside. But the door was silent. This time she didn't hear the loud squeal and slam. Of course not. That was a noise from her childhood, from the other house that they now used for guests. The main house was newer, the door well oiled and on a hydraulic hinge. The door on the main house closed with a gentle hiss. She felt tears spring to her eyes, that horrible hollow of sadness and uncertainty in her middle that she'd felt as a child. What had she seen? What had she heard? What was *wrong* with her?

A few minutes later, John was back on the porch. "It's clear," he called. "I'm going to check the other house and take a quick circle around the island. Are you okay?"

She gave him a wave because she didn't trust her voice. He looked off into the distance and pointed out toward the mainland. "Here come the police, Birdie," he said. "Everything is going to be okay."

She followed his line of sight and saw the white boat moving swiftly toward them, the red light flashing on the flat bimini top. Her hair was wet; the plastic bags on the dock were gathering pools of water in their folds. Drizzle was like that: It could almost fool you into thinking it wasn't raining. She brought her hood up, folded her arms around herself.

As the boat drew closer, she could see old Roger Murphy at the helm, and she felt a ripple of distaste. He'd grown up in the area on the mainland. But he was a townie, not one of the summer people, like Birdie's family. They'd known each other a long time. Apparently, he was quite high up in the police department, but she remembered him as a young man working in Blackbear marina, helping her father load the boat. He must have jumped at the chance to come out to Heart Island. Everyone did. There was no place to dock with both the cuddy and John's boat at the dock, so he tied off to John Cross's boat.

"Birdie Heart," he said. "It's been a long time."

He climbed from his boat to John's. She offered her hand to help him stabilize as he stepped onto the dock. The years had not been kind; he had an enormous belly, an atlas of lines on his face. His skin had the pasty cast of someone who didn't eat well.

Birdie Heart. She hadn't thought of herself that way in a hundred years. What a silly name. What had her mother hoped to accomplish by giving her a name like that? *It's a sweet, pretty name for a sweet, pretty girl.* Only her mother had ever called Birdie sweet. And other than her mother only Joe had ever called her pretty. Handsome, striking, attractive . . . she'd heard all of that. But she was never truly pretty, not like Katherine or Chelsea or Caroline. She'd never minded. Pretty didn't buy much these days, in spite of the way people chased after it.

"Birdie Burke now, Roger," she said. She gave him what she hoped was a friendly smile. Joe always accused her of grimacing when she thought she'd been smiling. *Why are you always giving people that appraising look, that tight sneer?* Birdie had no idea what he meant.

"Of course, of course." He cleared his throat and gazed up at the house. "Your neighbor John Cross said there was someone on the island? An intruder?"

John came through the trees then and jogged down the dock. The two men shook hands.

"I checked both houses and the bunkhouse, walked the perimeter. I didn't see anyone." John sounded a little breathless. "I think it's clear."

The men helped Birdie bring the groceries and laundry up to the house. One benefit, she supposed, of scaring herself witless. She was tired, and her sciatica was brutal, so she didn't fight Roger when he took the bags from her hand.

Up in the main house, she made coffee and told Roger what she'd seen that morning and again this afternoon. She didn't mention the screen door. She knew they both thought she was losing her mind, that she was old and dotty. Why confirm their suspicions? John Cross seemed to feel he was needed and hung around, looking at the artwork hanging on the wall, taking books from the shelves, glancing at them, and carefully replacing them. Nosy. He was a nosy man. As she watched him fondling her things, Birdie remembered hearing that he had more than a passing interest in the history of the area islands. She couldn't remember what the old woman at the marina shop had said about him, that he had a connection to someone eccentric who had lived here long ago. The woman had said that he'd been asking a lot of questions. A chatterbox, that's what she had called him. Bringing up things that people would rather forget. There had been something pointed about the way she said it, as if she were inviting Birdie to gossip. But Birdie didn't gossip, felt that it was beneath her.

"We've had break-ins, some vandalism, as I'm sure you both know," said Roger Murphy.

He sat at the long oak dining table. He looked too big for the chair; she imagined that if he leaned hard against the railed back, it would break into splinters. Birdie found herself remembering Roger when he was young. He'd often been shirtless, his well-muscled body the color of caramel. She and Caroline had always giggled, watching him, as he gassed up the boat or helped unload their luggage from the car. There had been something so handsome and virile about him then, something earthy and hardworking—so unlike the rich private-school dandies who populated their lives back home. And even though there were deep lines etched in his brow and under his eyes, and he was a shadow of the young man she remembered, she could still see him as he was. She wondered what he saw when he looked at her.

"Mostly, these break-ins are occurring in the late fall or after the first thaw, when many of the islands are empty."

John made some kind of affirming noise, and Birdie stayed silent. This wasn't news to her. The person she had seen wasn't a marauding teen or a vandal.

"What did you see from your place, Mr. Cross?" asked Roger.

"I was at my desk, which looks onto part of the Burkes' island and their dock. I saw Joe and Birdie leave; then a few hours later, I saw Birdie return alone. I happened to see her fall and came right over."

Roger wrote in a little leather book. "Nothing at the house?"

"I can't see up to the house from my island," John said.

Thank goodness for small favors. The whole point of having an island *was* privacy, wasn't it?

"Did you hear anything, Birdie?" asked Roger.

"Like what?" She hadn't meant to sound sharp.

He gave her a curious look, a little shrug. "Like a boat racing away?"

She shook her head. "No, nothing like that."

"That's the only thing I can think of," he said. "Whoever it was got away on a boat they had tied off on the other side."

Or that you imagined the whole thing. She was certain that was what he was thinking but didn't say. She wanted to rail that she *had* seen someone, flesh and bone, standing there this morning and just now. She wasn't crazy or senile. But she couldn't manage the appropriate bluster. They all knew no one could tie off on the other side of the island, which was treacherous and rocky. John's skeptical expression said it all.

"Maybe so," said Birdie unconvincingly.

Roger found it necessary to look through both houses and the bunkhouse again, as well as to take another turn around the island. She wondered if he did this to satisfy his curiosity about the new house. John Cross accompanied him, hands stuffed in the pockets of his jacket, looking grim and purposeful. His jacket was a pricey Burberry. She'd bought one for Theodore. He'd returned it. *It's not my style, Mother. Thank you, though.*

Birdie knew they weren't going to find anything or anyone. There wouldn't be any evidence that someone had been there. And they didn't, and there wasn't. To their credit, neither man sought to make her feel like a fool. She was glad Joe wasn't there to give her a hard time for inconveniencing everyone, causing a fuss. He'd have everyone joking around, cracking open cans of beer.

"Well, there won't be anyone heading out here tonight, that's for sure," said Roger. "Big storm coming."

Those clouds had been looming all day. They didn't seem to be moving at all, just a thick black cloak hanging over the mainland.

"Are you alone here tonight?" John Cross asked. He regarded her with an annoyingly concerned frown.

Birdie gave a quick, tight nod. She'd been weathering storms on this island since long before John Cross was born. "I'll be fine," she said. "Really. And I'm sorry for all of this. I don't know who it could have been. Or where he went."

"That's what we're here for," said Roger. He gave her a gentle pat on the arm. Then he climbed gracelessly over the Cross boat and onto his own. "Make sure your radios are charged in case you lose power tonight," he added. "Landlines will go down as soon as the storm gets bad, like they always do. And I know we're supposed to have cell service now, but it seems to be spotty."

Birdie hadn't been able to make a call since they'd arrived. They'd been communicating mostly via e-mail, Joe having bought them each a "rocket stick" that allowed them Internet access on their laptops. And the landline had been working fine, which hadn't always been the case.

"Something to do with the mountains." Roger was going on about the cell service and how bad it was, though Birdie had stopped listening.

"I hope you both have plenty of fuel for your generators and boats. Marina's still open, if not. Storm's still a few hours east."

John looked at the sky, then back at his house. He seemed worried. He was new to the islands. He and his wife were inexperienced, both as boaters and as residents. All their gear, boat, kayaks, outerwear, was expensive and brand-new. Birdie wasn't sure what the woman did; she hadn't paid much attention to her when they'd dropped by to introduce themselves. She was petite and plump, didn't seem to have much to say.

"You have my number, right, Birdie?" said John.

"I do. Thank you," she said. She had it somewhere. In a desk drawer, she thought. She'd find it if she needed it. She wouldn't need it, though.

First Roger pulled away. Then she watched John traverse the channel, tie up at his dock, and go ashore. He gave her a wave, pantomimed that she should call him, then disappeared.

She looked back at the tall pines and the rooftops peeking through the foliage. She listened to the boat bumping against the dock. In the distance, she could hear the hum of the generator, which, combined with the solar panels, powered everything on the island—all the electricity, the water pump, and the heater. She felt her isolation. She was alone with Heart Island. It was exactly—as she'd said so many times—the way she wanted it.

chapter ten

Emily knew that people made choices. She understood that. You chose to do well in school by studying hard and following the rules. You picked your profession, succeeded or failed by the amount of effort you put into it. You decided on the person to marry, whether or not to have children, how many. And all of those choices tangled and wrapped around one another, mingled with and impacted one another. And the resulting ball of twine? Well, that was your life. It all sounded right and perfect to Emily. *You don't always choose what happens to you, but you choose how you deal with it.* That's what her mother always told her, and it seemed true. Except that life, real life, wasn't like that. Moments spun out of control, looked like one thing and were really something else. You made mistakes, and there were consequences that could not be reversed. There were accidents of circumstance.

She was thinking about this as she sat in the backseat of her own car, with Dean in the driver's seat, Brad again on the passenger side. She was so tense that she was afraid she would throw up. Her stomach churned; she could taste the bile in the back of her throat. That had always happened to her, ever since she was a little girl. Whenever she got too worried or upset, whenever things were going really, really bad, she puked. It always made things worse.

There were some late diners in the restaurant. Emily recognized them as the husband and wife she'd waited on a few times. They'd recently had a baby, a sweet and pretty little girl. This was their date night; once every other week since the baby turned six months, they had a sitter. They always looked so giddy, so excited to be out, even though it was just for burgers at the Blue Hen. Emily loved the way the man looked at his wife when she ordered, as if she were the most fascinating creature he'd ever known. When they were there, Emily could hear them laughing, whispering. Once she'd seen the woman wiggle her foot out of her shoe and touch his calf with her bare toes. She watched them get into the car. He didn't open the door for her, and she shot him a look over the roof. He gave her a sheepish grin and ran around, made a show of sweeping his arm and offering a deep bow as she got inside. Her laughter carried on the cold night air, weird and echoey.

"The husband is still there," said Dean. He sounded stressed "There's his car."

Paul's new Charger was parked in the front. *Park in the back,* Carol always complained. *Those spots are for customers,* she chided. *But baby, then no one will see the new ride my sugar mama bought me.* She would always answer him with a smile, *Silly man.*

"They're not rich," Emily said. She knew that was what he thought. And she wanted to clarify for him that it wasn't true. He seemed to have a hostility about wealthy people, as though they had something he deserved instead. Maybe if she could convince him that they were just a normal couple who worked hard at their business, he would leave them alone.

Dean turned to glare at her over the seat. "Bullshit. We've been to their house."

In December, Carol and Paul had thrown a huge Christmas party at their home for family and friends and employees. Emily thought about their house sometimes. Not that it was so opulent; it wasn't. It was smallish compared to what the new homes on the market looked like. It didn't have that straight-from-the box-feeling, as if everything were picked brand-new from a catalog. Emily could tell that Carol and Paul had chosen each piece of furniture, art, even the hand towels in the bathroom with great care. Paul was an amateur photographer, so the walls were covered with framed shots of their travels around the world, their children and grandchildren. Every pillow, throw, and fixture was perfectly placed in its environment. Their two French bulldogs, Max and Ruby, happily tottered about seeking affection and scraps from the abundant spread. Each dog had a huge plush cushion beside the bed in the master suite with his or her name embroidered into the fabric.

"Look at this place," Dean kept saying. There was something odd in his tone, something darker than envy.

Their home *glittered,* with two huge Christmas trees, a lifetime of collected decorations and ornaments. The party was packed with friends and family, old employees who had remained in touch, vendors, and neighbors. Carol greeted everyone with equal enthusiasm. It was their home; they'd raised both their children within its walls. They'd devoted their time, their energy, and their love to making it a beautiful place where everyone who knew them felt welcome. It was the kind of home Emily had only dreamed of, the kind she hoped to make for herself someday. As she sat in the dark backseat of her car, that day seemed a long, long way off.

"He's leaving," said Dean. He exhaled his relief.

Emily watched Paul leave the restaurant, then close and lock the door behind him. She wanted to start screaming, try to force her way out of the backseat. She could envision the scene, hear her own voice slicing through the quiet, see herself running toward Paul. But she didn't do anything. She was paralyzed, strangled by her own fear.

"What if he recognizes my car?" she asked.

"He can't see it from where he is," said Dean.

He sounded very sure of himself. He always seemed so, even though his judgment proved fallible again and again. He never lost confidence. But Emily didn't think they were that far away, or that the few trees between the car and the restaurant were enough to block them from view. She said a silent prayer that Paul would look over in their direction. She willed it. But no. Emily felt her nausea increase as Paul gunned the engine and sped off in the opposite direction.

"They were going to stop doing it, you know," said Emily. "Paul was going to start taking the money to the bank every day, not just on Friday nights."

Dean spun around again to look at her. Brad was staring at Dean now. He hadn't said a word since they'd left the house. Since they'd parked, he'd sat there like a gargoyle, staring at the restaurant.

"You never told me that," said Dean.

"Why would I?"

He gave her a dark, threatening look, and she found herself bracing—for what, she didn't know. He'd never hit her, not really. He'd grabbed her hard one time. Once he'd pushed her. But he'd been so sorry afterward that he cried. He'd been so nice after that; for a full week, he was so sweet and considerate. It was almost worth it. Even her mother had never laid a hand on her. But you didn't need fists to hurt and scar, did you? Words could hurt worse. And those wounds never did seem to heal. *Sticks and stones can break my bones. But words can break my heart.*

"I hope you're wrong," said Dean. He got out of the car and pulled the seat forward for her. "Climb out."

She hesitated, wondering what he would do if she stayed rooted, started yelling and making a huge scene. She felt Brad's eyes on her and turned to look at him. She held his gaze and once more found it so disturbingly blank that she averted her eyes, lest she be sucked into the black hole of whatever he was.

Dean reached in and grabbed her arm, pulling her from the car. She struggled a second, then let him yank her out. Her arm ached from his grip. She rubbed it as she stood before him, fighting back tears of pain and anger.

"Why are you doing this, Dean?" She lowered her voice to a whisper. "It's wrong."

For a second, she saw something flicker across his face—sadness, fear, sorrow. Then it was gone. He was high, she realized. His eyes were red-rimmed and glassy. She had no idea what he was on; it could be any combination of their yield today. The man she loved, the one she trusted to take care of her, was nowhere to be seen. If only she could tell him how much she had loved him at the end of their workdays, when he came home tired and they cooked dinner together. She'd never loved anyone as much as she'd loved him on those nights.

"What you're going to do is knock on the door, okay?" he said. "When she opens it, go inside and give her some sad story, tell her you have no one else to talk to, that you need a friend. You know she won't turn you away."

No. Of course she wouldn't. Because that's the kind of person Carol was—a good person, a kind person. Dean and Brad would use the powerful instinct that Carol had to mother and help; they would use it to hurt her and steal from her. Because that's the kind of people *they* were.

"After a few minutes, excuse yourself to the bathroom," Dean said. He'd obviously given this a great deal of thought. That was why he'd kept coming to pick her up from work, gotten friendly with the kitchen guys. Even Paul had invited him back to see the office. All the while, he must have been planning. She'd had no idea. He went on, "When you go back there, unlock the rear door."

Who is this man? she wondered. He was cold and hard, a criminal, an addict. Had he always been this? Had her mother seen it all along? How could she have known when Emily had been so blind?

"Then go back to her and keep her busy."

She still didn't say anything. She was out of words.

"If you keep her out of her office, no one gets hurt," he went on. "There's no trouble at all. Right? So, that's your job: Keep Carol from getting hurt." He leaned in close and whispered into her ear. "Because you don't know this guy. You have no idea what he'll do if push comes to shove. Trust me." Emily wasn't sure if he was talking about Brad or about himself.

Dean's breath was rank; he was holding on to her shoulder.

"Don't worry about the money; they're insured," he said. "Just keep that bitch from getting her head blown off."

Emily's whole body throbbed with anxiety. If she stayed, if she did what Dean wanted her to do, she could keep Carol from getting hurt. If she ran to get help, what would they do to her? Would they chase her? The nearest establishment was a gas station about a mile up the road. How long would it take her to make it there? Ten minutes, at the very least. It would take the police another five or ten after she made the call. A lot could happen in fifteen minutes—if they let her get away at all.

"Okay," she said. "Okay."

He smiled, relieved. "Okay? Really?"

She nodded, and he leaned in to kiss her on the forehead. "Good girl."

She leaned over and vomited on the ground next to his boots.

"Christ, Em," he said, disgusted. "Pull yourself together."

When Emily got to the door of the Blue Hen and started knocking, tears streaming down her cheeks, her near hysteria wasn't an act at all. Through the glass, she saw some type of battle on Carol's face. There was concern first, then a flash of suspicion that faded quickly. She knew Emily. She trusted her. But she didn't want to deal with a drama at ten P.M.; she was tired. Finally, fatigue gave way to worry.

"Emily, honey? What's wrong?"

She opened the door, looking behind Emily. Would she see them? Would she know they were lying in wait to rob her? Emily stepped inside, and Carol closed and locked the door. They'd been robbed before, Emily knew. Not here in New Jersey, but in a place they used to own in New York City. They were cautious. There were security cameras outside. She wasn't sure whether Dean knew that. Had she ever mentioned it? Probably not; she would have had no reason to do so.

"I'm sorry," said Emily. Her voice caught and broke. "I didn't have anyplace else to go."

Carol led her over to the booth by the window. "What's happened? What's wrong?"

This was the moment, right here, before anything bad had happened. She'd dwelled in this moment before. Here she could make a choice. She could say, "Carol, you need to call the police. My boyfriend and some other addict ex-con are waiting outside to rob this place. I had no choice except to follow them this far. But they want me to open the back door and let them in so they can take your money. I'm not going to do that. You need to call the police."

That was the right thing to do. It was perfectly clear. But she didn't do it. Dean would get arrested and go to jail. Or they'd hear the sirens and get away. What would they do to her then? Dean would know that she'd betrayed him, and he'd hate her forever. Would he hurt her? Maybe not, but Dean couldn't stop Brad from hurting her. If she helped them, they'd get their money. Brad would disappear. Emily could convince Dean to clean up, get a job. Things would work out okay. After all, Paul and Carol *were* insured; a couple thousand dollars didn't mean that much to them.

She found herself sliding onto the vinyl booth. She made up a story for Carol, a fight with Dean that had gotten violent. In tears, Emily told Carol that she and her mother weren't talking. And she was so sorry to impose, but she *really* needed to talk to someone. Did Carol and Paul ever fight like that?

"I've never fought with Paul like that, no," said Carol gently. "But I've been in a violent relationship—when I was about your age. I will tell you that it rarely gets better. Once someone hurts you, chances are he'll do it again and again. And it will only get worse."

Emily knew Carol was right. She found herself nodding, the tears still falling. "He wasn't like this at first," she said. "At first he seemed like such a great guy."

"Honey, they all seem great at first," said Carol. "That's how they get you hooked."

"I don't want to give up on him. I love him," said Emily. "But I feel like I have to betray myself to be with him."

She hadn't meant to say that. She was sorry when the words were out in the air—they were too honest. She hadn't even realized she felt that way. But she did; she had for a while. Being with Dean made her do bad things. She was someone—even in this moment—who she didn't want to be.

"That's not a good feeling," said Carol. Emily could tell that Carol knew all about it. "And it's not love, either."

Emily felt a little rush of anger. She did love Dean. No one could tell her differently. Otherwise, why would she do all of these things for him? She wouldn't, not if she didn't know that deep inside, he was a better man. If they could just get back to that good place and forget all this other stuff, they'd be okay. She felt a renewed sense of purpose, of hope. In a few minutes, this would all be over. She'd get them back on track after that.

"Can I use the bathroom?" she asked.

"Of course," said Carol. "I'll get you some cocoa."

Emily walked down the narrow hallway where she'd dropped all those glasses earlier. It seemed like weeks ago, so much had changed between then and now. In the bathroom, she splashed water on her face and looked in the mirror. She dabbed at the black smudges of makeup under her eyes. She always hated the sight of her own reflection. Her face looked pasty and thin in the harsh fluorescent light. Her eyes were an uninspiring brown. Her mousy roots betrayed the fact that her blond tresses were store-bought.

Leaving the water running so that Carol would think she was still in there, Emily slipped from the bathroom and moved quickly down the hall and into the kitchen. Only the lights over the sink and stove were lit; the overheads were all off. It was dim and orange, quiet in stark contrast to the usual bright bustle when the restaurant was open. There was something nice, something intimate, about being there after hours.

Emily went to the metal back door. *Last chance,* she thought, looking at the dead bolt. It was new, still shiny and gold. She thought, *This is your last chance to do the right thing.* She'd stolen for Dean before—pills, jewelry, and cash from the houses she used to clean. She'd given him alarm codes—a family she babysat for who were away at Disney; a dress shop where she'd worked for a month. None of that was like this. It was all distant and theoretical. It had never felt like a personal betrayal, even though it was. All of those people had entrusted her with something, and for Dean, she'd betrayed them all. Why? Why would she do that, if not for love? She turned the lock on the knob and threw open the dead bolt and moved away from the door quickly. She didn't want to think about how awful this was.

When she pushed out into the hallway, Angelo was standing there. He had his headphones on and was mopping the floor slowly, almost lovingly. He raised his eyes to Emily, startled, and then smiled broadly when he recognized her. He reached up and pulled one of the headphones from his right ear. "Hey," he said. "What are you doing here?"

He wasn't supposed to be here. But it made sense. Paul would never leave Carol alone in the restaurant, not unless there was someone here to help her close up. Emily couldn't bring herself to answer or smile back. He looked confused for a second, his smile fading. Then his gaze drifted to the kitchen behind her. His eyes went wide. She didn't have to turn around to know he was watching Brad and Dean come in through the back door.

chapter eleven

Brendan was asleep. The girls were watching a movie in Chelsea's room, cuddled together on her bed like puppies. Kate remembered that physical closeness you had with your teenage girlfriends and experienced again with your small children. The unself-conscious melding of bodies, an acknowledgment that we were designed to wrap around each other for love and comfort more than anything else. She loved it when one of the kids got into bed with her and Sean, and they still did sometimes. Even Chelsea, who was too cool for school, sometimes slept with Kate when Sean was away.

Kate sensed that there was something going on in Chelsea's universe; she'd heard some excited chirping, some conspiratorial whispering. Something to do with boys, she was certain. She tried not to stick her nose in. She didn't try to act like one of the girls. She wasn't that kind of mom.

Sean had taken a call and was in his office. She could hear the low tones of his professional voice, as opposed to the "buddy" voice reserved for his pals, loud and mischievous, or his "dad" voice, soothing but firm, or the voice, sweet and strong, that he reserved for her. Kate loved this time of night, when everyone was safe at home. In this place, she felt as though she could release a breath she'd been holding all day. She might read or watch television with Sean. Or, like tonight, she might sit outside by the pool with a glass of wine and be still for the first time all day.

She'd tried to call her mother to see if there was anything she could bring, to assure her that whatever menu Birdie had planned would be just fine. But there was no answer. This was not unusual. Sometimes her mother didn't answer the phone, even turned the machine off so that no one could leave a message. As a mother herself, Kate couldn't understand. Why would you choose to be unavailable to your family, even if your children were grown?

It was a streak that ran through her mother's side, a fierce desire to isolate, the preference for solitude. There was a cold meanness to it. This violent assertion of their separateness from the people who wanted to love them had caused terrible, bitter estrangements among her mother's siblings, to the degree that Kate didn't have relationships with her uncle or any of her cousins.

Most of those relationships had crashed upon the rocks of Heart Island. Her uncle Gene and Birdie had fought a bitter court battle over Grandpa Jack's will, and they hadn't spoken again since terms were settled. Toward the end of her life, Aunt Caroline abandoned the place she'd always loved. *I'm sorry, Kate. But Birdie makes everything so ugly. It's not the same place it was, not for me.* Kate would learn that these estrangements were the least of it.

The August night was humid and thick. But after a day of darting between air-conditioned spaces, the real air felt good. *I am breathing in. I am breathing out.* She was aware suddenly of a leaden fatigue.

You're tired? her mother would say. *What did you do all day?* Birdie, who had never really worked and yet hadn't been a stay-at-home mother, either, seemed to have nothing but disdain for people who did "less" than she did. *Being a mother is not a job, exactly, is it?*

Birdie's day was and always had been a busy flutter of vigorous workouts with her personal trainer, various meetings for the charitable committees to which she devoted most of her time, expensive "business" lunches, and appointments to maintain her impeccable grooming . . . manicure, pedicure, facial, waxing, God knew what else. Theo and Kate had been more or less raised by nannies, a long anonymous string of them, since Birdie had trouble keeping staff. There was hardly time to attach to one before she fled. This was a fact that Birdie vehemently denied. *I had help, of course. Lord knows your father was never around. But I raised you children all by myself.* Maybe her mother believed that, but it was not true. And yet Kate had no harsher judge of her lack of professional achievement than her own mother.

At a certain point, people—including her parents—had stopped asking Kate what she was going to do with her life. By the time you reached forty, if you hadn't done anything to speak of, people figured you probably wouldn't ever do much of anything. Early on, the questions were always excited and hopeful. *What's your major? What are your plans after graduation?* Expectations ran high for the offspring of Joe and Birdie. The beautiful daughter of the wealthy, philanthropic New York City Burkes could do anything, couldn't she? That's what Mother always said, as if Kate's parentage were some ticket to ride.

Then, as the years went on and her college graduation was a distant point in everyone's past, the inquiries become more cautious. *Have you thought about what you might like to do? You were always such a good writer. Your parents always thought you'd go into publishing.* And, of course, there was the early and unplanned pregnancy. After that, her vicious public divorce from Sebastian. (*Se-bastard,* as she often thought of him; with a name like that, how could you *not* turn out to be a self-indulgent jerk?) Then she moved to the New Jersey suburbs and married a real estate broker.

She stopped attending her parents' dinner parties. In fact, they'd stopped mentioning the parties. By her early thirties, Kate knew she was no longer much of a showpiece, nothing to point to with pride. She was *justamom.* That's what she said when people asked what she did now. "Oh," she'd say with a self-deprecating smile, "I'm just a mom."

People knew all the right things to say about that. *Oh, well, that's the most important job in the world.* After Maria Shriver went on *Oprah* and said that mothers were on the front lines of humanity, people were *dripping* with respect.

Then there was some magazine article that said the job of stay-at-home mom was worth $110,000 a year. People seemed happy to trot out that statistic (she'd heard it at least three times, even though she'd never actually read the article), as if it meant anything at all.

The truth was that she'd meant to do so many things. She had fancied herself a writer, wrote prolifically at NYU—short stories, plays, poetry. She'd had some compliments, some encouragement from professors. But after college, there was Sebastian. She'd met him at one of her parents' parties. Her parents always insisted that it wasn't a setup, but they'd been thrilled when Kate started a relationship with him.

He was already famous; his first novel was the rare bird that critics laud and that also races up the best-seller lists. He'd made a fortune and was agonizing over his second novel, for which the expectations were so very high. She found his angst endearing; it never occurred to her at first that he had a problem with alcohol. Having just graduated from college, where drinking was the number one social activity, she didn't find it odd that he drank every night at dinner (someplace fabulous), then went on to the bars (dark ones, preferably belowground), then the giggling stumble through quiet city streets back to his apartment on Second Avenue, sometimes as the first light of dawn broke the sky. In his thrall, she lost herself completely. His success, his ambition, was a red giant, already bloated and dangerously unstable. The stars trembling in his galaxy hardly had a chance.

He'd read a bit of her work. *It's lovely, Kate. You have a delicate voice.* But what else would he say to the young woman ten years (twelve, actually) his junior as she lay naked in bed beside him, watching his face as he read? Anyway, what did that even mean? She took it to mean that he didn't think much of it, since she'd heard him describe other authors he admired as *muscular* or *powerful, masterful* or *mesmerizing*. Didn't she already know on some subliminal level that she wasn't allowed to have any ambition, any talent of her own, while she was with him? If she sought to be anything but his greatest and most intimate admirer, the delicate balance of their relationship would start to tip toward destruction. Chronic pleaser that she was, she couldn't have that.

And then there was Chelsea, the other supernova of Kate's twenties. Between Sebastian and Chelsea, their needs, their love for her and hers for them (there *was* so much love in her early life with Sebastian), Kate happily disappeared for a while. But at a time when she might have been forming herself, newly graduated, reasonably intelligent, with the desire and possibly even the talent to write, she didn't, she couldn't. Her parents *loved* Sebastian. He did know how to fluff and stroke them to purring and leg thumping. He knew how to be exactly what they wanted him to be. That was one of his many gifts.

And there was always money—his family money, the money from his obscene book advance (the kind of advance reserved for a beautiful male graduate of Princeton, so young that his talent staggered). Then there was Kate's trust. The truth was that she didn't *have* to do anything, ever. Her future was assured, regardless. A trust-fund baby never really had to make her way, find her path, or follow her dreams. The prize had already been given. In "The Artist of the Beautiful," Nathaniel Hawthorne wrote, "The reward for all high performance must be sought within itself or sought in vain." Even if that was an inherent truth of life, who believed it anymore? In a vain and corrupt society where people worshipped only wealth, beauty, and celebrity, who truly cared about high performance?

There were hands on her shoulders then. "Hey, why so serious?"

She tilted her head back to look at her husband. He smiled down at her and leaned in for a kiss. She thought of the *Spider-Man* kiss, which was the most romantic movie kiss Kate had ever seen. Just lips—every bit of passion and desire concentrated on the mouth, the body in exile.

Sean pulled up another lounge chair beside hers, stretched out his long legs. She reached for his hand, and he laced his fingers through hers.

"Are you going to tell them on this visit?" he asked. The question came from nowhere, but it was something they'd been talking about enough that she knew what he was asking.

"I don't think so," she said. She issued a sigh, felt it come up from the depths of her. "I don't know."

He didn't say anything. He wouldn't seek to influence her on this topic, knowing how fraught and personal it was. Because many years after people had stopped expecting Kate to do something—anything—she had, in fact, written a book. An agent had recently agreed to represent her. Soon after, there was a bidding war between several publishers.

She wasn't vain enough to imagine that this eagerness had anything to do with her literary talent. She suspected that it had more to do with her famed marriage to Sebastian. People in the industry felt as though they knew her, thanks to her ex-husband's memoir—which, as Kate saw it, was more fiction than fact.

Stealing time while the kids were at school, managing pages at night after everyone else was asleep, Kate had finally done what she'd always intended to do. It had taken over a year and had been both harder and easier than she'd imagined it would be to complete her novel.

A family drama, they were calling it—she'd heard her editor use the phrase a number of times. There was a true story at the heart of her novel. And this was, as far as her publisher was concerned, a very good thing. Apparently, people wanted to peek into your living room and watch the horror show you called your life, regardless of whether what they were seeing was truth or invention or some combination. These days, who could tell the difference?

"I guess I'll have to feel it out," she said.

Her husband was tapping a staccato beat on the armrest with his free hand. This was something he did when he was anxious or excited. It was one of the first things she'd noticed about him, a little tell reminding her that he wasn't always the mellow, devil-may-care guy everyone perceived him to be. He worried sometimes. He got as excited as a kid.

She looked over at him. He was staring up into the starry sky.

"What is it?" she asked.

"Well," he said. "I have some good news and some bad news."

He stretched his arms above his head, then turned to look at her. She couldn't read his expression.

"What?" she asked. She had a creeping feeling of trepidation.

"You know that five-thousand-square-foot mission-style home on Poplar? The one we've always loved?"

Oh, real estate. Fine. "Yeah, of course."

"The owners want to list it," he said. "They want to list it with *me*. Turns out they're friends of the Hamiltons, who told them I was the *only* man for the job."

He couldn't hold back the wide grin. Sean loved his job. He loved real estate—land, condos, houses. He was a matchmaker brokering happy unions between families and their perfect homes. He got crushes on properties, mooned over them. His excitement was contagious.

It was one of the things she first loved about him, that he had a passion for what he did. His success at his work meant something to him, meant a lot. The last couple of years in the worst market ever had been hard on him. She felt the same wave of excitement that she felt when her kids were happy about something.

"Oh, Sean, congratulations. That's fantastic!" she said. Then, "What's the bad news?"

His smile faded a bit, and he raised his eyebrows. "They're very motivated," he said. "They want to do their first open house on Sunday."

It took a second for the meaning to sink in.

"Oh," she said. "*Oh*."

It wasn't disappointment or anger that she felt. It was fear. She didn't know if she could handle the island, or her parents, alone this year. He must have seen it on her face. His smile dropped, and he quickly raised a palm.

"I *told* them we had a family trip planned and that I'd ask my wife what her thoughts were," he said. "So say the word, and I'll tell them it will have to be next week."

She looked up at the stars overhead. There would be so many more in the Adirondack sky, an eternity of glimmering lights. She and Sean would lie on the rocks after the kids went to bed and stare into that vast beauty, soaking up the silence, the peace of the place, cherishing the utter disconnection from the bustle of their modern life.

"Honestly, it wouldn't be that big a deal," he went on when she didn't say anything. "I'd just meet you up there on Monday. Brendan could chill with me and give his ankle an extra day of healing. We'd be there by Monday dinnertime, Tuesday morning at the latest. A day behind you."

He looked so glad, so animated, like a kid asking for a puppy.

"It's fine," she said. She tried for a smile. "Really."

"Seriously, Kate." He tightened his grip on her hand. "Just say the word, and I'll tell them to find someone else."

The thing was, he meant it. Even though he wanted it, he'd walk away, zero attitude, if she said the word. That's who he was. That was precisely why she couldn't ask him to do it, as badly as she wanted to. She wouldn't cling to him and force him to be her lifeline.

"What about your 'disconnect'?" she said. "You *do* need some time off."

"I do. But—" he started.

She interrupted him with a squeeze on his arm. "No, it's okay," she said. "I want you to do it."

He hadn't had a listing he was enthusiastic about in a while, mostly foreclosures and short sales, houses in disrepair owned by folks who didn't have the money to maintain them and then looted them when they left, taking appliances, fixtures, even trees from the landscaping. During the boom, he dealt in dream homes. These days he was scraping those dreams off the concrete and selling them to the highest bidder.

"Really?" he said.

"Really."

He leaned in for another kiss. How could she say no? The island was a chore for him, laboring under her parents' disapproval. *He's a Realtor?* her mother had said with such disdain that her tone could have peeled paint off the walls. Somebody who sold things for a living was worse than a domestic, according to Birdie. As if everybody weren't selling something. (Nor was there anything wrong with being a "domestic," as far as Kate was concerned. Work was work.) As if Birdie's own father, Grandpa Jack, hadn't made all his money in real estate. He *bought* real estate, Birdie said, and hired *others* to sell it. There seemed to be some important distinction that was lost on Kate. Her mother just needed to feel better than other people; Kate didn't know why.

"There's cell service on the island now," Sean went on, thinking aloud. He was in full planning mode. "So I can field any interest from there. If anyone wants a showing, Jane can do it. And then we'll head back in time for the second open house next week."

"Sure," she said. "That's fine. That's perfect."

He talked then about the house, its vaulted ceilings and stunning landscaped pool area. About the marble master bath, the steam shower, and the gourmet kitchen. The four huge bedrooms, two with their own attached baths. He'd obviously been stalking the house for a while. He raved about the clay tile roof, three-car garage, media room, and gargoyle doorknocker; he was practically swooning. A straight man in love with design—it was cute. When she met him, he'd shown her the house they lived in now. He'd said, "It needs work, but the bones are there." She had felt that way about Sean. She'd thought he was a bit of jerk during the showing, but somehow, even before she'd spent an hour with him, she could see that the structure was solid.

"Maybe we should buy it," she said.

He gave her a look. They'd agreed before they married that Kate's trust was to be reserved for the kids, their education, their needs growing up (although Chelsea and Brendan had no idea the money even existed). For Kate and Sean's purposes, they'd use the money for emergencies and, if they needed it, in their retirement, trying to leave as much as they could to Chelsea and Brendan and various charitable organizations. *I want to build a life with you, not live off what your parents earned.* She loved him for that. Sebastian never had any similar thoughts. In his life, money was a river that flowed with no beginning and no end. He rode its current; it had no meaning.

Sean and Kate *had* relied on her money a bit in the last couple of years, as Sean's income waned, to pay for the kids' private school tuition. Sean hadn't been happy about it. He'd come the closest to sulking and moping that she'd ever seen.

"Not from the trust," she said. "You know, sell this place, use that and the book advance to make a big down payment."

He gave a slow nod as if considering it. Which she knew he wasn't.

"Our property taxes would triple," he said. He was very practical about these kinds of things, unlike Sebastian, who'd felt that money had no value until it was spent. Nothing Sebastian ever made was enough to sate his appetite; it had kept Kate in a constant state of anxiety—what would he want next, what would he buy now? It wasn't about whether they could afford it or not. It was about that inner hunger of his that could never be satisfied. Nothing was ever enough.

Sean went on, "And I love our house." He was nothing if not faithful.

"So you'll flirt—*oh, baby, I love your doorknocker*," she said. "But you won't divorce and remarry?"

"What can I say?" He reached for her hand. "I guess I'm a one-house guy."

Her book advance was impressive but not staggering. It was a solid amount and, she was embarrassed to admit, the first money she had earned in her adult life. She was surprised at how good it felt to get paid for her work. It made her think her mother had been right about that, at least.

While Sean went to his office to fax the contracts to the new clients, Kate went upstairs. Theo had backed out of the trip. Now Sean and Brendan would be arriving late. She'd had a text from her father saying: *I needed to get away from your mother. Buckle up; she's got some bug up her ass. See you Wednesday. Probably.* It was not unexpected. Her parents could not be on Heart Island alone together for more than a couple of days.

She thought her father could have called rather than sending a text. That was what people did when they wanted to impart information but not *talk* about it. Her father was the master of that, hiding in plain sight. She found it interesting that Theo believed she and Joe were so close, that Kate was his favorite. Even Birdie had expressed jealousy over the years of their relationship. Kate loved her father. He was always kind to her, always reasonable. The truth was that he was like the sun: warm and nurturing but just as distant, just as unreachable, and at times just as harsh and unforgiving. Ironically, she was closer to Birdie in some ways. At least her mother engaged, even if it was only to be a total witch.

Kate knocked on Chelsea's door and pushed inside without waiting for an acknowledgment. Chelsea, not very subtly, closed the lid on her laptop as Kate moved into the room. The movie the girls had been watching apparently had been abandoned.

"What's up, Mom?" Chelsea was all sweet, wide-eyed innocence. *Hmm.*

Kate told her about the male exodus from Heart Island. "On Sunday, it's just going to be the two of us," she said.

"Brendan is going to freak out," said Chelsea mildly. "But that's fine."

"Can I go?"

Both Chelsea and Kate turned to look at Lulu. She offered a sheepish shrug. Lulu had no boundaries. She practically lived at their house, had been Chelsea's closest friend since kindergarten. Kate wasn't always thrilled with Lulu's influence on Chelsea, but she did have an affection for the kid, who wasn't nearly as worldly or as confident as she wanted everyone to think.

"I don't know, Lulu," said Kate. "It's not like the other trips we take. Heart Island is not for everyone." Lulu had been with them to Disney World, the Grand Canyon, even to the Caribbean with the Burke-Abbott family (Kate had never changed her last name, not for Sebastian and not for Sean).

"I can handle it," said Lulu. "It'll be fun. Besides, you know how Chelsea's grandma *loves* me."

Chelsea let go a little laugh at that. Strumpet. Ditz. Stray. All words Birdie had used to describe Lulu over the years, never to her face, naturally. But Birdie didn't need words to communicate her dislike. It didn't seem to bother Lulu; she seemed to enjoy getting under Birdie's very thin skin.

"I'll think about it," said Kate. She glanced at her daughter, who appeared to be thinking about something else, staring with a slight frown at the ceiling. Kate couldn't read her expression. "We'll see."

"Lemme know," Lulu said, and went back to tapping on her phone, the permanent condition of the teenager.

"I'll call your mother," said Kate.

"She won't care." Lulu didn't look up from her device.

Kate considered screen etiquette to be as important as a reasonable bedtime or limiting television and sugary treats. It was her personal "broken windows" theory of parenting. Meaning, if you didn't have at least some control over the little things, you couldn't hope to manage the big things. Chelsea and Brendan were not allowed to text or play games at the dinner table, when other people were talking to them, or until homework was done. It was a matter of priorities.

When Kate looked back at Chelsea, her daughter was watching her in that careful, sensitive way she had. Even when Chelsea was a baby, Kate felt as if her daughter could read her mind.

"It's fine, Mom," Chelsea said. Her daughter gave her a sweet, comforting smile. "It's going to be fine."

"Yes," Kate said. She clapped her hands together and forced a bright smile. "Just us girls."

chapter twelve

"What the fuck?" Angelo said.

His face went slack, but he lifted the mop like a weapon. Emily spun around to see two men in masks walk through the back door. Fear rocketed through her before she realized it was Brad and Dean; she almost let out a little shriek. Angelo grabbed her by the arm and pulled her behind him. He obviously hadn't put the scenario together and was moving to protect her. There was a yawning moment of silence as Brad pulled the gun from his pants.

"Emily?" It was Carol coming up behind her.

"Carol, stay back," she managed to say. Her voice didn't sound right, as if she were listening to herself underwater. She heard Carol come to a stop with a gasp.

"We just want the cash and nobody gets hurt." Emily recognized Dean's voice.

"Angelo and Emily," said Carol. Her voice was cool and level. "Step back toward me and let them pass. Let's go have a seat in the dining room until they're done."

She could have been talking about the cable guy or a visit from the plumber. The three of them moved backward down the hall. Brad kept step with them, as Dean hung back.

"The money is in a cloth envelope on the desk, through that door to the right," said Carol. "There's quite a bit of cash. We'll just have a seat and wait for you to leave."

If you didn't know her, if you didn't hear the slight tremor in her voice, you'd never know she was afraid, thought Emily.

The three of them walked into the dining room and had a seat at one of the four-tops. Emily could hear Dean and Brad move heavily down the hall and enter the office. The pie case was humming. Carol tapped her fingers on the wood, her breathing quick and shallow. Neither of them said a word at first. Emily felt Angelo's eyes settle on her.

"You let them in," he said. He sounded hurt, sad, but not angry.

"That's your boyfriend, isn't it?" said Carol. "I recognized his voice."

"No," Emily lied. "No."

She'd had only one thing to do to make this okay, and she hadn't done it. Now they were all totally screwed. She couldn't bring herself to meet Carol's eyes, just kept her gaze on the table between her outstretched fingers.

"I trusted you," said Carol.

Emily had heard this sentence before, said in the same sad, bemused way. It never failed to flood her with shame. She thought of all the meals Carol had served her, all the pats on the back and the words of encouragement. Even tonight, though she must have been tired and in no mood for drama, Carol had opened the door and let her in. Emily's despair and regret were a well within her.

Angelo got up quietly and moved behind the counter. "They can't do this."

"Stop, Angelo," Carol said. "Just sit down. The money doesn't matter."

But he already had the gun in his hand, a look of grim determination on his face.

"Goddammit," said Carol. Her voice was a frantic hiss. "That stupid gun. Put it *away*."

"You're going to let them rob you?" said Angelo. He was angry now, indignant. "Just let them come here and take the money *you* earned?"

Emily could see how young he was then. She hadn't noticed before, even though she saw him every time she worked. He was younger than Emily, who wasn't quite twenty-three. He was only a kid.

"Yes," Carol said. "If money's all they want, let them have it. It's not worth our lives. Or theirs. Sit down."

Or theirs? Carol was concerned about Brad and Dean's lives as well. Emily found herself staring at Carol, trying to understand how someone in her position could be thinking about that.

Angelo came back to the table, but he had the gun in his pants.

"Give it to me," Carol said. She reached her hand across the table.

"If they walk out, I'll let them go. I swear it," he said. He put his hand on hers, and they locked eyes. "But I'm not going to let them hurt us."

"Angelo." Carol smiled at him as if he were the sweetest, saddest thing she'd ever seen.

"I promise," he said.

Carol drew her hand back, wrapped her arms around herself, and gave a slow, sorry shake of her head. "Oh my God."

"Let's go," said Dean from the doorway. Emily thought that was incredibly stupid. Because weren't they supposed to pretend that she didn't have anything to do with this? What were they supposed to do now? Go on the run?

Then she realized with a horrible, sinking dread that no one had thought this through at all—not Brad, not Dean, certainly not Emily. Brad and Dean were junkies; they needed money. They hadn't planned a thing, hadn't anticipated a single consequence. They'd used her: her car, her knowledge of the restaurant, her relationship with Carol. And Emily was the fool who'd gone along for the ride. She was totally and completely screwed. She thought about those tumblers of ice water falling to the floor, shattering into a thousand shards. That was her heart in this moment. That was her life.

Angelo had his eyes on Emily. "You don't have to go with them," he said.

"Shut the fuck up," said Dean. "Let's go."

"If you go with them, Emily, that's the end of you," said Carol. "That's your whole future in flames. There's still a way out."

Emily looked at the other woman and could see the sadness in her eyes, the fear. Carol's hands were shaking. She was probably thinking about her children, who were grown, in college but home all the time. And yet she was also thinking about Emily, a girl who had betrayed her trust and her friendship.

"Shut up," said Dean. He sounded panicky, his voice going a bit high. "Let's go."

"Leave her," said Brad, coming up behind him. "We have to get out of here."

She knew they couldn't leave her; if they did, she would have to tell the police everything. If she stayed, Brad would have to kill her, Angelo, and Carol. Brad had the gun in one hand and the envelope in his other.

Emily stood, and Angelo did as well. She mouthed to him, *Don't.* She was thinking, *Don't be stupid. Let me go.* But she saw something on his face, something like pity. A communication passed between them. Angelo wasn't stupid; she was. Brad and Dean were just trying to get Emily out of the room before Brad started shooting.

As Angelo started to turn around, he pulled the weapon from his waist. His face was a dark mask of determination, his mouth a thin, pressed line. She could see the sweat on his forehead, the fear in his black eyes, the gold cross hanging around his neck. *No, don't. Please.*

The rest of it was a blur, the sharp details of the moment fading into a carnival ride of light and sound. She didn't know who shot first, but the sound of gunfire—deafeningly, brutally loud—

rocketed through her. Her hands flew to her ears, and she dropped to a crouch, wishing she could squeeze herself into a ball so tight and so small that she would cease to exist. It went on, the gunfire, the yelling. It went on forever.

When it was quiet again, her head was filled with a high-pitched ringing. She opened her eyes to see the white of Angelo's uniform blooming a dark, angry red. Carol, her face blank, stunned, crashed across the table, falling heavily to the floor, knocking down chairs. *This is not happening,* thought Emily, even as Carol came to lie still on the floor. *This is not happening.*

Brad and Dean disappeared around the corner; she heard their pounding footfalls. Angelo followed them, though he was injured, into the hallway. Emily crawled to Carol, tugged on her hand. *Get up, get up,* she heard herself pleading. Her ears were still ringing. *Please, Carol, I'm so sorry.*

There was blood on Emily's shirt, on her hands, on the floor and wall. *So much blood.* How was it possible? How did this happen? The smell was somehow sweet and metallic. *Oh, God. Oh, please, let this not be real.* She heard three more shots ring out, and then there was silence.

Emily crushed her eyes closed. She wished she'd go blind. She wished that river of blood were flowing from her and that the scene around her, the world itself, would fade to black.

"Come on, Em."

Dean had come back and was pulling at her. She was holding on to Carol, who was still and heavy. At least it was quiet; at least that horrible, nightmarish screaming had stopped. Who had been screaming like that? Emily realized it had been her.

Dean lifted her from the ground, and she pounded and kicked and screamed at him as he carried her over his shoulder from the restaurant. It was a horror show. Carol lay where she'd fallen. Angelo slumped against the wall, his palms turned toward the ceiling.

"Oh, no, no, no," she heard herself saying, dragging her hands on the wall, leaving three long trails of blood on the paint. "No, *please*, no."

"Shut her up."

In the fog of her awareness, she knew it was Brad. She hated him. Why wasn't *he* dead? Why wasn't *he* lying in a bloody heap on the floor? Why did people like him always win?

"Hush now, Em," said Dean. "It's okay."

What a ridiculous thing to say. She found herself laughing. Things would never be okay again. That much should be obvious even to a pill junkie. Then her laughter turned to sobbing.

"I'm serious," said Brad. He was so calm. "Shut her up or I will."

She felt all of her sound and tears dry up. They were at the car now. The air had turned cool while they were inside. A wind washed over her and felt good. A cold front was moving in; all the humidity had dissipated, and it felt like rain.

"Don't cry, please. Please be quiet." Dean put her down gently and took her face in his hands. There he was, the man she'd loved and thought would take care of her. But it was too late for him. "It wasn't supposed to be like this."

He pushed the seat back for her, and she fell inside. Her face, her hair, her arms were bloody. She used her jacket to wipe herself off. She remembered when she'd carelessly tossed the garment in the back, in case she got cold at the Blue Hen, which she often did. It seemed like another universe in which she'd worried about little things like catching a chill.

The two men climbed into the car, and Brad unzipped the envelope. Dean rested his head against the steering wheel. She'd seen tears in his eyes inside. She heard him take and release a long breath. He hadn't meant for things to go like this. If it hadn't been for Angelo, it might have been okay. Sweet, stupid Angelo. If only it had been just her and Carol there. Brad and Dean would have come and gone quietly. No one would have known that the money had been stolen until they were gone. That was how it was supposed to be.

Emily let herself believe that was what had happened. She imagined that she had let Dean and Brad in and returned to her conversation with Carol. And a while later, she'd left Carol there as if nothing had happened. She'd left the back door open, so Carol didn't suspect her. They'd given Brad his money, and he'd driven away, never to be heard from again. Dean was making promises. He was going to get a job. Things were going back to the way they were in the beginning. Why hadn't things happened that way?

"There's five grand in here, man," said Brad. "Five grand."

Emily couldn't tell if he was happy or not. Dean had told him ten thousand; she'd told him a couple hundred. So it was right in the middle. Five thousand was nothing. Even she, who had nothing, knew that. You couldn't buy a house, a car—you couldn't even live well for a few months. But, she supposed, to an addict, it was like winning the lotto. You could stay high for a while with that.

"Just take it," said Emily. "Take it and leave us alone."

Brad spun around to say something to her, his face an ugly scowl.

"Shit," said Dean, interrupting whatever Brad was about to say or do. "Do you hear that?"

She did. It was the faintest wail of sirens. She felt a potent rush of fear and relief. Maybe Carol or Angelo was alive and had called the police.

"There must have been some kind of alarm," said Brad. He looked accusingly at her, as if she'd had some part in the planning and execution of this nightmare. Emily didn't know whether there was an alarm. If there was, the employees hadn't been notified. The sound of the sirens was definitely growing louder, heading in their direction.

"What are you waiting for, asshole?" Brad said. His voice was quiet but white-hot with menace. "Drive."

Dean did as he was told. Thinking about the words Carol had spoken to her, Emily turned around to watch the Blue Hen disappear.

chapter thirteen

Whenever there were games, Caroline always lost. She was the smallest, the most prone to tantrums, and the clumsiest. She couldn't run without tripping. She couldn't hide without laughing. She tried to cheat at board games, would fly into a rage if caught. And she always, always tattled. Gene was the oldest; Caroline was the baby. Birdie was the middle child.

In Birdie's memory, they never got along. Gene was impossibly bossy, always trying to control everyone, always acting bigger, older, and more knowledgeable than he was; that never changed, even into adulthood. Caroline was everyone's pet. She'd be an absolute terror, wrecking every moment of fun and pleasure for Birdie, then acting the perfect angel for the adults. How they fawned over her, her cherub cheeks and golden curls, her blue, blue eyes. Even as a child, Birdie found it disgusting. People were so easily fooled by a pretty face.

On the island, they used to play a game they called Castle. Birdie always wanted to be queen, and Gene always wanted to be king. But they didn't want to rule together. No, if Gene were king, then Birdie had to be the serving wench. And if Birdie were queen, Gene had to be the knight at her command. Caroline always wanted to be the baby princess, so that was fine. She'd just lie in the hammock, linking flowers for her princess crown or, later, scribbling in her journals. The game always ended badly, with Birdie and Gene engaging in physical combat and being yanked apart by Mother or Daddy. *What is wrong with you two? Why can you never get along?* their mother would ask in distress. *We raised you to love each other.*

Birdie could concede that it was true. Their parents, Lana and Jack, were loving and kind. They never played favorites or took sides, though everyone doted on Caroline because she was the baby. That seemed right somehow, even to Birdie, who hated her for it. Her parents never, in Birdie's memory, had more than the most banal arguments. Once her mother had slammed a door. But there was nothing like the verbal and physical battles she would experience in her own marriage to Joe. So Birdie and Gene were not mimicking some bad behavior on the part of their parents. It was just that the chemistry wasn't there, she supposed. She never liked him. And she never wanted him to win, even though he was bigger and older and a boy.

There was an album, a large clothbound book in which their mother had painstakingly organized all their childhood photographs. Each photo was lovingly affixed with paper corners. Her mother's careful handwritten notes were written beneath each image. *It's important that you have this, that you always remember your childhood,* her mother had said, ignorant of the fact that there was nothing Birdie, at least, wanted less.

It was the sound of the squeaking screen door that had Birdie looking for the album now in the boxes stored in the bunkhouse. The wind had been picking up as she walked the path from the main house, gun in her pocket, flashlight in her hand.

She wasn't afraid, in spite of everything. She refused to be afraid on Heart Island, which belonged to her. She unlocked and opened the wooden door and flipped on the light switch. She was greeted by the chill of an unused, uninsulated cabin. It was a small but cozy space, with a desk along the left wall and two tidy bunk beds on either side of a large picture window. There was a small fireplace and an intimate sitting area. Everything was draped with white cotton slipcovers, since the bunkhouse was rarely used.

She knew the album was there. Joe had suggested that they leave it out on the coffee table so their guests could see what the island looked like back then, compare the old black-and-white photographs of the house and island to the stunning professional color shots in the coffee-table book in which their Heart Island home had been featured as one of the jewels of the area: *Great Adirondack Island Homes.*

Joe wanted to do that only to feed his ego. He loved for guests to see how he'd had the original structure remodeled into a modest guesthouse and then designed the main house himself. Everyone would know that he'd put his indelible stamp on her island. Ostensibly, it was his twentieth-anniversary gift to her. But by that point in their marriage, extravagant gifts had lost their meaning somewhat— not that she didn't love the new house. At least until recently, it was free from the ghosts of memory.

She found the book in the third box she opened. Caroline had desperately wanted it. She'd asked for it again and again over the years, especially after their mother's passing. But Birdie, though she could barely stand the sight of the thing, had kept it from her, even as her sister lay dying. *I've looked for it everywhere, Caroline. I'm sorry. I've no idea where it is.* It was something she felt terribly guilty about when she allowed herself to think about it. It had been cruel and cold, a vicious act of withholding, proving her sister's most furious, desperate recriminations true. But if that was what they thought of her, then why shouldn't she be that?

She lifted the album from its box, marked *Memorabilia,* and turned her head away from the powerful smell of mold and dust that lifted into the air. She issued a shuddering sneeze and then sank back onto the floor with the album in her lap.

The story was that her mother had inherited the island from her uncle, who had won it in a poker match from its drunken owner. Whether that was true, Birdie didn't know. But it was the story her mother told. She told of that and the island ghosts. Birdie had been thinking about it since the dock incident.

There was a little girl her mother had seen playing naked near the rocky shore where Birdie always waded in to swim. The girl came when the fog was thick. A young woman stood at the highest point, which the children called Lookout Rock, and gazed back toward the mainland. *She's anxious,* her mother would say. *She's waiting for someone who never comes.* There was an old man who, forever restless, tirelessly walked the perimeter when the moon was full.

Mother was delicate, prone to terrible headaches and spells that sent her to darkened rooms. The only other person who claimed to see the island spirits was Caroline. And no one believed her because she was Mother's pet and would do or say anything to please her.

Much as Birdie had never believed in Santa (Gene took care of that early) or the Easter Bunny, she had never believed in Mother's ghosts. She'd never seen anything even vaguely resembling a spirit during her summers on the island.

Sometimes the mournful call of an owl would scare her senseless late in the night. She'd climb into her sister's bed, and Caroline would wrap her warm body around Birdie. *Don't be scared, Birdie,* she'd say in her sweet voice. *I won't let anything hurt you.* Birdie did believe that, even though Caroline was two years younger and much smaller. She had always been braver and fiercer. But until today, Birdie had never seen anything on Heart Island that she couldn't understand or explain.

In the main house, she could hear the phone ringing, a low chirping in the quiet. It could only be Kate, since Joe wouldn't bother to call to check on her. Theo had already phoned to deliver his news.

And no one else would call so late in the evening. But thinking of Caroline had Birdie feeling annoyed with Kate (Kate and Caroline had always been thick as thieves; even her own daughter preferred Caroline's company). She didn't bother to make the dash to the main house. Let Kate wait until morning with whatever she wanted to say. If she, too, was calling to abandon Birdie, that could wait until she was feeling less vulnerable.

Birdie flipped through the thick pages separated by dusty vellum sheets. There they were, all skinny legs and mussed hair, wide smiles, funny shorts and vests for Gene, matching dresses for Birdie and Caroline. Were they ever so young and small? Gene was a beautiful boy, towheaded, with brown skin and flashing green eyes. He grew into a heartbreakingly handsome man, until he allowed wealth and success to make him fat. Even then, everyone always seemed to swoon around him.

Caroline was a little porcelain doll of a child who grew into a pretty woman, if not a great beauty. And Birdie—well, was she frowning in every picture? Or wearing an expression that could only be read as antagonism? There were a few of her smiling, yes. But it was that forced photograph smile, stiff and wan, threatening to flee in a moment if the shutter didn't snap quickly enough. Often her eyes were closed. Well into adulthood Caroline accused Birdie of doing it on purpose, of willfully ruining every family photo. *I have sensitive eyes,* Birdie explained. *The flash makes me blink.* But it wasn't true. Birdie hated to be photographed, especially next to Caroline, who was always so pretty, forever younger and more joyful-looking. Beside her, Birdie looked like a hag. *Can you give nothing, Birdie?* It was one of the last things Caroline had ever asked her. She still wasn't sure what Caroline had meant. Birdie had devoted her life to charitable causes.

On the island, the falling of night was thick and total. When there was no cloud cover, there were more stars than sky, it seemed. For a city girl, the starry night was the most magnificent sight on earth. But tonight there were no stars and no moon, everything obscured by the thick cloud cover that had rolled in, threatening but so far dormant. Through the picture window, the other islands were points of light in the distance. A glow emanated over the mainland. Out here, night was black when the moon had waned. Flashlights seemed to cut through a velvet cloak that had settled over everything. Outside the smaller window that faced the main house, Birdie could see only the porch light. The guest cabin was totally dark.

In the album, she found the picture she was looking for. Once upon a time, the old house was the sole structure on the island, except for the outhouse. (Gene always had to take the girls to the bathroom in the night, groggy and annoyed, carrying the flashlight. *Hurry up, Birdie. I'm freezing.*) There were three bedrooms. Their parents took the largest, of course. Birdie and Caroline shared the small one next door. And Gene slept, to his great pleasure, in the attic room, because he was the oldest. In the photo, Birdie was touching the old door. No matter how often it was oiled, it would issue a long squeal and bang loudly if you didn't hold it as it closed, which Mother was always begging them to do. Even when you tried to make it close quietly, it seemed to have a way of pulling away from you and slamming anyway. *Children, the door! Please!*

There were certain sounds in the night. Her father snored. The water knocked the boat against the dock. Caroline breathed deep and even, always in Birdie's memory, soundly asleep. And then one night the sound of that door. It woke Birdie; she heard it echoing in her consciousness, though the house was silent. Who would be out and about in the night when everyone was sleeping?

Birdie climbed from bed and slipped from the bedroom in her bare feet. There was a high full moon that night, and everything was cast in the silvery glow. She peeked in on her parents. Her father lay on his back with his arms flung wide, chest bare. Her mother was gone.

Even as a child, she met her fear head-on. She stepped out into the chilly air, onto the splintery porch. She saw her mother making her way down to the dock, her white nightgown shimmering in the moonlight. She was ghostly and weightless. Birdie wanted to call out to her but couldn't. She almost couldn't imagine her voice slicing the darkness, carrying over the air, probably waking everyone in the process. So she followed behind.

Her mother got into the boat, untied the lines, and soundlessly crossed the channel. A man waited on the shore of the island now occupied by John Cross and his wife; there was no dock back then. She threw him a line, and he pulled her boat to shore.

As Birdie watched, her mother fell into the open arms of this strange man. She tilted her face up, pale and glowing in the moonlight. Birdie gasped, nearly shrieked in surprise, as this man—dark-haired, tall, and slim—pressed his mouth to hers. It looked to Birdie as though he were trying to devour her mother, to swallow her whole. Her mother seemed to give herself over, the white of her nightgown nearly enveloped by the black of his coat.

The stranger and her mother disappeared into the trees. Birdie thought that she'd never seen her parents kiss like that, not even close. There was the occasional chaste peck on the cheek or lips. Randomly, her father might pat her mother on the bottom. She might move the hair from his eyes. But a full kiss on the mouth—never. Birdie could hardly imagine her mother as that kind of creature, one who would be the object of such passion, one who would return it with equal fervor. Birdie found her way down to the dock. She would wait, shivering, until her mother returned. She found an old blanket in the dock box, sat in one of the Adirondack chairs they used to watch the sunset. She waited and waited, but her mother did not return.

Birdie must have drifted off to sleep. When she woke, the sun was breaking the horizon. The boat was neatly tied off as though it had never left. Would her mother have passed her sleeping without seeing her? Or left her out there on the dock?

"Birdie! Birdie!"

She heard her mother calling and looked up at the house to see her standing on the porch. She was dressed in slim white pants and a blue-and-white-striped shirt, red Top-Siders.

"Mama! I'm here."

"Birdie Heart!" her mother said, catching sight of her and jogging down the steps. "What on earth are you doing out there? I've been scared witless," she added as they reached each other. Birdie let Lana take her in her arms and basked in that rare moment of her complete attention.

"I've been looking all over the island for you," Lana said, squeezing Birdie tight. "My goodness, Birdie, you're frozen."

"I saw you with him, Mama," said Birdie. She pressed her head into her mother's shoulder. "You took the boat to the other island. He was kissing you. Who was he?"

Her mother drew back, held Birdie's face in her hands. She had a sweet, amused smile on her face. "Oh, Birdie," she said. "No, darling, you were dreaming."

"I wasn't," she said. "I wasn't dreaming."

"Of course you were, sweetie," Lana said. She sounded so light and sure. She wrapped her arm around Birdie and led her up to the house. Birdie waited, even as she shivered with cold, for her mother to say something. But all the way, her mother was quiet. Inside, Lana moved quickly, wrapping Birdie in the blanket draped over the couch. Birdie watched carefully as her mother made her hot cocoa in the galley kitchen that was part of the main living space. The other children were still sleeping.

"I saw you," said Birdie. She realized her mother wasn't going to say anything at all. Birdie needed to understand what she had seen.

Her mother's hair was dark and full. It fell about her shoulders as she shook her head. None of the children had inherited those luxurious tresses, all of them with baby-fine hair of gold. "There's no one on that island," said her mother. Her tone had gone a little more stern. "You know that."

Her father came out of the room, looking tousled and groggy. "What's the matter?"

"I found Birdie asleep on the dock," said her mother. There was the faintest shadow of something across her face, then that famous smile. "Our daughter thinks I dashed across to the other island for a secret rendezvous."

Her father opened the cupboard, rubbing the crown of his head. "Is that so?"

"Yes," her mother said. Birdie could see that her brightness was forced. "But, of course, she must have been dreaming."

Birdie's father was silent a moment, and she was sure a slew of questions would follow. She knew her father to be a very curious man.

"We're out of powdered milk?" he asked. But was there something stiff and strange about him? Was his air of indifference put-on?

This was not the type of reaction Birdie expected from her father. Not that he'd ever displayed much of a temper. But still. It took her a second to realize that he didn't believe her. It did sound outlandish, since no one had ever inhabited that island. And back then, there were very few people in the area at all.

But Birdie knew what she saw.

"He kissed her," Birdie said. "Not like you kiss her." Her father raised his eyebrows at that. Then both her mother and father were staring at her, her father frowning. Her mother's expression was unreadable, a smile that didn't reach her eyes.

"It was a movie kiss." Birdie said, since the adults seemed at a loss for words. She thought they'd get angry, but both of them began to laugh. Birdie felt tears of anger and shame spring to her eyes.

Her mother, giggling a little, walked over and offered her the cup of cocoa. "Well, Birdie," she said. She sat on the sofa. "It seems to me that you've seen some of the island ghosts."

Birdie got up and ran to her room, slamming the door and waking Gene and Caroline. When Caroline wanted to know why she was crying, Birdie refused to answer. A while later, she heard them all laughing over breakfast. No one believed her. No one ever took her side.

Even at seventy-five, she could feel the anger and shame as if it all had happened yesterday. To this day, the sound of laughter in another room made her feel annoyed, even when she knew it had nothing whatsoever to do with her.

Why had she come up to the bunkhouse looking for the silly album? The light from the desk lamp was dim and flickering. Outside, the wind was picking up. The air felt like rain, had that clean, light scent. They'd had the bunkhouse built some years ago, with the idea that the children would sleep here during their visits. Once upon a time, Birdie had imagined that Chelsea and Brendan would feel the bunkhouse was an adventure, their very own place.

"They're children, Mother," Kate had said in that annoyed, superior tone she always seemed to take with Birdie. "They aren't sleeping in a separate house from us."

The children *were* young at the time, Birdie realized now. Chelsea was nine, so that meant Brendan was four or so. Maybe three.

But she'd said, "What could happen to them here?"

"Oh, Mother," said Kate. She'd looked at Birdie as though she were depraved or idiotic. "Really."

Kate always did smother the children. Probably since she had nothing better to do than focus her attention on them. So the children hadn't yet slept in the bunkhouse, preferring to stay with Sean and Kate in the guest cabin. The bunkhouse had become more of a storage depot for linens and spare supplies, old items that had belonged to her parents, framed photos that she could neither bear to look at nor discard. There were some old clothes that she, Caroline, and Gene had worn as children. They were threadbare and moth-eaten, not even suitable for donation. But they remained in the trunk they'd inhabited for decades.

It was on the last page of the album that Birdie found the picture she was looking for. It had lingered in her memory, like so many things about her childhood that she tried not to think about. The events of the day brought it back to mind. Beside each of the photos were her mother's meticulous notes: *Gene and Birdie, first sailing lessons! Lana and Jack (Mommy and Daddy), renewing our vows! Caroline, our little flower!* All but one of the pictures were in summer; they were never on the island in winter. It was Joe who had winterized the homes so they could come if they chose. But when the weather was cold, to Birdie, Heart Island was just a dream of summer, something unreachable, almost unimaginable, until the thaw.

The picture was of her mother standing beside a tall, dark-haired man. He was lean with long, pale features. Lana sat on the rocker that Birdie remembered on their porch, and he stood beside her. He looked off, up and away from her. She stared at the lens. There was nothing intimate about it, nothing incriminating. Except. Except the small upturn of her mother's lips. Her left hand gripped the armrest. Her right was lifted toward him. He was drawing his hand away. It was as if they'd been touching moments before the shutter had snapped. There was a thin line of snow on the windowsill. Lana was there in winter. When? Birdie didn't remember her mother ever going away from them.

Beside the photo, there was no note in her mother's delicate, looping cursive. It was out of place among the summery, happy pictures. There was something strange and unsettling about it. Birdie heard the first drops of rain start to fall. It started its tap-tap-tapping on the tin roof. Birdie lifted the photo from its place, and it came away with a slight crackle. She turned it over. Her mother had written there, *It wasn't a dream, darling. I'm so sorry.*

chapter fourteen

Sean had been talking a lot all morning, which they both knew he did when he was feeling nervous or guilty. Today he was both. He was nervous (and excited) about the open house; he felt guilty and uneasy that the girls were going up north alone. Brendan was sulking and limping, in varying degrees of intensity depending on who was watching and to whom he could put the screws for the unfairness of the whole situation.

Do you have the navigation computer? Is the address entered correctly? Do you have enough snacks? You're really taking Lulu? Really? Don't let your mother get to you. Seriously, we're right behind you. We'll be there tonight or tomorrow morning at the latest. He was rambling like a crazy person. Every time he tried to be quiet, some other thought bubbled out of his mouth. *I'm sorry. I'm talking too much.*

Kate was being quiet, which they both knew *she* did when she was nervous or feeling guilty. Sean knew that she was nervous about going to the island without him and feeling bad for leaving Brendan behind. Her silence only caused Sean to talk more, desperate to fill the void of quiet between them. *It's okay, honey. We're fine. Don't worry about it.*

Chelsea and Brendan were fighting over whether Chelsea should be able to take the iPad to watch movies on the trip, or whether it should stay with Brendan to play games.

"You have the iPhone!" Brendan yelled suddenly, their argument reaching a crescendo. "You don't need it. You get everything. She gets everything. She *always* gets *everything*."

"That's it!" said Kate. In her anger, her tone reached an uncharacteristic pitch and volume. All three of them turned to stare at her. "You two—figure out a way to share that thing, or I'm *donating* it to kids who have *nothing*."

Brendan and Chelsea watched her gape-jawed as she proceeded to slam the rest of the dishes into the dishwasher. It was not yet six A.M., the golden morning light dappling the floor. Sean moved to Kate and put his hands on her slender shoulders, which were tight and hiked up high.

"Sorry," she said after a moment. He felt her take a deep breath; her shoulders released a bit beneath his touch. "Sorry for yelling. But I meant it."

"Okay," said Chelsea. She sank onto one of the kitchen chairs, kept a watchful, worried stare on her mother. Chelsea was usually the one to relent, the one eager to keep the peace. Sean thought maybe it had to do with the battles between Kate and Sebastian, the classic behavior of a child caught in conflict. Brendan, on the other hand, had never had to mediate or to please warring personalities. "You can keep it."

Brendan was as sore a winner as he was a loser. He took the iPad from his sister and stormed, as best he could with his terrible limp, from the room. Chelsea followed him out, casting a quick glance behind at her mother.

"Everyone's stressed," said Kate when they were gone. She brought a hand to her forehead and rubbed.

"They'll get over it," he said. "We'll get over it. This time tomorrow, all of this will be forgotten, and we'll be relaxing at the island."

"Right," said Kate. "It's going to be *so* relaxing."

"Look," he said. "Why don't you just wait? We'll all go tomorrow."

He knew before the words were out of his mouth that it would never fly. He could already see the etching of worry in her brow. God forbid she should disappoint her parents, make them wait for anything they wanted. They'd all be subject to the famous full-throttle Birdie meltdown.

"No," she said. "The car is packed. We're ready. I hate to leave him, but it's better for him to have another day to rest."

"Okay," he said. "It's all going to be fine."

She melted into him. "Is it?"

"Of course." He squeezed her tight. "Of *course*."

The first time they met had been in this very house. It was empty then; the owners had moved out west. Realtors didn't do much staging in those days, setting up rented furniture so that people could envision how the houses would look when they moved in. The walls needed painting. The floors were older. But it was a nice house in a good neighborhood. In the market as it was then, it would sell no matter how much work it needed.

Sean's assistant had made the appointment, and Sean was waiting on the porch when Kate and Chelsea pulled up. He saw Kate first as she stepped out of her old but well-maintained Mercedes, having pulled up alongside his brand-new Porsche Spyder. She wasn't his type. She was sweet-looking, with wheat-blond hair and a cute body. She wore a flowered dress over leggings, a denim jacket. Cute, nice, the kind of girl his mother would like. But he wasn't into cute. The redhead he was dating at the time was rocking his world; she was a five-foot-ten lingerie model with a real kinky streak. Honestly, he could think of little else.

Then he saw Chelsea in the car seat in the back. She was pouting, clutching a stuffed dog. There was some negotiation at the car door.

"Just one more," he heard Kate say. "Then we'll go for ice cream."

He remembered thinking that was the problem with modern parents, always bribing and negotiating. No one had negotiated with him when he was a kid. He just did what he was told or he got his ass kicked.

But as they approached, something happened. Kate smiled and shook his hand, but she didn't really look at him. Chelsea scowled at him, apparently unimpressed by his bright and, he thought, charming "Hi, there, princess." That guy, the one he was then, was such a clueless jerk. And Chelsea, not yet four, could see it clearly.

There was something about them. Even now he couldn't say what. It was in the way Chelsea held Kate's hand, leaned her body against Kate's leg. It was in the way they whispered to each other, walking slowly from room to room. *That's a nice big closet,* Kate said. *All my toys could go there,* answered Chelsea practically. *You'd have fun in that tub,* said Kate. *Oh, yes,* Chelsea said. *I would.*

"My daddy isn't going to live here," Chelsea told him in the kitchen. "It's just me and Mommy now."

"Oh," said Sean.

"I'm sorry," said Kate. She smiled at his awkwardness.

"It happens sometimes," said Chelsea. She put up a hand, ready to explain. "Sometimes grown-ups don't want to live together anymore."

"That's true," Sean said.

When he looked back at Kate, she seemed to be studying him in a way he was not used to. It was as if she were trying to figure out the exact nature of his character.

"Do you have kids?" she asked him.

"No," he said. "Not even close. Someday, though, I hope. And I hope they're as cute and smart as this little girl." He added that last part to be connective; it was a sales trick. Relate. Relate. Relate. Chelsea's frown was back. Kate gave him a slow nod. There was that smile again, amused, understanding. A little condescending? She thought she was smarter than he was. Maybe she was.

"I like this house," she said. She put her hands on the granite countertop (the very same one they were leaning on now). "It's the nicest thing I've seen in a week. It feels . . . safe."

He'd wondered what she meant by that. She hadn't meant the

neighborhood or the new security system. She meant something else, something bigger. And it *was* a nice house, though he hadn't thought much of it until he saw Kate in it. It wasn't big and flashy, like some of the other houses he'd recently sold in this wealthy New Jersey suburb. But it had good bones. It was solidly built, unlike the new McMansions that looked stunning but had paper-thin walls, fixtures and baseboards that started to pop out after a year or so. It was a real house. With a little love, someone could turn it into a home.

"Make an offer," he said. "The sellers are very motivated."

He always said that. But in this case, it was true. She did make an offer, a good one. She didn't lowball. She'd done her research and knew what the house was worth. Later that afternoon, the seller happily accepted. There was none of the usual back-and-forth. He knew before they'd all left the house and gone their separate ways that the place belonged to Chelsea and Kate. It was like that with people and houses. When it came to real estate, he believed in love at first sight.

That night he'd had drinks with the redhead—he couldn't even remember her name now. It was the name of a month, he remembered that: April, May, June? He found himself distracted, elsewhere, during that date, which he'd been anticipating with a voracious appetite all week. That night, and every night after that, he was thinking about Kate.

"Just promise me one thing," she said now. Looking out the window, Sean saw an enormous Escalade drift into the driveway.

"Anything," he said.

"Just don't drive if you're tired or if things run late. Wait until morning."

"Don't worry," he said. Between the two of them, they'd probably said that ten times.

"Just promise."

"I promise," he said.

The slamming car door rang out in the quiet morning. The kids rambled down the stairs, making, it seemed, as much noise as humanly possible. Then the doorbell was ringing, and Chelsea and Lulu were carrying their huge, overstuffed baggage out to the car. Lulu's mother waved but didn't get out of her car; she rarely did. She was already talking on the phone, smiling but distracted.

Sean felt a wave of sadness that he couldn't explain as her car pulled away. *She's missing out,* Sean thought. But then his own phone was beeping with a text from his partner, Jane, another early bird with a big day ahead of her. And the next thing he knew, he was sending her a text while hauling Kate's bag to the car. Kate was saying something to him that he didn't quite get.

"What was that, babe?"

And then the girls were all in the car, Kate futzing with the navigation computer, the girls giggling and chatting. Then he was giving hugs and kisses goodbye: *I love you. No arguing with your mother. Keep your seat belt on. Read a book, for crying out loud. Don't just fry your brain with those machines.*

"Why do I have to stay?" Brendan was saying, holding on to Kate.

"I just need you to rest today, get that ankle iced and feeling better," said Kate, running her hands through his wild curls. "You can drive up with your dad, keep him company."

Sean could hear the uncertainty and concern in her voice. He was sure Brendan could, too. Kids had a knack for that, knowing where you were soft. He clung to Kate a minute longer, then limped off to the stoop.

With Brendan pouting by the door, the girls laughing at something on Lulu's iPad (iPad problem solved—of course Lulu had one), Sean leaned into Kate's window.

His wife had a way of giving him her complete attention, making him feel like the only guy in the world, even with everything in chaos around them. She was the only person he knew who wasn't constantly diverting her attention to a screen. She had a cell phone but rarely used it. She hated to text.

In his reflection in the mirror that morning, Sean had thought he looked more tired and stressed than he felt. But Kate always gazed at him as though he were man of the year.

"You're a killer," she said. He *felt* that smile of hers. "You're going to rock that open house."

Right then, at that moment, he almost threw it all in. He could turn the listing over to Jane, make her the senior broker, and assist her when he returned. He could grab his and Brendan's suitcases and pile into the car with the girls. They'd be on their way to a place they didn't necessarily want to go. The kids would fight the whole time. They'd eat junk food. But at least they'd be together.

He didn't do that. For a hundred reasons that all meshed together and were indistinguishable from one another: He'd felt like a failure at work for a year. He wanted to make his own money and not rely on Kate's trust. He didn't want to go to the island and face Joe—Mr. Success, Man of the House—feeling like he had this year. He wanted to go with a success under his belt. He hadn't even realized it had been eating at him until the listing came up.

Kate must have seen it all play out on his face. She lifted a hand to touch his cheek.

"Don't worry," she said again. He loved her pale skin, the pink blush of her lips, the icy blond of her hair. "This is good. Maybe this is a trip I need to make alone right now."

It was true. She had a lot to face on the island, a lot to share with her parents. He wanted to be there with her, and he would be. But maybe she needed a little time there on her own as well.

He gave her a last kiss and then went to stand by Brendan. Sean dropped an arm around his son's shoulders, and they watched Kate pull away. The SUV made a turn at the end of the road; with a honk, and three hands waving out windows, they were gone.

"This sucks," said Brendan. He bowed his curly head and lifted his swollen ankle to regard it resentfully. Sean agreed wholeheartedly but caught himself before saying so.

chapter fifteen

When Emily awoke in a dim, milky light, there were a few seconds when she didn't know where she was. In those moments, her life was a blank. She could have been in her own bed. The day might have stretched ahead of her—having a nice hot shower, making breakfast, getting ready for work. But slowly, reality crept back in, and the weight of everything that had happened, everything they had done, put a terrible crush on her heart. *Oh, God,* she thought for the hundredth time, *oh, no.*

She was alone in a grimy motel room. Where were they? They'd driven north; she remembered that much. Dean had given her something, a pill she'd happily taken, not even knowing what it was, even though a day ago she never would have done that. She didn't care what happened to her now. And sleep had come for her, thrown itself over her like a black cloak.

She vaguely recalled Dean carrying her from the car, and feeling that she was unable to rouse herself. Even now she felt artificially groggy, her limbs so heavy, her thinking dull. Had Dean left her here? She almost didn't dare to hope. What would she do then? She'd go back, turn herself in, and accept her punishment. She'd try somehow to make amends. She tried not to think about the restaurant, the blood-soaked floor. But the image was seared in her mind's eye. She wondered if she'd ever think about anything else again.

She wrapped her arms around her belly, curled into a ball. "I'm so sorry," she whispered. "I'm so sorry."

The door opened then. She glimpsed Brad's tall, hulking shadow before she clamped her eyes closed and pretended she was sleeping. She felt her heart start to pump when the door closed with a click. Where was Dean?

She could hear Brad breathing, standing at the foot of her bed. The sound of his breath mingled with the whispering rush of cars speeding on a highway. It sounded like the ocean, which Emily had not seen since she was a teenager. Somewhere outside, she heard a television, a door slam. Her whole body tingled with tension. She wondered if he could see her shaking.

"I know you're awake," he said.

She tried to hold herself as motionless as possible.

"You have to get up. We can't stay here much longer."

His voice sounded different, more gentle. She opened her eyes. He looked cleaner; he'd showered. But he had that vacant look to him, the one that so unnerved her. He was wearing other clothes than he'd been wearing last night. It looked like a shirt that belonged to Dean. She remembered that they'd stopped back by her house. She remembered wailing on the bed while Dean shoved their clothes into a duffel bag. *Em, be quiet. Be quiet, please.*

"Where's Dean?" she asked. She tried to keep her voice flat. She wouldn't show him her fear.

"He went to get supplies and gas up the car." He leaned against the wall as though he didn't have a care in the world. "Better we're not seen together. The police know there were three."

The police. They were on the run from the police. It was so far outside of what she had ever hoped for, ever expected of her life, that it didn't seem quite real.

"They don't know who we are?" she said.

"Not yet." He ran a hand through his hair, was looking at her with an expression she couldn't read.

"They're dead?" The word was heavy on her tongue. She sensed a falling feeling inside, a horrible emptiness.

"The kid's dead," he said, no emotion, not even fear. "The woman is in a coma."

She let it sink in, the knowledge that Angelo was dead because of something that she'd done. She thought of the gold cross around his neck, the goofy smile he always wore for her. Carol was fighting for her life. Emily thought about poor Paul, how sad and scared he must be.

"It's on the news?" she asked. "That's how you know?"

She tried to imagine her mother seeing it on television. Would she remember that was where Emily worked? Would she try to call? Emily would give anything to call her mother right now. Even a verbal lashing would be better than this feeling of free fall.

"How else would I know?"

She didn't answer him, just closed her eyes. He climbed onto the bed, keeping his eyes on her. How could Dean have left her alone with this monster? Dean knew what he was, and still he left her to him.

He lay the full length of his body alongside hers, and began to draw a finger up and down her arm. She stayed perfectly still. Never run from a junkyard dog. She could smell him—soap and cigarettes.

"Please leave me alone," she said.

Brad laughed, and it wasn't a nice sound. "You're funny," he said. "But the good-girl routine is getting old."

She sat up and pulled her legs in, burying her head in her arms. She didn't want to hear him talking.

"You were with us every step of the way on this," he said. "You unlatched that door. I honestly didn't think you would. But you did."

It was more than he'd said to her since he walked into her living room yesterday. She wouldn't have imagined him to be able to string as many sentences together.

"Fuck you," she said, looking up. "Fuck. You."

He grabbed her hair hard, and her hands flew to his. He brought his face in close to hers. There was a deep red scar on his cheek beneath the stubble. His eyes were red around the rims.

"You're every bit as rotten at the core as we are," he said into her ear. His breath was hot on her neck, the stubble on his jaw like sandpaper against her skin. "You just can't admit it to yourself."

"Let go of me," she hissed. Then louder, "Let go of me!"

He was straddling her suddenly, sitting heavy on her thighs, holding her arms down. He must have outweighed her by a hundred pounds, was so strong that she could barely move. Rage, fear, shame shot through her in one pulse, then left her weak and sick to her stomach.

"Let me go," she said again. Her voice was just a whisper, like in those dreams where she wanted to scream and strike out but couldn't. He leaned down and pressed his mouth hard against hers. She felt his teeth, his hot tongue. It wasn't a kiss but some kind of ugly, violent hunger. He grunted like a rooting animal, burying his mouth against her neck. Emily started to thrash and sob. When he tried to put his mouth on hers again, in an unthinking moment of struggle, she bit down hard on his lip. He roared in pain, railing back. She tasted his blood in her mouth.

"You crazy bitch," he said, more amused than angry. He smacked her hard once across the face.

She let out a wailing scream, made a futile effort to push him off of her, just as Dean walked in. He paused in the doorway for a second, then dove for Brad. Dean was smaller, lighter, but his fury turned him berserk. He started pounding at the back of Brad's head, and the two men fell off the bed as Emily rolled away from them. Dean wound up on top of Brad and started pummeling, panicked and merciless, at the other man's face until Emily pulled him away.

"Stop," she screamed. "Stop!"

Brad was still, blood gushing from a cut on his face. Dean

panted, chest heaving. "Did he hurt you?" he said through his labored breaths.

"I'm okay," she said, but she didn't recognize the sound of her own voice. Her jaw ached; it would probably start to swell and bruise.

Brad issued a low moan but stayed still.

"Ah, God," said Dean. He put his head in his hands. "We are so massively screwed. So deeply, totally fucked. Em, what are we going to do?"

Even though she was almost sick with anger for him and for herself, she wrapped her arms around him and held on hard. She buried her face in his neck, grabbed the soft cotton of his shirt with her fingers. She felt like she was drowning and clung to him. Brad's words were ringing in her head. Was it true what he had said about her?

"Where's the money?" she asked. The question seemed to come from outside herself.

"Under the seat in the car."

"And the gun?" she asked. "Same place?"

He nodded slowly. Emily recognized it as another of those moments. They could go back now, turn themselves in. Brad had been neutralized as a threat for the moment. He was the triggerman holding the gun that had injured Carol and killed Angelo. They were accomplices, but hadn't they been acting under duress? Wouldn't there be some way to explain what had happened? How everything had spun out of control?

The door to the motel room stood ajar; a thin line of light shone into the room. Her head felt heavy, hungover from whatever Dean had given her. The light looked like a beacon. If she moved toward it, she'd be safe. There would be hell to pay, but she'd survive it.

"I can't go back to jail," Dean said, as though reading her thoughts. She didn't say anything. "But you could go back," he went on. "You've never done anything bad, Emily. We forced you to do this. You tell them that; they'll believe you."

She leaned against the wall, keeping her eyes on Brad, who hadn't moved. She wondered if he was dead. She didn't dare get close enough to him to check. She could feel the ache of his hands on her body, his teeth on her neck. She hoped he was dead. Dead and already on his way to hell.

She didn't know how long they both sat there, lost in their own dark thoughts. Then Brad issued a low groan, and Dean's gaze fell on the other man. Brad tried to rise, lifting one hand and shoulder, but fell back to the ground. He wasn't getting up anytime soon. Maybe never, Emily thought hopefully.

Then she had another thought. That they should smother him and make sure of it. She looked over at the pillows on the bed and imagined herself taking one and using it, leaning all her weight on his face, feeling him convulse and kick beneath her until all the life drained from him.

"Emily," said Dean. He was looking at her with frightened eyes. "What are you thinking? You don't even look like yourself."

Emily shook off the image and rose, started to gather her things: her bag, her cell phone, which had died hours ago. She walked into the bathroom and stared at her reflection. Even though she was wearing fresh clothes, she was filthy with blood. It was in her hair, in the crease of her nose, under her nails. She took a few minutes to wash, leaving the stained washcloth and towels in the sink. She couldn't get the blood out from under her nails.

When she returned to him, Dean leaned against the wall, as if drained of all his energy. "We need supplies," she said.

"I got all that. It's in the car," he said. Then, "I'm sorry I left you alone with him."

There were so many things to be sorry for now, she couldn't imagine why he'd chosen that. "Let's go," she said.

"Where?" he said. He looked at her uncertainly. "I can't go back, Emily. I can't do any more hard time. I won't make it."

He looked like a boy sitting there. He'd cleaned himself up, had on a new shirt. His blond hair was cut close, darker stubble on his face. He had these clear blue eyes that always managed to look young and innocent.

"I know a place," she said.

He looked away from her. "You go back," he said. He got to his feet and came toward her. "I'll drop you somewhere, and you call the police. Tell them we let you go."

He put his hands on her shoulders, pulled her in to him. She rested her weight against him. What was there to go back to? She'd have to face the shame of the terrible things she'd been a part of. Even if she didn't go to jail, she'd have to move back in with her mother, who'd told her—promised her—it would all go bad. Emily had dropped out of school. She had no job. As sorry and pathetic as he was, all she had was Dean.

"I won't leave you," she said. She hated herself, her own weakness and desperation.

Dean put his hands to her face, pushed the hair back from her eyes. "I'm going to make this up to you," he said. "You'll see."

She could tell by the earnest look on his face that he really believed he could do that. If it weren't so tragic, she might have laughed.

chapter sixteen

Every time I arrived at the marina, I was filled with a giddy rush of excitement. I knew the weeks before me were a sunny stretch of sleeping in and cool swims, picnics, and card games. There'd be late nights, camping trips, ghost stories, and flashlight tag. School and all its requirements and restrictions were a distant dream. We'd race from the car to the waiting cuddy, with Mother calling us back to help unload the car and begging us to watch our steps on the floating dock. One year Gene fell into the drink and got such a chill that he had a cold all summer. Anyway, that's how I remember it. Gene, to this day, claimed that Birdie tripped him. She, of course, denies it. Of the two of them, I never know whom to believe, even now, when all those childish things ought to have been put aside.

And then we'd all pile in the boat, Daddy at the helm, Mother with her hand on his shoulder. All of us in the bow, life vests fastened. How she came alive as the island approached! All the tired tension in her face seemed to lift; a certain smile found its home in her lips and would stay there all summer. It wasn't that she ever seemed unhappy back at home. She just felt that she only truly belonged on Heart Island, that the cells in her body longed for it. For Mother, every summer was a homecoming, a return to her true nature. New York City robbed her of something. Heart Island recharged her. It invigorated all of us. We were all different there.

Kate had spent so much time with her aunt Caroline's journal that she knew whole passages by heart. And these words were in her head as she, Chelsea, and Lulu pulled into the marina and found a place to park, even though she didn't share any of her aunt's feelings.

"We are *seriously* in the middle of nowhere," said Lulu. She pushed her way out of the SUV. She sounded a little nervous, looked anxiously down toward the water.

"I told you, Lulu," said Chelsea. She stretched her arms high over her head, turned a playful smile on her friend. "Not a decent mall for *hours*."

"My cell phone isn't working." Lulu held the phone up to Chelsea, whose smile widened.

"Service is spotty," said Kate. "Supposedly it's fairly good on the island now."

She acknowledged a low-grade buzz of anxiety, a kind of simmering tension that always preceded a visit with her mother. Would her mother comment on her weight or her outfit? Make some quip about the gray in Kate's hair or the fact that it was too long? *You never did have the face for long hair, Kate,* she insisted. In pictures of herself as a child, her hair was always boyishly short, unevenly chopped. Kate remembered screaming matches when Birdie forced her to have it cut or permed into short, tight curls when Kate wanted it long. As soon as Kate was out from under Birdie, she'd let her hair grow long, as long she'd always wanted it. *Oh, Katie,* Caroline had said. *You look just like your grandma Lana. She had glorious hair like yours.* Kate had always felt safe with Caroline, at ease—the way she imagined some people felt with their mothers.

"Mom," said Chelsea. Kate realized she was standing at the car trunk, zoning out while Chelsea and Lulu waited for her to open it so that they could start unloading. She took a deep breath. Here, the air was fresh and wet. It smelled green. The marina was surrounded by tall trees—pine, sycamore, maple—the swell of low mountains, the foothills of the Adirondacks. A heavy quiet amplified every clanging halyard, the lapping water, the approach of a boat, the crunch of gravel beneath her feet. She opened the trunk.

As Chelsea and Lulu unloaded their suitcases, Kate watched the boat approach the dock, Birdie at the helm. Her mother was, as ever, perfectly outfitted for her environment. A bright red all-weather jacket, cropped white pants, navy Top-Siders. Her frosted blond hair (dyed, of course; no one could remember Birdie's natural color, and she would never tell) was clipped into a smart pixie cut (no fuss, no muss). Her handsome face was a landscape of deep lines. She refused to go under the knife for vanity, one point at least on which Kate and she agreed.

Birdie looked well, as always. She was impossibly slender and unmistakably wealthy. She charged up the dock toward them. She lifted her hand in a wave, wore that tight smile Kate knew so well. She would not be happy to see Lulu. Kate didn't care. There was something about Lulu that comforted Kate. She found the girl's aura of absolute self-assurance, her impenetrable cockiness (even if it was partly an act) in the face of Birdie's disdain, admirable to the point of being inspirational. There was so much to learn from this generation of girls.

Chelsea ran to her grandmother, and Birdie took her in a close embrace. For whatever reason, Birdie was very affectionate with Kate's children, though she hadn't been with her own. Kate thought it represented some kind of personal growth for her mother. Or maybe it was because Birdie's self-esteem wasn't tied up in her grand-children. She didn't see them as a poor reflection of herself.

"Hello, darling," Birdie said, approaching Kate and planting a perfunctory kiss on her cheek.

"Hi, Mom," said Kate. She closed the trunk and bent to lift one of the suitcases so she didn't have to endure her mother's appraising gaze.

"You're looking well, dear," said Birdie. "Not as broad in the beam."

"Uh, thank you, Mother," said Kate.

She watched Chelsea and Lulu exchange a wide-eyed look. Lulu started to cough and Chelsea to laugh. It took an expert to hear Lulu conceal the word "bitch" in her fake hacking.

Birdie's face froze when her eyes fell on Lulu. "Well," she said, narrowing her eyes. "This is a surprise."

Kate filled her mother in on the fact that Sean and Brendan would be late and that they'd invited Lulu to join them. "I thought the girls could sleep in the bunkhouse," she said. "When Sean and Brendan get here, the boys can share the guesthouse with me."

Birdie frowned. "It would have been nice if you'd let me know. The bunkhouse hasn't been used for anything but storage. It's not suitable for guests at the moment."

"I tried to call you," Kate said. "In fact, I've been trying to call you since Friday night. We'll make it work."

"Well," said Birdie. "The phone's been down."

"Since when?"

"For days." Kate could always tell when Birdie was lying. "Well, since late last night."

"Hi, Mrs. Burke!" said Lulu with exaggerated enthusiasm. "Can I call you Grandma?"

"You may not," said Birdie.

Chelsea and Lulu dissolved into giggles again, and Birdie looked at them, puzzled as to what could be so funny. She brought a hand up to her throat. "I suppose there's little to be done about it now. I don't know what we'll do about food."

"It should all work out, since the boys aren't here," said Kate. She tried to keep the annoyance out of her voice—and her heart—but she found it so challenging. Why couldn't Birdie just go with the flow? "Shouldn't it?"

"Don't worry about it, Grandma," said Chelsea. She draped an arm around Birdie, gave her a kiss. She was easy with Birdie, light in a way Kate never could be. She saw Birdie's mouth turn into a reluctant smile. "Lulu doesn't eat."

The four of them brought the suitcases down to the boat and

loaded it up. Birdie handed out the life jackets, and they all piled on board. Kate undid the lines.

"Would you like to captain, Kate?" asked Birdie. There was the hint of a smirk in her voice.

This was a big bone of contention between them and always had been. Kate didn't actually like the open water, was uncomfortable around boats. The rocking motion unsettled her; the cuddy especially seemed inherently unstable, though it wasn't. She could swim, but it wasn't exactly her favorite activity. Water was silently malicious; it could take you. It could swallow you. It would do so when you were at your most relaxed. One moment you could be floating, peaceful, and the next your lungs would fill with water. All your panic and fight would pass quickly. You'd have no choice but to surrender to its terrible, quiet weight.

"Sure," said Kate. She saw surprise and skepticism on her mother's face. Birdie stepped away from the helm. Kate took her place, easily backing the boat from its slip, then guiding it out of the marina.

"Well," said Birdie. "More surprises."

She hadn't expected her mother to be pleased. Birdie was happy with herself only when someone else had failed. But Kate had managed to take those boating classes. She and Chelsea had gone together to a school in Connecticut and were both doing pretty well on the water, having learned navigation, docking, knot tying, and emergency procedures.

As they pulled from the cove, Kate saw Heart Island looming ahead of them. It looked different to her. She'd made the approach many times, always filled with a riot of emotions. But this was her first time at the helm of the boat that took them there.

On the dock, she and Birdie unloaded the suitcases as the girls tore, shrieking with pleasure, up the rocks. *They should stay and help,* thought Kate. But she liked to see them so exuberant, so free. It often seemed that their young lives were lived with a screen before their eyes or while being shuttled endlessly from activity to activity. She liked that this place unfettered them. Even she felt a freedom here she didn't know anywhere else. She'd sent a text message to Sean on arriving at the marina: *The eagle has landed.*

Don't let her get her claws in, he wrote back. *Enjoy what you love, ignore everything else.*

It was sage and simple advice, as always, from her husband. Why was it so hard to follow?

"Why did Dad leave?" asked Kate.

Her mother didn't answer, was staring intently at the main house. "Mom?" Birdie liked to be called Mother and had insisted on Mommy until Kate went to college. It had turned out that Kate could call Birdie Mother only when she was angry.

"Who knows why your father does the things he does?" asked Birdie. She didn't have her usual tough tone. Today she sounded sad. It caused Kate to cast her a second glance. Did she look thinner? Frail? She noticed that Birdie's movements were stiff. Kate wondered if her sciatica was acting up but knew better than to ask. Birdie didn't like to talk about her physical weaknesses.

"What are you looking at?" asked Kate. Her mother hadn't taken her eyes from the house.

"Nothing," Birdie said. When she looked back at Kate, she wore a fake smile. "I didn't sleep well. The storm was brutal."

Kate had seen the branches down along the road, one fallen tree, on the way into the marina. The island had that scrubbed-clean look that it usually did after a good rain. Kate remembered how frightening and powerful they'd seemed when she was young. How the thunder boomed and the lightning crackled. They always lost power, and the landline went down right away. She remembered wondering how they would get off if they had to, if lightning struck the house and there was a fire while the waters were rough.

"I can helm the boat in any storm," Birdie used to say to ease her fears. "And have."

"Yes," agreed her father. "The natural disaster has yet to be invented that can defeat your mother."

"You never need to be afraid in this place," Birdie had said. "You are always safe here."

Kate had wondered what she meant. They were surrounded by water, frequently cut off from the rest of the world, at the mercy of the weather. Other islands had been decimated by fire, two during Kate's childhood. But because her mother said so, Kate believed her.

"You did well with the boat, Katherine," said Birdie. But her mother wouldn't meet Kate's eyes, as though the paying of a compliment pained her.

"Chelsea and I have been taking lessons," Kate said.

"Well," said Birdie. "About time."

Kate rolled her eyes. Together, they hauled the luggage up to the house. Kate made sure to take the heaviest cases and insisted on going back for the second load. Birdie didn't put up a fight. When she thought Kate wasn't looking, a hand flew to her back, and she winced in pain. *Why did she have to hold everything in?* Kate wondered. Why could she never be vulnerable, even with her own daughter? Kate almost said something but then didn't.

"Need help, Mom?" asked Chelsea, falling into step beside Kate as she headed back to the dock.

"Yeah," said Lulu, behind them. "Let us get the rest."

Kate felt that urge to brush them off: *No, go play, girls.* But she remembered how it felt when she was younger to offer help and be refused. There was always a sense of rebuff from Birdie: *You won't do it right, so I'll just do it myself.* It wasn't just an intuition on Kate's part; her mother had said as much a thousand times. There was something controlling about wanting to be the one to do everything, to refuse assistance.

Yes, Birdie, play the martyr, her father always said. *It's so endearing.* Meanwhile, where was he? Always in front of the television or reading a book with his feet up. In her life, Kate had never seen her father touch a dish, wash a floor, or make a bed. Had he just given up long before they were born?

"That would be great, girls," she said. Kate dropped one arm over each narrow set of shoulders. "Thanks."

The girls ran the rest of the way, light, dancing over the rocks utterly without fear of losing their footing. They looked like fairies in the sunlight. They laughed, landed heavily on the wood, their footfalls and peals of laughter echoing across the bay. She turned to look back at the house. Birdie stood on the porch, her hand shielding her eyes from the sun. Kate couldn't tell if she was smiling or frowning.

"It's Birdie Burke, from across the channel," she said. From the desk in her bedroom, Birdie could hear Chelsea's and Lulu's voices, the sound of their laughter like the tinkling of bells somewhere off in the distance. Kate was in the guesthouse, unpacking and getting settled.

"Oh, hello," John said. "Is everything all right?"

"Yes," she said. She gripped the phone. "How did you fare in the storm?"

It had been a battering, howling affair, keeping Birdie up most of the night. It wasn't just the weather that had her tossing and turning into the wee hours. It was the intruder, the photograph, the pending arrival of Kate and her family. Birdie couldn't keep her mind quiet. She'd always been this way, unable to control the churning of her thoughts. And then there had been her sciatica. The fire from her back down her leg that took her breath away. It wasn't quite as bad as the pain of childbearing, but it was damn close. They had only Tylenol on the island; it was no match for what Birdie was suffering.

In spite of the storm and the pain, she'd finally drifted off sometime after three A.M. The morning had dawned clear and chilly, no visible wind damage to any of the structures, just leaves and branches tossed about. The pain, too, had disappeared as quickly as it came.

"Well enough," John said. "No damage. You?"

"All fine here," she said. "Look, thank you for your help yesterday. I'm a bit embarrassed about the whole thing."

"That's what neighbors are for," he said. He sounded distant and distracted. She'd expected him to be more loquacious on the phone. In their few encounters, he'd always struck her as a talker.

"I was wondering," she began. But suddenly, she felt silly. She didn't go on, and the silence on the line seemed to yawn awkwardly.

"I saw you arrive back with your family a little while ago," he said.

"Yes," she answered. She wanted to clarify that Lulu was not her family, but she didn't bother.

"Perhaps you'd all like to come over for cocktails this evening? Around five?" John asked.

Birdie found herself accepting even though she normally would have declined. At the best of times, she didn't like to socialize with the neighbors. And she was lost without Joe, who had a special gift for small talk and making everyone feel at ease, especially when he'd been drinking a bit.

"I was wondering," she said again. "About your island."

"Oh?"

"Its history and former owners."

"Ah," he said, but didn't go on.

She found herself chattering to fill the silence. "It's a bit of a pet project for me to learn about the various island histories."

This was actually true. Birdie had amassed quite a knowledge of some of the properties with more storied histories. The little island across from them, uninhabited for as long as she could remember, had never piqued her curiosity. Or had she, for some subconscious reason, avoided it?

There was another long silence on the line.

"John?"

"Funny you should ask, Birdie," he said. "I've been doing some research of my own. I've learned quite a bit about this island." She thought he'd say more, but instead, "I'll look forward to chatting about it tonight."

She wanted to press, but she was loath to seem overeager. She never wanted people to feel that they had something she needed or wanted.

"Very well, then," she said lightly. "See you at five."

She stepped out of her bedroom to find Kate in the kitchen, which was open to the great room. From the floor-to-ceiling windows on either side of the room, they had a panoramic view. The green of the trees, the blue of the sky, the gray of the rocky islands filled the room with a fresh, soothing beauty.

"Tea?" Kate asked.

"Please," Birdie said. She sat on the sofa and watched her daughter move about the kitchen. It was hard for her to sit while someone else was in the kitchen. She leaned forward to straighten the magazines on the maple coffee table, fixed the pillows on the plush sofa. She noticed that the antler chandelier (Joe's choice) hanging over the long dining table needed dusting, and that some of the books on the floor-to-ceiling shelves were out of order from John Cross's snooping. She got up to fix them.

She strode over to the sidebar near the dining table to check the levels on the liquor. The Scotch was low. The port hadn't been touched in months. Then she went back to the couch, keeping her eyes on her daughter.

"Let it steep awhile," she said when Kate poured the hot water from the kettle into the pot. "The matching cups are in the cabinet to the right of the sink."

Kate looked into the cabinet, but Birdie could tell she didn't see the cups, just stood there looking. Must she do everything?

"Well," said Birdie. She rose and walked over to the kitchen. "Just have a seat. Let me do it."

Kate got that stone-faced look she shared with her father, and without a word, she took the seat that Birdie had so briefly occupied. *Better to let her do it herself, whatever it is,* Birdie remembered overhearing Joe say to Kate. *You'll never do it quite right, and you'll never hear the end of it.* The memory smarted, as so many memories did.

She retrieved the cups and saucers, the tea tray, the spoons, and put together the service. She took the creamer and sugar bowl from the refrigerator and carried it all to the coffee table. Kate moved to clear the magazines (which Birdie had *just* straightened—never mind), and Birdie set the tray down with a satisfying clink.

Birdie knew that Kate, left to her own devices, would have brewed the tea right in a mug, then tossed the tea bag in the garbage. But a tea bag could make many cups of tea in a pot. And the ritual of the tea service was calming and centering. These things were lost on Kate's generation. Everything was a rush, the shortest distance between two points. Why dirty cups, saucers, spoons, teapot, and tray when one mug would do? Why boil the water in a kettle that would take ten minutes when you could heat it in the microwave in two? Because there was a right way to do things. And doing things the right way was its own reward. This was something that could not be explained to young people.

"We'll be going over to Cross Island at five," she said. She poured the tea and handed it Kate.

"Oh?" said Kate. "I thought we didn't socialize with the neighbors."

Kate and Theodore had always wanted to play with the children on the neighboring islands, and Birdie had never allowed it. When they were older, they'd take the boat themselves. It had annoyed her to think of them associating with the caretaker's son or the daughters of the man who ran the marina. The children never seemed to perceive boundaries like that. You couldn't make them understand why it was awkward to share a meal with people, then direct them properly when they were your employees. Kate and Theo thought their mother was a terrible snob.

"He knows Sebastian," said Birdie. She watched for Kate's reaction, but there wasn't one.

Kate peered over her cup. "How?"

"They move in the same publishing circles, apparently. How *is* Sebastian?"

"Sober. But otherwise unchanged."

"Remarried?"

Kate offered a shrug. "Living with someone. She's fine. She's kind to Chelsea, which is all that matters."

"Hmm," said Birdie. "Such a shame."

A younger Kate would have bitten. *What do you mean by that?* She'd have wanted to know. A fight of some kind would follow. But motherhood seemed to have mellowed her daughter. Maybe "mellowed" wasn't the right word. She was more distant, less easily engaged. She and Theo had this in common, this subtle drift away from Birdie and her influence. Maybe that was the way with grown children, or maybe just with hers. Her acquaintances always seemed so busy with their grandchildren, taking care of them, planning big family vacations, arranging for visits, or planning to go stay with their grown children. Birdie tried not to notice that she was rarely making those kinds of plans with Theo and Kate. They came to the island or for brief visits in the city. But that was it.

Kate leaned back easily and crossed her legs. "That's fine. The plans you made, I mean," she said, ignoring Birdie's invitation to rumble. "I assume we'll leave the girls behind."

"Of course," said Birdie. She couldn't have that trollop socializing as though she were a member of the family. Birdie didn't have to say as much; Kate knew.

Here, suddenly, Birdie had a strong desire to tell Kate about the events of yesterday. Part of her wanted to share about the photo album and the childhood memory and how all of it seemed connected. She felt that she needed to share it with someone. It had all been knocking around in her head, like birds fluttering, panicked in an attic, looking for a way out. But the words didn't come.

"She's not that bad," said Kate, answering the comment about Lulu that Birdie hadn't bothered to make.

"I thought this would be a family time," said Birdie. She smoothed out her pants leg and tried for a slightly injured look.

Her daughter rolled her eyes as if nothing could be more laughable. "It still is. Or will be when Dad, Sean, and Brendan get here."

Birdie gave a dissatisfied grunt. *Why are you always making that noise?* Joe wanted to know. *Why don't you just say what you're thinking?* Then, "Theodore has taken a pass. Do you know why?"

"He said he couldn't get away from work," Kate replied. She was gazing out the window. Birdie thought she would say more, but she just took another sip.

"And you believe that?" asked Birdie.

Kate turned a cool gaze on Birdie, offered a slight lift of her eyebrows. "What else, Mother? Can you think of another reason he might not want to come?" Her tone said it all.

Birdie went silent. Somewhere one of the girls shrieked in that way that could be terror or could be delight. Birdie watched them out the window, walking near the shore, the sun behind them. They were lovely, slim-bodied and with flowing hair, faces lit by the afternoon sun. Birdie couldn't even remember what it felt like to be that young. *You were never that young,* Joe would undoubtedly say. And maybe he would be right.

"I wrote a book," said Kate. She said it softly, almost musing. Birdie nearly didn't hear her. But the words lingered.

"Did you now?" she said.

"I did." Kate looked solemnly down at her cup. "I always wanted to write. But then I just didn't."

Birdie knew all about wanting to do things that never got done.

When she was a girl, she thought she'd be a dancer. She'd had ballet shoes on her feet since she was four years old. They said she didn't have the body for it, legs too short, bosom too big. She didn't have those lean lines, that effortless carriage, though she'd had the talent. Everyone acknowledged that. Biology was an exacting bitch, wasn't she?

"Life can be like that," Birdie said. Kate looked at her, surprise lighting up her eyes. What had her daughter expected her to say?

"Yes," Kate said. "It can."

"Do you have an agent?" Birdie asked. She was aware of a flutter of anxiety, though she couldn't have said why. "Your father knows some people."

"I do have an agent." Kate wore the slightest smile. "And a publisher. There was an auction, actually. And the book will be released next summer."

Birdie felt a wave of surprise, followed by an unexpected flash of jealousy, which she could barely acknowledge. "You are just full of news this visit," she said. Her voice sounded tinny, even to her own ears.

"I guess I am."

"Well, congratulations, dear," Birdie said. "It must feel good to have *finally* found your calling."

She saw that tentative smile on Kate's face fade, and she felt a rush of regret.

"What type of book is it?"

"It's a novel," said Kate. "About family. Caroline left me some journals that belonged to her and to Grandmother Lana. The journals—inspired me."

"You've written about *our* family?" asked Birdie. She felt something akin to horror.

"No," said Kate quickly, lifting a palm. "No, not about us. Not exactly."

Birdie found that she couldn't say more. She couldn't bring herself to ask more about what Kate had written, or what the advance had been, or any of the things an excited and proud parent would ask. She *was* excited for Kate, and proud. Wasn't she? She didn't even know why, but all she wanted to do was take her leave.

"Well," said Birdie after an awkward moment of silence passed between them. "I'll go see to the boat."

"You do that," said Kate.

Kate looked more like Caroline than she did like Birdie, which made an odd kind of sense, since Kate had always preferred her aunt's company to her mother's. She was pretty the way Caroline was, with an upturned nose and pink cheeks, full lips. Birdie searched for something else to say. What would Caroline have said? Something gushing and effusive, something kind. But Birdie found herself, as usual, lost to bridge the distance she felt between herself and her children. Her cup sat untouched on the tray.

Kate turned her gaze back from the window. "Call if you need help," she said.

"Why would I need your help?" Birdie said. She got up quickly and pulled on her jacket. She hadn't meant it the way it came out. She'd meant that she could handle it, as she had since she was a child. And just because she was older, she was no less capable than she'd been once. But the words, the sharp tone, the misunderstood meaning all hung in the air between them, and she wouldn't clarify. She shouldn't have to.

"Of course you wouldn't," said Kate.

Her daughter turned away again, picked up a magazine, and started flipping through the pages. Birdie hastened from the room.

chapter seventeen

Emily remembered that both visits had been around this time of year, in the waning days of summer when it was still hot, before the leaves started to turn. As a girl, she'd always suffered motion sickness. She was queasy in the backseat, even with all the windows open and the clean air rushing through. She remembered vomiting in the car.

But that wasn't what she remembered most. Most of all, she remembered him and the way her mother was someone all new when he was with them. When he was around, her mother smiled and laughed like a girl. He wore a shiny gold ring on his left hand, and a thick gold bracelet. He didn't smell like the other men she knew, who all smelled like cigarettes and booze. He smelled like perfume. *That's the smell of money, honey,* her mother told her when she mentioned it. *Lots and lots of money.*

His skin was always richly tanned, and his eyes were a smiling, sparkling sea green. *Where's my little Em?* he'd call, and she'd run to him. He'd lift Emily high in the air as if she weighed nothing, and then he'd hold her tight. How old was she when she last saw him? The last time he took her there? Maybe she was four or five? And that last time, something happened. Something awful. She couldn't remember quite what—there were raised voices, the sound of something thrown and shattered. After that, she never saw her father again. *He doesn't want us, Emily,* her mother told her. *He never wants to see us again.*

Since Emily never heard another word from him, not another phone call, no cards or gifts, she had no reason not to believe that. He was the sandman, appearing to her as a bright and silvery memory right before she'd fall asleep. Just a dream she had.

There were other men in her mother's life. They were always fine. Emily didn't have any horror stories to tell about abuse. But they were stick figures that came and went, leaving behind nothing except a few awkward snapshots and cheap dolls she hadn't wanted in the first place.

"We have to get rid of the car," said Dean.

They'd been driving for so long. The motel where they'd left Brad was in New Jersey somewhere. They had just entered a town called The Hollows, where they'd stopped to get gas, and food at a McDonald's drive-through.

"They'll be looking for it," he added.

She'd already thought of this but hadn't said anything. She didn't want to steal a car, which was what they'd have to do if they wanted to keep running. And wasn't there part of her that was hoping they'd get caught, that all of this would soon be over? She'd thought the drive-through girl had looked at them oddly. She wondered if there was some kind of bulletin out. But then she realized that the girl must have been looking at her swollen jaw. She'd covered it self-consciously with her hand, and the girl looked away.

Dean pulled the car over to the side of the road.

"What are you doing?" she asked.

"I saw a nice one back there."

"No," she said. "Keep driving. If we steal a car from someone's house, they'll report it. Then the police will be looking for that car. They'll find the Mustang nearby, and they'll know it was us. Better to steal one from a parking lot somewhere. Right?"

She thought it was logical, but Dean looked at her uncertainly. What did she know about stealing cars? Or what the police would be looking for?

On the radio, they heard that the police didn't know who had robbed the Blue Hen and killed the young employee, leaving the owner in critical condition. The security camera had captured two masked men entering the back door and leaving, carrying a young woman from the restaurant. They thought she was a hostage. Carol obviously hadn't emerged from her coma to tell them differently. And Angelo wouldn't be telling anyone anything ever again.

Dean kept driving. Since the motel, he'd been pliant. But he was starting to seem edgy and jittery. He chewed mercilessly on his thumbnail while he drove. "How much farther?" he asked.

Emily glanced at the navigation computer that sat on the dash between them, another bizarre gift from Dean. She had no idea where it had come from, but it was new, in its box. So she'd kept it in her car, in case she ever needed it. She really hadn't thought she would—she never went anywhere she hadn't been a hundred times before. But it was coming in handy now.

"Not far," she said.

For many years, she told anyone who asked about her father that he was dead. He'd died in a car accident when she was little, she'd say. She didn't even remember him. People, especially adults, found that so sad. She got a lot of attention and sympathy, which she enjoyed. The truth was that her mother had an affair with a married man. Emily was the product of that affair. When his wife found out, there was a terrible drama. To save his marriage, he had to promise never to see them again. He'd kept his promise. That was what Emily had pieced together from the little her mother would tell her, from overheard conversations between her mother and her aunt. She had his last name, different from her mother's.

When she was thirteen, she'd found a check on her mother's dresser. It was written in the amount of five hundred dollars; at the top of it were his name and address. The information was all so black-and-white, printed words on a slip of paper. He was real, a real man with a checking account. She had always thought of him as existing someplace unreachable and so far away. She never imagined him nearby, living a real life.

She was nodding against the window when she smelled smoke and gasoline. She sat up. This had happened before. A moment later, the car started to stutter, then rattled to silence.

"Fuck!" yelled Dean. "Fuck me!"

He steered the rolling car toward the side of the road, where it drifted to a halt. Dean tried the ignition a couple of times, and a terrible grinding sound came from the engine. He popped the hood, and Emily watched big plumes of black smoke billow into the sky. They got out of the car, coughing. Dean covered his mouth and leaned over the hood, cursing. Neither one of them knew anything about cars, but only Emily seemed to realize that.

After a few minutes of staring pointlessly into the engine compartment, Dean came away coughing harder. It was dark, with only the dim light from a streetlamp up the deserted road a bit. There was nothing around them but trees. An old mailbox tilted up a bit at the end of someone's long driveway.

"Now what?" Dean said. His voice echoed in the quiet night, and something in the bushes moved. Emily figured he'd get angry with her, start yelling like he usually did when things went wrong. She braced herself for it, but when she glanced at him, he looked as lost and desperate as she felt.

"Maybe this is it. We're done. We have to turn ourselves in," she said. She hadn't meant to say it: The words flew out.

"No," he said softly. "I can't."

He sank down on the grass by the side of the road and put his head in his hands. She sat beside him, rested her head on his shoulder. They weren't going to make it to the place they were headed. It didn't exist. Like everything else she'd ever wanted, it was too far away for her to ever touch. She thought they could go there, and hide through the winter. The idea of that, that she could visit and be with Dean, live there, just the two of them even for a short time, filled her with a luminous joy. Everything good and right lived in that place. Even people who weren't happy, like her mother, were happy there.

"What do we do now?" asked Dean.

She was about to say she didn't know when she heard a car approaching. Without thinking, she moved into the road, Dean leaned into the car. She saw him grab the bag with the money and the larger one with all the supplies. He had the gun at his waist.

Emily watched the headlights draw closer and started waving her arms. Dean leaned into the car one more time, then moved out of sight.

It was as if they'd done this before, even though she didn't have a plan. She'd pulled back her hair, managed to get the rest of the blood out from beneath her nails. She knew she looked young and clean-scrubbed, except for the bruise on her face. Who wouldn't stop for a stranded girl with a broken-down car on a dark stretch of road?

The other vehicle, a beefy maroon SUV, came to a halt, and she ran toward it. She couldn't see who was in the driver's seat, and she had no idea what would happen next. She didn't know what she would say when she reached the car. It seemed to Emily that some moments were an eternity; they stretched and yawned with possibilities. And something about that simultaneously terrified and thrilled her.

chapter eighteen

Mother and I shared something that she didn't share with Birdie or Gene. Even though it wasn't my fault, or hers, I think Birdie and maybe Gene, too, hated me for it a little bit. There was something kindred between us, something beyond even the mother-daughter bond. It's why she left her journals to me. I think she wanted me to know her as a person, as Lana, a young woman who made choices and mistakes, not just as my mother. She wanted me to know about her, her joys and sorrows, her failures and successes. You can't really know your mother that way until you're grown, maybe not until she's gone.

You're the closest thing I have to a daughter, Kate. That's why I am leaving my journals and hers to you. I know that you, and maybe you alone, can understand and appreciate the things written here. I know you won't judge me—or your grandmother. You told me that it was your worst nightmare to think you'd one day be like Birdie. You could never, ever be that. You're nothing like her. You're not like your father much, either. In fact, I think you're the perfect product of their incompatibility. Somehow, darling, you're the very best of both of them.

Since Kate had arrived at the island with the girls, Caroline's words had been alive in her mind. It was the first time she'd been back here since completing her novel, and she was seeing the place with fresh eyes, with the eyes of an adult and not a child.

She'd been living inside the pages of Lana's and Caroline's journals, and the island seemed electric with their recorded memories.

Their words mingled with Kate's own recollections of all her summers spent here. The island was alive in a way it never had been.

At this point, Kate knew more about her mother's sanctuary than Birdie did. This thought brought a mingling of emotions—sadness, fear, and a little bit of glee.

She'd wanted to share it all with her mother, even though she knew it wouldn't be easy. Sitting there, with a pot of tea between them, it seemed like the perfect time to tell her: about Caroline's and Lana's journals, about everything written there and how it had inspired Kate in so many ways. In fact, she had brought the journals to the island with the intention of giving them to her mother. But Birdie had practically fled from Kate's news. The moment, uncomfortable and not at all what she had hoped, had passed.

Birdie left the girls with specific instructions on how to prepare dinner. And now Kate listed the rules for them to follow while she and Birdie were across the channel: *Clean as you go along. Don't leave dishes in the sink before dinner begins. Make sure the lettuce doesn't have any grit in it. Turn off the oven as soon as the ham is done. No smoking in the house, Lulu.* She'd seen Lulu smoking down by the shore earlier and was glad to note that Chelsea had not been smoking with her.

If it were up to Kate, the girls would come to Cross Island. But Birdie didn't think children should socialize with adults. And Kate could tell that Lulu was already regretting coming along.

"I thought you said there was cell service," she said to Kate. Lulu was wearing an apron Birdie had insisted she wear; it was too big for her and covered in a hideous floral pattern. It made Lulu look like the child she actually was.

"It's intermittent, apparently," said Kate. Lulu gave her a blank stare. Kate clarified: "It comes and goes. It might be because of the storms. Or because of the mountains."

Lulu looked down at her phone. "Oh."

Chelsea plucked it from her hand and put it on the counter out of reach. "Let it go, Lulu. Help with the salad."

Lulu gave the phone a longing look, then turned her gaze reluctantly to the tasks at hand. "What do I need to do?" She sounded truly mystified.

Kate heard a too-familiar, high-pitched whistle and looked out the window to see Birdie sitting in the skiff at the dock, exuding, even from a distance, annoyance at being kept waiting. All of Kate's life, Birdie had used that whistle on the island to call the children from wherever they were. It was maddeningly rude and imperious when they were young; it was insufferable now that Kate was an adult. She *was* an adult, wasn't she? As soon as she was in Birdie's thrall, she never felt like one.

"You're being summoned," said Chelsea.

"That's messed up," said Lulu. She was chopping carrots. "I mean, seriously, who does she think she is?"

How can you stand it, Kate? Theo had asked. *I hear that godddamn whistle in my nightmares.* Kate should have known after last summer's visit that he'd never come again. *Maybe when they're gone,* he'd said. *Maybe I'll come back then.* He'd said it without a hint of emotion during the conciliatory conversation they'd had right before she left for the island. He would come back to the island after their parents were dead. *How sad,* she'd thought. *How terribly sad.*

Down at the dock, Kate climbed into the skiff. It wobbled beneath her weight, and she felt a familiar flutter of nerves.

"I've been waiting," said Birdie.

"Everyone knows, Mother," said Kate. "We heard your whistle."

Birdie gave an annoyed grunt and started the engine.

"Can I see that?" asked Kate. She held out her hand, and Birdie handed her the whistle from around her neck. Kate regarded the slim silver missive; it was warm from Birdie's skin, gleaming in the waning light. Then, without a thought in her head, she tossed it in the drink. Birdie looked stricken.

"How—" she said. "How could you? That's for emergencies."

Kate felt a wave of regret, a kind of fearful feeling she got when she stood up to her mother. She pushed it down hard, the way she'd promised herself she would. An odd feeling of pleasure took its place.

"If there's an emergency, Mother," she said, "try screaming. Otherwise, try politely waiting, as you would expect others to do for you. I had to speak with the girls. They've never been alone on the island."

"There are other whistles," said Birdie. She hadn't taken her eyes off of Kate, nor could she seem to lose the look of shock that pulled her features long.

"Well," said Kate, "don't use any of them to *summon* me again."

The water lapped against the side of the boat. Above them, a hawk circled slow and easy on the air.

"I didn't realize you found it so offensive," said Birdie.

"Really," said Kate. She'd meant to say no more. But she couldn't let Birdie have the last word. "How could you not?"

She turned to face the Crosses' island and saw John waving from the dock. He knew Sebastian, her mother had said. But Kate didn't recognize the name or the face from her years with her ex. Publishing was a small business; at a certain level, everyone knew everyone, it seemed. But she didn't know him.

By the time they reached the shore, Birdie had a bottle of wine tucked under her arm and her game face on. She was all smiles, compliments, and polite conversation. *Well, this is a sturdy dock! Who built it for you? Oh, what a lovely home. I just adore those picture windows. We used to have a weather vane like that. We lost it in a storm a few years back.*

While Birdie was a guest in their home, the Crosses would find her irresistibly charming, impeccably well mannered, and delightfully funny. But when they were out of earshot once again, Birdie would tell Kate in unsparing detail what she really thought. Birdie Burke took merciless measure.

The Cross home *was* lovely: high ceilings, panoramic views, plush surfaces. Kate was thinking that Sean would be impressed, angling for a tour of the rest of the house. It was quite a bit nicer in some respects than the house on Heart Island. More spacious, more comfortable, newer—facts Birdie was sure to observe. Whether it was a mark for John Cross or against him depended on how he scored elsewhere.

"So how are you doing after yesterday?" asked John. He wore a concerned frown that Kate felt was not quite sincere, though she couldn't have said why.

"Oh," said Birdie. "Fine."

"What happened?" asked Kate.

"Your mother didn't tell you?" said John. He was oblivious to the fact that he had misspoken—or maybe not. Birdie turned away, pretended to regard a piece of art. "She thought there was an intruder on the island. The police were out."

"It was nothing," said Birdie. "Just an old woman's mind playing tricks on her."

"Well," said John, "there *have* been a number of break-ins in the area, some vandalism. You never know."

"Yes," said Birdie. "I suppose. So, is your wife not joining us?"

A deft change of subject. How could Birdie not have told Kate about this? Now the girls were alone on the island. She felt anxiety start to rise.

"She had to pop back into the city," John said. He ran a hand through his thinning hair. "She'll return by the weekend."

"Mother," asked Kate. "What did you see?"

Birdie reluctantly recounted the events, ending with a shrug. "I haven't been sleeping well. My blood sugar was low yesterday. I really *don't* think anyone was there, now that I'm better rested."

Kate watched her mother uncertainly. Birdie did not seem well rested in the least. She seemed vulnerable and pale, and for a moment, Kate regretted tossing her whistle in the water. It was a little over the top, and not very nice.

"Should the girls be alone?" Kate said.

"Oh, Kate," said Birdie. She rolled her eyes elaborately at John. "Don't be such a nervous Nellie."

John seemed embarrassed for Kate, threw a sympathetic look her way. She felt heat rise to her cheeks. Now she wished she'd held on to the whistle and thrown her mother in the drink.

John put a comforting hand on Kate's shoulder. "We can see the island from here," he said. "And we can be there in a flash. Nothing to worry about, I'm sure."

Kate thought about how the landline was down, and about the bad cell phone service. Chelsea knew how to use the radio, but that was inconveniently located in the bunkhouse.

She tried not to think about it as John poured each of them a glass of wine and they came to sit on the plush brown sofas, facing out the window. But she found it hard to take her eyes from the window. Heart Island *was* visible (perfectly centered in the frame) and, beyond it, the vast expanse of the lake and other islands in the distance. The setting sun was painting the water golden, violet, and rose.

Kate could see the roofs of their main house and the guest cabin. The glow from whatever lights were burning lit the darkness between the trees. While John and Birdie chitchatted, Kate's thoughts remained with the girls.

Kate took a long sip of wine and felt its warming effect almost instantly. They'd stay another fifteen minutes, and then Kate would insist on going back, whether Birdie liked it or not. Kate kept staring at the darkening sky, unable to focus on the conversation. She'd managed to talk briefly with Sean earlier on her cell phone. It seemed to work fairly well from Lookout Rock, which she hadn't shared with the girls. She didn't want them racing up there at every opportunity to use their phones.

"The ankle is still bad," Sean had told her.

"Really?" She had been gripped by guilt. She shouldn't have left them. She should have waited until Monday morning, and they all could have come together. Why hadn't she?

"Don't worry," Sean had said, understanding her tone. "I'm sure it's fine. He's tough, our guy."

Brendan hadn't sounded tough when she'd spoken to him before Sean got on the phone. He'd sounded like a hurt kid who needed his mom but was trying to be brave.

"We shouldn't have come without you," she said to Sean. Regret flooded through her. "I'm sorry."

"It's okay," Sean had said. His voice alone soothed her. She had sighed into the phone. "We're right behind you. It's no big deal."

"The story is that my great-uncle won Heart Island in a poker game," Birdie was saying. "I don't know if that's true or not. But it's a story Joe loves to tell. My parents gave it the current name, my father's last name, of course. And from the air, it looks to be in the shape of a heart. So it was quite serendipitous."

Kate had heard the story many times. She gazed over at the shelves and shelves of books that lined the far wall. Sebastian's books were face-out on a shelf at eye level. She wondered if John had done that intentionally for her visit.

If he had read Sebastian's most recent book, which she didn't see there, his so-called memoir, he knew all about Kate—or thought he did. He would know Sebastian's version of who she was—a doormat, an enabler, and finally, a deserter. He would imagine that he knew the intimate details of her first marriage and its unraveling. This didn't make her as uncomfortable as she would have imagined. She didn't think of the woman in that book as herself, just a character Sebastian had created. And if she'd ever been that woman, that girl, she wasn't anymore. The woman in that book was a ghost, a sad and silly specter.

"Ours is the first structure on this island," said John. Kate could feel his eyes on her, but she looked down at her glass. "We bought it from the estate of a man named Richard Cameron. Does that name ring a bell for you, Kate?"

"Of course," she said. She looked up at him; he was smiling as if he had a secret. The name did more than ring bells. It set off a jangle of alarms. If John noticed, he made no sign.

"Who's this now?" asked Birdie. She looked over at John with a frown, but he hadn't taken his eyes off of Kate. She was uneasy, but she wouldn't give him the satisfaction of seeing that. She held his eyes, offered an easy smile of her own.

"Richard Cameron was a very dark but brilliant writer," said John. He shifted his gaze to Birdie. "Some people think of him as writing noir fiction. But his books were really just these beautiful, searing character portraits. He never had much success or acclaim while he lived, though he came from tremendous wealth. He died many years ago." He took a sip of wine. "He has a big cult following now. And a long list of famous fans, including Kate's ex-husband, who cites him as a major influence."

"Is that so?" asked Birdie.

Kate met her mother's inquiring glance. "Yes," she said. "That's true."

Usually, Birdie took a kind of malicious glee in conversations that disconcerted other people, especially Kate. She also lapped up any island lore that came her way for her pet project, a journal about the islands and their histories. But now Birdie was distant. Though Kate was sure her mother would have at least *heard* the name, she seemed honestly in the dark. Birdie was clicking her nail against her wedding ring, which she did when she was angry or impatient.

"His granddaughter claims that he came here to write," said John. He seemed like the type to go on and on, oblivious to whether people were interested. "He brought a tent and enough supplies to last him the summer. But I wonder if she told me that to drive up the price."

He gave a hearty chuckle. Birdie wasn't laughing. She was watching John with an odd intensity, her eyes shining. Now that Kate was thinking about it, she was sure Birdie knew that much. Hadn't Sebastian told them about it? It was one of the reasons he was always so keen on coming to Heart Island and kayaking over to Cross Island. Admittedly, they hadn't talked about it in years. And Birdie *was* getting older.

"How did he die?" Birdie asked.

"He drowned," he said. The room felt very still.

"Here?"

John offered a somber nod. "That's the prevailing theory anyway. He disappeared one summer. They found his body after the thaw, when it washed up on one of the neighboring islands."

He stood up suddenly, startling Kate. "Just a minute," he said as he left the room. Kate heard him moving heavily down a hallway. Birdie was looking at some indeterminate point across the room.

"Mom," said Kate. "What is it?"

"Nothing," Birdie said. She rubbed at her temples, as if she were in pain. "I'm fine."

John returned with a framed photograph that he handed to Birdie. Kate rose and went to stand by her mother. She wanted to leave. She was concerned about the girls, as well as tense and hoping to be on the way before this unwanted conversation continued or another about Sebastian cropped up. John Cross had the look of a fanboy, the kind of man who developed male crushes on successful authors and fawned over them like groupies. For whatever reason, Sebastian had a legion of them, as many as Richard Cameron had. And they turned up everywhere, even here.

"Is that him?" asked Kate, looking over Birdie's shoulder. She knew it was. She'd seen many pictures of him on the Internet in her research.

John nodded.

"So interesting," said Birdie. To anyone else, she'd have sounded light and casual. But Kate could hear the strain, and was surprised to note that her mother's hands trembled. Kate knew better than to call attention to it.

The man in the photo was long and lean, wearing a black coat. He had a black shock of hair and eyes just as dark; his face was ghostly pale. The shot must have been taken on the island. He stood with his hand on the bark of a tree, the water glittering gray and white behind him. He wore the slightest shade of a smile.

"He supposedly was always alone here," said John. "This is the last picture of him. It is the only photo on a roll of film in a camera found among his belongings. But no one knows who took it. Murder, suicide, accident—no one will ever know how he died."

"What year was it?" asked Birdie

"Nineteen fifty."

They were all silent, until John released a startling laugh. He lifted a glass. "Now, how's that for a good ghost story?" he said. "You can see, I'm sure, why I *had* to have this island. I fancy myself a bit of an amateur sleuth, you know."

Kate looked at him hard. He had an agenda. What was he trying to say? Did he somehow know about the journals? About her novel? The silence among the three of them deepened and grew.

"I know Sebastian has visited here," said John. "Long before we bought the place."

"Ah," said Birdie faintly. "Fascinating."

"Yes," said Kate. There was something about John Cross. She didn't like him at all. "So, John, how is it that you know my ex-husband?"

She had to ask; it was killing her now. John cleared his throat and looked down at his feet.

"Oh," he said. "We're friends on Facebook."

"Oh," said Kate, relieved. Facebook, or Fakebook, as Sebastian liked to call it, the place where you could be *friends* with people you'd never met or hadn't seen in decades. The guy was a poseur. She should have known. "And you're in publishing?"

"My wife and I are starting our own company. We're going to reissue some classic crime novels to start, including some of the out-of-print Richard Cameron titles."

"How interesting," said Kate. Now she sounded like Birdie, and for once she didn't mind. She wanted to keep her distance from John Cross.

"Well," said Birdie. The firm, purposeful tone was back in her voice. Usually, Kate found it annoying. At the moment, she found it comforting. Birdie never stayed anywhere if she wanted to leave. Kate was forever stuck, enduring endless conversations, dinners, and personal encounters out of politeness. Like this one.

"I can see my daughter is worried about the girls, more so after all of this. And I'm worried about dinner being ruined."

Sure, Mom, blame it on me.

"So soon!" he said. Kate noticed that his face had gone noticeably redder, whether from the wine or something else, she didn't know. But he didn't move to stop them, trailed them out of the room, Kate leading the way, her mother right behind.

"You have a lovely home," said Kate without turning around. Behind her, she heard a soft thud.

"Oh, my," said John. His face pulled long with worry and surprise. Kate turned quickly to see that Birdie had collapsed on the floor.

"My mom said there are ghosts on this island," said Chelsea.

Lulu was sitting on a bar stool near the counter. She was completely useless in the kitchen but had done a fairly decent job of setting the table. Now, in a caricature of herself, she was simultaneously filing her nails and relentlessly checking her cell phone for service.

"My mother told me there was a tooth fairy," said Lulu. She didn't bother to look up from her tasks. "Do we still believe the things they say? No."

"There's a lady who watches the mainland from Lookout Rock, the highest point on the island," said Chelsea, undaunted. "A man who walks the perimeter. And someone else I can't remember. It's in the book she wrote."

Chelsea checked the ham. It looked to be nearly done. She wondered if she should take it out. Mom and Birdie were ten minutes past when they said they'd be back. Which, in a way, was a little paralyzing. She'd never known either her mother or her grandmother to be late. And with no cell service, she couldn't call. She decided to take the ham out, reached for the oven mitts. She hefted the sizzling roasting pan from the oven and set it with a heavy clang on the stovetop.

Lulu looked up from her nails with mild interest. "Oh, right," she said. "The scathing tell-all."

"No," said Chelsea. "It's fiction. Sort of."

She wasn't supposed to have read her mother's book. Nobody had said that she *couldn't,* precisely. But she had sneaked into her mother's office and read it as it was being written. It was one thing for her father's life to be a mystery, filled with dark places into which she wasn't allowed to pry, passages that needed to be blacked out. But her mother had always been wide open. Chelsea wasn't able to handle the idea that there might be things about Kate that she couldn't know. She understood that some parts of the book were fiction and some were true. She wasn't sure which was which. She hadn't been able to bring herself to ask.

"Oh," said Lulu, going back to her nails. She didn't like to read or care about anything that had to do with books unless it was *Twilight* or *Harry Potter*—and really, she only liked the movies. Even though she had pretended not to be interested: "Have you ever actually seen anything? I mean, any ghosts?"

"No." Chelsea wished she could have said yes.

She knew to cover with tinfoil dishes just removed from the oven, so she did that, feeling somewhat proud of herself for taking the initiative. Wasn't that what her mother was always saying? *I shouldn't have to ask you to clear the table, take out the garbage, empty the dishwasher*—whatever it was she was mad about. *At this age, you should be able to observe what needs to be done and do it. Take the initiative.*

After she had done that, Chelsea looked out the window and saw the red and green navigation lights and the white bimini light. The boat was coming across the channel.

"I'm going to go down to the dock so they can throw me the lines."

"I have service," Lulu said, excited. She drifted over to the couch, not offering to come, as Chelsea would have. Lulu's thumbs were going furiously as Chelsea headed out.

It was that time of night when the sun hadn't totally set but was low enough in the sky that the areas of the island under tree cover were darkening. She walked down the lighted path, and was glad for a minute to herself. She felt like the island had been waiting for her and was disappointed that she'd brought along someone who not only couldn't appreciate it but also wanted to distract her from it.

When Chelsea was showing Lulu around, she could tell that her friend couldn't see what was special about it. Chelsea tried to tell her about the butterflies and how sometimes, around this time of year, you might see thousands of them. Lulu didn't seem to understand how beautiful, how magnificent, that was. All she wanted to talk about was Conner Lange and Chelsea's cyber boyfriend, Adam McKee. Chelsea hadn't heard from him since she'd told him she couldn't meet him. She'd pretended not to care. Because she knew the minute Lulu sensed that she cared about something, she'd start to cut that thing down. Right now it was a game that they were playing, one that Lulu was directing. As soon as it seemed like something Lulu couldn't control, she'd get sullen and slicing.

Down at the dock, Chelsea saw that her mother was at the helm as the boat approached. At first she didn't see her grandmother. Then she realized that Birdie was sitting slumped in the back, her head resting in her hand. It sent a shock through Chelsea. She wasn't used to seeing Birdie any other way than perfectly erect and in motion.

Her mother managed to throw the lines to Chelsea while still at the helm. Kate cut the engine, and Chelsea pulled the boat in, tied off the lines on the cleats.

"What's wrong?" Chelsea asked as she helped her mother get Birdie off the boat.

"Nothing," said Birdie. "Everything's fine."

"Your grandmother is not feeling well," said Kate. She had the brisk, officious tone she got when she was super-stressed and trying to hide it.

"Did you take out the ham?" Birdie asked. She sounded odd, like she was talking in her sleep. "It will get dry."

"Oh, Mother," said Kate, supporting Birdie's weight up the dock.

"I did take it out," said Chelsea. She was happy to be able to say so. "I wrapped it in tinfoil."

Chelsea and Kate walked Birdie up to the house, an arm over each of their shoulders. On the stairs, they practically had to carry her like a drunk, her feet dragging behind them. "I'm fine," she kept insisting. "Put me down."

Lulu looked up as they entered. She stood and opened the door to Birdie's bedroom at Kate's direction. "What's wrong?" she said. "What happened?"

"Chelsea," her mother said at Birdie's bedroom door. "Give us a minute."

Kate helped Birdie down onto the bed, and Chelsea stood helpless in the doorway. She fought down the rise of worried tears. "Mom," she said. "Is she all right? Should I call someone?"

Her mother didn't answer as she lifted Birdie's feet onto the bed and took off her shoes.

"Should we call a doctor?" asked Lulu. She'd come to stand behind Chelsea.

"I don't know," said Kate. She wiped a hand across her forehead. She seemed frazzled, not sure of herself. Another first. "Give us a second. Girls, go see to the boat."

Chelsea and Lulu both stood there, watching. It was weird when the grown-ups didn't seem to know what to do. Chelsea often felt that her father, Sebastian, had no idea how to handle things. She had never felt that way about her mother or grandmother. She didn't like it. She wanted to call Sean, to tell him to forget about that open house and come now.

Birdie said, "It wasn't a dream."

"It's okay, Mom," said Kate. But confusion and worry were etched on her face. "Chelsea and Lulu," she said. Her tone had an unfamiliar stern quality. "Go see to the boat."

Chelsea moved quickly toward the door and pushed outside. It was dark, and the air was cold. There was nothing to do with the boat. It was tied off. There was no sense in securing the cover if they might have to take Birdie to the mainland. Chelsea figured that Kate had just wanted them to go while she decided what to do.

Lulu followed close behind. "What's happening?" she wanted to know.

"I have no idea," said Chelsea. *I am breathing in,* she thought. *I am breathing out.* "I think my grandmother is sick."

As they rounded the bend, Chelsea saw someone standing on the edge of the dock. He was a dark tower against the blue of the night sky. Chelsea stopped in her tracks, and Lulu crashed into her. She felt her throat go dry.

"What the frak, Chaz?" said Lulu.

Chelsea grabbed Lulu's hand and took a step back. She turned around quickly and started pushing Lulu back up the path.

"What?" Lulu was searching her face, and Chelsea thought

how her friend looked pale and so young in the moonlight. "What's wrong?"

Chelsea whispered, "There's someone on the dock." She didn't dare look back. Who could it be on the island when there was no other boat at the dock but theirs?

Lulu looked past her, still holding her hand tightly. Then, "I don't see anyone."

"Right there," Chelsea said, spinning around to point.

There was no one there; the dock was empty. Just then it started to rain.

chapter nineteen

The sight of the marina filled Emily with an irrational sense of relief. As soon as she heard the gravel crunch beneath their tires, she was overcome by the strong feeling that everything was going to be all right. She let herself sink into it.

Dean was sleeping, head lolled against the window, mouth hanging open. He was snoring softly. How he could sleep, she didn't know. When he'd been driving, every time she closed her eyes, she was shocked awake by the sound of gunfire, or fighting off Brad, or staring down at Carol's bleeding body. She wondered if she'd ever sleep again.

Maybe she should take what he was taking, whatever it was he'd given her last night. But one of them, at least, needed a clear head. She knew he had a stash of pills somewhere. He was surreptitiously popping them, thinking she didn't see. She wasn't going to say anything. What worried her was what would happen when he was stressed, on the run, and needing some kind of fix. She didn't want to think about it.

She hadn't checked the news in a couple of hours. As of the last broadcast she'd heard on the radio, there was no mention of their crimes or their flight. She'd listened for a whole hour while the announcer listed off news events—a plane was escorted by fighter jets, a terrorist plot was thwarted, two men were on trial for murdering a family, the Democrats lost the Senate in the midterm elections. She hadn't heard a single thing about an armed robbery in New Jersey, one man killed, a woman injured, the perpetrators on the run. When the newscast was over, she allowed herself to fantasize that none of it had happened. Or that, compared to other horrors in the world, it didn't even rank.

You don't want to do this.

She thought again of the man as she pulled the SUV into a space at the far corner of the lot and killed the engine. The way he had looked at her, like he knew all about her. The way he'd run a hand along his own jaw, as though wondering about the bruising and swelling on hers. His expression had told her that he'd known a hundred sad and sorry girls who had laid waste to their lives, and she was just another face in the crowd.

He'd pulled to a stop in front of where she stood in the street, waving her arms. She couldn't see him at first, because the lights from his vehicle were so high and blindingly bright. But when she came up to the driver's-side window, she could see that he was a big man, broad through the shoulders and tall. He looked at her with a calm, interested gaze and then cast his eyes to the Mustang and beyond, scanning the side of the road. Smart.

He rolled down the window. "Car trouble?" he asked. He kept his hands on the wheel. The wedding ring on his right hand looked tight. There was a picture of a pretty woman and a young man taped onto the dash. The guy in the photo looked like a younger, leaner version of the man in the car. Emily found she couldn't answer the question; she stared at him, the lines on his face, the gray in his light brown hair.

"Are you all right?" he said. She had forgotten about her jaw, that it was swollen from where Brad had hit her. "Is there something wrong?"

She watched Dean come up to the passenger window, gun drawn. He tapped on the glass with the barrel, and the man at the wheel turned slowly to look at him. He didn't jump or start at the sight of Dean. There was just a narrowing of his eyes when he turned back to her, a slight humorless upturning of the corners of his mouth.

"What is this?"

"Get out of the car," said Dean.

His voice sounded young and distant through the glass, a little boy playing cops and robbers. The man at the wheel did not look afraid. There was something about him. Yes, that was it. He was a cop or had something to do with the military. There were a few regulars like him at the Blue Hen. She'd always loved those guys, the way they seemed to know and understand things that other people did not. They had their crazy stories, brushes with death, had glimpsed elements of life that most were shielded from ever seeing. This man had *that* kind of look to him, cool and knowing.

Emily moved to stand in front of the car. She was banking on him not gunning the engine and running her down. He turned his eyes on her, held her in a level, assessing stare.

"We don't want to hurt anyone," she said. But it wasn't her voice. It belonged to someone else, someone she didn't know well and didn't like at all. "We just need a car."

He seemed to consider his options. Then he opened the door and stepped from the vehicle. He wore a barn jacket and jeans, sensible brown shoes; a pair of work gloves peeked out of his pocket. He seemed so strong and safe, so good. Emily suddenly wanted to throw herself in his arms, turn herself in, and let him take her to jail, where she belonged. She was thinking that when he said it.

"You don't want to do this."

"No," she said. She fought a rush of tears. "I'm sorry."

"Stop talking," said Dean.

"There are people who are no good," the man said gently. "And people who have, for whatever list of bad reasons, *thrown in* with people who are no good."

"Shut up, old man," Dean had said. He came around from the side of the car; the gun was shaking. He crossed between Emily and the man and headed for the driver's-side door.

"Which one am I?" she found herself asking.

Dean shot her a look. *What are you doing? Shut up.*

"You tell me."

"Give me your cell phone," said Dean, pointing the gun.

The man reached into his pocket and handed Dean an old flip phone. Dean dropped it to the ground and crushed it beneath his boot.

Emily thought that most people would be having some kind of emotional reaction: anger, fear, begging for life. But this guy was calm, observant.

"I don't know what you're running from," he said. Emily knew he was talking to her. He'd given Dean a single glance and dismissed him as a lost cause. She'd seen that play out on his face as Dean had passed between the older man and the car. Even though Dean was holding the gun, the other man barely glanced at him a second time. "But whatever it is, you won't get far."

"Get in the car," said Dean. He was sweating, getting ever more agitated, shifting from foot to foot. For that reason, Emily moved toward the door. She couldn't stand for anyone else to get hurt. But something in her was disappointed that the man wasn't putting up more of a fight. She thought about what Carol had said when Angelo went for the gun. *It's not worth our lives or theirs.* She was right. Nothing, no possession, no amount of money, was worth someone's life. Emily could see that now that her whole life was gone. She wouldn't have thought she had much to lose. But she'd do anything to get back to the place where she at least had hope for the future. This guy wasn't going to fuss about his car, not when he had a wife and a son waiting for him to come home. He already knew what was important.

"Are you sure you want to do this?" he said.

She paused at the door.

"What the fuck?" Dean said. "Let's go."

There must be something about her. People were always giving her unsolicited advice. Maybe it was because she was young, or because she was small, barely a size four. People always seemed to think she needed help, even when she viewed herself as handling things fairly well. She had gotten him to pull over, after all. They were about to drive off in his vehicle.

"You don't know me," she said. It was true. No one did. Before yesterday, even she hadn't known what she might be capable of doing. Maybe Brad was right about her after all. "Why are you still talking to him?" Dean was holding the gun high and breathing hard.

The man looked down at his feet, moved to put his hands in his pockets.

"Don't move your hands," Dean screamed. It sounded shrill and girlish, and it almost made Emily laugh out of sheer nerves. Dean could not handle being laughed at. He'd pull the trigger to get her to stop. Emily closed her eyes instead. She didn't want to see what was going to happen next. How could you feel so in control one minute and so out of control the next? How could everything go from so ordinary to so chaotic in the space of a day? She rested her head against the door. The moment simmered with everything that could go wrong. She braced herself for the gunshot.

"It's okay," the man said. Emily started to breathe again. "You can have the car. I'm going to stand here and let you go."

When she opened her eyes again, the man was staring down at his shoes, trying to avoid eye contact. He'd identified them as something wild, something to be soothed or avoided until they decided to move on. She climbed inside. The interior was warm, the seat big and plush. It was nice inside, maybe the nicest car she'd ever been in. Everything soft and clean with bright dashboard lights, red,

green, white. Clean, organized, well maintained. Dean climbed inside, keeping the gun pointed out the open window. He couldn't hit
the side of a barn that way. Didn't he know that? He wasn't just a bad
person. He was also an idiot. The guy was letting them go, that was
the only reason they were driving away in his car.

"Give me the gun," she said.

When he did, she tucked it down under the seat. He locked the
doors, put his hands on the wheel. The man moved closer to the
shoulder to get out of their way, and Dean roared off. Emily watched
the other man disappear in her side mirror. Just like that, he was
gone. She wondered how he would get home. He had a long walk
ahead of him; they were in the middle of nowhere.

"We should have killed him," said Dean. He sounded angry and
regretful, as if it was her fault that they hadn't. Maybe it *was* her.
That was what she'd wanted to say to the other man. *There are bad
people, yes. And there are good people who get tangled up with bad people, sure. But sometimes can't good people help bad people to be better?*
Maybe if she hadn't stayed with Dean through all of this, even worse
things would have happened. Maybe that man would be dead.

"He can identify us," Dean said. "They'll put it together."

"He'll have to walk hours before he gets anywhere."

"Unless he gets someone to pull over."

"No one pulls over anymore."

"He did," said Dean.

"They don't pull over for a man walking in the road. Maybe a
girl. Maybe."

She didn't say anything else. She was glad that Dean hadn't had
it in him to hurt an innocent person, whatever the reason. Brad had
done all the shooting at the Blue Hen. At least Dean had that going
for him—he wasn't a killer and a rapist.

That got her to thinking about Brad. She reached for the radio,
hoping for some news. But Dean reached out to stop her. His fingers

were long and thin, and the skin on his hands felt cold and dry. "Let's wait a minute," he said.

She didn't want to know, either. She didn't want to know what had happened to Carol or if they'd found Brad. She didn't want to know how much the police had figured out by this point or if they were looking for the Mustang. Maybe, for a little while, they were better-off without the answers.

She opened the glove compartment, started rifling through the neatly stacked papers. She found the vehicle registration. Jones Cooper—it was a good name, a solid one. The name of a person who had never done anything wrong in his entire life. Tucked in the far corner, she felt a compact leather folder and opened it to see a gold shield. The space where the number would have been was replaced with a plate stamped "retired" in red. She closed it and put it back where she had found it.

"What's in there?" He seemed calmer now that they were moving. Or maybe he'd popped a pill in his mouth. Who knew? But she wasn't going to get him upset again.

"Nothing," she said. She shut the door. "Just some papers— receipts and whatnot."

He didn't say anything, just stared at the road ahead. "Turn on the radio," he said. She did.

Remarkably, Dean had had the foresight to grab the Garmin from her Mustang. So they easily found their way to the marina. It was nearly midnight, and so quiet. There were a few other cars in the lot. Most of the summer people were gone by this last week in August. She remembered that. The air was already cool, the water colder. Once winter settled, the area was virtually uninhabited. They needed supplies, more than what they had. They needed enough to last them the winter. But Emily hadn't wanted to risk stopping and being spotted. She felt paralyzed, drained. Her plan hadn't involved anything further than their arrival.

"Is this it? Are we here?" Dean asked, sitting up and looking around.

"Yes," she said. "We're here."

All they needed to do was find themselves a boat that could take them to Heart Island.

heart island

The island was, for each of us, a personal fiction. We each wrote a story about it in our minds. And so it belonged to each of us in a different way. That's why, when it came time to share it, we just couldn't do that. We all fancied ourselves kings and queens of that place, our siblings playing only supporting roles in our memories. Each of us imagined that one day Heart Island would be ours and ours alone. And only one of us was right.

FROM THE JOURNAL OF CAROLINE LOVE HEART
(1940–2000)

chapter twenty

*M*aybe that's why she told me things she never could tell them. About the affair she had, about the dark things that happened. She waited until after Daddy was gone. Only Mother and I knew that she'd married Daddy for all sorts of good reasons—position, family, friendship—but passionate love was not one of them. Those days, she said, romantic love wasn't the most important thing when it came to marriage. In all her life, she truly loved only one man, someone she never could have married. But "affair" is too tawdry a word for what my mother shared with Richard Cameron, so wrong for what they were to each other.

They're all of them gone, and only I know the truth. And now, Kate, you know, too. I hope it's not too much of a burden. I know I can trust you not to judge them, because you have a poet's heart, like mine. You see it all. It's funny how, as time rushes on, even the biggest things matter not at all. When you read this, we'll all be gone. Isn't that funny? And once upon a time, there was all this terrible pain and trauma, love and grief. And now it's just a dream we all had. An awful, wonderful dream.

The journals sat in a box in Kate's closet for more than two years before she found them. She had taken the box with her name on it from Caroline's apartment when she and Theo cleaned it out after Caroline's death. She had watched as Sean carried it to the trunk of their waiting car, then brought it into their house. Still, she couldn't bear the thought of looking inside. Caroline had left all her money, possessions—even her small Manhattan apartment—to Kate and Theo, a fact that had inexplicably enraged their mother.

"Not even a piece of jewelry for her sister," Birdie had said. She had everything money could buy and turned up her nose at any gift anyone ever dared to give her. No one gave her anything anymore, least of all Caroline.

In Caroline's final days, Birdie had sat with her, reading from a book they'd loved as girls, *Rebecca of Sunnybrook Farm*. Watching her there, peaceful, reading to her dying sister, Kate could almost see some capacity for tenderness that Birdie had never exhibited. Birdie even found it within herself to hold her sister's hand. When they were both in good health, one of them would storm off inside an hour, or an uncomfortable silence would fall over the gathering, one of them stewing about what the other had said or hadn't. The endgame of Caroline's illness was the only time the two of them had occupied the same room without an argument erupting. Of course, she was in a palliative state, barely aware of her surroundings.

"Mom," Kate had said. In the war between Birdie and everyone else, even Birdie's dead sister, Kate always tried to smooth things over. "You can choose any of the pieces you want."

Caroline had an entire dresser full of jewelry, some of it valuable, some of it costume. All of it large and chunky, glittering, the exact energetic opposite of anything Birdie owned or liked.

"That's not the point, is it?" Birdie said. For a second, Kate thought Birdie sounded almost grief-stricken. Then her mother shrieked into the phone, *"She looked like a gypsy with all that garbage on her hands and around her neck. And those long skirts, ridiculous scarves. She was a circus act."*

How could Birdie rage while her daughter grieved? Kate wondered. It was pathological that Birdie could even make her own sister's death about how *she'd* been slighted. Had the long hospital visits been an act, something she did because it was appropriate? Or had she been able to contain her vitriol, even remembering happier times between them? Or was this how she grieved, her rage a kind of catharsis?

"So why do you want her jewelry, then?" It was all Kate could think to say. Her mother had hung up the phone.

Kate knew that the box contained correspondence, among other things. Her aunt had published some poetry in small journals. Kate assumed that the original drafts, along with stories Caroline had made up for her and Theo when they were young, were all in there. She expected love letters (Caroline had a number of searing love affairs in her time, another thing that drove Birdie mad), cards, pictures Kate and Theo had drawn for her as kids. Because those were the types of things that Caroline saved, the emotional detritus of life, the things that Birdie discarded as clutter.

Kate couldn't stand it to see how Caroline's rich and beautiful inner life had been reduced to piles of paper in a box. So the box sat waiting. Every time she went into the office closet, it sat there—an invitation, a recrimination, and a plea all at once. Until finally, one afternoon when she was alone, she opened the box.

The journals were sealed inside another box within the larger one. The box was buried, as though hidden, at the very bottom beneath the predicted piles of letters (tied, of course, with red ribbon), chapbooks of poetry, envelopes of old photos. There was Kate's christening gown wrapped in white tissue and Theo's baby shoes. Written across the top of the smaller box, in Caroline's scrawling cursive: *For the eyes of Katherine Burke only.*

Upon retrieving it, Kate felt a flood of guilt. It had the essence of urgency; it was something Caroline had wanted her to see. And Kate had let it sit there unopened. Yet even when she had it in her hands, feeling how much her aunt wanted her to read what was inside, it still took another few months for her to break the seal. Why? She didn't know except that she had a kind of dread in her heart when she looked at that box.

Kate couldn't have known that within it were all sorts of secret things, little and big. That when she opened Caroline's and Lana's journals and started to read, she would see her family, her mother,

her history in a whole new way. She would learn things about her grandparents' marriage that Kate was sure even Birdie never knew. She would learn, in Lana's own words, about her affair with Richard Cameron. There was no way to know any of that at the time, and still, she shrank from whatever was inside.

Clothbound and stained, pages covered margin to margin with almost identical handwriting, the journals opened doorways in Kate's perception she didn't even know were closed. They answered questions Kate had about her mother and introduced more. Kate had only the vaguest memory of her grandparents. But through Lana's journals, they both came to life, full-bodied, flawed, and fascinating. Caroline painted a vivid picture of her childhood memories of Heart Island, and Kate saw Birdie through fresh eyes. The middle child, Kate's mother was always crushed between Caroline's beauty and sweetness and Gene's expansive, athletic golden-boy personality. In all her life, Kate had never thought of her mother as a little girl and how she might have been formed.

In important ways, the histories she'd uncovered were Kate's own, even though most of the players were long gone. Because it was her story, she felt she had a right, even a compulsion, to tell it. Kate wondered whether Caroline knew that the journals she'd left to her niece would cause her to reconnect to her heart's first desire, to write. Kate suspected that Caroline *had* known, all too well.

"Are you feeling better, Mom?" Kate asked. She sat in the small sitting area off to the side of her parents' king-size wood-framed bed.

They'd barely extracted themselves from John Cross, who had wanted to escort them back to the island. Birdie, once she came to, had been a bit sharp with him. *We'd like our privacy, please, Mr. Cross,* she said when he tried to help her down to the boat. They'd left him looking somewhat miffed on the path down to his dock. *I'm sorry,* Kate said. *Don't apologize for me,* whispered Birdie.

Birdie's eyes were open now; she was lying on her back, arms folded over her middle, gaze fixed on the ceiling. "I'm fine," she said.

"I haven't been feeling well since yesterday. Since I saw him. Maybe before. Then my sciatica."

"So there *was* someone here?"

"Yes," Birdie said. "No." The wrinkle of a frown, an annoyed exhale. "I don't know. I really don't know what I saw."

"Tell me what happened."

Kate wanted to reach for Birdie's hand, pale and delicate, palm turned up on the sheet. But she couldn't. She couldn't touch her mother that way; there was no precedent for physical closeness. She knew only how to kiss her mother quickly on the cheek, perhaps squeeze her bony shoulders. Kate's own children draped themselves over her at every opportunity—even now, when Kate's friends were complaining of adolescent and teen children who couldn't stand to be in the same room with their parents. Kate still kissed them both on the mouth, pulled them into long body-connecting hugs. Birdie was ice; if you held on too long, it hurt.

She didn't expect Birdie to talk. She expected Birdie to say that she wanted to be alone. But her mother told her about the events of yesterday: a man near the shore, then disappearing into the house. It did sound frightening, unsettling.

Still, none of that was enough to get to Birdie like this. If it was some problem with her vision, or even if there had been an actual intruder, it didn't seem like any match for the formidable Birdie Heart-Burke. There was something else.

"Did they ruin the ham?" Birdie asked.

"No," said Kate. She didn't know if they had or not. "Dinner's fine. Maybe you'll feel better if you eat."

Birdie turned to look at Kate, her expression unreadable. Kate was silent, wondering if her mother would say more. Birdie went back to staring at the ceiling.

Kate thought she heard something, the way her children's voices carried through the walls at home. She listened, but she didn't hear anything more. She walked to the window and looked down toward the dock. All she could see was black. A thick cloud cover blocked the stars.

"It feels like rain again," said Birdie.

As if on cue, a few drops tapped on the windows, just a drizzle. Hopefully nothing more. Kate hated the island in a storm, especially with Sean and Brendan someplace else. When it stormed, she felt cut off, trapped.

"If you're all right," said Kate, "I'll see to getting dinner on the table."

"Do you think there was someone here?" asked Birdie. She sounded anxious. "Or am I losing my mind?"

Everything in the room was made from wood—the walls, the dresser, the bed on which Birdie lay. It was rustic, lodgy, not what her mother would have chosen but just as her father liked it. He fancied himself an outdoorsman, though he seemed to wilt outside of Manhattan. He called himself a chef, though most nights at home, they had a cook or ate out. He liked to think of himself as an opera aficionado, but more often than not, he was soundly asleep before intermission. Of course he'd want a big log house for the island, something perfectly befitting his idea of who he was here—even though he could never seem to get off the island fast enough. Birdie looked somehow out of place in the room, sunken and small.

"I'm sure you're not losing your mind," said Kate. "But that doesn't mean there was someone here, either."

"Oh, that's right," said Birdie. She issued a disdainful snort. "You believe in Caroline's ghosts."

"That's not what I meant," said Kate. She was trying to be patient, to remember that her mother wasn't feeling well. "I just meant that there are more than two possibilities."

"John Cross thought I was batty," said her mother. "You should have seen the way he looked at me."

"I'm not sure I like that guy," said Kate.

Birdie raised her eyebrows in surprise. "I don't like him one bit," she said. "New money annoys me. Where did he get that money, anyway? Certainly not from publishing. The wife must come from wealth."

Kate had to laugh. No matter what, Birdie was always Birdie. There was thunder. No. It was the girls storming up the steps, heavy and fast. Kate walked out of the room to greet them.

"Those girls sound like a herd of rhinos," Birdie mumbled as Kate closed the door behind her.

"What is it?" she asked. They were both pale and breathless, as if they'd sprinted from the dock. They exchanged a look. Lulu shot a worried glance out the window behind her.

"You look like you've seen a ghost." Kate was trying to be funny, but the girls didn't laugh. She glanced around the room; she hadn't noticed as she brought Birdie in, but they'd set the table. The ham was wrapped on top of the stove, the salad sat waiting on the counter. She was proud of them.

"Maybe we did," whispered Chelsea. She cast an anxious eye toward Birdie's room. "On the dock."

Chelsea told Kate what she'd seen, someone on the dock—a man, tall and thin. Then there was no one there at all. It was an encounter just like what Birdie had described. Was there really someone on the island? It was hard to imagine. The island was so small, the terrain rocky and somewhat inhospitable. Other than the clearing around the buildings, and the lighted path that led between them, the land was wild, heavily wooded, and rocky. There was no place even to pitch a tent comfortably. But still, there had been three different sightings by two different people in different areas at different times of the day.

Lulu was shivering—from nerves or the cold, Kate couldn't tell. She moved to put her arms around Lulu, and the girl sank into her and clung. Kate couldn't believe how small she felt in her arms.

"Okay," said Kate. "That's it. I'm calling the police."

Lulu shook her head. "You can't. I had cell service for like one minute. Now it's gone again."

"We'll use the radio," said Kate. She moved toward the door.

"Mom," said Chelsea. She lifted her palms in a gesture that reminded Kate so much of Sean. Her husband and daughter both had a dread of unnecessary drama. "I'm not even sure what I saw."

Though Kate wouldn't have dreamed of calling the authorities under normal circumstances, she told the girls about Birdie's experiences the day before, keeping her voice low and her eye on the door to her mother's room. Birdie wouldn't want them to know. The girls watched her with wide eyes.

"There's no one on this island," said Lulu. "It's a rock in the middle of nowhere. I didn't see what Chelsea saw." Her voice sounded shaky; she kept her eyes on the door. She sounded like she was trying to convince herself.

"We were all over today," said Chelsea. "We didn't see anything unusual . . . until just now."

Kate pulled her phone from her pocket and saw that Lulu was right about the cell service. She thought about walking the perimeter of the island with a flashlight and checking things out for herself. But she didn't want to leave the girls alone. Tamping down a rising sense of dread, she walked over to the door and shut and locked it. Then she leaned against it for good measure. The door felt flimsy and insubstantial, as were the knob and the lock. She couldn't remember ever locking it, or any other door on the island, until they were ready to leave for the summer. There had never been any need.

Chelsea went to the back door beyond the long dining table and locked that as well. Both the girls were watching Kate as if she should know what to do. Ghosts, intruders, her mother going senile, the girls hallucinating—not a comforting list of possibilities. *I am breathing in. I am breathing out.*

Or maybe none of those things. The island had a way of making problems seem worse, more dire, than they actually were. With the sudden and violent storms, myriad strange noises, and the play of light and shadows, it was easy to get spooked here. And Kate, as the adult, had to be the one to keep her cool.

It's a crucible, Caroline had written. *Everything is broken down there to its essential nature. And it's not always pretty.*

"Look," said Kate. "Let's just eat. We'll keep checking our cells. And the second there's a signal, we'll get someone out here."

"Okay," said Chelsea. She didn't look convinced that it was the best plan. "I mean, maybe I didn't see what I thought I saw."

"Exactly," said Kate. "Exactly."

Birdie opted out of dinner, so the three of them ate quietly on the back porch, which was roofed and screened in. The trees were black, wild, and whispering against the sky. Before Kate served the ice cream, the rain was pouring down so hard that it sounded like a hundred people dancing on the roof.

chapter twenty-one

Emily's mother had been beautiful. Martha did some catalog modeling in the sixties. She was thin, like Emily, but tall and regal. She had big feline eyes, a long wide mouth, jutting cheekbones. Emily used to stare at the pictures from her mother's modeling book. She often wondered what had happened to that girl in the pictures, so gorgeous and self-assured, so elegant and worldly. Where had she gone?

It was more than just faded beauty. It was as if a light had drained from her, as if disappointment had sucked her dry. The woman Emily knew bore no resemblance whatsoever to that girl. The skin on her face had grown loose and dry. There were deep lines around her mouth. There wasn't a shade or shadow left of Martha the stunning model, Martha who loved Joe Burke, Martha with everything ahead of her. That girl was Holly Golightly, a fiction. She was someone who only wished she existed, and could survive only in memories.

Thyroid problems wrecked Martha's figure. Smoking drew her face long and etched valleys in her skin. Drinking made her angry and depressed. But Emily loved her. None of that mattered to a daughter. If only Martha hadn't been so mean. The stinging slap of her words still rang in Emily's ears. *You're useless,* Martha would complain when Emily hadn't done something right. *You have delusions of grandeur,* she might say if Emily told her of a dream to be a ballerina, or a scientist, or a movie star. Then there were the days when her mother stayed in bed, barking orders from her darkened room.

When Emily was little, she used to wish that she could know the young woman in the pictures. That girl was happy and kind, laughing and light. The girl with a champagne glass on a picnic blanket, the one holding a bouquet of roses, the one on Santa's lap smiling in a way that said sometimes naughty *is* nice. Right now *that* was the woman Emily wanted to call. "Mama," she wanted to say. "I've done awful things, and I'm in terrible trouble." And her mother would say, "Come home, baby. I'll take care of everything."

No, that wasn't how it would go. Her mother would say, "You idiot. What have you done? I told you he'd ruin your life." The worst part was that she'd be right.

Emily and Dean walked down the floating dock, each of them carrying a bag. Emily had their few supplies. Dean had the bag with the money and the gun. The dock wobbled beneath them; the water, black as tar, slapped hard against the side. Conditions were bad: A high wind lashed at them, and the rain felt like needles on her face. Maybe tonight was not the night. It couldn't be more different than the other times she had come here. Maybe it was an omen. She yelled to Dean that maybe they should find someplace else to spend the night. He either didn't hear her or didn't feel like answering. Since awakening, he'd been edgy and cross.

The rain had worsened by the time they found a boat with a key on board. He'd chosen a boat called *Serendipity*. Emily had always loved that word. It spoke of when unexpectedly good things happened, things that were surprising in a happy way. Or something like that.

"These are the kind of people who leave a spare key somewhere," said Dean when he read the name. He said it with a smirk, as if all people who looked for good in the world were fools who deserved to have things taken from them. Sure enough, when he unsnapped the canvas cover and climbed into the hull, he found one under the captain's bench.

Emily remembered that, too, from her visits here. That people left keys in their boats and cars, left their doors unlocked. It was isolated, and everyone knew everyone, her father had said. Emily remembered thinking how that was so nice, and about the gates on her mother's windows in their house on the bad side of town. How did you wind up in a place where you didn't need to lock yourself in and gate the world out?

She and Dean were loading their gear into the boat when they heard a shout and saw the beam of a flashlight moving toward them. Dean quickly took the gun from the bag and shoved it in his pants. As a lightning bolt sliced the sky over the distant mountains behind the approaching front, Emily felt that familiar lash of hope and fear.

"Let me do the talking," said Dean. He climbed back up onto the dock. He waved his arm in greeting, as if he had every right to be there. Emily felt as though fear had turned her to stone. She stood rooted with the boat rocking beneath her. *Go away,* she thought. *Please, please go away.*

The hooded man approached. "What's going on here?"

"Hi, there," said Dean. "We're Anne and Rob Glass? We're doing a home exchange on Heart Island?"

Emily couldn't see the other man's face. But she imagined a deep frown of skepticism and distrust.

"No one told me about any exchange. Far as I know, the Burkes are still on the island. And it's the middle of the night."

His voice was gruff and unpleasant, but something soared inside Emily. Did that mean Joe was here? She imagined herself running into his arms, his big warm embrace. *My little Em!* She started to shiver. Everything on her, from her jacket to her underwear, was soaked through.

"I know," said Dean with a little laugh. He was such an easy liar. Even she would believe him. "We had bad weather. And we got lost . . . those damn navigation computers. They are always wrong, aren't they?"

The other man was silent for a minute. Did he not notice that Dean had his hand in his pants? *Let us go,* prayed Emily. *How much are they paying you to be the night watchman here? Let us go.*

"And this is not the Burkes' boat."

"Right, right," said Dean. "They told us to look for *Serendipity,* that the key would be under the captain's chair. And here it is." He held up the key. The other man didn't say anything. Dean was so sure of himself, so convincing, that Emily thought the other man was going to let them go, maybe with some warning about the weather.

"I'm going to have to check on this," he said.

"Don't do that, man," said Dean. "Like you said, it's late."

Emily heard how his tone had shifted from amiable to menacing. It was just a shade's difference, but Emily's heart started to thrum. She heard a rushing of blood in her ears.

The man started to back away from Dean, who took out the gun. "Don't move, man," he said. "Just stay where you are."

The other man raised his hands in the air, the flashlight beam shooting off into the night sky, leaving them dark.

"Give me the lines," said Dean.

"The what?" said Emily.

He turned to flash her an angry look. "The rope, for Christ's sake," he snapped. "Don't you know anything?"

The man on the dock took advantage of Dean's momentary distraction and started to run up the dock toward land. He was slow and limping. Dean gave chase, and Emily watched them both lumber up the dock while it rocked violently beneath their footfalls.

Just as the man reached land, Dean was on him. Emily saw them both go down, though it seemed to be happening on a small screen far away. It was a movie she was watching with the sound down, strange and slow.

Violence in the real world was clumsy and awkward. Flesh on

flesh didn't make much sound, she was thinking when she heard a high-pitched scream. It was girlish, and it radiated through her as something inside recognized a primal yell of pain. She was startled, knocked from the trance she'd been in, and ran after them. She found herself stumbling along the rocking dock, and the distance between her and them seemed to stretch and go.

"Don't, Dean," she yelled. She wasn't sure what it was that she wanted him to stop. She couldn't see what he was doing. She just knew that it was bad and wrong.

As she approached, she heard the gun go off. It was a sharp, quick sound that seemed to echo all around them and then be absorbed completely by the rain. She stopped running. She could hear Dean panting as she approached, see him straddling the other man.

"Stupid motherfucker," said Dean. "Why'd you have to run like that? I was just going to tie you up."

He sounded sad and desperate, like a little boy, and Emily was seized with a terrible hatred for him.

"What did you do?" she asked. "What did you do?"

Her voice, shrill and loud, sliced through the darkness, and Dean turned, startled. The man beneath him was utterly still, his legs splayed as if he were running in a weird, twisting gait. Life recognizes death, somehow.

"What did you want me to do?" he screamed. He stood and moved toward her. "He was going to call the police." He came up close to her. "I had to do *something*."

She hauled back and slapped him hard across the face. He stared stunned, stricken, lifted a hand to his cheek.

"Look what you've done to us," she shrieked. The words were bursting out of her, like they'd done at her mother's. She couldn't stop herself from screaming with all her rage and sorrow. "*You've ruined us. You've destroyed us. How could you do this to us? I loved you.*"

"Emily."

She started pounding on his chest, beating at him in all her fury.

She was screaming about how she had wanted so much for them and why had he done this and they could have had everything. The rain poured down on them, and the lightning and thunder seemed to ramp up with her growing misery. Dean just stood there until she exhausted herself, her arms aching from hitting him, and laid her head on his chest, weeping. She felt his arms close around her.

"I'm sorry, Em," he was saying over and over. "I'm so sorry."

"I'm pregnant," she wailed. Because it didn't seem right to say it that way, as if the words were too weak to make him understand, she said, "I'm carrying our child inside me."

He held her tight, and then she felt him start to shake, too. At first she thought he was laughing. But then she realized that he was crying. And they stood like that, the rain coming down on them, the water splashing over the dock and the seawall, the boats rocking in their slips. They might have stayed there forever if Emily hadn't seen someone else approaching in the darkness. It was a large man moving toward them quickly.

"Dean," said Emily. "There's someone else."

Dean spun around and drew the gun again. Emily's stomach clenched when the other man walked into the light. His face was swollen black and blue around the eyes and jaw; his hair hung in great wet chunks around his face. And he had that same blank, empty stare, that same mirthless, hungry smile. Seeing the gun, and the body on the ground, Brad kept his distance.

"You always were dumb as dirt, Dean. You never should have told me where the marina was. I never would have found you."

"Brad." Dean lifted his free hand. "You should have kept your hands off my girl."

"You told him about this place?" she asked. It wasn't possible. "When?"

"Shut up," he hissed at her.

The guilty, angry look on his face told her everything she needed to know. They were coming here all along, she realized. It was all part of his plan with Brad. She hated herself in that moment for loving a liar, for betraying Carol, for allowing an innocent boy to lose his life. She'd made the mistake of sharing her dreams about this place with him. And, now, after he'd taken everything else, he was taking that, too. And it was right, because she deserved to lose it all.

"Where's the money?" said Brad. "I just want my cut."

"I don't think so," said Dean. "You fucked it all up, man. It wasn't part of the plan for those people to get hurt."

"Just give him the money," Emily whispered. "What difference does it make now?"

"It's all we *have*." It was true. Five thousand dollars was all they had. They were bankrupt in every other possible way.

Brad was fast, too fast for Dean. When Brad rushed him, Dean fumbled for the gun, and it fell on the dock, nearly sliding into the black water. Brad dove for it and Dean for him, with Emily screaming again.

"*Stop it! Stop it!*" She looked up into the rain. "Help!" she wailed. "Help us!"

Why did no one come? Why was there just the black shadow of the mountains around them and the rain? Why was the rain so loud that it swallowed her voice?

As the two men struggled, Emily thought about running from them, leaving them to kill each other. She could do that. It was another of those moments, and this time she chose right, she did the right thing. She was going to run and run until she found someplace to turn herself in. She began to back away from them. And when she felt firm land beneath her feet, she started to sprint.

It was the shot ringing out in the night that stopped her in her tracks. It was so loud that the sound seemed to stop the rain. She hid behind a car in the lot, a red Toyota. She sat on the wet gravel, and all she could hear was her labored breathing. Then approaching footsteps.

"Emily." His voice was sickly sweet, a terrible singsong. "Oh, Emily!"

From where she crouched, she could see that Brad had the gun and was holding it to Dean's head. "My old friend Dean tells me that your family is rich, rich, rich. That your daddy has lots of money."

She felt a sob rush up from her chest into her throat. She clamped a hand over her mouth.

"He says there's money on the island, and jewelry."

She found herself standing, even though she knew she should hide and try to run again when she had a chance. "That's not true," she said. "It's just not."

It wasn't true, as far as she knew. She didn't know anything about that and had never said anything that might have made Dean think that. She'd said that Heart Island was a place that was full of treasures. She meant butterflies and beautiful sunsets, golden memories and wildflowers. That was what she meant. Had he misunderstood her? Was he so empty inside that he'd mistaken her meaning?

Brad was walking toward her, holding Dean with an arm around his neck and the gun to his head. Dean was clawing at Brad's arm but couldn't speak. He was kicking out and kicking back toward Brad and missing every time.

"Dean's been researching Heart Island for a while now, ever since you told him about it. Just like he was casing the restaurant where you worked. He knows more about it than you do."

Dean wanted to take everything from her, didn't he? He wanted to destroy everything. She didn't bother trying to stop the tears.

"Why would they keep any money or jewelry on that island?" she said. God, they were both idiots—mean, murderous fools without a thought in their heads. "They're only there in summer. It's locked up most of the year."

Brad seemed to consider this. Dean was making a strangled grunt, still trying to break free.

"Who knows where rich people keep all their money?" Brad said a little defensively.

"They keep it in a *bank*," she said. She practically spat the word. "So that maniacs like you can't get their filthy hands on it."

"There's a safe in the bunkhouse," said Dean, who'd finally found his voice. "I read it in a book: *Great Adirondack Island Homes* or something like that."

"Shut up, Dean," said Emily. He was a fool. What book? There was no "bunkhouse" on the island—whatever that was. He didn't know what he was talking about.

Brad laughed an ugly little laugh, as if he'd caught her in a lie. But he looked a little less sure of himself. "I like you, Emily. I don't want to kill your boyfriend and anyone I find on that island. But I think you know I will."

The man Dean had killed had said that the Burkes were on Heart Island. Was it true? Was her father there, a boat ride away?

"And in case you think I don't know how to get there, I do. We've been planning this a good long time, haven't we, Dean?"

"The storm," she said weakly. "It's too rough."

"Dean and I grew up on boats," he said. "You know that. Or maybe Dean didn't tell you how far back we go. Trust me, you haven't seen a storm until you've seen a storm in Florida."

She floated above herself to see the three of them standing, a sick triangle of bad intentions and ugly mistakes. She tried to run through her choices, the right ones, the wrong ones, what she could do, what she wanted to do. But she found that her mind had gone blank. There was no path except the one that she found herself on. There was no way to go but forward. She couldn't run and leave Heart Island to those two, especially Brad. No, she had to go with them. She had to salvage what she could of this place she cherished. And maybe, somewhere deep inside, there was a little girl who thought that it might be—as dark and twisting and fraught with peril as it was—the road home.

"The girl didn't present like a hostage," said Jones Cooper.

"We have footage," said Special Agent Eliza Griffin. She was young—very young, too young, surely, to be on the job. When Jones first walked in, he thought it was Take Your Daughter to Work Day. Since when did they let kids join the FBI? "They carried her screaming out of that place."

"Well, between then and now," Jones Cooper said, "something's changed."

He was mad about his SUV, first of all. It was a nice car, paid for, and in good condition. Second, he was feeling like he could have done more than let those two drive off.

Fact was, as soon as he saw the girl in the road, he knew who she was. He'd been following the story since yesterday, monitoring the police scanner. He'd had a hunch they were headed north and figured it was possible that their flight would take them right by The Hollows. And third, adding insult to injury, he was answering questions from a federal agent who was about half his age but appeared to think she was about twice as smart as she actually was. She had that look about her, that cocky, overeducated, self-righteous look that could only get her into trouble. All the young ones had it. Even he'd had it once, to a lesser degree. But that was a long, long time ago.

"*He* had the gun, right?" She was staring at her notepad.

"Right."

"And you said that her face was bruised, as though she'd been hit." The agent had a habit of grabbing at her thick dark ponytail and bringing it over her shoulder and twisting it hard around her finger.

Jones gave an affirming nod. He would have liked to believe that the girl was a hostage, a sweet-looking young person like that. She might have been acting under some threat that was unclear to him at the time. But he didn't think so. She was desperate, that was his read. Her life had spun out of control, and she was flying blind.

"So she was under duress." The agent pushed up her dark-framed glasses. Most young women wore contacts these days or had Lasik surgery. Jones found himself wondering why she had chosen otherwise. The frames dominated her face; when you looked at her, they were what you saw. Maybe she wanted it that way.

"Well," he said, "maybe in some sense. I doubt she was the architect of this mess. But she's along for the ride now. She loves him. She thinks she can save him."

The girl looked at him with raw skepticism. "And you know this how?"

He gave a shrug. "Experience, instinct. It's an old story."

She smiled in a way that she might have thought was polite but was really just condescending. "An associate of Dean Freeman says that Freeman had been planning this robbery for a while and that he called a friend, Brad Campbell, to come up from Florida and help him pull it off."

That didn't ring true for Jones. He knew the Dean Freeman type, bad news but weak and not that smart. He wasn't masterminding a robbery or anything else. It might have been his idea, but without someone else calling the shots, he never would have had the guts or the drive to do it alone.

"He didn't seem like the sharpest tool in the shed," said Jones. "He was skittish, panicky. I can't be sure, but he might have been on something."

"The restaurant security cameras show two men entering through the back, then exiting again, carrying the girl. But you say it was just the two of them?"

"That's right," said Jones.

"They were spotted at a motel south of The Hollows," said Agent Griffin. "According to witnesses, Emily Burke and Dean Freeman left alone. By the time we got there, there was evidence of some kind of struggle—furniture knocked over, blood on the rug and the wall. But all three of them were gone."

Jones wasn't sure why she was telling him this. Was she asking for his opinion without wanting to ask for it? "A fight over the money, probably," he said. "Someone always thinks he deserves more."

The young agent regarded him as though she found him amusing. "That's what I was thinking. Or the girl. A fight over the girl."

"Could be," he admitted. Emily Burke was a very pretty girl.

"What were your impressions of her?" she asked.

"She was sober. Fairly coolheaded. Like I said, not a hostage, to my thinking. She seemed more in control than he did. He's about five minutes from losing it completely."

The agent sat up a little straighter, glanced down at the file on the table between them. Jones followed her eyes to the mug shots of Freeman.

"This is the worst thing he's done," she said. "He had a robbery charge as a juvenile in Florida, but no one got hurt, and he wasn't the gunman. Then there was a possession with intent to distribute a few years back in New Jersey. This is a new level for him."

Jones kept thinking about the girl. Why was she involved with a man like that? If he'd had more time, if that bozo hadn't been waving the gun around, he could have talked her in. She wanted a way out of the mess; he could see that in her. His wife, Maggie, would laugh at him. *Another damsel in distress? You never can resist one, even when she steals your car.*

"And they gave no indication where they were going?"

She'd already asked him this—twice. "No," he said. "But my guess is they'll keep going north."

"We'll know soon enough," said Chuck Ferrigno. He was the lead detective at the Hollows Police Department, a post he'd taken when Jones retired almost two years earlier. He'd been sitting in the corner of the room, tapping away on his BlackBerry. "LoJack says they'll activate the device and get back to us with a location within the hour."

"It's been four hours since they took the vehicle. They may have ditched it by now," said Jones.

It was the main reason he hadn't put up a fight for the Explorer. He'd had the device installed when he got his private detective license last year, figured it might come in handy. Of course, that was part of his fantasy about what private detective work would be. He hadn't taken a case in over six months, except for the occasional consulting work he did for the understaffed police department. In the last year, he'd investigated two cold cases.

"Even so," said Agent Griffin, "we'll be closer to them than we have been in two days." She got up from her seat and stuck out her hand. "Thank you for your help, Mr. Cooper. And thanks for keeping a cool head yourself."

He stood and took her hand. Her grip was strong, but her fingers felt small and delicate. "I think you'll be able to talk them in," he said. "Especially if you appeal to the girl."

"Mr. Cooper," she said, as if taking him to school, "these people have committed an armed robbery that left one man dead and a woman in a coma. We'll bring them in by whatever means necessary."

She was puffed up with her own sense of self-righteousness. It wouldn't take much to deflate her. But he didn't have the heart.

"Of course," said Jones. He lifted a deferential palm.

"Please give the people at LoJack my telephone number and have them call me, Detective Ferrigno," she said. She gathered up her files and hugged them to her chest. "I'll be waiting in the parking lot with the federal team for their location."

"Will do," said Chuck easily. "Should be anytime now."

She left the room with a slam of the door.

"Christ, were we ever that young and stupid?" asked Chuck after she'd left.

"No," said Jones. "We were always the geniuses we are today."

"That's what I thought." Chuck rubbed his forehead. Every time Jones saw the guy, he had less hair and looked a bit bigger around the middle. The job was not good for anyone's health.

"Can I get a lift home?" asked Jones.

Chuck lifted his eyebrows. "Don't you want to wait this out?"

The truth was there was nothing to go home to at the moment. Maggie was taking their son, Ricky, back to school. So Jones sat back down. He'd spent a lot of hours in the interrogation room over the years, although this was the first time he'd been the one answering the questions.

"Sure," he said. He felt that old tingle of excitement. "Why not?"

"I wonder about the other guy," said Chuck. He tapped his pen against the table.

"Brad Campbell," said Jones.

"He's a real bad dude. You saw that record?"

"I did." Armed robbery, assault, attempted rape, grand theft auto—a list of charges that seemed to go on and on. That he was walking around free was a living indictment of the penal system. A man like Brad Campbell either ended up killing someone, getting himself killed, or serving out the rest of his life in prison. It was that simple.

"The kid's knuckles were split wide open," said Jones. "There was probably a fight, like Agent Griffin said."

"Tell you what," said Chuck. "Let's hope they went their separate ways amicably. Otherwise, I bet he's after them. Especially if they have the money."

chapter twenty-two

The island, the island, the island. As long as Lulu could remember, Chelsea had been talking about it. In Lulu's imagination, it had taken on mythic proportions, like some kind of fairy-tale place where only Chelsea could go. It was perfect and beautiful—and exclusive—somewhere Lulu was never invited. She had a sense that Chelsea hadn't wanted her there, that there was something on Heart Island Chelsea wanted to keep for herself. Secretly, though there was no way she would ever admit it, Lulu had always been jealous. She acted like she thought it was the lamest thing, this yearly family trip that Chelsea had to take. But every year Lulu hoped for an invitation that never came.

Now that she was finally here, she was mystified. The place was a rock in the middle of a cold gray lake. Sure, there were lots of pretty trees and clean air. But it had a strange vibe, a lonely, isolated feel. There was no television or cell service. The Internet service they got through Chelsea's rocket stick was so slow that it almost wasn't worth having. It was a tease. And worst of all, there was no Conner Lange.

The truth was that Lulu had invited herself along only to spite him. He'd gotten pissy with her when their plan to get Chelsea to sneak out had flopped. That night he'd wanted Lulu to dump Chaz and come out anyway. There was a party with alcohol that older kids from another school were having. She'd badly wanted to go, to be with Conner, to have a good time and lose herself for a while. But she wouldn't go without Chelsea.

I don't dump Chelsea, she'd written. *Learn that now.*

Fine. See you whenever, he'd written back.

That was when Chelsea's mom had come in and Lulu had invited herself to the island. She would show Conner how little she cared. It had worked. He'd left about a hundred messages. But now she was in exile. And that little sophomore slut Bella was making flirty eyes at Conner, according to him.

Meanwhile, Chelsea's grandmother was a total bitch. And the whole place was an obstacle course of rules. Five-minute showers (as if Lulu could wash and condition her hair in five minutes). Don't flush the toilet every time you pee (so gross). Don't run the water while you brush your teeth. Be careful on the rocks; don't yell too loud even if you're having fun. It was too cold to swim. And then she and Chelsea had to make dinner? What kind of *vacation* was this?

Chelsea's mom had made a fire in the guesthouse. Now Lulu and Chelsea were huddled in front of it while Kate tried to call Sean. Chelsea kept reaching in with the fire poker to stoke the flames, as if by keeping them warm, she could erase their deep sense of unease. It wasn't working.

There had been a brief window of connectivity when Lulu had talked to Conner.

"I love you," he said. "Come back."

"I can't," she said. "I'm stuck here."

That was when he'd said the thing about Bella flirting with him. So basically, if Lulu wasn't around to put out, someone else would. That's what he was trying to tell her, right?

She played it cool. "Oh, yeah?" she said. "She's hot. You should tap that. I hear she'll do anyone."

"I only want you, baby."

But that wasn't true. He was a whore. He'd go with anyone hot who wanted him. All men were whores.

After a while, Chelsea moved over to the couch with her book, and Lulu felt that empty place open inside of her. Usually, when

Chaz was around, she felt calm and secure. But even Chelsea was different here, distant somehow, more interested in the island than she was in Lulu.

Lulu was starting to wonder if Chelsea knew about her lie. That thought filled her with dread.

"Stop worrying, Lulu," said Chelsea.

Lulu knew Chelsea thought she was worried about Conner and Bella. When Lulu looked at her friend, Chelsea was peering over her book with a reassuring smile. The girl was always reading. Lulu didn't understand the appeal of books. All those words swimming on a page, someone's lies. B-O-R-I-N-G.

"I'm not worried." She was trying the same attitude she used with Conner. The difference was, she couldn't fool Chelsea. "She can't compare to me."

"Of course not," said her friend. "No one can."

"I know."

She almost told Chelsea then. But she couldn't. She put her head down on the pillow she'd dragged onto the floor and closed her eyes. She hadn't seen what Chelsea had glimpsed on the dock. But the look on her friend's face was enough to scare her. Lulu had been spooked ever since, jumping at every little noise, even though she'd just been making fun of Chelsea for believing in ghosts.

There was something about this place. The quiet was oppressive. When she couldn't get cell service, it felt malicious, like the island wanted them to be disconnected. She almost said it out loud. But she could just hear Chelsea. *You've seen too many horror movies,* she'd say.

"Why do you like this place so much?" said Lulu. "I don't get it."

She was staring at the high wood-beamed ceilings, listening to the pounding of the rain. Out the window, there was only black. All Lulu could see was the reflection from the inside. Chelsea didn't answer right away, and Lulu glanced back at her friend, who was staring at nothing.

"I don't have to be anything here," said Chelsea finally. "I don't have to be anything other than who I am."

This answer surprised Lulu. When was Chelsea ever anything other than who she was? She said as much.

"You know," said Chelsea. "I don't have to shave my legs or put on makeup. I can wear whatever, and no one cares. I don't have to *maintain*."

The idea that Chelsea had to maintain was news to Lulu.

"You're perfect," said Lulu. "Without even trying."

"Yeah, right." Then, after a loud exhale, she said, "He never wrote again. After I wouldn't go out to meet him."

Lulu knew she was talking about Adam McKee, and she felt a powerful rush of guilt. She was *such* a horrible friend.

"Forget him," Lulu said. "He's probably a loser. He's not good enough for you."

"Yeah," said Chelsea. She sounded thoroughly unconvinced. "I guess."

Lulu almost told her then. But she couldn't. "I'm going to bed." She stood and walked toward her room. She wanted Chelsea to come with her, to curl up beside her and go to sleep like they used to when they were young. But Chelsea didn't follow.

"Okay. I'm going to read awhile and wait to see if Mom got in touch with my dad." Chelsea had seemed distant and unsettled since the dock, as though she had things on her mind that she didn't want to discuss.

The floor beneath Lulu's feet was cold, and she knew the bed in her room was hard and unwelcoming. "Are you all right?"

"I'm fine," said Chelsea. She said it in the way that Lulu knew meant she wasn't. Lulu lingered a minute, but Chelsea went back to reading. Lulu went to her room, got under the covers, and wrapped herself up tight. She was so tired that even with all the things bothering her—the stupid island, her faithless boyfriend, ghosts, the terrible thing she'd done to Chelsea—she fell right away into a deep, heavy sleep.

In the night, something woke Kate. What was it? She could feel the imprint of sound on the silence all around her. The rain had stopped. Chelsea was pressed up against her, her arm draped across Kate's middle. She'd crept into the room shortly after Kate turned off the light. Now she was snoring lightly.

In the moonlight, she looked just like she had as a toddler—her creamy skin, her unfurrowed brow. She was in that innocent, impenetrable slumber. Nothing followed Chelsea into her dreams; she'd always slept a deep, untroubled sleep. Brendan, the worrier, still woke up in the night during times of stress. He got that from Kate.

She listened to the quiet, hearing nothing. She slipped from the bed and padded over to the window. She could see the main house and the bunkhouse, dark and undisturbed.

She'd decided that in the morning, they'd get in the boat and go to the mainland and talk to the police. There was something off about the island, something unsettled. She couldn't explain it, but she could feel it. Caroline had believed that Heart Island had moods and feelings. Kate wouldn't go that far, but something wasn't right.

She moved back to the window, folded her arms, and watched the sway of the trees, the drift of the clouds, the solid triangle of the main house roof, the glittering water. She thought again about walking around the island with her flashlight. But what would she do if there were an intruder hiding in the trees? She'd still have to leave the girls alone. When she and Theo were children, they'd sneak from their beds and walk around the island in the dark. With flashlights, they'd revisit all their daytime spots and find them new under the cover of night. Never once were they afraid. They felt sheltered and protected here, as though nothing could ever go wrong. Caroline talked about the island ghosts, but neither Kate nor Theo had ever seen anything, in spite of every effort to find them.

She walked from window to window, taking in the different vantage points. She could see the western shore, the main house to the south. To the east, there were only trees and the path to Lookout Rock. It was the point where, according to Lana, her affair with Richard came to its ugly end. Kate wondered if reading about him, writing about him, however indirectly, had resurrected him. Was it Richard Cameron wandering the island, wanting to make himself known after all these years? Both Chelsea's and Birdie's descriptions matched the photos Kate had seen. But it wasn't. That was the silly imagining of an overtired mind. Still, Kate wondered what Caroline would say. No doubt she'd think it was true. She'd want a séance or a Ouija board. *Richard,* she'd say, *is that you? We're so sorry for how you suffered.*

Kate wondered how much, if anything, Birdie knew about her mother's affair. Birdie had seemed genuinely clueless when John mentioned Richard's name, as though she'd never heard of him. But why had she experienced such a powerful reaction to the story John had to tell? Was it because the picture reminded Birdie of the man she thought she saw on the island the other day? Or was it more, some instinct, some neglected memory? To open the conversation with Birdie would be to admit that Kate knew almost everything about the affair, even Grandma Lana's version of how it ended. Kate wasn't sure she was ready to get into all of that. The story, though heavily fictionalized, was at the heart of her novel. It was a conversation she needed to have with Birdie before the book hit the shelves.

Now that they were away from him, Kate allowed herself to wonder if John Cross knew about her novel. The publishing world was so small. She wouldn't think he'd have access to her manuscript at this early point, but she couldn't be sure. Of course, everything was heavily fictionalized, names changed, scenarios invented. And yet there were shades of truth. She'd been very honest with her editor, and maybe rumors were circulating. The best fiction, her editor assured her, read like nonfiction. The best lies contained a kernel of truth.

She was so deep in thought that she almost didn't see it at first, the movement in the trees—a shadow that was static and then not, slipping between the trunks. She felt her throat go dry and her chest lurch. And then there was nothing, no movement, just the same endless stillness that began before she was ever born and would live on long after they were all gone. What had she seen?

Quickly, quietly, she moved to the mudroom and pulled on her jeans, shoes, and coat. From the shelf above the utility sink, she grabbed a flashlight and a flare. As far as weapons went, a flare gun wasn't much of an option. But it felt like something, the heft of it in her hand.

Then she exited the house, locking the girls inside behind her. In addition to fear, she felt anger, a sense of violation. As she marched out into the dark, she acknowledged that there was more of Birdie in her than she liked to admit.

Birdie hadn't slept much. She would fall into a fitful doze, then startle awake. She couldn't bring herself to move from the bed. She'd listened to the girls talking quietly, then eating dinner. She'd listened to them cleaning up, using too much water—didn't they know that the pump was solar-powered? They'd figure it out when they turned on the spigot and nothing came out.

Then they'd all left for the guesthouse, and she was alone again, finally. Anything but quiet made her edgy. She had always been that way, never able to bear Gene and Caroline's roughhousing, or Kate and Theo's exuberant running and laughter. It hurt her; it caused her to cringe. She supposed that made her some kind of monster, someone who couldn't stand the sound of people having fun. She didn't know how to be any other way.

She'd wanted so badly to tell Kate about her childhood memories and how that photograph John Cross had shown them was of the same man she'd seen in her mother's photo album. The same man she'd seen her mother kiss, and the same man she'd seen—maybe, *maybe*—on her island. But how could she tell anyone those things? They sounded crazy, even to Birdie.

Who was he to her mother? Her lover, obviously. That much was clear. What did it mean? She remembered the kiss, that passionate movie-star kiss. In some ways, all her life, she'd been waiting for a kiss like that. With Joe, she'd never had anything like it. And now she never would.

You had to be a certain kind of person to give and receive so much heat. She knew that she wasn't that kind of woman, lusty and wanton. She was narrow, hard to the touch, not soft and yielding. Her lips were thin, as though designed only to deliver hard words, reprimands, and complaints. She was nothing like her mother, who was full-bodied and passionate.

Caroline was. Caroline was just like their mother, every bit as radiant, every bit as full of emotion and laughter. Caroline had gotten it all because Birdie had gotten nothing. She had the slender, cold features of her father's family, the rigid posture, the pinched features, the ice-blue eyes. *Why couldn't I have been thin like you, Birdie?* Caroline always lamented the battle she fought against her body's desire to expand. But Birdie, once upon a time, would have given anything for Caroline's full bust, her pouty lips, her flushed full cheeks. It was only recently that strangled thinness had come into fashion.

Once the rain stopped for a brief time, she might have dozed for a while. Then the moonlight shone through the dissipating cloud cover. She dreamed of her mother and Richard Cameron kissing on the shore. She dreamed of her father, who was so kind but always from a distance. In her dreams, he was slipping around corners, swift and straight-backed. She could never see his face or get him to stop running. She dreamed that Joe was beside her. *Ah, Birdie,* he said. *Do you have to be so cold?* It was so easy for him to say she was cold.

She wasn't. She was anything but. He was the cold one, never with her when he was meant to be. He'd always given the best of himself to someone else. Just like her mother, Joe had loved another person more than the one he married. It was all so clear now that Birdie knew what she'd seen so many years ago wasn't a dream.

What did it matter? They were gone, all of them—her mother, her father, Richard Cameron. Even Joe, in his way, was gone. Any love that had existed between them had drifted away long ago, leaving them with a mutually beneficial business relationship. *But it does matter,* thought Birdie, *because the island remembers. Love and lies never die. Their legacy just grows like vines through generations, twisting around and strangling us.*

Caroline knew, Birdie thought with a sudden clarity. She finally understood the superior, knowing tone Caroline always used on the rare occasions when they discussed Mother and Daddy. And she had dropped little hints. *There were things about Mother that you never knew.* Or *Mommy and Daddy didn't have such a perfect marriage.* When Birdie pressed, Caroline would get vague and take her leave. Birdie had thought her sister was being a drama queen, or trying to remind Birdie that she had always been Mother's favorite child. As if anyone could forget such a thing.

Caroline knew because Mother had told her. Among all the things that pained Birdie, this hurt more than anything else. Caroline had gone to the grave with the secrets Mother had shared with her and not with Birdie. Yes, Birdie had withheld her love, her affection, her friendship. But Caroline had withheld the most important thing of all: the truth about their mother and about that night. She had a knowledge of Lana that Birdie had been denied. Didn't Mother know that no one loved her as much as Birdie did? How could she not have known?

Amid this mosaic of thoughts and dreams, something woke her, some sound. She sat up in bed and listened to the silence. She couldn't hear anything. But she knew something wasn't right. She could feel it in her bones, just as she could feel when the rain was coming. She lay still and waited.

Chelsea woke to find her mother gone. She rolled onto her back and listened. She could hear Lulu breathing deeply in the next room but nothing else. Her mother was not in the bathroom. Where was she? She got up and went over to the window. She saw the beam of a flashlight moving through the trees. Kate was probably going to check on Birdie.

"Do you want me to stay here with you tonight, Mother?" Chelsea had heard Kate ask before they left the main house.

"Don't be ridiculous," Birdie had snapped.

Chelsea loved her grandmother, but it made her angry to hear her talk that way to Kate. Chelsea hadn't said good night, had just walked out with her arm looped through her mother's. She'd never heard Kate talk that way to anyone, even when she was angry. No one in her immediate family talked that way—not Sean, not even Brendan. Sebastian could be nasty like that. She remembered that about him, even though he walked on eggshells with Chelsea now. She remembered the voice-mail messages he used to leave for her mother when he'd been drinking—the vitriol, the rage, was palpable. She didn't like to think about that, though. That was the past. Her mother always said that the past was gone. Chelsea liked the idea that every ugly and awful thing disappeared when the tide came in. Like sand castles, it all just washed away.

She walked into the next room to check on Lulu, who was soundly asleep. Chelsea took the cell phone from her friend's hand, and Lulu groaned, turned over, and pulled the covers tight around her.

Lulu had talked to Conner and seemed satisfied that he still liked her and wasn't running around with Bella. *She can't compare with me,* she'd said. But there was something sad around her eyes that told Chelsea Lulu didn't quite believe it. She'd felt really sorry for her friend, not for the first time. *No one can,* Chelsea had said to soothe her. *You know that.* Lulu had flashed her a grateful look, but there was something else there. It looked for all the world like guilt, but maybe Chelsea was imagining things.

Imagining things, like the figure she saw on the dock. How could you be so certain one minute about what you saw and so doubtful the next? She'd been afraid; she'd wanted to run. But then it was gone, and even as she and Lulu were racing back to the house, she'd felt silly, as though she'd made the whole thing up.

She'd always wanted to see the ghosts on Heart Island that her great-aunt Caroline believed in. But she didn't truly believe in them herself, much as she'd never truly believed in Santa Claus. But she'd gone along with the Santa story for years because she'd so badly wanted to it to be true: the flying reindeer, Santa coming down the chimney, how he knew when you'd been bad or good. There were so many holes in the story, but she'd wanted to be convinced, so she allowed herself to be. Maybe that was what happened tonight. After all those years of *wanting* to believe, she'd finally seen what she'd wanted to see.

Like what she did with Adam McKee. In the brief moment of connectivity they'd had, she'd checked to see if he'd left her a message, and he hadn't. He hadn't posted on his own page, either.

"Forget it," Lulu said. "He's a loser."

Chelsea didn't forget it. She carried the disappointment around in her middle like a stomach virus. What was wrong with her? Boys chased after Lulu, did backflips for her attention, even as she used, abused, and discarded them. Lulu would move on to the next and obsess about him as she was doing with Conner now. Once she was sure he belonged to her, she'd lose interest immediately.

Chelsea had never actually had a boyfriend. She probably never would. *You're not like other girls.* In his online silence, what she'd taken as a compliment suddenly had new meaning. She wasn't like other girls . . . she was a freak, a weirdo. No one would ever want her.

"What's going on?" Lulu had come up behind her, put a cool hand on the small of her back. Chelsea jumped, startled. "Where's your mom?"

"I think she went to check on my grandmother." She didn't turn around, kept her eyes trained outside.

Lulu moved in close to her, shivering. "I'm freezing."

Chelsea looked out across to the main house. She didn't see the bobbing light of her mother's flashlight. She didn't see any lights go on in the main house, either. There was some energy that Chelsea didn't quite understand, as if a breath had been drawn and held. Lulu was tugging at her, pulling her away from the window.

"She'll be back in a minute. Come cuddle with me," she said. "Warm me up."

They got into her mom's bed and huddled together under the covers. Lulu's hair smelled like strawberries. When they were younger, they'd often slept together in the same bed, and Chelsea was used to the feel of her friend's body curled up against hers. They used to practice kissing on each other. But that was a long time ago. Neither of them ever talked about that anymore; it was unspoken. It was embarrassing to the point of being shameful. But then it had been warm and wonderful. Not sexual at all, Chelsea didn't think. But even remembering it caused heat to come to her face.

"This place really sucks," said Lulu. She sounded desolate, mournful.

Chelsea didn't say anything. If you couldn't see what was wonderful about Heart Island, then it *did* suck. She knew that. Plenty of people she loved—Sean, Uncle Theo, even her father in some ways— had similar feelings about the island. But no one hated it completely. It was just so fraught to spend time there. *It's like loving an addict,* she'd overheard Uncle Theo say to her mother. *You know how good it can be when it's good, how truly beautiful it is. But the ugly stuff is just not worth it.*

"We're trapped here," said Lulu.

"We're not trapped." Even as Chelsea said it, she wasn't sure that was true. It seemed like a lot of people were trapped on Heart Island or in their idea of it.

"Your mother said the water was really rough," said Lulu. "We can't take the boat back to the mainland."

Chelsea knew that was so. Although they'd left the island once during bad weather, when they knew a worse storm was coming and they felt they had no choice but to get off while they could. It was a frightening trip, with Sean white-knuckled at the helm, the water washing over the sides of the small boat. Chelsea and Brendan had clung to Kate as the cuddy pitched and rolled in the big water.

Birdie had stayed behind and weathered a storm that kept her trapped on the island for a week by herself. Chelsea had wept to leave Birdie. *She wants it this way,* Kate had told her. *We have to respect that.*

Chelsea hadn't understood. She *still* didn't understand why Birdie had wanted to be left behind. *She loves Heart Island more than she loves us,* Brendan had yelled over the weather. Neither Kate nor Sean had answered him.

"We'll be able to leave eventually," said Chelsea. "It's okay. Nothing bad happens here. We're safe."

Lulu snorted. "Sure, except for the ghosts or the stranger lurking on the island."

Chelsea didn't say anything. Lulu's fear was contagious. Maybe they *were* trapped. Maybe there was no way to call for help. The emergency radio needed to be kept charged. Maybe since everyone seemed to think there was cell service (even though there obviously wasn't), it had sat neglected.

Chelsea lay listening for her mom to come back. Before Kate had given permission for Lulu to join them on the trip, she'd called Chelsea into her room. "Do you really want her to come? Or do you need a break?" she'd asked.

Kate had sat with her legs crossed on the big chair over by the fireplace. Chelsea had felt a rise of indignation, of defensiveness about Lulu. But it had dissipated quickly. *Had* she been looking forward to a week without her friend?

"I don't know," she said. "I guess I want her to come."

"Why?"

"She'll be lonely without me."

Kate had pressed her lips together and looked at her with sad eyes. "It's not your job to entertain Lulu," she said. "Is she going to make the trip better or worse for you?"

"Better?" Chelsea said. It came off sounding like a question, and Kate frowned. "Better." Chelsea firmed up her tone. "I want her to come."

"You're sure."

"Yes."

It wasn't a lie. Well, it wasn't a lie she told her mother. Maybe it was a lie she told herself. Because hadn't she been a little disappointed when her mother told Lulu she could come? Hadn't she, on some level, wanted her mother to say: *Sorry, Lulu, this is a trip for family*? Why hadn't she just told her mother that? It wasn't as if she weren't free to speak her mind.

"Chaz?" Lulu was touching her hair, a soft, soothing, stroking movement.

"Yeah?"

"I have to tell you something."

Lulu had that tone, that sheepish, too-cute tone that she used when she'd done something awful.

"What?" said Chelsea. She was bracing herself. She couldn't imagine what Lulu had done. She'd used the same tone in telling Chelsea that she'd lost her virginity, and when she'd confessed to smoking a joint. What now?

"That guy? Adam McKee?"

"Yeah?" Oh, God. Chelsea felt a flowering of dread. What was she going to say—that she knew him, that she'd slept with him, that he was flirting with her online, too, and she'd decided that she liked him?

"He's not real," she said. "He's not a real guy."

"What are you talking about?"

Even as she said it, Chelsea knew it was true. Of course he wasn't real. Smart and kind, sensitive, into art and music—boys like that didn't exist. Someone who thought she was cool, different in a good way. She should have known.

"Conner made that page. It was Conner sending you those notes."

That she hadn't expected. She felt a boil of anger and shame. "Why?" The word barely squeaked out of her throat, which was constricting.

"He wanted me to sneak out last night from your place. We thought if you had someone you wanted to meet, you'd do it."

Only Lulu could have known the exact kind of boy Chelsea would want to meet. Only Lulu would know all the right things to say. Chelsea, on the other hand, didn't have any idea what to say. The anger, the disappointment, was too much. She didn't trust herself to speak without crying.

"I'm sorry," said Lulu. "Conner was going to bring a friend for you to meet, someone from another school. We thought you'd like him. We used his picture. You thought he was cute."

Still, Chelsea couldn't say anything. Her mind was racing back through everything she'd written. What had she revealed about herself? What had she shown Lulu and her asshole boyfriend about herself that they hadn't known? Really, it was her own eagerness that embarrassed her more than anything else.

"Please don't be mad," said Lulu. "I didn't think you'd really like him. I didn't think you even cared about boys."

Chelsea found her voice again. "I *don't* care."

She couldn't believe her own level, easy tone. She had always been able to do this, hide her feelings, keep them locked tight inside. It was so much safer that way. No one could ever know the power they had to hurt her. She'd learned it when she was little, to never let anyone who'd proved untrustworthy see her cry.

"Chelsea."

"I don't. Really," she said. She pushed out a laugh, but it sounded strangled and sorry. "I'd almost forgotten about the whole thing." She knew that didn't hold much weight, since they'd just been talking about it before they went to bed. She could hear Lulu breathing.

"Come on," Lulu said. "I'm sorry."

Some people knew her—Sean, her mother, Lulu. These were the people she couldn't and didn't want to hide from. That was why it hurt so badly that she now had to protect herself from her oldest friend.

She could feel Lulu looking at her in the dark. She could see the crown of her head, the round of her shoulder. Lulu put a hand on Chelsea's arm. The gentleness of the touch made something go dark and angry inside Chelsea.

"Seriously," Chelsea said. "It's no big deal. I'm not like you. I'm not a slut for any cute boy who comes along."

She wanted to take those words back. But they were out, shattering in the air all around them, slicing them both. Lulu didn't say anything, just left the bed and the room. Chelsea had never felt so alone.

chapter twenty-three

Emily's fatigue was like an unbearable weight she carried on her back, one she couldn't put down. She'd never wanted to sleep so badly—just to rest her head on something soft and drift away for hours. But everything was different; nothing was as she remembered it. The island was dark and cold. There were three structures instead of one. And yes, there were people here. Was her father among them, sleeping peacefully somewhere? She looked from house to house, wondering where he might be. It was probably the biggest one, the one to their left. For a moment, she felt a vague sense of relief, as if she had arrived home after a long, tiring journey.

Open your eyes, Emily, her mother always said. *See what's right in front of you.*

The weather had grown wild. They'd barely made it here, with Dean at the helm and Brad holding the gun to Dean's back. There had been water washing in over the sides of the boat, the vessel bucking in the heavy chop. Emily had felt a terrible surge of nausea, but she'd managed to keep herself together.

As soon as they'd pulled away from the marina, she'd seen the dark, hulking shadow of Heart Island. Or maybe it was just her imagination. She knew it was the largest island and that it would lie straight ahead once they hit the open water. She sat quietly beside Dean, who hadn't dared to look at her. But all her anger had drained. She just felt numb.

Finally, after what seemed like hours, they crashed the boat against a rock as they ran aground at the only place they could. The sound was so loud, the impact so jarring, that she was certain she'd see lights come on in the houses. But all was quiet. She wasn't sure if the hull had been breached or if the water collecting in the bottom had rushed in over the sides. Now it was beached and tilting on the rocky area.

Brad climbed off the boat first, never turning his back on them. Dean and Emily followed.

Brad stowed the money on the boat, which she thought was idiotic, since it might sink or wash away. *Five thousand dollars,* she thought. She and Dean had ruined their lives for five thousand dollars. She thought about that college fund her father had set up for her. Emily's mother controlled the money, so she had no idea what was in it.

There's enough for school and a head start after you graduate, her mother had told her once. *It's what I didn't have when I was your age. If I'd had a leg up, maybe I wouldn't have made so many mistakes.*

Emily didn't know what those mistakes were and how they had affected the course of Martha's life. Naturally, Emily had asked. Martha had said: *I'll tell you when you're older.* But that day had never come.

"What do we do now?" Dean said.

Brad didn't answer right away, just looked at them with some unreadable expression. *He's wondering if he should just kill us both now,* she thought. *He's wondering what use we are to him.* Her numbness gave way to a feeling of desperation. She had to get them out of this. Not her and Dean—her and her baby.

Dean put his head in his hands. She hated him in that moment. What had she seen in him? What was it about him that had caused her to fall in love? He was like a drug she'd become addicted to, so good the first time. Every time after that was just a poor facsimile of that initial high. What had Carol said? *They're always nice at first, honey. That's how they hook you.*

She wrapped her arms around her belly. She'd missed her period last month, and a week ago, when the day came and went again, she'd taken a pregnancy test. Positive. She was pregnant at the same age her mother had been pregnant with her, in spite of Martha's many warnings.

It didn't feel real. She didn't have a sense of connection to the life growing inside her. She'd always loved the look of pregnant women, so flushed and full-bodied, so aware of the passenger within. She loved the careful way they lowered themselves into chairs, how they rested possessive hands on their bellies. But she didn't feel like one of them. It felt like a lie or a dream.

"Okay," said Brad. Apparently, he had some reason why he still needed them. "This is how things are going to go."

Birdie was sitting at the table with her tea service when Kate walked in. In the dark, she looked slight and stooped like a much older woman, as though the costume of the younger, more vital self she wore during the day had been cast aside.

"What are you doing, Mom?" Kate closed the door behind her.

"Remembering," Birdie said.

It was a short answer, but it revealed more than Kate had come to expect from her mother. It was an invitation, wasn't it? It seemed as though Birdie had been waiting for her, as if she'd known Kate would come, in the way that only mothers know what their daughters will do and when. There was some uncanny connection that way, in spite of the distance that always had been between them.

"I thought I saw something—someone," said Kate. "I came to check on you."

"You're seeing things, too?"

"I don't think so, no." Maybe she was. She hadn't seen anything on her walk down the lighted path. There had been only the rain, the wind bending the trees, and the sound of her footfalls on the rocky path. She'd beamed her flashlight between the trees, but she only frightened a rabbit who hopped away into the black. She'd felt the aloneness, the isolation. Whatever she'd seen, there was no sign of it as she made the trip from the guest cabin to the main house.

She told her mother all of this, but Birdie didn't seem to be listening. Kate sat across from her mother, thinking not for the first time that the chairs at this table were hard—uncomfortable and unwelcoming.

"Remembering what?" Kate asked.

She left the flashlight on the table between them and placed the flare gun beside it. Birdie turned the light so it was facing away from them, as though its brightness pained her. The beam cast odd, ghoulish shadows on the far wall. The rain persisted, tapping on the roof and windows.

"What did she tell you about Richard Cameron and my mother?" Birdie asked.

The question sent a shock wave through Kate. It was both expected and unexpected. The answer was right on her tongue and, at the same time, buried deep.

"Who?" asked Kate. She was stalling; she already knew the answer.

"Caroline," said Birdie. "You two were always thick as thieves."

If anyone knew how to embed an insult, it was Birdie. Thieves. All they'd ever taken from Birdie were the things she'd already tossed aside. The truly sad part was that Birdie could have had them both—Kate and Caroline—had she ever put down her guard and opened her arms. They'd both been waiting all their lives to love and be loved by Birdie.

"We were close," said Kate. "That's true."

Birdie let out a grunt. It sounded sad as much as disdainful. In front of Birdie was a photo album. It was the album that Caroline had wanted for years. Birdie had always claimed it was lost, but here it was. It probably had been in the bunkhouse all this time.

Her mother opened the book to its final page, spreading her jeweled fingers wide across the photographs. Kate had always admired Birdie's hands, white and long-fingered, with delicate ropes of veins pressing against the translucent skin, always perfectly manicured. As she aged, Birdie's hands only seemed more regal. Kate had gotten the Burke hands, wide and too thick, she'd always thought, to be attractive on a woman.

Your father's people come from peasant stock, Birdie always said. So Kate thought of her hands as peasant hands, designed for hard labor. She imagined generations of thick-handed women beating laundry and diapering babies, milking cows, tending fields, cooking stew, serving meals. In another century, maybe she would have been one of them.

Birdie thinks that anyone who works for a living is a peasant, her father said. *But our people built this country, carried it on their backs. You can be proud of that.* Kate didn't know if that was true. Her grandfather on her father's side was a Wall Street man. Her great-grandfather was with the railroad. It seemed to her that the Burke family had always found ways to make money, peasant stock or not.

"A long time ago, when I was a child," said Birdie, "I saw them together—Richard Cameron and your grandmother. My mother slipped away in the night and met him on that island where John Cross built his house. Until two nights ago, I thought it was a dream. That's what my mother told me, that I was dreaming."

Birdie flipped the photo over, and Kate saw what her grandmother had written there: *It wasn't a dream, darling. I'm so sorry.*

"All these years, I remembered that morning with such shame," said Birdie. "They all laughed at me, mocked me. But I *did* see her run away to him."

Kate was startled by Birdie's hand on hers. "What do you know?" her mother asked.

Kate took her hand away. There was a time when she craved contact from her mother. But now she could hardly stand it. "Does it really matter, Mother?"

"It matters," said Birdie. "I need to know."

In Kate's mind, the story was a romantic one, tragic and violent but somehow beautiful. She knew it wouldn't be that for her mother. It would be the story of betrayal and infidelity. Birdie could only find it ugly and wrong and would judge the players harshly. She would indict Lana and Richard and maybe even Jack.

But Kate didn't have any choice now; she couldn't control how others would view her grandmother's affair with Richard Cameron.

"They were lovers," said Kate. The words sounded weak and ordinary, not right for how she understood the relationship. "They met here, on these islands, when they were children. And they loved each other."

It sounded so simple. In her journals, Lana had painted such a picture of the two of them swimming and climbing rocks, knowing even then that they were meant to be together. Kate, in this moment, did not feel up to the task of telling it. The journals she'd brought for her mother were tucked away in the upstairs bedroom. Kate had figured that if she didn't have the nerve to talk to her mother before she left, she'd tell her about the journals once she was back home. Sometimes, when it came to Birdie, Kate felt like a coward.

Kate went on. "But ultimately, she married Grandpa—who came from a better family and who was a better man. She tried to give Richard Cameron up. But she couldn't. He waited for her here every summer until he died."

Birdie released a long slow breath and, for a long moment, didn't say a word. The rain had started again. "Did my father know?" she asked finally.

"I'm not sure what he knew. Something," said Kate. "I only know what Caroline wrote in her journals and what Lana wrote in hers."

"I always thought they loved each other," said Birdie. She sounded grief-stricken. "Their relationship was always so tender."

"She loved Grandpa Jack," said Kate. Caroline hadn't thought so, but Kate believed differently. "She did. They were great friends. She admired him, considered him her partner in this life, the father of her children. But did she have with him what she had with Richard? I don't think so. They were different men. She loved them differently."

Birdie didn't say anything, her eyes cast down to the table.

Kate went on, "On the other hand, her relationship with Richard was tempestuous, unpredictable. There was violence between them. When it was time to choose, when she had to decide between them, she married Jack."

Kate thought of what Caroline had written: *She chose sanity, security, the kind of gentle and easy love my father offered. It was enough for her in so many ways. But at the same time, her appetite for Richard never died, not until he did. She wilted all year without him, coming alive again only in the summer. It was their stolen time. I wonder if my father knew all along. If it was a bargain he made to have her with him the rest of the year.*

"She told you all of this?" asked Birdie. "Caroline confided all of this to you?"

"No," said Kate. "Not while she lived. It was all in the journals she left to me."

Birdie leaned away from the table. In the dim light, her face was a blank mask, no emotion registering at all. Kate knew her well enough to understand that her anger was gathering like a storm. The rage would come later, someplace unpredictable, chosen for maximum impact.

"And you didn't think I'd want to know about this?" Birdie said.

"I've been searching for a way to tell you," said Kate. "I knew it would only hurt you. I felt that you wouldn't understand—or forgive."

"And this book you've written," Birdie said. "I suppose now I know what it's about."

Kate smiled, though it almost hurt to do so. How could Birdie know that? Was Kate so obvious, so transparent? This was not the conversation she'd wanted to have with her mother about her book. She'd imagined it so differently. But that was just a fantasy, one of many she'd had about her mother. It was a fantasy to imagine her mother as proud, excited, and giving. It had been silly to hope that Birdie could share Kate's passion for the story that had reignited her will to write. She wanted to tell her mother about the emotional journey she'd taken via Caroline's journal. And how Lana's words had been an intimate window into a time before Kate was ever born. But she couldn't do that. She said instead what she had intended to say to anyone who asked about the inspiration for her novel.

"My book is a work of fiction. It is inspired by actual events from journals left to me by Caroline. But the characters in my novel and its events are fictionalized to the point of being unrecognizable. It's not about anyone or anything real, not truly."

"That's convenient."

"It's true," said Kate.

"Don't pretend you don't want to hurt me," said Birdie. "It's all you've ever wanted. To get even because you think I was a horrible mother."

The accusation stung, and Kate felt tears spring to her eyes. How was it that her own mother knew her not at all? "You're wrong, Mom," she said. "I've wanted so many things over the course of my life, but revenge was never one of them. I know you did your best, as we all do with our children."

Birdie let out an ugly laugh. "Oh, that's rich," she said. But she didn't go on.

Kate wasn't sure what Birdie found so funny and disdainful. She'd learned long ago not to answer those goading statements that implied she'd done or said something awful, laughable, or insulting.

Instead, Kate asked a question she'd been wanting to ask for as long as she could remember. "Why are you so angry, Mom? Why have you always been so angry at everyone? Why do you push everyone away and then act surprised when they finally go?"

The questions seemed to drain the energy from the room, and Birdie's head sank into her hands. "I don't know," she said at last. "I really don't know."

Kate didn't have time to be surprised by Birdie's answer. There was a loud knock on the door. Birdie looked up at Kate, startled. It took a second for Kate to register that there was somebody standing on the porch. Two people. She could see them through the glass.

"Who is that?" asked Birdie. Her voice was thin and shaky. Kate got up, but Birdie reached across the table and put a hand on her arm. "Don't," she said.

"We need help." It was the voice of a young woman, her tone desperate and afraid. "We've crashed our boat. We're stranded."

Kate reached for the flare gun, but Birdie stopped her. "There's a gun in the cabinet."

"Who's with you?" Kate called as she reached for the weapon. She was surprised by its weight as she brought it down. A quick glance at the chamber told her it was fully loaded.

"My fiancé," the voice from outside replied. "Please. We're in trouble. Our boat—it's sinking."

Kate looked at her mother, who was standing, staring hard at the door. Birdie reached out for the gun, and Kate handed it to her.

"Should I go to the door?" she asked. Birdie looked her straight in the eye; Kate could see the uncertainty, the hesitation.

"What choice do we have?" said Birdie finally. "They're on the island."

Kate knew what she meant. If it was trouble, it was already here; the perimeter had been breached, and they had no choice but to face it head-on. Kate walked over to the door and opened it.

Heartbroken

Two young people in their mid-twenties stood wet and shivering on the porch. The girl looked sad and frightened. The young man was nervous, fidgety, with the eyes of a con man. Kate would look back and think she knew in that moment that nothing good could follow.

chapter twenty-four

Sean had a feeling he should leave after the open·house. It was something in his gut that told him he should go straight over to his mom's, pick up Brendan, and get right on the road. But Kate had made him promise, if he was tired, to wait until Monday morning. And for a number of reasons, he *was* tired, bone-tired.

He hadn't slept at all the night before, going over details in his mind for the open house—what to serve, what needed staging, what needed tidying or rearranging. He'd run around like a crazy person all day, getting everything ready, putting up signs, sending e-mails to his favorite clients, making calls to people who'd reached out to him in the past. *It's one of my favorite houses ever,* he'd said about a million times. And it was true.

By the time four o'clock rolled around, everything was perfect. He was hopped up on Red Bull. His partner, Jane, was there, ready and raring to go. It was the first house of the year that wasn't being sold out of sheer desperation. In his heart, he felt it heralded a recovery for the market. He couldn't have said why; there were still plenty of foreclosures. It just felt like a new beginning.

But then it was four o'clock, and then it was five. One couple walked through quickly. He could tell by the woman's shoes and bag that it was a curiosity sweep. They didn't have the money to even *dream* about a house like this. As he stood at the bay window, a few cars cruised by, obviously attracted by the open-house signs. They slowed down, but no one stopped to come in.

Closer to six o'clock, Sean was sitting on the couch, looking out the picture window to the beautifully landscaped pool and hot tub. He didn't bother to wait by the door.

"If you don't need me," said Jane at six-thirty, "I think I'll go."

Jane was younger than Sean by about ten years. She was usually bubbly, unflappable. But tonight she looked tired, too. She hadn't yet ridden the highs and the lows of the market; she'd come in on the boom. The last year had been really hard. Sean was disappointed that the open house had been a flop. But Jane looked devastated.

"It's just the first showing," said Sean. He put on his pep-talk smile, but it felt as fake as it was. "Don't be discouraged."

"I'm not," she said. She gave him a quick wave, forced her expression to brighten. "Oh, no. I'm fine."

She was sweet, a nice girl with a husband and small kids. She was great with clients, but this was just her sideline. She was all about staying home and being a mom at the moment, which was nice. So few people seemed inclined to do that anymore.

"You'll see," she said. She gathered up her bag, her reusable coffee mug. "Next week it'll be a mob scene."

"Definitely," he said.

She headed toward the door, then turned back to him. She had a wild head of copper curls, a face of freckles. Everyone loved her, both women and men. It was a good trait in a salesperson, to be able to connect with everyone. If you were too sexy or good-looking, same-sex clients hated you and opposite-sex clients hit on you. She was right in the middle, attractive enough but solid and real, reliable. She had a mom-next-door energy.

"You okay?" she said.

"Yeah," he said. "I'm great. The house looks good, the price is right. We'll get some action next week." He got up to see her out.

"Have a good trip," she said. "Try to disconnect. I'll call right away if there are any bites."

And then she was gone. He watched her climb into her late-model BMW and drive off. Her husband made money, something to do with finance. She didn't have to worry. He was glad about that, at least.

When he couldn't see her car anymore, he let himself deflate. He was too experienced to be this disappointed by a bad open house. But he was. He cleaned up the deli platter, the cooler of water, and carried them to his car. He called the clients and told them that things had been a bit slow, no bites today, but the ads would all start running on Monday, and he was sure the week ahead promised good things. He wasn't sure of that at all.

After the call was finished, that was when the fatigue set in. He'd let the girls go on alone to the island for nothing. He hadn't felt good about it, but it might have been worth it for a killer first showing. Since things had gone badly, he felt like he'd wasted his time and let Kate down. He tried to call, but it went straight to voice mail, which meant that either her battery was dead or service was out. Kate would not be out of touch when she was separated from him and one of their kids. A tickling sense of unease started inside him.

But when he'd picked up Brendan, the kid looked like death warmed over. His ankle was more swollen and he was in more pain than when Sean had dropped him off.

"What's up, buddy?" he'd said. "Did you take it easy today?"

"Yeah," Brendan said. "It just hurts."

Sean had known as they pulled out of his mother's driveway that they should just get on the road. Brendan could rest in the car and take it easy on the island. But on two past occasions, Sean had fallen asleep at the wheel. Once, he drove onto the shoulder and came to a harmless stop. The next time, he'd nearly drifted into oncoming traffic, pulling out just in time. Kate and Chelsea had been in the car. He could still feel that rocket of adrenaline, the weak relief after disaster was avoided. He knew he couldn't take a chance. And Brendan easily agreed to wait until morning, which meant his ankle really hurt. If Kate had stayed, they'd be canceling the trip. But she was already up there.

At home, Sean gave Brendan some Tylenol and parked him in front of the television. He ordered Chinese food and tried to call Kate, then Chelsea, then the house. The calls to the girls went straight to voice mail. He got a perpetual busy signal at the house. It was normal for communications to be haywire on the island. It was like the place wanted to isolate you, to keep you for itself.

"Can we call Mom?" asked Brendan during dinner. They tried again. Still nothing. "I want to talk to Mom," he said miserably.

Sean put a blanket over him, a fresh ice pack on his ankle, and sat beside his son. "I know, pal," he said. "We'll get her in a bit."

The kids were attached to Kate in a way they couldn't be to Sean. It was a mom thing. He didn't take it personally—he had his own special bond with each of the children. But when comfort was needed, Mom was the only one who would do. Hell, even Sean wanted to talk to Kate and metabolize his feelings about the shitty open house. He wanted to hear her say, "Hang in there, babe. It's a great house, and you're the man to sell it." Maybe it wasn't fair that they all leaned so heavily on her, but that's the way it was.

While watching *The Lord of the Rings* for the hundredth time, they both fell asleep on the couch. When Sean opened his eyes again, it was midnight. He managed to get Brendan up to his room and into bed. After that, he found an e-mail from Kate, telling him that service was intermittent and he shouldn't be worried that he couldn't reach them and she hadn't called.

But Sean, she wrote. *Leave first thing, if you're not on your way already. This place . . . I don't want to be here without you. Mom's not feeling well and things are weird. I'm worried about Brendan. How's his ankle? Why didn't we just wait and come with you?*

He wrote back: *I was too wrecked to drive tonight. I'm going to get some sleep and be on my way before the sun comes up. Hang in there. I love you and I'm with you.*

There was no response. He set his alarm to get four hours of sleep, but he just lay there staring at the ceiling, where a hairline crack was starting near the light fixture. *A crack on the ceiling had the habit of sometimes looking like a rabbit.* A line from a book he used to read to Chelsea. What was it? *Madeline,* of course.

He closed his eyes finally and fell asleep with the phone and laptop on the bed beside him. He began to dream fitfully. He was on the island with Kate. They were standing on the dock, looking up toward the house.

"I don't want to come back here anymore," she said.

"We don't have to," he answered.

Just as he said those words, he saw flames jutting up from the roof of the main house. He smelled smoke, hot and acrid in his nose.

"It's on fire," he said. He felt utterly calm.

"I did it," Kate answered. She looked peaceful in a way she never had there. "I'm burning it to the ground."

In his pocket, his phone was ringing and ringing. It was a strange, bubbling noise, like an electronic ripple underwater. "Aren't you going to answer that?" said Kate. But Sean couldn't find a phone in any of his pockets.

It went on and on until Sean woke up and saw that it was the Skype phone on his computer. The window on his screen said, *Chelsea's laptop calling.* He dove for it and clicked on the accept button. He expected to see Kate, but it was Chelsea on the screen. She looked pale and tired; she was looking at something off camera. "Dad?" she said. "Daddy?"

"Hey, kiddo," he said. He was so glad to see her, felt flooded with relief. "What's going on over there? I've been trying to reach you guys all night."

"Dad, listen," she said. She moved in close to the camera, but she was looking at his image on the screen, not into the lens, so it had the effect of her looking down. There was something odd in her tone of voice.

"What is it?" He felt the first jangle of alarm.

"Dad," she said. "There's someone on the island. I saw them walking toward the main house. We're in trouble."

"What are you talking about, Chelsea?" he said. Was this some kind of joke? It didn't seem real. "You're freaking me out."

"Something woke me up, and I was looking out the window," she said. "I saw Mom go to the main house. Then a little while later, I saw two other people. I don't know what to do. The phones aren't working. But I got Skype to work with that rocket stick you gave me. Should I go after her?"

"No, no," he said. He felt a blast of adrenaline; pure fear pulsed through his system. "Just stay on the line with me. Tell me what you heard. I'll call the cops." He was reaching frantically about for the phone. Where was it? It had fallen to the floor. "Daddy?" she said. "There's a bad storm, but I don't think what I heard just now was thunder. What should I do?"

"Listen—"

"Can you hear me?" He saw her pick up the computer and give it a little shake. "I can't hear you."

"Oh, Christ."

"Dad," said Chelsea, "I'm scared. I think there's something really wrong."

In the next second, her image froze. The screen read, *Connection lost.*

chapter twenty-five

Roger Murphy had always been a deep, heavy sleeper. Once upon a time, he used to lie down beside his wife, Lydia, at ten P.M. and wake up exactly eight hours later in the same position, on his back, arms over his head. But since his wife had died two years ago after a protracted battle with cancer, insomnia was his new roommate. He knew the night in a way he never had. With Lydia, he lived his life in the daylight hours, like everyone else. Without her, he roamed the house in the dead of night, sifting through their drift of photographs, old cards, and love letters, waiting for the first break of dawn. Grief was too shallow, too weak, a word for what he knew after Lydia's death. He was halved, cored out. He was the walking dead.

He was so relieved for her when she finally passed. Her illness had taken over their lives, turned their home into a hospital, every shelf and surface a resting place for bottles of pills, books on dealing with cancer, holistic remedies, meditation CDs—later, the morphine ampoules he'd learned to inject, the final soldiers in the legion of pain-relief drugs.

When she released her last breath, he'd been so happy that she didn't have to suffer anymore that he'd actually experienced a few hours of joy for her. It was as if she'd gone off on a wonderful journey, and he was so relieved for her that it hadn't dawned on him yet that he'd been ruthlessly left behind. The next two days, he thought about joining her. But in the end, he was a coward, rooted to this death in life without her. She'd always been the brave one, the adventurer, the daredevil. He was always on the ground watching her skydive, or ride the roller coaster, or climb the bridge. *You're my rock,* she told him. *You're the place where I am moored.* They had no children. It had just never happened, and neither of them spent much time trying to figure out why. He was glad for that, too, after she passed. There shouldn't be anyone else left in her wake, floundering, wondering how life could possibly go on, angry that it did for everyone else with such ease. Lord knows he wouldn't have been much use to anyone needing comfort from the loss of her.

Now he was just marking days. His pension was fully vested; he could retire anytime. He knew his superiors *wanted* him to retire, that he was widely regarded as so far past his prime as to be a liability. He was pushing sixty-five and dangerously out of shape. Still, no one in the department knew the town or the community the way he did. That could not be denied. He was mainly behind a desk, anyway. Besides, if he gave up the job, the only constant in his life now that Lydia was gone, what would he become?

The younger guys took the occasional calls for break-ins—recently an armed robbery, some domestic complaints. It was a small town with little crime, and the young guys were sitting on their hands until they transferred out to someplace with more action. But today he took the ride out to Heart Island because he hadn't seen Birdie Heart in years. John Cross had made it clear that it wasn't an emergency situation. Roger was fine on calls like that.

Insomnia had given him the gift of reading. He'd taken to buying books online, since there wasn't a decent bookstore for miles. He had a great stack collecting around the big old recliner by the fireplace. Lydia had always begged him to get rid of that chair. It was a terrible eyesore, brown and morphed to the shape of his body from hours of unapologetic lazing and dozing. Lydia claimed that it gave off an odor, which he had never been able to detect.

Now that she was gone, he sat in the thing most nights, reading—Lee Child, Michael Connelly, George Pelecanos, Stephen King, and

Elmore Leonard. He liked the old greats, such as Ross Macdonald, James Lee Burke, and Raymond Chandler. He liked his books dark and easy, written by men, full of guns and women. He didn't mind Patricia Highsmith. Even though she was a woman, she wrote like a man. He wanted to go someplace when he picked up a book, anyplace but where he was.

He'd read almost all the Richard Cameron books. The author had spent his summers on the island now owned by John Cross. Roger remembered, as a kid, seeing Cameron and thinking he was a weird one. Cameron had come and gone without a word of thanks, never tipped Roger at the fuel dock.

There had been rumors that he and the Heart woman were lovers. Roger had never seen any evidence of that. He'd always tried to ignore local gossip. Of course, the rumor mill had gone wild when Richard Cameron's body was found. Some people said that Jack and Lana Heart had visited their island in the beginning of winter on separate boats. Some suspected that their visit had something to do with Richard Cameron's death.

By that time of year, Roger was back in school, so he never saw anything. It sounded to him like the noise of too many mouths that talk and too few minds that think—a line he loved from a book he read once. Bored people looked for drama and caused trouble. He was no better. When John Cross had asked about Richard Cameron, Roger had told him all the rumors that had floated around back then. What did it matter now? It was ancient history. The guy had a lot of questions, and Roger had been all too happy to answer them. Why was he so interested? Roger didn't know. There were plenty of rumors about John Cross, one of which was that he was a distant relation of Cameron's. But Cross had made no mention of that.

There had always been a lot of attention paid to the Heart family. Caroline and Birdie were the prettiest girls he had ever seen. Their mother, Lana, looked like a movie star, with her wavy hair and red lips. The girls were like flowers, sweet and willowy, always flanking their much taller brother, Gene. Jack was a big tipper with a booming voice and an easy laugh. Everybody loved them. They spent a lot of money in town and were always friendly, not like some of the other New York summer people. If anyone ever suspected that they really had anything to do with Richard Cameron's death, nobody ever said a word to the authorities. Richard Cameron was a drunk and a depressive. His death didn't come as a surprise to anyone, nor did anyone in Blackbear mourn him.

Roger was at the beginning of Ross Macdonald's *The Drowning Pool* when the phone rang. He looked at the clock: one A.M. He couldn't remember the last time the phone had rung in the middle of the night. It took some effort, but he hefted himself up to answer.

chapter twenty-six

It was nice to be welcomed, offered a seat and a cup of tea. Emily felt so warm and comforted that she could almost forget that Brad was waiting outside.

Emily didn't remember this house; it wasn't the house she'd visited when she was a girl. She couldn't help staring at Kate, who she could tell was Joe Burke's other daughter. *You're my sister,* she wanted to say. But the timing wasn't right.

The other woman, Birdie, was looking straight at her. They'd never met; Birdie couldn't possibly recognize her. Still, she stared at Emily intently, as though trying to place her face. Perhaps she saw some resemblance to her husband. Whatever Birdie saw, it didn't make her warm to Emily. Her gaze was severe and unyielding; it made Emily squirm inside. Birdie was the woman Joe had picked over her mother; she didn't see how it was possible. Where was he? Surely, if he were here, one of them would have gone to wake him. She looked around at the closed doors, wondering whether he was sleeping behind one.

"We rented an island," said Emily. "But we got lost on the way there." It sounded lame, like the lie that it was. She had never been a very good liar; even necessity hadn't helped with that.

"What island?" asked Birdie.

"Cooke Island," said Emily. She just made it up.

"I've never heard of it," said Birdie. "And I've been coming here all my life. You must have come in at the wrong marina."

"Yes," said Kate. She was kinder, softer. She'd been the one to offer tea and a blanket. She'd started the fire. "It's easy to lose your way out here, especially at night."

Dean was tense and silent beside Emily. She could feel his leg twitching. They were supposed to lead someone outside, where Brad was waiting to subdue the family one by one. He would tie them up and take whatever money and valuables they had, plus the money from the Blue Hen. Then he would take the boat on the dock and leave. That was his promise. He swore he wouldn't hurt anyone. Emily wasn't foolish enough to believe that, not after what he had done. She was just biding her time. When her father appeared, she was going to tell him the truth. And he was going to fix everything. That's how it was going to go.

"We're a bit stuck until morning, I'm afraid," Kate went on. "Hopefully, by then the bad weather will have cleared, and communications will be restored."

"It's odd that you would venture out into unfamiliar waters in weather like this," said Birdie. "Most people would stay on shore until morning."

"Rob grew up on boats," Emily said. She tried for a smile that said, *Men. What are we to do with them?* "He thought we could manage."

"We found the boat we rented in its slip," said Dean. "We had the map. It seemed doable."

It was the first time he'd spoken since introducing himself as Rob. Emily was Anne, her middle name.

"I'd like to see that map," said Birdie.

Dean shrugged. "It's on the boat, which is half under water by now." There was no trace of the lie in his voice. Emily marveled at that. How many lies had he told her, just like that? It came so easily to him, more easily than the truth, it seemed.

"We should try to see to that," said Kate. There was a flash of lightning and a powerful clap of thunder.

"Leave it till morning," said Birdie. "You shouldn't be mucking about in this weather."

"I think Rob and I should try to rescue the boat."

Emily wanted to jump up and stop her. *No,* she wanted to say, *don't go out there.* But she was afraid. Brad had said he'd be listening at the door. "You say one word I don't like, and I'll kill them all," he'd promised her. That, she believed.

Kate was looking at Birdie, who was frowning in return. The look on the older woman's face was harsh and disapproving. In the moment, Emily felt kindred to Kate. She knew what it was like to grow up under the frown of disapproval. You imagined it everywhere for the rest of your life.

"It's not a good idea," said Birdie. "You won't pull it out if it's sinking."

"But we could tie it off," said Kate. Her tone was brisk, brooking no further discussion.

"Isn't there someone else?" said Emily quickly. "Someone stronger."

Kate was already moving toward the door, pulling on a rain jacket. For some reason, she didn't answer Emily. Kate looked so much like their father. She had his powerful, purposeful way about her, a kind of quiet strength and confidence. Kate had his sunny blond hair, his tanned skin. She had the same aura of wealth and ease. Emily knew that she herself didn't look anything like Joe; she hadn't inherited her mother's beauty, either. She was surprised by a dizzying flash of jealousy for this woman, her half sister, who had gotten all of Joe Burke for herself. For a second, Emily felt a welling of anger and sadness that their paths should cross this way. In another life, they might have been close. Emily wouldn't be such a wreck, her life about to burst into flames, if things had been different.

"Is there anyone else on the island?" asked Dean. He seemed to realize that it sounded like an odd question. "Someone who could help?"

"No," said Kate. She looked away from them. "There's no one."

Kate Burke wasn't a good liar, either. Emily's heart soared. He *was* here. He was. Kate looked at Emily now. It was a searching gaze, a wondering.

"Of course, there's always John Cross," said Birdie, too quickly.

"Yes," said Kate. She glanced out the window, as if to catch sight of him.

"Our neighbor," said Birdie. Her voice sounded a little high, had the pitch of nervousness. "He's quite the busybody. He seems to see everything that goes on over here. But he's quite helpful. If we need him, he'll come right away."

Emily knew the old woman was trying to tell them that they were not as alone here as they imagined. That if they were up to no good, the neighbor across the water might be watching. These people were frightened. Two strangers had shown up on their island in the middle of the night. Who wouldn't be concerned? And they didn't know the half of it.

"You said the phone lines were down," said Dean.

"We can always take the boat across the channel," said Birdie. "Even in this weather. After all, you made it from the mainland."

There was an electric tension in the air.

"Well," said Kate. She looked at Dean. "Shall we?"

Dean and Kate walked out onto the porch, and Emily heard them going down the stairs. Then there was silence. She had the urge to run after them, to stop Brad from doing whatever it was he was planning to do. But she stayed rooted, pulled the blanket tighter around herself. It was a second before she sensed Birdie's gaze on her.

She turned to face the older woman. She wasn't pretty at all, and Emily couldn't imagine that she ever had been, not the way her mother had been.

"Now that he's gone," said Birdie, "why don't you tell me who you are and what's really going on here."

The boat was grounded on the east side of the island, taking on water. It listed to the side, and Kate could see that there was a breach in the hull where it had hit a rock. It was swaying in the choppy water.

Her intention was to retrieve the lines for the boat and tie it to a nearby tree. Now she could see that it was a dangerous errand, maybe a foolish one. The wind had picked up again, and when she yelled to the young man, asking him where the lines might be, he shrugged. It had been a bad idea to come out here alone with him; she knew that. But she had wanted to see the boat, to see if they were lying. Here it was. The vessel was clearly in distress. She felt some measure of relief. Maybe they *were* just a young couple in trouble.

She waded into the water while the young man waited on shore, looking useless. The wind was a sound vacuum. It was all she could hear in her head. She could no longer see his face, lost as it was in the dark of his hood. The cold water soaked through her shoes, her pants legs, and her feet started to ache with it.

She called to him to help her push it farther up on shore. He just stood there. Did he not hear her? Her heart was starting to thump. She glanced back at the guest cabin, which was dark. She hoped the girls were asleep and that they would stay where they were until morning, or at least until she knew what was happening.

In the next lightning flash, she saw the whole island bright as day. The rumble of thunder followed. She walked around the back of the boat. Why was he standing there? She was about to push when she noticed the boat name: *Serendipity*. With a flood of dread, she recognized it as belonging to friends of her parents who lived several islands away. They definitely did not rent out their island or their vessel. Shit.

Another skein of lightning, flashing like a strobe, was followed by a loud crack. Something had gotten hit; Kate couldn't see what. When she looked back toward shore, Rob was gone. Her breath was coming shallow and fast. She quickly grabbed the lines that were still tied off on the cleats and got out of the water. Maybe he'd run, afraid of the storm, or afraid that she'd discovered his lie. If she were smart, she'd get inside, too.

She brought the lines around and tied off on a nearby birch that leaned toward the water. The rain was coming hard and fast, still deafening. In the next wash of light, she saw someone moving toward her fast.

The next thing she knew, there were hands on her, dragging her back toward shore. This man was bigger, stronger, than the one who'd come in out of the rain. He was impossibly powerful, lifting her effortlessly as she screamed and thrashed, writhing to be free of his grip around her chest.

Her mind was a siren of panic, but it caused something primal to come alive in her, forcing her to fight with all her strength. It was not enough. Her breath was coming hard and too shallow; his arms were a vise.

In the next lightning flash, she saw Rob standing on the shore.

"Rob!" she yelled. Her voice sounded like a whisper to her own ears. She could hardly draw a breath into her aching lungs. There was a dancing of white stars before her eyes. "Help me!"

Finally, he came toward her, holding a coil of rope in his hands. A scream escaped her, but it sounded strangled and weak. Anyway, who was there to hear her—her teenage daughter and friend, her seventy-five-year-old mother? No one would hear in the storm. Kate was on her own. She thought about Brendan and Sean, wished for the hundredth time that she had waited for them. What were these men going to do to her? To all of them?

Instead of reaching for her, Rob looped the rope around the larger man's neck and started pulling hard. The man released Kate suddenly, and she fell to the ground. She felt a blessed relief from the crushing grip on her chest as air swept into her lungs.

She lay weak and helpless for a moment as the two men struggled and then fell to the ground. Every nerve ending in her body throbbed with fear while she watched them in their horrifying dance. She started crawling away, the breath slowly returning to her body. She saw a flash and heard a sharp report.

Her mother had taught her how to shoot a gun on this very island, and she recognized the sound. But where the shot came from, she couldn't tell. The two men still struggled, one mass of rage in the storm.

Crushed by sound and wind, by a white bolt of terror that shot right through her, she didn't know what to think or do. She found herself obeying the only instinct she had: get to her child. She gathered her strength and started to run as best as she could for the guesthouse.

chapter twenty-seven

In all his life, Dean Freeman had wanted only one thing: to not be the worthless piece of crap his father always thought he was. But that desire seemed a distant memory, a dream he'd had and couldn't quite remember. He felt tired now, and so cold. Brad loomed over him like some kind of ghoul, panting and staring down at him. A long time ago, they'd been friends. Not that Brad hadn't always been a cold-hearted bastard. But Dean remembered liking the guy once. This was not how he'd thought things would go between them when they used to drink beer under the palm trees on Clearwater Beach, hiding the case under a blanket so the cops wouldn't see.

The pain in his center was so intense that there was no sound he could make. It seemed to spread from his middle and down his legs like some kind of silent scream. With every breath he took, he felt more blood gush from his side. It was thick and warm against his hand. He wasn't afraid. Maybe he should be, but he found he wasn't. *I'm sorry, Emily.*

How was it, with every good intention every time, he'd wound up here on this rock in the middle of a lake, on the run from the law?

If he looked back, it was that day with Ronny that had led him here. If Dean had only been able to hold his temper, to take whatever criticism the man had offered and done his job, none of this ever would have happened. Because of all the times in his life, only when he was working and living with Emily was he ever happy. He could see how people, normal people, did it—how they worked and fell in love, got married and had a family. He could see how people just lived without some big scheme on the horizon or something from the past chasing them. It had seemed, for a little while, that Dean could be one of those people.

"Tell me where the safe is." Brad's voice sounded gravelly and strange. "There are three houses. Which one has the safe in it?"

Dean wanted to answer, he really did. But he couldn't. All he could do was look at the shadow standing behind Brad. It was a tall, dark smudge against the night sky, and Dean couldn't think of who it might be or why the person would be standing there in the rain.

"Can you tell Emily that I'm sorry?" said Dean. Except he didn't say the words; he spoke them in his mind. Of all the many things he regretted, he regretted the most that he had let her down. He regretted dropping out of school and letting those losers talk him into coming along on the armed robbery. He regretted the first pill he popped into his mouth and every one after that. But more than anything, he had wanted to be a good man for her. It was simply that on some very deep level, he didn't know what that meant. It had always remained just out of his reach.

"Answer me, asshole," said Brad. He leaned heavily on the wound, and Dean felt a bottle rocket of pain from his gut to his toes. He let out an inhuman scream, a sound he couldn't believe came from his own body, and Brad—he smiled. Now Brad pressed the warm muzzle of the gun to Dean's head.

The black form moved closer to Dean and towered over Brad. Maybe it was Dean's eyes playing tricks on him, because Brad didn't seem to notice.

Dean was happy about one thing, though: that he'd brought Emily home. She had always talked about this place like it was some kind of paradise. She'd idolized the father who had abandoned her to her shitty childhood growing up with Martha—a meaner or more morose bitch he had never known. He could admit to himself that his intentions had not been honorable; he'd wanted to come here and take what should have belonged to Emily anyway. He wanted to make those people pay for what they'd taken from her. If he was honest, that had been his intent long before Brad had shown up and made it possible. Even though he had not planned it as a homecoming for her, maybe that's what it would be. Maybe now that she was here, her father would be forced to accept her and help her. If not for Emily's sake, then for their baby's.

He started to cry then, to blubber like a girl. Brad turned his face away in disgust. The dark shadow began spreading like a fog, and Dean felt it settle over him, cool and comforting. He closed his eyes and surrendered to it, thinking it could hardly be worse than other places he'd been.

chapter twenty-eight

Kate crashed into the guesthouse and locked the door behind her. The thin wood frame with glass panes wouldn't keep anyone out. She peered into the rain, but she had no more than a few feet of visibility. She leaned against the door and then sank to the ground, trying to catch her breath, to calm her mind. Her chest ached, and each breath was painful. Around her, a mass of jackets hung on hooks; a clutter of shoes lined the baseboard. The water from her clothes ran off onto the floor. She tried to notice the details around her in order to expand the moment, to conquer the panic clouding her mind. It wasn't working.

"Mom?" Chelsea stood looking small and terrified as she appeared at the end of the hall. "What's happening?"

She dropped beside Kate and climbed into her arms, not seeming to care that her mother was soaking wet. Kate held on tight. Her first instinct was to lie. *Nothing. Everything's fine. Go back to sleep.* The thought of telling Chelsea what had just happened, what she had seen, went against every desire she had to shelter and protect her child.

"Did you see him?" Chelsea asked. "Did you see the ghost?"

Kate *really* wished she'd seen a ghost. She told her daughter what had happened, starting with the knock on the door and the stranded couple, whoever they were.

Chelsea sat up and stared at Kate, her face still and calm. "There's a gun," she said when Kate was done. It was not what she had expected Chelsea to say. "In the main house."

"We saw it when we were getting dinner ready." It was Lulu, who had come to join them.

"Get down," said Kate. "Come here." She held out her arm to Lulu, who crawled over to Kate. The three of them huddled together in front of the door. It was then that they heard footsteps on the porch. Chelsea issued a little whimper as they listened to the sound of someone heavily climbing the steps, then walking the length of the house. They saw a shadow pass in front of the window above them, listening as the footfalls continued on and then stopped again.

Kate could hear the sound of the blood rushing in her ears, the girls trying to control their frightened breathing, the rain on the roof. The moment seemed unreal, took on a dreamlike quality. She thought of the flare gun, which she'd left on the table in the main house. She should have kept it with her when she went out to the boat. She was defenseless here with the girls. At least Birdie was armed.

It seemed like days ago that she had been sitting there, telling her mother about Richard Cameron's affair with Lana. What had seemed grim and serious not an hour ago seemed silly now—luxury worries, as Sean would call them. The kinds of things that people who had no business worrying worried about.

Kate carefully extracted herself from the girls, who both clung a moment and then let her crawl away, keeping herself below the windows that lined the hallway.

"Mom," Chelsea whispered.

Kate held up a hand. She had to see where he was, what he was doing. She couldn't sit there and wait for him to come in after them, the three of them helpless and afraid. She peered over the sill in time to see him standing, looking over toward the main house. She could see the soaking strands of his hair, the profile of a broken nose, the large square shoulders. Who was he? What did he want here? He turned back toward her, and she froze. He seemed to be staring right at her, though he stood as still as stone. He seemed oblivious to the rain. Finally, he started moving down the far stairs.

She watched him until he was swallowed by darkness. From the porch, he must have seen the light burning in the main house. That must be where he was headed. She felt a rush of raw adrenaline. "Girls," she said, "I need you to get to the bunkhouse and call for help on the radio."

She didn't want them coming to the main house with her, if that's where the danger was. She'd send them in the opposite direction, keeping them away from the threat. At least that was her thinking.

"I called Dad on Skype a while ago," said Chelsea. "I couldn't hear him. I don't know if he could hear me, but I told him that I thought someone was on the island, that we might be in trouble."

"Okay," Kate said. She thought about Sean, how frantic he must be. What would he do? He'd call the local police if he'd heard Chelsea at all. "Where was he?"

"Home, I think."

Kate remembered asking him not to get on the road if he was too tired to drive. For once, he must have listened. It figured that this would be the time he took her advice on caution and safety. She bent down in front of the girls. "We have to operate as if he didn't hear you," she said. "Can you handle it? Can you make it to the bunkhouse and call for help?"

Lulu looked down at the ground, then up at Kate. Chelsea took Lulu's hand.

"We can do it," said Chelsea.

"Yeah," said Lulu. "We can handle it."

Kate felt a little shock at the strength, the mettle, she saw in her child's eyes. There was enough of Birdie in her to get them through this. There was enough of Birdie in Kate, too. Kate stood and fished through the jackets on the hooks and found what she was looking for: two whistles, one red and one silver. She hung one around Lulu's neck and one around Chelsea's. "If you get into trouble, blow, scream, make noise," she told them.

Lulu looked pale and shocked in spite of how confident she'd seemed a moment ago. Kate knew she could trust Chelsea to keep her cool and do what needed to be done. She hoped Lulu was up to the task as well.

"Stay together," she instructed. "Don't separate. And once you get to the bunkhouse, lock the door and don't leave. No matter what you hear, stay inside."

"What are you going to do?" asked Chelsea.

"Your grandmother is alone over there," she said.

It was all she could come up with. She had no idea what she was going to do. She didn't think it was a good idea to say so. Chelsea and Lulu looked at her uncertainly, as if they knew she was flying blind. The girls pulled on raincoats and shoes, and then they all left the guesthouse together.

My husband always had a soft spot for strays. The words kept ringing in Emily's ears.

When Emily was small, she used to have nightmares in which she was falling. Not those short, jerky dreams that left her flailing out arms and legs. They were long and slow; at first they felt like flying. But they didn't end, and she couldn't control them. She just went down and down and down. That's how she felt now, staring at Birdie.

"I remember your mother," said Birdie. "She thought she'd won the jackpot."

Emily watched her. Birdie sat perfectly erect, her shoulders a straight line, her elbows resting lightly on the table. Her gaze was cool and level, like that of an executive in a boardroom, a judge at her bench.

"Little did she know that everything belonged to me, including this island."

All of Emily's words were jammed in her throat.

"Joe earned a good living," said Birdie, "but the real wealth came from my family. Joe wouldn't give that up. Not for something as worthless as love."

There was something about the way she had said it. *Now that he's gone, why don't you tell me who you are and what's really going on here.* It had sounded to Emily as if Birdie might understand, or maybe she already knew. Emily felt a strong desire to confess, as if in doing so, she might be welcomed here, to take her place among the family. She thought maybe Joe could be called and there would be some way to work it all out. Because if anyone could fix the things that had gone so terribly wrong, surely he could.

When Emily had said nothing at first, Birdie went on. *Let me help you, dear.*

We're lost, Emily had said. *We're stranded.*

And this was the God's honest truth, wasn't it?

Maybe Birdie could see that Emily was in dire straits. Truth be told, it was Dean's fault. She certainly wouldn't have been here if not for Dean and the things he'd done and asked her to do. Maybe Birdie could see that. And maybe, even though it was very hard to believe, maybe Birdie, too, had been in a circumstance beyond her control, following a man who was on the wrong path. Maybe once she'd needed a guiding hand, someone to help her out of a terrible mess she'd made. Emily allowed herself to believe that maybe, on some level, Birdie knew who she was and was offering to be that helping hand.

"I'm Emily," she said. It was almost a whisper. She saw Birdie lean in closer and narrow her eyes. "I'm Emily Burke. Joe Burke's daughter."

The other woman had frozen where she sat. Emily swore that when she looked into Birdie's eyes, she saw an iron gate come down. Her face turned into a blank mask, a shield. And Emily knew she'd made a horrible, horrible mistake. Outside, the rain was pounding on the roof, and the thunder was crashing.

"My husband doesn't have a child outside of our marriage," said Birdie. There was no heat, no emotion, in her voice. It was a cool statement of fact.

"He does," said Emily. She was drawing on a strength she didn't know she had. "And I would like to call him. I'm in trouble, and I need my father. He owes me that much. A phone call, at least."

Birdie smiled, but it wasn't warm. It was mocking. Emily felt a rise of shame, and with it came a lash of anger.

"My dear," said Birdie, "Joe Burke is *not* your father. I understand that perhaps your mother told you that—and indeed it seems that she gave you his last name. It would be just like her, considering what she tried to do to us. And I can see that you believe it to be true. But no, the tests were clear. I have no idea who your father might be. But it is not my husband."

"You're lying," said Emily. She felt an unwanted quaver in her center, a welling of tears. "He wrote checks every year, money for my education."

She saw a flicker of something across the old woman's face— anger, surprise. That was when Birdie said the thing about her husband having a soft spot for strays. And then she went on.

"Martha tricked him. She might have been another of his dalliances." Birdie gave a little laugh. "Of which, trust me, there were many. But his believing that her child belonged to him kept him around for a while. Eventually, she wanted more than the secret night out, a couple of weekends away. But by then he was on to the next. She tried a paternity suit. Hence, the tests. And the bitter out-come. I daresay that she believed you were his as well."

"This is a lie."

"But Joe is a softy for little girls," said Birdie. She still wore that unkind smile, offering a sad shake of her head. She either didn't hear Emily or didn't care. "I'm not surprised to learn he gave Martha money. Though I would have fought him tooth and nail had I known. Not that he has ever listened to a word I say."

There was a leaden silence between them. Birdie sniffed. "Joe will have his way. And I have been weak with him. That's my genera-tion, I suppose."

"You're lying."

It was all Emily could think to say. The sinking, empty feeling threatened to swallow her whole. There had been so many crushing disappointments in her life already. But to lose this—she didn't even know who she was without this. Without her memories of Joe and this magical place, there was nothing golden, only ash.

"Anyway, the money was enough for your mother," said Birdie. She played with a heart locket she wore around her neck, moving the clasp between her fingers. "We never heard from her again. So, I sup-pose, in that way, it was worth it. It spared me further humiliation."

He doesn't want us, Emily, Martha had told her. *He doesn't want you.* Emily had carried this with her, the idea that her father hadn't wanted her. It had taken on a shape and a form inside her, a kind of ragged hollow, a valley she had spent her whole life trying to fill. That was why she'd come to Heart Island, for him. She had thought he'd be here to save her from the awful things she'd done.

"Why did you come here?" Birdie asked, reading her mind. "What did you think would happen? That you'd be taken into the fold?"

"I didn't think anything," Emily said. She sounded weak and foolish. She was in the principal's office after cutting, or facing off against the woman whose ring she'd stolen, or trying to explain to her soon-to-be-former boss why she was snooping around the office. She was in the wrong again, trying to make herself understood. There were reasons, good reasons, why she did the things she had done. Or so it seemed in the doing. In the aftermath, under the microscope of judgment, those reasons always seemed so flimsy, so *wrong*.

Emily stood quickly and saw Birdie lean away from her, a startled look of uncertainty flashing across her face. Emily realized that Birdie was frightened, wasn't sure what the younger woman might be capable of doing. That thought frightened Emily.

On the table, Emily saw a flare gun. It was big and thick and looked like a toy. It was out of Birdie's reach where she was sitting. Emily found herself diving for it. The older woman stood and backed away, moving toward the kitchen.

"I'm not going to hurt you," said Emily. She looked down at the flare gun in her hand. "I never wanted that."

"It's far too late to be making assurances," said Birdie.

Emily heard something outside, a loud crack, different from the thunder they'd been hearing, something loud enough to be heard over the wind and the rain. The sound sent a shock of fear through Emily. What had he done?

She was running then, away from the frightened stare of that horrible woman and her lies. She was out in the rain, which poured down on her in great sheets. She slipped, her right foot shooting out from underneath her on the slick rock. She came down so hard that it knocked the wind from her. As she lay there, breathless, a form moved out of the rain.

"What did you do to her?" she yelled. "What have you done now?"

He bent down and yanked her up roughly. She let out a wail of pain and anger, started to struggle against his hands on her. It took her a second to realize that it wasn't Dean. It was Brad.

In his face, she saw everything ugly and awful in her life. It was almost a relief when he put his hands to the back of her head and started pulling her toward the house. She couldn't fight him; her pounding fists and kicking legs felt like they were hitting the thick trunk of a tree, rooted and immovable.

"Who's in the house?" he said into her ear.

"No one," she yelled. "There's no one here."

"Bullshit."

His grip was tight around her hair, and the crown of her head was screaming with pain. It felt like her hair was going to come out by the roots. Still, she pushed back against him, digging her heels into the ground. Finally, he knocked her down, and the ground rose hard, pushing the wind from her chest, leaving her gasping.

He dropped his weight on top of her. "You know where that safe is," he said, his voice a deep, threatening rumble. His knees were resting heavily on the crooks of her arms.

She let out an enraged scream: "*Get off of me.*"

"Just tell me where the goddamn safe is, Emily." He sounded tired, his breath coming in ragged bursts. "What do you care about these people?"

"Okay," she said. "I'll show you." It was a lie. She didn't know anything about the safe. There it was again, that horrible, ugly smile of his.

"I knew what you were the minute I saw you."

The words drained the energy from her, and she felt herself go limp. She'd been fighting all her life, swimming against the current that wanted to take her to a place of despair and disappointment. She'd been so sure she could find something better. But no. Here she was, on the island she'd always held in her imagination as a kind of heaven, and it was worse than any nightmare she'd ever had. She'd brought destruction here. She'd wreaked havoc.

It was then, in the moment when she was about to surrender, that the idea of the child inside of her became more than an abstraction. There was a voice calling out to her, and it offered something

she was sure she'd lost: hope. In hope, she found an unexpected re-
serve of strength.

He grabbed her hard by the hair again and yanked her up so
hard that she heard her neck crack. "You better not be fucking with
me," he said. "Or I'm going to burn this place to the ground."

Summoning all of her will, she issued a guttural moan and began
thrashing. She was going to fight him—and everything he thought
he saw in her.

chapter twenty-nine

Sean had called his mother, who'd rushed right over to stay with Brendan. Now he was racing up the highway. The road was lightly traveled, bathed in amber light. He was just over the speed limit, reminding himself that this was probably nothing—a teenage girl afraid in the night.

Even at seventy-five miles an hour, weaving past the stray car on the highway at four in the morning, he felt like he was wading through tar, time and distance expanding to confound him. The last call from Roger had said that he was on his way to the marina, that he'd call when he knew something. Sean fought the urge to call again. Instead, he called his father-in-law. "Call Joe," he told the voice dialer.

"Calling Joe," it responded. For once, it actually worked.

The phone rang, and the car sped. The landscape was a dark blur studded by streetlamps. It was hypnotic.

"Joe Burke." The old guy always sounded like he was at the ready, and Sean felt a familiar internal cringe at the sound of his voice— like the recruit in front of the drill sergeant, the employee in front of the big boss, the student before the teacher. Sean had never felt this way with his own father or anyone else. He didn't owe anything to Joe: He didn't take his money; hell, he didn't even let Joe pick up the dinner bill. And still.

"It's Sean." There was a pause when he considered adding *your son-in-law.*

But then, "What's wrong?"

Sean ran the situation down for Joe, listened to the other man breathing on the line.

"Did you call the police?" asked Joe when Sean was done. He didn't sound the least bit concerned; maybe he sounded a little annoyed.

"I did," said Sean. "I'm on my way up there now."

"Don't overreact," said Joe. It was his way, Sean knew, to be cool, level, to assess and analyze before acting. But Sean felt himself bristling at the implication that he was overreacting. "Have you tried to reach Birdie?"

"I've been trying to call since last night," said Sean.

"Why did you not go up with them?" asked Joe.

"I had a showing," Sean said. The words practically stuck in his throat. It sounded so stupid and lame—because it was. Why did he not just go with them? Why did they not wait for Sean? What was it about that stupid fucking island and Kate's awful parents that had them all jumping through hoops all the time? Whatever the reason, it was the last time they would. "I had to work, Joe."

He heard Joe give a sniff that to Sean was the very sound of disdain. As if Joe ever did anything but work, as if he hadn't always put that before everything. He just didn't think anyone else's work was as important as his.

Sean was in no mood. "Why did *you* leave?" he asked. He was surprised at the anger in his own voice. "You were supposed to be there."

It could have been any number of "important reasons"—a golf game, a massage, or a "business lunch." Joe had been semi-retired for years but still managed to act like he had no end of critical things to do.

"The place was closing in on me," said Joe. "It's oppressive to be there alone with Birdie."

Sean didn't say anything; he couldn't. In over ten years, those might have been the only real and honest words his father-in-law had ever said—not some rambling story designed to show off something about himself, some vague pleasantry or adage, some declarative about the weather. Maybe that was what happened when you woke someone in the night. He didn't have time to put on his mask.

"Okay," said Sean, for lack of anything better to say.

"So," said Joe. Sean heard the rustling of bedcovers. "You called the police. And they're sending someone out?"

"I spoke to Roger Murphy. He was going to take a boat over there."

"And you're on your way, so that's covered," Joe said. "Call me when you get there."

"What are you going to do?"

"I'm going back to bed, son. Let me know if there's something to worry about. Not much I can do now."

He heard Joe hang up the phone. After a moment of stunned silence, Sean started to laugh. He wondered, not for the first time, where Kate had come from, how she had turned out the way she had. It was a miracle.

"Call Kate."

"Calling Kate."

"Hi, it's me." She sounded strong and clear, and he felt a blessed rush of relief. Then, "I can't talk right now. Leave a message."

He fought back the crushing disappointment. "Hey, it's me," he said. He ran a hand through his short dark hair, which felt stiff and a mess. "I just wanted to tell you that I'm sorry. I'm sorry I didn't go with you. I'm sorry I didn't make you stay and wait. I'm on my way. I don't know if there's really something going on there, or if Chelsea was just freaking out for nothing. But I'm coming. Brendan's at home with my mother. Even if I get there and this is all some crazy misunderstanding, you guys are coming home with me. Because you know what? We need a break from your parents and from Heart Island. We really need a break. Okay?"

He felt exhausted and overwrought and a little silly. Maybe Joe was right, maybe he was overreacting. He had to believe that it was better than underreacting. He didn't want to be the guy who underreacted when people he loved might need him. "And Kate, I love you. I love you so much."

The silence on the other line crackled. He pressed the button on the steering wheel that ended the call. It was under two hours to the Blackbear marina. He inched his foot down on the gas.

Kate approached the main house along the path. Though the rain had lessened a bit, she could hear the water slapping against the rocks. Across the channel, Cross Island was dark. It was a ten-minute swim in calm water. One might shout from island to island. But it seemed liked another planet, unreachably distant.

After she watched the girls head away from the house, an odd stillness had settled over her. It was very clear what she needed to do. She needed to get the gun, get her mother, and get all of them off the island, even if that meant taking the boat out in a storm.

The open water had always been a problem for Kate, She was comfortable in a pool, a safe and predictable small body of water. But the wide expanse of a sea or the lake, with its incalculable volumes, its deep mysteries, caused a rising tide of panic within Kate. As a child, she'd refused to swim at Heart Island, was white-knuckled on the necessary boat rides (and often seasick), absolutely rejected the kayak. Kate remembered Birdie raging at her refusal to jump off the dock and swim with the family. Once, in a fit, Birdie pushed her. *You can swim, Katherine,* she shrieked. Kate remembered how the dark water seemed to engulf her, to pull her down. Her panic caused her to take in water, her mind growing blank with fear. It was her father who dove in after her, lifted her onto the dock, and held her while she threw up lake water and bile. Her mother stood by, arms crossed, the ugliest twist of anger and disapproval on her face. How Kate hated Birdie in that moment.

"You can swim, Katherine," Birdie had said. She walked up to stand before Kate and Joe. "You know you can."

"Shut up, Birdie," said Joe. Kate buried her head in his chest. She thought, *If not for him, she would have let me drown.*

"You would rather she gave in to her fears?" said Birdie. She sounded indignant, as if she had been wronged. "We face the things that frighten us, Kate. Or they swallow us whole."

Kate could hear the gulls calling, the generator humming in the distance.

"Are you trying to prove to everyone what a monster you are?" Joe asked.

"This is ridiculous," said Birdie. She marched off in that way she had, stomping her big feet, her whole body and aura stiff like an exclamation point. She called back, "*I'm* a monster because I don't want my daughter to be a sniveling invalid standing on the shore of life."

Joe raised Kate to standing, wrapped her in a towel, and led her back up to the house. How old had she been then? Maybe ten.

"What happened?" he asked her.

"She pushed me," said Kate.

"I know," he said. "But why didn't you swim back?"

Kate couldn't answer him. She didn't know why. The water had seemed so black, so dense. It seemed to want to pull her down into its depths.

"I don't know," she said. "I was scared."

"Are you sure you're not doing this just to spite her?" he asked. But his tone was gentle. "Maybe you didn't swim because you knew how badly she wanted you to."

"No," she said. "I was *scared*." She'd been adamant. But even then hadn't she wondered if, on some deep level, maybe it was true?

She was shivering from the cold. The skin on her hands looked blue and was covered with gooseflesh. The dock was hard and splintery beneath her bare feet.

"Okay, kid," said her father. "Okay."

On the porch, he knelt down in front of her, moved the wet hair back from her face. "She loves this place. She wants you to love it, too. She wants to know you'll come here and take care of it when she's gone."

Even at ten, Kate knew he was making excuses for things that could not be excused. He wanted to make it all better, to make it seem less awful than it was.

"She loves it more than she loves anything, even us," Kate said.

"That's not true," he said, his tone growing cold. "Now go get yourself dried off and dressed for dinner." He stood and turned away from her, looked back toward the dock. She felt in that moment, as she so often did in her childhood, that there was no soft place to put her head down and be safe. She had felt that way until she met Sean.

As she was coming around the side of the house, she heard a high-pitched scream. It rocketed through her, and she pressed her body against the shingled wall, feeling her heart start to race, her mouth go dry. When she looked around the corner, all she could see in the dim light shining from the porch were two forms—a man and a woman.

The larger form was clearly the aggressor, with a hold on the other's neck. The smaller was all flailing limbs, uselessly trying to break free. Her helplessness awoke something within Kate, some powerful desire to protect and defend.

She could see that it was the girl who'd called herself Anne. The woman looked so small; she could have been a child. Kate remembered how strong he was, how merciless: This was the man who'd attacked her by the boat. Her whole body remembered the crush of his arms around her chest.

Unthinking, Kate found herself hurtling toward them, crashing her body into him with the full force of her fear and anger. They both went tumbling, rolling and coming to a hard stop against a tree. Kate felt a sharp pain in her side, but adrenaline kept it at bay because he was on her again, his weight bearing down like a stone. His face was eerily blank as she flailed at him, trying to get out from under him.

She heard the girl screaming. *Get off of her! Get off of her!* It struck Kate as a powerless and nonsensical demand, as though he might abruptly abandon whatever agenda had brought him here and they'd work everything out. Panic began to crowd out other thoughts as she struggled to take a breath. The girl leaped on top of the attacker, knocking him down. Kate saw the flare gun lying beside her, and she crawled for it. It was beneath her fingers when the monster was on top of her again, landing on her hard, knocking the wind out of her.

She felt her head knock heavily against the rocky ground. For a moment, everything was scattered, a puzzle of sound and motion—a woman screaming, his breath on her face, the smells of sweat and blood and rain. There was a loud pop, a hiss, and a violent flash of orange. Then it all went dark.

chapter thirty

Joe Burke had stopped loving his wife so many years before that he couldn't remember what it was like to feel anything but indifference for her. When he looked back on their life, even the night they met, he couldn't remember ever loving her, not really.

He remembered that when he first saw her there was some spark, some energy, that drew him to her. There was something about her—slim and patrician, practical and smart—that appealed to him. She wasn't like the other girls he knew, puffs of perfume and makeup and crinoline. When Birdie smiled, there was real depth. She had thoughts, opinions, ideas, and she didn't hide that fact to make herself pretty, more desirable. Her whole bearing felt like a dare: *Come and try to have me, if you think you can handle it.* And Joe Burke was not a man to back down from a challenge.

She'd been right—right for his parents; she was attractive, came from wealth, stood to inherit. Marrying her was "marrying up," as his mother liked to say. Birdie and his mother hated each other on sight. Maybe that was right, too. Joe's mother was a doormat. She'd let her husband beat their children and run around on her and put her in an early grave. No, Joe was not one of those men who wanted to marry his mother. He had wanted an interesting woman, a strong woman, and a woman who would be his match. What he hadn't realized was that Birdie, who was all of those things, was also cold and withholding. That wasn't clear to him until long after he'd made his vows. And vows, as far as he was concerned, were not meant to be broken. Stretched, maybe bent, but not broken.

He hadn't been able to sleep again after Sean's call. Birdie was one with the island. Frankly, he pitied the idiots who would breach that boundary—if that was the case. But Kate and Chelsea did not have the same constitution as Birdie. They did not belong to Heart Island in the same way. Chelsea was a reasonable girl; if she said something was wrong, maybe there was.

Sean's call had been the second unsettling one of the day. Joe had just returned to the blessed noise and bustle of the city after the oppressive quiet of Heart Island. The island always seemed so nice at first. Then it started to weigh on him—the silence, the isolation, Birdie's endless litany of demands and complaints, her deafening silences.

Even though he hadn't heard from Martha in years, he recognized her number. It was seared in his memory. He had called it so many times with such breathlessness. The voice on the other line had brought him so much pleasure, so much comfort, and in the end, so much misery. He almost didn't answer; it couldn't be anything but bad news. Why else would she call after all these years?

"Joe?" she said. Her voice sounded older, smokier. But he remembered when it had been sweet and young. When she'd been everything that Birdie wasn't—soft, yielding, eager. He remembered the feel of her lean body, that velvet skin beneath his fingertips. Even now, a lifetime later, he could feel the tickle of arousal.

"Martha," he said. He used to call her Martie, a sweet diminutive of her name that seemed more in line with who she was then. "Why are you calling?"

He heard her take in a breath. "Emily's in trouble, terrible trouble."

He'd thought of Martha's little girl, too. She was nothing like his Kate. He always knew Emily wasn't his, but he played along because it was a game he enjoyed. The game of house with these other two, the two who wanted him so desperately, who needed him. He'd often thought Birdie could replace him with anyone. Not his Katie. The moment Kate was born, he'd looked into her eyes and felt as if he'd always known her. But with Emily—*my little Em,* he used to call her—though he loved her, he knew that she was not his. But he *could* love her, because she loved him so much.

"What kind of trouble?" he asked.

Martha told him, and he could hardly believe it. He felt a rush of sadness, of guilt.

As if she sensed his sorrow, wanted to use it against him, she said, "She needed a father."

"I'm not her father, Martha."

"But you could have been."

He felt the old rise of anger; all the things he'd said a million times lodged in his throat. *You knew I was married. I told you I wouldn't leave my family. I always knew the baby wasn't mine. I cared for you both anyway. All these years, I've sent you money.*

"I'm sorry," he said instead. Because really, what else was there to say? He listened to her crying on the other line. She should know not to do that. Tears made him go cold inside; they always had.

"I wanted you to know in case she came to you. In case she called."

"Why would she?" he asked. "How could she even remember me?"

The silence on the line told him everything.

"She has your last name," Martha said. "I never had the heart to tell her she wasn't yours after all."

He let the words, their implication and meaning, sink in. Somewhere down on the street, he heard a fire engine roar.

"So all these years, she thought I was her father," he said. "And what? That I abandoned her, didn't want her? That's what you call having a heart?"

"You did abandon her, Joe." There it was, the cloying, self-dramatizing tone that came out in her when things got ugly.

"And you lied to her, manipulated her—just like you did me." How quickly old angers rose from the buried depths. You thought you'd forgotten about the ancient hurts and disappointments, but brush back the dirt and there they are, calcified, harder than ever.

"If she calls or comes to me, I'll let you know."

"Joe," she said. "Do you ever think about me?"

"Martha," he answered. "Do you ever think about anyone but yourself?"

He had hung up the phone, slamming it down hard. Then he'd picked it up and slammed it again. She called back once, twice, three times. And then the phone fell silent. He'd gone to the gym and worked out with his personal trainer for an hour and a half. Then they got in the boxing ring.

"Joe," the younger man said. He was sweating and breathless. Joe was nauseated from the effort. "Got something on your mind?"

Joe had taken Martha and Emily to the island twice. Birdie had accused him of doing it purposefully to hurt her. At the time, he denied it. It was circumstance only, a private place where they could be alone and not seen. But that wasn't true, because the harbormaster *had* seen them. Joe had tipped him handsomely but apparently not enough to keep him from running his mouth off. Heart Island, it seemed, had a history. Another affair had played out there and ended badly. He wasn't sure how, but it had gotten back to Birdie. And the shit had hit the fan.

But his time there with them was something he visited in his memory more often than he cared to admit. Without Birdie and her rules of order, it was a beautiful place, the island, peaceful and embracing. He could relax with Martie and his little Em. He could breathe, just breathe, and be there in a way he never could with Birdie. She was always taking measure of him, how he spent his time, what he was doing or wasn't doing to facilitate her endless catalog of chores and activities. Martie didn't care if there were dishes in the sink, if the bed was unmade. She didn't care if they ate tuna-fish sandwiches for dinner, a baked potato on the grill, drank beer from the bottle.

He remembered those late-summer sun-soaked days, the air still warm, Birdie back in the city gearing up for the fund-raising season and the holidays. He remembered them with joy, with nostalgia. Heart Island had let him fantasize about being with Martha and Emily, about what he would be if he'd chosen a different life, a different kind of woman. Birdie was fully occupied by that time of the year, didn't think twice about his golfing clinic, or business trip, or whatever it was he'd told her he was doing. All he had to do was show up in a tux at some appointed date and time, to take her to some endless dinner for Africa or AIDS or inner-city schools. Before then she wouldn't have thought to look for him.

And there was little Em, who hadn't needed to be entertained, was happy to color or swim with them or just nap on the blanket. She wasn't like Theo and Kate, with their endless list of activities, their at-home schedules so packed with tennis and horseback riding and ballet and drama that they didn't know what free time was. They always needed an activity, something to *do*. It was his fault, he supposed. He could have taught them that, at least. They'd certainly never learn it from Birdie, who'd been in perpetual motion since the minute he married her. *Daddy, will you take me kayaking? Daddy, will you play hide-and-seek with us? Daddy, will you pitch the tent?* Sometimes he thought they all kept moving so Birdie's critical eye wouldn't fall on them and find a reason to complain.

Later, after Martha's call and after the gym, he met his old friend Alan for dinner. He barely heard his friend rambling on about his stock losses, his new ski gear, his kid finishing medical school but wanting to join Doctors Without Borders after Alan had spent untold amounts of money on his education "so the kid can just run off to the third-fucking-world and take care of the natives."

Joe was thinking about Emily on her own, out there with some shithead who had trashed her whole life. And about how things could have been different for her if Joe had ever once done what he wanted to do rather than what he felt he should do or *had* to do. If he had ever done anything that was in his heart rather than following the rules that had been clearly set out for him. He wondered if Emily still thought about the island and the time they spent there. But no, he told himself, she wouldn't remember. She couldn't. She had been a little girl. She wouldn't remember Heart Island. It wouldn't have cast a spell on her like it had on so many. It was just an island in the middle of a lake. It didn't have that kind of power. It didn't have any power at all.

From his bedroom window, he could see the Chrysler Building. It was a sight he'd always loved, an art deco reminder of the shimmering beauty of New York City. He got out of bed and stepped into his slippers, padded over to the window. Below him, Park Avenue teemed with traffic even though it was only after three. He always wondered at the throngs of people living inches apart, the full rainbow of experience playing out on every block, stories into the sky. No matter what time of day it was, someone was headed somewhere for some reason. Where were they all going? Didn't they realize that none of it mattered?

Heartbroken

He picked up the phone and dialed the island but got only the fast busy signal that told him the lines were down, as they often were. The sound of a horn drifted up. In the distance, he heard the wail of a siren. Joe Burke just stood there with the phone still in his hand, watching.

chapter thirty-one

Her mother always told her that her life would boil down to just a few moments, just a few choices. Those choices, usually made in a split second, would change everything that came after. Those moments were blurs, clear only after the consequences had been dealt. As Emily watched the flare shoot into the sky, casting the world in an eerie orange, she wondered if all her moments had passed. She was sure they had. Now there was nothing to do but play out the rest of her terrible hand.

Brad disappeared into the dark like a frightened animal. He'd had the gun once. Where was it and why hadn't he used it in the struggle? She tried to think of how many rounds he'd fired at the Blue Hen. Four, she thought. Or maybe five. Which meant he had maybe one or two left in the chamber. Had he used the gun again? Was he out of bullets? And where was Dean?

Kate lay motionless on the ground. Emily felt the cool rain on her face, the painful ache where Brad's hands had squeezed her neck. She been losing strength when Kate came from nowhere and knocked Brad down, breaking his grasp. Why had she done it, risked her life to save Emily's?

"Put your hands where I can see them." It was the old woman. Emily dropped the flare gun and turned around. The other woman had a gun, a real one. Emily held her hands up and stood staring. She had no words; she was spent, stunned.

Birdie said something to Emily as she rushed past. But Emily didn't hear; she was listening to the trees whispering and feeling the rain wash over her. It was dark, and the island was nothing like she remembered it. But she recognized its song, the sound it made when everything else was silent.

Emily watched Birdie kneel beside her daughter and put a hand to her throat, push back her hair. "Katherine," she said. "You stay with me." When she looked back at Emily, the old woman's face was a scowl. "Help me get her back into the house," Birdie snapped.

It was an order from the lady of the house to an errant servant, full of anger and disdain. Emily obeyed. But she was on autopilot. Again she wondered where Dean was. She could use his help right now. With effort, they managed to lift Kate and bring her up the stairs.

A wound on the side of Kate's head gushed blood; it was on Birdie's clothes—Emily's too, she noticed. Big drops had fallen to the floor, leaving a smearing trail from the door over the carpet. Someone, thought Emily, would need to clean that up.

Kate issued a low groan but didn't open her eyes. Birdie rushed off and then came back with a first-aid kit. She was calm and purposeful, not at all a woman looking at her possibly badly injured child. She removed a role of gauze, a jar of antiseptic.

"Katherine Elizabeth," she said. In the sound of that name, Emily heard all of Birdie's fear and regret. "Open your eyes."

Kate was still and silent, so very, very pale. Emily kept a careful eye on the door. Birdie placed the gun on the table beside Kate. Emily could take it and go after Brad and maybe find Dean. Instead, she sank against the wall, the terrible fatigue weighing her down again. More than anything, she wished she'd come back to find the house as she remembered. Not this place that was so different from anything else.

———

"You know, we never realize how bad they are until it's too late," said Lana.

They sat where Kate and Birdie had sat earlier that afternoon, the same tea set between them. But the room wasn't the same; it was some dream hybrid of the old house Kate remembered from her childhood and from old photographs, and the new one her father had built. But she felt utterly relaxed and at home.

"When you're young," Lana went on, "it's easy to confuse passion for love."

Lana's beauty was musical, with her clear, dark eyes and the same milky skin Birdie had inherited. The delicate line from her neck to her shoulder, the sheen of her hair, the elegance of her fingers were an exquisite combination of grace and innocence. Kate was mesmerized by her grandmother.

"I know," said Kate. "I thought I loved Sebastian. You couldn't have convinced me otherwise."

Lana put her hand on Kate's. It was a warm, loving gesture, and Kate felt Lana's compassion move through her. "You think you're swimming at first," said Lana. "And then you realize it's the undertow pulling you out to sea."

"Yes," said Kate. "It was just like that."

The light from the windows was so unnaturally bright that Kate had to close her eyes against it, and even then it seemed to burn through her lids. In her head was a searing pain that had achieved what felt like a dangerous decibel. Kate had a growing sense of unease, the vague idea that something was terribly, terribly wrong.

"When I tried to give him up," said Lana, "he just wouldn't let me go."

Kate couldn't answer. The pain was so distracting.

"It wasn't that he loved me so much. It was that he *needed* something from me that no one else could give. I filled something empty in him; isn't that what we all do in love?"

Yes, it had been true with Kate and Sebastian, too. He had wanted everything from Kate. The very size of his soul demanded a sacrifice like an angry god. Maybe it was like that for Lana and Richard. Kate didn't say this.

"I'm not sure if I could tell you what the thing was, precisely," said her grandmother. "I needed what he offered as well. But I needed Jack and the children more. It was Birdie who made me choose, though she never knew it. And she was right to demand that."

Why was Lana telling her this? Kate knew; she'd lived Lana's journal. But more than that, she knew it in her own heart. Because it was Kate's love for Chelsea that had forced her to leave Sebastian. Even though Chelsea was Sebastian's daughter, Kate needed to get the girl away from his tortured instability, his rages, his addiction. Only true love could rescue you from the masquerade of love. She knew. And her heart's knowledge was the reason why she'd connected to Lana's story, why, when she wrote it, it was as if she were telling her own.

"I didn't mean to kill him, Katie." She was crying now. "It was an accident."

"It was self-defense, Grandma. You were fighting for your life. It wasn't your fault."

The gratitude on her grandmother's face brought Kate to tears. "Make her understand it, darling," said Lana. "Please, Kate, make her understand all of it."

"I will," she said. "I promise."

But honestly, Kate wasn't sure she could make Birdie do anything she didn't want to do. She rested her head in her grandmother's lap, and it felt so soft and warm. She felt herself drifting, the pain easing. A long sleep, that's just what she needed. But no. She shouldn't. There were things that needed her attention. What were they?

"Katherine Elizabeth Burke, you open your eyes this second."

Lana was gone, and Birdie was standing in the doorway with

her usual scowl. Kate pulled herself to a sitting position as her dream began to fade and the real world started to leak back in. Did Birdie always have to be so goddamn bossy?

"Katherine, I am your mother. You do what I say."

And like the good girl she had always been, she obeyed.

chapter thirty-two

"Chelsea," said Kate.

She sat up suddenly, a look of fear on her face, and then sank her head into her hands with a groan.

Emily moved away from them and stood by the door. She felt distant from this scene and the people in it, including herself. Where was Dean? Dread had settled in her center, was spreading through her like poison in her blood. Outside, it was still dark. Would the sun ever come up? She felt as if, when it did, everything would seem better.

"Chelsea's in the bunkhouse with Lulu," said Kate. "I sent them to use the radio. I need to go get them."

The bunkhouse—wasn't that where Dean had said the safe was? Emily wanted to tell them that was where Brad might go next, but she stayed silent.

"Who was that man?" said Birdie. "He wasn't the man you came here with."

It took Emily a second to realize that Birdie was talking to her. "Where is he?" Emily spoke to Kate. Kate and Dean had left together, and she had come back without him. What had Dean told them his name was? "My f-f-fiancé? Where is he?"

Birdie walked over to Emily quickly, holding the gun in her hand. "You need to tell us right now what in God's name is happening here. We are all in danger, including you. *Who* was that man?"

"Whoever he is, he shot your boyfriend," said Kate. She was

standing, supporting herself on one of the tall chairs by the bar. She was pale and shaky, with a dark swath of blood down the front of her shirt. "What does he want?"

The words didn't sink in right away, that Brad had shot Dean. "He wants the money," Emily said. "He thinks there's a safe here on this island, in the bunkhouse."

"The bunkhouse," said Kate. She looked at Emily with something like horror. Emily wanted to tell them the whole awful story. She wanted to make them understand. But she knew she couldn't do that.

"Why did you do this?" asked Birdie. She sounded desperately sad. "Why did you bring this nightmare here?"

Emily couldn't answer that. It hadn't been her intention to *bring* anything here. All she'd wanted to do was to come to the place, maybe the only place, where she'd ever been happy and safe, where she'd ever felt loved. She'd wanted to come to the pretty house with the wind chimes, where the air was so clean it had a scent like a perfume, and the sky was a blue that she'd never seen anyplace else. Why was she being punished for that?

Rather than trying to answer, she turned and ran out into the night. She wasn't afraid of the storm or Brad or what he might do. She heard the door slam behind her, felt the wood and then the stone beneath her feet. She was going back to the boat. That's where Dean would be, waiting for her. She didn't remember that Kate said he'd been shot. She'd pushed it from her mind.

But as she approached the boat, she saw someone on the ground. Her whole being rejected the sight of Dean lying still in the rain. Then she knelt beside him. He was already cold, his face white and motionless. He had his arms folded over his bloody middle, but his face was slack and peaceful. The rain had slowed to a drizzle, and somewhere she heard the sound of a boat.

"Dean," she said. "Dean, honey, don't do this."

She pulled at his jacket. The weight of his body seemed immense, as though the earth had already claimed him and was pulling him down, down inside itself.

"I think it's a boy," she whispered to him. "I really do."

When she pulled her hands away from his chest, they were slick and wet with blood. In the night, it looked as black as tar. She realized that she was kneeling in a pool of it that had flowed from him—a pool where all his life had drained. Somewhere from deep inside, a terrible wail, a cry of pain and sorrow and unfathomable regret, escaped her like vomit. She couldn't stop it, nor did she want to.

She stood and stumbled away from him, back to the main house. Dazed but in the grip of a terrible rage, Emily moved through the trees unseeing. She had no thought for the child inside her. She climbed the stairs to the porch and entered.

The place was empty; both women were gone. How long had she been out there with Dean? She looked around and hated everything she saw, everything that was not as she remembered it. What a terrible trick this place had played on her, living all this time in her memory as a shining beacon of what her life could have been. It was just another lie, like the one her mother had told her about who she was. She was fatherless now in a whole new way. She didn't even have the fantasy of Joe Burke.

She was sobbing. Great heaving moans escaped her frame; her face was hot and wet with tears. She started frantically opening cabinets and drawers in the kitchen. In the drawer by the stove, she found what she was looking for—a large box of matches. Under the sink, she found a small tin of lighter fluid.

She looked around at the plush sofas, the walls covered with tasteful art and professionally shot family photos, the embroidered pillows, the coffee-table books. All pieces of a life that had been dangled before her and cruelly snatched away. She wanted it all to turn to ashes.

Chelsea remembered how, only a couple of days ago, she'd been arguing with her mother about the sweater she was going to wear. She'd wondered then how one event linked to the other to create the life you had. Now, as she and Lulu crossed the threshold into the bunkhouse, she wondered how things could go so wrong, how dark things could creep in and change the whole world as you knew it. She tried not to worry about her mom, whom she'd watched disappear into the rain. She couldn't think about her grandmother, either. Only the idea of the gun made her feel better. Her mom would get it, and they would all be safe.

She found the radio on the desk toward the back of the room and led Lulu there. Lulu was crying, had not once let go of Chelsea's hand. Her friend was afraid. Chelsea was surprised to note that even though she was angry beyond measure, she still loved Lulu. It was comforting to know that.

She used to believe that anger was the absence of love. Her parents had been so angry with each other. She remembered the sound of their voices, the looks on their faces, even though she was very young when they divorced. Anger broke you apart, she'd always thought. Recently, she'd come to understand that sometimes love and anger wrapped around each other and became one living thing in your heart. It was her father, Sebastian, who had taught her that. Because that was how she felt about him.

Chelsea powered up the radio, and it came to life with a whine. She pressed down the transmitter, as she'd learned to in boating class—it was very similar to a nautical ship-to-shore radio, like on the boat where she and her mom had taken lessons.

"Heart Island to Blackbear Police," she said. "We have an emergency, three intruders and a stranded vessel."

There was only static for her answer. She waited a moment and then repeated herself. She looked around at the stacks of boxes, the bunks that had never been used, the refrigerator that was unplugged. The place was bare and cold, the bunk beds and their thin mattresses uninviting. More static.

Lulu sat on the ground beside Chelsea and rested her head on her friend's lap. Chelsea stroked Lulu's hair; it was so soft that the feel of it between her fingers gave her comfort, even though an hour ago she'd wanted to pull it out by the roots. Chelsea pressed the transmitter button again. "Heart Island to Blackbear Police," she said. She felt less sure of herself, her voice wavering. "We need assistance."

"Why aren't they answering?" Lulu asked. "The police are supposed to answer when you call."

Then, "Blackbear Police. We read you, Heart Island." A male voice, staticky and far away.

"There are intruders on our island," she said. "Please help us. Over."

There was that whispering static again; they might as well be on the moon, isolated and unreachable. Why didn't he say something?

"Are you safe for the moment?"

They weren't safe. They weren't safe at all, maybe for the first time ever.

"For the moment," she said. She had to be grown up; she had to be strong. She would be. "My friend and I are in the bunkhouse. My mother is trying to find my grandmother on the other end of the island. She says two people, a man and a woman, came to the door. When she was trying to save the boat that they ran aground, another man shot the first man."

If you listened to the white noise long enough, it started to sound like voices.

"Understood, Heart Island," said the police officer "Stay where you are. The weather is bad, but there's a boat on the way. The people on your island are possible fugitives. Stay away from them at all costs. Can you lock the door?"

They'd thrown the inside latch on entering. She told him as much.

"If your situation changes," said the male voice, "radio back. I'll be right here."

"Okay," she said. She wanted to say more. She wanted him to say more. But he was just a voice on the radio. He couldn't help her. "Heart Island out."

She turned down the volume on the radio so that the hissing wasn't so loud. She sat for a second, listening.

"If we're going to die," said Lulu, "I don't want you to die mad at me."

"We're not going to die," said Chelsea. She walked to the window and gazed outside. She willed her mom and grandmother to come out of the trees. But there was only the dark, the leaves tossing and whispering.

"I'm really sorry, Chelsea," Lulu said. She came up behind her friend and wrapped her arms around her middle. "It was so stupid."

"I liked him," said Chelsea. "Figures he wasn't real."

Lulu buried her face into Chelsea's neck. "I didn't think you even cared about boys."

"I don't," she said. "But I'd never met a boy like him. And now I know it's because he doesn't exist."

"I'm sorry," said Lulu.

"You lied to me. You used private things you knew about me to trick me." Saying it made her feel angry and hurt again, which was fine, because it was a good distraction from the real matters at hand.

"It's not like that," said Lulu miserably. She pulled away from Chelsea and sat on the chair by the radio, wrapping her arms tight around herself. Chelsea turned to watch her. She felt cold in the absence of her friend's body against hers. "It really isn't."

"It is," said Chelsea. She felt stubborn and mean; she didn't want to forgive her friend, not yet. Lulu got away with too much.

"Do you know what it's like to be your friend, Chelsea?" Lulu was looking down at her feet.

"What it's like to be *my* friend?"

"Yes," said Lulu. She looked up with those glittering movie-star eyes. "What it's like to be friends with someone so *perfect*."

For a moment, Chelsea thought Lulu was making fun of her. But one look at Lulu's face told her otherwise.

"You're gorgeous, you're *smart*," said Lulu. She held up a hand and started ticking items off on her fingers. "You have a perfect family. Your parents love you. Your father is a celebrity. You have *everything*, and you don't even know it."

Was Lulu really this stupid?

"You think it's so great that I have boyfriends?" Lulu asked, raising her voice a little. Then, more quietly, "Boys like me because I sleep with them. That's why. My parents don't have time for me. My brother is in and out of rehab. I'm barely passing school. My life is a *mess*."

Chelsea walked over to Lulu, who rose and sank into her arms.

"I'm sorry," said Lulu. She drew in a deep shuddering breath. "I would never hurt you. I didn't do it to hurt you. I'm a moron."

As she said it, they heard something at the door.

"Shh," said Chelsea. She switched off the light by the radio, and they stood, frozen, as the knob on the door started to turn.

Lulu pulled Chelsea toward the back of the one-room cabin. They hid behind the corner of the thick stone fireplace jutting out about two feet from the wall. They pressed their bodies tightly against the wall and gripped hands. The turning of the doorknob became a kind of rhythmic thumping, as if someone were trying more forcefully to enter. Then there was an awful silence. *Am I dreaming?* Chelsea thought. *Please let this all be a dream.* She found herself leaning forward. Lulu started tugging at her. *Don't. Don't move, Chelsea, please don't move.*

She reached out, snaking her hand around the cold stone and finding the wrought-iron stand that held the fire poker and the heavy ash shovel. She felt it at her fingertips. *What are you doing? He'll see you.* If she could just stretch a little farther, she could get it. They'd have something to defend themselves with.

As her mother had said a hundred times, those doors wouldn't keep out anyone who really wanted to get in. And the two windows, one beside the door and one over near the bunk beds, could be easily smashed. No one ever cared, because they were safe on Heart Island. No one who didn't belong here would come here, until tonight. Chelsea's heart was thumping so hard that it felt like a bird in her chest. Just a little bit more, a little more.

Then the pounding started, a heavy kicking like a boot against the door again and again. Of course, Lulu couldn't help but scream. Chelsea started and reached too far, tipping over the stand. She held her breath as it banged loudly over the stone hearth and onto the floor. God, how could it be so loud?

The pounding suddenly stopped; Chelsea and Lulu held one collective breath. How much time was passing? It seemed like hours. With her ears ringing and Lulu weeping softly, Chelsea got to her knees and reached for the poker. As she did, the pounding started again, hard and slow. One: The whole bunkhouse seemed to shake. It was a house of sticks, and they were the two little piggies. The big bad wolf was outside: *I'll huff and I'll puff and I'll blow your house down.* Two: A picture of her grandparents fell from the wall, and the glass shattered. Chelsea had the poker in her hand and was handing the ash shovel to Lulu, who was shaking so hard she could barely hold it. It seemed too heavy for her, like she might not be able to lift it. Chelsea could barely see her friend's face in the dark. *Oh, God, oh, shit, this isn't happening, Chaz, tell me it's not happening.*

Three: Chelsea started moving toward the door, with Lulu following. She raised the poker high like a softball bat. What was it that her coach always said? Don't hit the ball. *Smash* the ball. *Pulverize* it. Send the little shreds of it into outer space.

But when he came through the door, splitting the wood in two and sticking one booted leg in through the hole he'd made, then trying to squeeze his body through, he was every nightmare she had ever had, everything they ever warned you about. Here he was, the stranger, the one who wanted to hurt you and take you from your parents. Chelsea froze; she couldn't breathe as she watched him fit one arm through, his hand searching for the doorknob to try to unlock it. She thought, *That's it, we're going to die.*

It was Lulu, who had just been crying a minute before, who let out a kind of warrior's yell, a guttural scream. She moved by Chelsea fast. She was on the same softball team, and maybe she had the same words in her head. Because she held that shovel just like she held the bat, and she started pounding on that intruding arm and leg like she wanted to turn them into hamburger.

The sound of her, the sight of her, put air back into Chelsea's lungs. With her free hand, she put the whistle in her mouth and started to blow and blow with all her might. And then she joined her friend in beating back the wolf at the door.

chapter thirty-three

Moving toward the bunkhouse, Kate heard Anne issue a horrible keening wail from behind them, so primal that it cut a swath through her. Kate could imagine her bent over the body of her fiancé. And Kate, even in this moment, could feel her grief.

She could tell by the look on Birdie's face that her mother felt it, too. It was the very sound of grief and rage. But it was happening on another planet. She could think only of that monster headed for the bunkhouse where Chelsea and Lulu were. The world seemed to impede her progress, distance and time pulling like taffy. She'd vomited twice since leaving the house.

"I'll get them," Birdie had said after Kate vomited the second time. Birdie had the gun now.

"We stay together," said Kate. Besides, Birdie wasn't moving that much faster. She was limping badly.

Above the sound of her own labored breathing, Kate thought she heard the sound of a boat. She prayed she did, but the water played tricks with sound. Boats too far to be seen could sound as though they were nearby. Even the screaming seemed to echo on the night air. It was possible that the harbormaster had seen the flare or that Chelsea had managed to contact the police.

"Do you smell smoke?" Birdie had dropped behind and was looking back in the direction of the main house.

Kate did smell smoke. She looked back and thought she saw a golden glow. Then it was dark again. She didn't trust her eyes. There was that siren of pain in her skull and an odd fuzziness to her vision. She was keeping herself upright to get to Chelsea. But fire was the thing to dread on the island. The trees, the wood-framed buildings, everything would be consumed.

"It's nothing," said Kate. She didn't care about the house; all she cared about was getting them all off the island and away from the nightmare that had come ashore. "Not with all this rain. Let's just get the girls and go."

As they started to move again, Kate heard the sound she'd always hated and dreaded. It took a moment for fear to replace annoyance. It was the panicked shrilling of a whistle.

Kate started to run, and as she drew closer, she heard the girls screaming. On her approach, she could see that the door to the bunkhouse had been smashed open. She ran up the stairs, yelling for Chelsea.

"Mom!"

She heard her daughter's terrified voice and pushed her way through the smashed center of the door. It was quiet inside, only the sound of someone crying. She flipped on the light and first saw the girls huddled by the back window. Then she saw the man who had attacked her lying prone on the floor in front of them. Lulu gripped the iron fireplace shovel, Chelsea the poker. The intruder lay sprawled by the hearth. Kate didn't bother to check if he was breathing.

He'd been looking for a safe, the young woman had said. It was amazing to Kate that he even knew about it. The sad thing was that they never kept anything in it. Maybe her mother might put in a piece of jewelry, so as not to misplace it, but rarely. And they never brought anything of value here. What would they keep on the island? It amazed her that these people had come here looking for some prize that had never existed. That all of them had destroyed themselves for nothing.

The girls seemed paralyzed, afraid to move. They both had their eyes on the intruder, as if waiting for him to get up again.

"He got up once," said Chelsea. "I don't think he's dead."

"Chelsea hit him on the head with the fire poker," said Lulu. "It was amazing. She held it just like a bat."

They seemed a little unhinged, on the verge of hysteria.

"Girls," Kate said gently. They looked at her. "Let's go."

Chelsea ran to her, and Lulu was close behind. She took them into her arms. She looked down at the man on the floor. She thought of taking that poker in Chelsea's hand and driving it through his heart. He was a mad dog, and the world would be better without him. Wasn't that what anyone would do? Kill the man who'd tried to hurt her child? But Kate lacked whatever element that existed within a person that might allow her to kill or hurt someone when he was unconscious on the floor. She felt as though it might be a weakness within her. Certainly, Birdie would put a bullet in him. But Birdie had the gun and was nowhere to be seen.

"It's okay," said Kate. "We're okay."

The feel of Chelsea in her arms melted away all her panic and tension. There was a physical release in her shoulders and her chest, a lightening of her breath. All she wanted to do was get them out of this horror show. That was just what they were going to do. They were going to get on that boat, and she was going to take them away from this place. She pulled the girls along.

It was when they were outside the bunkhouse that they saw the first lick of flames through the trees. The smell of smoke was strong, the wind carrying it north toward them. They all stood there staring, disbelieving. A moment of unreality settled over Kate; she heard Chelsea start to cry again. Then Birdie joined them, silently coming to stand beside them.

"Oh my God," said Lulu. "It's burning."

It seemed to Kate that she had been here before, watching the flames rise from the trees, listening to the girls crying, feeling Birdie steady herself against Kate's shoulder.

Kate knew there wasn't time for tears. She was surprised to feel nothing for the house or anything inside it. Everything that was important to her was right beside her or, mercifully, out of harm's way. She found she couldn't care less if the whole island turned to dust as long as she'd gotten them safely off before it did.

Birdie could tell that the main house was on fire. Though the rain had slowed to an almost imperceptible drizzle, the trees on the island were saturated with moisture, so maybe the damage would be contained. When she was a girl, her family had watched a fire rage on a neighbor's island. Even though the season had been wet, the house was consumed. The fireboats arrived too late, and when the fire had burned out, the trees were nothing but black lines against the sky. The structure disintegrated; only the charred skeleton remained. It had always been her worst nightmare, a fire on the island.

Somehow she'd known that Joe would manage to take even the island from her. Watching the fire through the trees, she almost could have predicted it. The three girls stared, the glow reflected in their eyes. Birdie had a wave of déjà vu—the three of them staring in horror into the distance.

Hadn't Caroline claimed there was a fire once, the original shack owned by her mother's uncle that burned after being struck by lightning? Birdie had never really listened to her sister, who always seemed like she was speaking a different language, always looking for beauty and meaning where there was only the cold, dull ordinary. Caroline would have liked that the island—well, the new house that Joe built—was burning. Even Birdie could see that there was a kind of poetry to it.

"Mom," said Kate. Her voice was strained with fear. "We can't get back to the dock that way."

It was true. Even if the fire hadn't spread to the trees, which it may have, the smoke could overcome them. Or it might have spread far enough to block their way to the dock. If that were the case, they couldn't escape that way, either.

"No," said Birdie. "You'll have to swim around the perimeter."

Kate looked out into the blackness. On her daughter's face, Birdie read the fear she'd always seen when her child looked at the water. But this time some mettle Birdie hadn't known Kate possessed settled into her features. Birdie wondered if they were so different after all. Kate had Caroline's beauty and Joe's expansiveness, but she had Birdie's strength. Why hadn't she seen it before?

"Good girl," she said. She reached out to touch Kate's cheek. "Get the children to the boat."

Kate's brow wrinkled into a worried frown. "What are you going to do? You're coming with us."

"No," said Birdie. She looked back at the house. "I have to try to put out the fire."

"Mom," said Kate. Her eyes followed Birdie's gaze. It looked bad enough that no sane would person would consider moving in that direction. Fire demanded that you go the other way. "No."

"Please," Birdie said. A sob in her chest surprised her, but she choked it back. "It's all I have. This place."

"You have *us*, Grandma," said Chelsea. "You have your family."

The look on her granddaughter's face, bewildered and sad, almost moved her to go with them. Lulu was already walking toward the water. The girl was a survivor, at least. The other two would go down trying to save people who didn't want to be saved.

"I'll meet you at the boat," Birdie said. "I promise. I have to see if there's anything I can do to save the house."

She tried for a smile, though she was sure it didn't come off that way. Anyway, it was a lie. She wouldn't meet them at the boat. She wouldn't try to put out the fire, either. It was too late; she could see that. What did she plan to do, then? She honestly didn't know. She just knew she couldn't leave, not like this.

"Don't do it," said Kate. There was pleading in her tone that

Birdie wasn't sure she'd ever heard. She tried to hand the gun to Kate, but Kate pushed it back; she handed the flashlight over as well. "They'll both be ruined in the water. We'll take our chances. If we can't get to the boat, we'll swim to Cross Island."

The water was frigid. They'd have to swim fast and hard. And Kate had never been a strong swimmer; plus, she was badly injured.

"The key is in the ignition," said Birdie. "You'll have to move fast."

Kate had that look again, the one that Birdie was sure she reserved for her mother. Her expression managed anger, sadness, and bafflement, as if Birdie were impossible for her to fathom. But that was all. There were no more words of protest or argument. Kate had learned long ago—she must have—that there was no arguing with Birdie once she'd made up her mind. Kate started pulling Chelsea toward the water.

"Grandma!"

"Chelsea, let's go."

"*We can't just leave her.*" The girl was shrieking, and it broke Birdie's heart.

She heard Kate's tone, soothing and measured. But she didn't hear her daughter's words, because Birdie was already walking away from them toward the main house. A captain didn't leave his ship just because it was sinking. Birdie wouldn't leave Heart Island—not to fire, not to intruders, not for any reason except her own.

chapter thirty-four

"**M**om," begged Chelsea. "*Please* go after her."

Kate stripped off her jacket and shoes, then pulled off Chelsea's coat. The heavy outer layers would drag them down in the water. Her daughter was sobbing, and the sound of it was causing Kate physical pain.

"I can't, Chelsea," she said. She put her hands on her daughter's shoulders. "Not yet. When you and Lulu are safe, I'll go back for her. I promise."

How could she explain to her daughter that in the choice between whose lives to save, her children would come before anyone, including Sean, including herself? No one but a mother could ever understand. Kate wouldn't—she couldn't—risk herself for Birdie, not unless she knew Chelsea was safe. Her children needed her. Her mother, clearly, did not.

"She'll *die*."

Chelsea sounded like she had as a little girl, her sadness so total, so despairing and innocent. Kate thought of a moment a lifetime ago when Chelsea had carried a dead fish from the shore and set it into the ocean. "I'm giving it back to the universe," she had said in a sweet mimic of something Kate had once said to her. She stood up, looking despondent. "I don't like it when any creature gets dead."

"No," said Kate now. She couldn't allow herself to believe that. The water felt frigid to her feet as she inched toward it, pulling Chelsea with her. "She won't die. There's nothing and no one tougher than Birdie."

"Chelsea, *come on*," said Lulu. She was sobbing, shivering in the cold. She had her hands on Chelsea, too. They were pulling her toward the water while she looked back after Birdie. "She wants to stay on this island. Let her."

Finally, the girl relented and came of her own volition. Lulu shrieked as she forced herself into the water. Kate, too, felt the painful shock of cold against her skin, tried to ignore the fact that the blackness seemed to stretch into eternity. She knew how that could take you down, how heavy it was, how total was its darkness. She forced those thoughts out of her mind.

"Swim as fast as you can, as hard as you can," she said. "Don't look back for me. I'm right behind you. If there's fire on the dock, or if you see anyone there when you round the island, swim across the channel."

It would be best if they could get to the boat. If they couldn't, they'd have to try to get across. The water was rough but, luckily, somewhat sheltered in the channel between the two bodies of land.

Kate had always found that in caring for her children, anything that she was afraid of, or any shortfall she had, simply became irrelevant. She would be what she had to be, do what she had to do, to get them through any crisis, large or small. Adrenaline held all the pain in her head and body at bay. She hardly noticed that she was being tossed by the water, taking in huge gulps as the waves hit her. She ignored the heavy fatigue settling in her limbs.

She watched the two bobbing heads of the girls as she kicked and stroked with all her strength. The water was likely around sixty degrees; it wouldn't take much longer then ten minutes for their core temperature to start dropping.

She could see the flames topping the trees, and she was almost overcome by fear and sadness. The orange of the fire glowed on the black water. The moon was white and high, the cloud cover clearing. A million stars winked, oblivious. She kept her eyes on Chelsea and Lulu. The dock wasn't far; she could see it now. It was empty, free from flames. The cuddy bucked and bounced, waiting for them. She almost yelled out at the sight of it.

It was then that Lulu started to struggle. Kate saw her head go under, then come up, then disappear again.

"Mom!" She heard Chelsea's voice, panicked and faint on the air.

Pure adrenaline allowed Kate to double her speed and come upon them quickly. Chelsea was trying to hold on to Lulu, who had stopped moving. She wasn't unconscious, but her eyes had a glassy stare, and she was coughing up water.

"Stay with us, Lulu," Kate said. "We're almost there." She took the girl, turned her, and held an arm under her neck, keeping her face out of the water as best she could.

"Swim," she yelled to Chelsea. "Swim."

Life's not so precious, Birdie was thinking as she watched the flames eat the main house from the inside. Everyone always seemed so convinced that it was. Maybe it seemed precious to people like Caroline, who were prone to magical thinking and believed that every moment was a *gift* and that we were all part of some *spiritual net,* our actions affecting every other soul on the grid. For Birdie, the world was rock-hard. What you saw was what you got. And she truly believed that when the time came for lights-out, there was nothing. No heavenly light. No "other side." Just the end. Why was that such a bad thing? Who would know the difference? When she would say this to people, notably her husband, they would look at her blankly, as though the thought had never occurred to them.

She'd pulled the collar of her turtleneck up over her nose. Even so, she could taste the smoke at the back of her throat. She'd never liked the main house, not really. It belonged to Joe; it was a monument to his gigantic ego. It was right that it should burn, that its burning should be the direct consequence of his philandering, his myriad infidelities.

There were fire buckets near the well, a manual pump that would operate even when the generator was down. Inside the house, there were fire extinguishers in every room. All of this assumed that you were there when the fire started, that you could keep a cool head and act quickly. Even if she ran to the well and ran back with two buckets, which was reasonably all she could carry, it wouldn't matter.

She saw the lights of the police boat approaching. It must have taken them this long because of the weather. Though the rain had ceased, the water was rough, the winds high. They would radio for help from the fire department, but they would be too late to save the main house. Perhaps the other structures could be salvaged.

She found herself running up the stairs of the front porch. The photo album lay on the dining table. It was all she had left of her childhood, the only photos of her parents, of her siblings. Gene and Birdie hadn't talked in over a decade. He was dead to her and she to him. Still, she didn't want to lose the last remnant of her childhood, even if her parents did have a sham marriage.

The screen door was hot to the touch, but she pulled it open and walked inside. Flames climbed up the drapes on the far wall, were already licking at the landing of the loft. The house was groaning, picture frames cracking and popping in the heat. She saw the album on the table. And then she saw the girl on the floor.

She grabbed the album and clutched it to her chest. Her eyes were watering, and she started coughing from the smoke. She could see that there wasn't much time, how quickly she might be overcome. The portrait over the fireplace, a younger Joe and Birdie standing stiffly together on the dock, began to burn.

I love them, he'd wept to her a lifetime ago. *Martha's a woman, a real woman. There's blood running through her veins. She laughs, she cries, she doesn't stiffen at my touch. Christ, Birdie, I wanted to love you like that.*

How she had hated him at that moment. Every breathless moment of love between them—there had been those, hadn't there?—was a distant memory. She couldn't remember what it felt like to want him. How she had wished he would leave her and never come back. But no, she couldn't have allowed it. She couldn't allow the shame, the disgrace. The very idea that he'd leave her for a shopgirl, someone who worked in a boutique, was intolerable.

And what are you? The fucking aristocracy? he'd wanted to know. *What did you come from?*

She'd come from more and better than he had. All the wealth belonged to Birdie; the real money was hers, inherited from her father's real estate investments. Even in the split with Gene and Caroline, there had been millions, though she never would have known it when they were young.

Her father, wise man that he was, had never liked Joe Burke. Her father had demanded that Birdie protect her inheritance with a prenuptial agreement, something that was far ahead of its time. She didn't understand it then, but she always did what her father told her to do. If Joe were to leave her, he'd get none of her money. Not a penny. He made a good salary, to be sure. But there would be no Manhattan penthouse, no sailboat kept on Long Island or ski trips to Switzerland—not for him. Even the island, which he never loved, really, but about which he loved to say: "Oh, we have an island on the lake." When it came down to it, he couldn't give up all of that. Not even for "true love."

Her cough worsened; the smoke was growing thicker. The air around her was so hot, her body felt soaked in sweat. The house was turning into an oven. An ache had started in her sinuses and was clawing its way over her crown. How long until she would be overcome? It was meant to be fast, mercifully fast. And peaceful. But no, she wouldn't let Joe off the hook that easily. She fully intended to outlive him. She walked out the door and tossed the album onto the ground below, heard it land with a thud. Then she went back inside.

She grabbed the girl by her hands. For such a tiny thing, she seemed to weigh a ton. It took all of Birdie's strength to pull her from the room. She didn't look back at the burning structure, couldn't care less about the clothes, the furniture, even the jewelry on her nightstand. She dragged the unconscious woman down the stairs and over the rocks. There would be bruising; it wasn't a graceful or particularly gentle descent. But it was the best she could do. Birdie pulled her down, down and away from the house, until she came to rest on the large smooth rocks at the shore. The girl groaned. No, life wasn't precious. But sometimes it was the punishment you deserved.

chapter thirty-five

John Cross wasn't sure what woke him from his sleep. Some type of popping noise. He'd lain there for a while, listening but hearing nothing. He'd just started to drift off again when he saw a strange orange glow from outside. He stumbled down the stairs and to the picture window, where he saw the house on Heart Island in flames. At first he almost didn't believe his eyes. And then, as if propelled by some unseen hand, he was running out of the house and down to his own dock.

From his right, he watched the slow approach of emergency boats, their flashing lights bouncing in the rough water. On Heart Island, the flames looked like dancers, tall and lithe, reaching up into the sky. He stood at the edge of the dock, heart pounding and panic keeping him paralyzed. What should he do? What *could* he do?

He heard the sound of voices yelling. Was someone calling for help? Unthinking, he began untying the lines of his boat. He was inexperienced in such choppy water. But he could hardly stand here when people were in trouble. He searched the water and thought he caught sight of swimmers, their cries echoing and carrying over the night. The wind had died down, but the water was rough. And cold. No one could stay in it long without being overcome.

He started the engine on his boat and backed out of his dock, knocking twice against it, then revving the engine to give himself enough power to pull away. He pointed his spotlight and saw two heads bobbing in the water, clearly struggling.

Slowly, he moved toward them, the boat rolling and bucking beneath him. He felt a wave of nausea but bit it back. He felt ill equipped to the task. How could he man the helm and help the people aboard, whoever they were? He couldn't anchor in water like this. The water would wash in and sink the boat.

As he approached, he saw one of the swimmers waving a frantic arm. Closer still, he could see that it was a woman. With a deftness he didn't even know he had, he tossed out a life ring and tied it onto one of the cleats. Then he let down the ladder on the side and raced back to the helm to correct the boat, which was veering away from the swimmers. He brought it back around and watched as one of them grabbed the ring and then grabbed the other person and started pulling toward the vessel.

It was the girl who climbed out first. She looked so young and terrified. Her hair hung in sodden rivulets, her wet clothes clinging to her thin body.

"My friend is drowning," she said, her voice shrill with panic. "We can't pull her out."

"Can you take the helm?" he asked.

"Yes," she said. "I can."

"Try to keep it steady."

She took it with a confidence beyond her years, and John climbed down the ladder. He saw Kate Burke trying to keep the head of an unconscious girl above water. He climbed into the water, still holding on to the ladder, and took hold of the girl, then dragged her back onto the boat. It was pure adrenaline. He hadn't a thought in his head as he lifted her over the side. If anyone had asked him yesterday whether he could have done it, he'd have said no. It was a good thing the girl was light.

He helped Kate up, and she knelt beside Lulu. "Mom," the girl yelled from the helm. "Is she all right?"

Kate started pumping on her chest; John watched, stunned, as she performed CPR. He walked over to the weeping child and moved her away from the wheel. She fell on her knees beside her friend. "Lulu," she said. "Please."

He began steering toward the emergency boat he'd seen. As he approached the island, he heard the girl start to sputter and cough. The other two let out loud cries of joy and relief. He found that his hands were shaking and that his heart was a turbine engine in his chest. Great flames were rising into the sky. It was the most beautiful and terrible thing he'd ever seen.

Birdie was having trouble catching her breath, and the girl was starting to stir beside her. "You burned down my house," she said.

Emily didn't move again or make a sound. Birdie found she couldn't muster any real anger. She felt blank and empty, as if it were all happening to someone else, another Birdie, another life.

That was when she noticed him, standing just as he had when she first saw him. Who was he? What did he want? Was this, after all, one of Caroline's ghosts? The ghost of Richard Cameron, come to haunt her. If he'd died the summer Birdie had seen him kiss her mother, was she somehow responsible for his death? Had he killed himself? Maybe her father had killed him? Maybe her mother had? All because she'd discovered their affair that summer night? But that was her imagination running wild.

"Who's there?" she yelled. "What do you want?"

She took the gun from her waist and held it. How silly, an old woman holding a gun against a ghost as her island burned. Her hands were shaking. If she were smart, she'd get in the water and swim like the girls. If she were smart, she'd have done so when they had. But she was in so much pain, and so tired. She thought, *No, I'll just sit here and see what happens.*

The girl was moaning, and the form started moving toward them. It had the purpose of a man. It was no apparition.

She heard voices drawing near. They were yelling, and it sounded like someone was barking orders. But the man kept moving closer.

"Stay back," she said. "Stay where you are."

As he came into view, she could see that it wasn't poor Richard Cameron at all. It wasn't a ghost haunting Heart Island, not tonight. She realized that he must be the man who'd been chasing Emily, the one looking for money. He didn't have some generation-old grudge to satisfy. What did he want? The money the girl had mentioned—Birdie didn't know where it was. Did he want the girl? What could he possibly want with her now? And no, there was nothing in that safe. It was empty, always had been. All of this nightmare, caused by people who knew only how to rob and steal, to kill each other, to set things on fire. It made her angry, so angry. She let that rage fill her and bring her to her feet.

"I have a gun," she said. Even with her anger, that was all she had the strength to say.

A long time ago, her father had taught her, Caroline, and Gene how to fire a gun. They'd line up bottles on the rocks and shoot. Birdie had loved the loud concussion, the smell of cordite in her nose. Gene was a horrible shot, always flinching from the noise and the recoil. But once they got the hang of it, Birdie and Caroline hardly ever missed. Birdie loved the way the glass shattered.

"I don't have any money," she said. "And neither does this foolish girl."

He stopped for a moment. "Where is it?" he asked. His voice sounded like a growl.

"How should I know?" she said.

"I have it," said Emily. "It's here." She pointed to a bag she had strapped around her body. Birdie hadn't noticed it when she pulled the girl from the house. The girl opened the flap and found the canvas envelope inside. She took it and flung it at the man.

"How much is it?" Birdie yelled. "Was it worth all of this?"

She thought he'd take the money and leave them, try to make his escape. Anyone would have done that. But he kept moving toward them, leaving the envelope where it lay. Birdie warned him one more time. He didn't stop coming. So she raised the gun, aimed center mass as he drew closer still and showed no signs of slowing. Finally, she opened fire.

Roger Murphy heard the shots ring out. The sound carried, echoing the way it did on the bay. He moved heavily over the rocks. His breathing was labored, and he refused to acknowledge the stitch in his side. He didn't like to be reminded how out of shape he had allowed himself to become.

The Burke girl—she wasn't a girl anymore—yelled to him from the Cross boat that her mother was on the island. She still looked like a child to him; he'd known her all her life. Just as he'd known her mother when she was a girl. But Kate Burke was a mother herself, and Birdie was an old woman. Everything had changed except the islands, which were the same as they'd always been. Except now they were occupied by the huge homes of the wealthy.

There had always been some resentment among the townies toward the rich people buying up the islands. Used to be when he was young that the islands belonged to whoever might land upon them. You could take your run-down old boat and have your choice of picnic spots or campsites. You could pitch a tent. All of a sudden, that was considered trespassing.

But he always liked to watch the summer people arrive. He'd see them come in the early days of summer, when they would arrive pale and tired-looking. Months later, they'd depart brown and smiling. He felt sorry for them, having to leave. He knew they felt sorry for him, having to stay.

The Heart girls were untouchable, the sun and the moon. But he watched them. He thought of the rumor again, that Lana Heart had been running around on her husband with Richard Cameron. Having read Cameron's books, Roger felt sorry for any woman who was foolish enough to get involved with the author. The women in his books were all whores and murderesses; they were crazed and died violent deaths, were brutalized and raped. Richard Cameron was ghostly and strange, never smiled, came in early summer, left just before the cold settled. Until the year he didn't leave at all.

Three more shots rang out. Roger's radio crackled at his hip, and he heard the chief's voice. "We have a body on the northwest coast of the island. The stolen vessel *Serendipity* is in distress, taking on water."

Roger moved through the trees. He saw two forms on the ground and one sitting by the shore. He drew his gun. "Police," he said. "Don't move."

His wife always said that his voice boomed. It didn't feel like that now. The night swallowed it. Nevertheless, the seated figure stretched arms to the sky. "You're a bit late."

He recognized the voice.

"Birdie Burke?" said Roger. "Is that you?"

"Who else?" she said. "Watch your step. I think I just killed a ghost."

Roger looked down to see a dead man at his feet. A large man with long hair, a battered face, and a chest full of lead. There was a horrible gurgling sound coming from the man. Roger had heard it before. It was the sound of the end, the death rattle. The man's chest was black and wet in the moonlight. Roger had always heard that the Burke girls were dead shots. He knelt beside the man. As he did, the labored breathing came to a shuddering end. Roger put a hand to the man's neck and felt no pulse; his skin already had a chill to it.

"Who's that beside you?" he asked.

"A girl," she said. "One of the intruders."

Roger tried to take in the scene. Usually, on these calls out to the islands, you found some teenagers high and making love on the beach. Or maybe there was a vagrant taking up residence in the house. Tonight, a fire and dead people. Heart Island, which always seemed to him so idyllic. Not the biggest but somehow the most beautiful island in the area.

"Is he real?" asked Birdie. "That man there?"

It was an odd question, and Roger wondered if Birdie was going into shock. "He looks real to me."

Roger approached and saw that she didn't look well. She'd aged since he saw her yesterday. The smoke was blowing their way, and Roger found himself coughing.

"It's time to go, Mrs. Burke," he said, leaning down to help her up. "Fire department is on the way." The girl beside Birdie had her eyes open but was staring blankly at the sky. "Can she walk?"

"I don't know," said Birdie. "I pulled her from the house and dragged her this far. Ask her."

The roar of the fire was loud, its sound filling the night. The cracking and shattering of the building, the odd moaning sound that a burning structure made, was ghostly and strange. There was enough distance between the trees and the house that the fire was contained to the structure. But if the fireboat didn't get here soon, they might be looking at a total loss.

He was about to radio for someone to bring the police boat around when John Cross pulled his vessel up as close to the shore as he could. He was alone on his smaller outboard craft. He hopped out with the line and splashed through the water, coming to shore.

"Let's get Mrs. Burke on board first," said Roger.

"I'm not leaving," she said. Her tone was stubborn and imperious, but he saw that she was shaking badly and holding back tears. He felt a flash of pity for her, something he never thought he'd feel for someone like Birdie Burke. But there she was, as old and as alone as anyone else.

"Yes, you are," said Roger. He pushed her gently toward John, who lifted her like a child and carried her to the boat.

"Put me down right now, young man!" said Birdie. Her indignation rang out, echoing over the other sounds.

Roger looked down toward the girl at his feet. *This* was the fugitive—this tiny, helpless girl? Her eyes were open but unseeing. She coughed, a horrible hacking sound, clearing smoke from her lungs. Then she turned on her side and started sobbing. He felt a tenderness for her, akin to what he might feel for a wounded animal.

It was then that he wondered how she had the same last name as the family who owned the island. There was more to this story than met the eye, he guessed. He hesitated before cuffing her; it was unsafe to have someone handcuffed in a small boat. She looked harmless enough. There were two people dead and a house on fire. She was the one left to answer for all of it. He closed the bracelets around her wrists gently and, with John's help, got her on the boat.

"It's gone," she said as they pulled away. "It's all gone."

Roger Murphy heard her despair, her hopelessness, and it was a note he felt reverberate in his bones.

chapter thirty-six

Birdie had no choice now but to watch Heart Island burn. The three of them sat on the police boat, wrapped in thick gray blankets, watching as the flames raged from the main house. The great plumes of water from the fireboat seemed to do nothing. Just when it seemed that one part of the fire had been extinguished, another leaped to life.

Birdie had never felt so powerless. She found herself holding on tight to Kate's arm. Chelsea had buried her head in Kate's lap and could be heard softly crying, as she had been since Lulu was taken by boat to a waiting ambulance. Chelsea and Kate would be following her soon.

Birdie didn't cry; the tears she'd shed as she left the island seemed to have dried her out. She searched inside for some kind of emotion, but it was as if everything in her had turned to stone.

"It was him," she said. She hadn't meant to say it out loud, but the words escaped her mouth, and she was glad for it. She couldn't have that thought knocking around inside her head; it would drive her mad.

"Who?" asked Kate. She wasn't crying, either, Birdie noticed. Everything was suffused with orange light. The men calling back and forth in their tasks sounded like strange night birds.

"The ghost," Birdie said. "It was Richard Cameron."

"Mom."

"I'm serious," she said. She faced her daughter. "He was warning me. I took what he loved the most. He took what I loved the most. Now we're even."

"You didn't take anything from him."

"Didn't I?"

After that summer, the summer of 1950—the summer she'd seen her mother with him, the year Richard Cameron's body was found—Lana was never the same person again. It was nothing that Birdie could point to, really. She was just *less* somehow. She said all of this to her daughter.

"Still," said Kate. "It was Lana who chose. She chose Grandpa Jack and all of you."

"But it was because of me, what I saw, that she had to choose," said Birdie.

"No, Mom," said Kate. "It was right that she chose. What she was doing was wrong; she was betraying everyone, even herself. Richard Cameron was violent, prone to depression, and an alcoholic. She never could have been happy with him, not truly."

They were both quiet for a moment.

"She came back that winter," said Kate. "That's the picture in your album, I suppose. They must have put the camera on the porch rail and timed it to snap. It looks like that, doesn't it, like they weren't quite ready for the shot? I can't think of anyone else who could have done it."

"We did have a camera like that," said Birdie. "Not many people had cameras back then. But we did."

Kate drew and released a long breath. "In her journals," she said, "she wrote down everything that happened after the night you discovered them. I brought them for you."

"Don't," said Birdie. She lifted a hand. "I don't want to know."

"I need to tell you what happened."

"Not now."

"If not now, then when?"

"Maybe never," said Birdie.

Kate stayed silent and looped her fingers through Birdie's. Birdie squeezed her hand tight.

"He was a destroyer," said Birdie. "This is his legacy. These are the consequences of infidelity, of betrayal. Everything burns."

"Everything burns," said Kate. "But most things can be rebuilt."

They sat like that awhile more. Eventually, it seemed that the firefighters might be making progress, getting things under control from the barge circling the island.

Chelsea wanted to go be with her friend, who she knew must be afraid and needing her. Roger Murphy said they could take the cuddy when they were ready, as long as they stayed at the marina to answer questions. He'd moved their boat to the other side of the Crosses' dock. It sat, ready to carry them back to the mainland.

"I'm going to take her, Mom," said Kate. "Come with us. There's nothing more to see here."

"I can't leave until it's done," said Birdie.

"Mom," said Kate. She held out a hand. "Please."

But Birdie turned back to the fire, watching the flames against the sky.

"Why does she always want to be left alone?" asked Chelsea.

Kate watched as her daughter undid the lines, steady even though the water was knocking the boat against the dock. There was no trace of fear in Chelsea. As Kate looked out at the dark water, the burning island, she was surprised that she didn't feel much fear, either. Not of the boat, not of the open water, and not of life without Heart Island as she knew it.

Kate remembered that when Chelsea and Brendan were small, Birdie had insisted on being left behind on the island during the worst storm in a decade. Pulling away from her, Kate had been riven with anger and fear and sadness. Tonight she found she could accept Birdie's decision without any of that. A constant puzzle in her life, her mother suddenly seemed less mysterious. She was as lost as anyone, as tethered to the past, as clueless about the future as Kate herself. She, too, was struggling to find some modicum of control over the chaos of action and consequence.

"That's just her way," said Kate.

"It's not okay," said Chelsea. "She's abandoning us for that place."

"It's not so cut-and-dried," said Kate. She remembered feeling the same way so many times.

"Yes, it is," said Chelsea.

"When you're older, things don't seem as black-and-white."

"You always say that."

Chelsea was crying in the stoic way she had developed as a teenager. As a toddler, she'd let out these earsplitting wails, releasing all the noise of her anger or disappointment or pain into the air. Kate had almost rejoiced at the sound, the fearlessness of it, the proof of life, of heart. She supposed everyone learned silence over time, learned to hold it all back, hold it in. All those powerful negative emotions leaked into their lives in other, less obvious places. You ate, or drank, or worked too hard, maybe you bullied others, maybe you had affairs, maybe you robbed and killed, went on the run from the law.

She pulled the boat away from the dock. In her boating lessons, she'd learned how to make mistakes and how to correct them. She'd learned how to clip the dock, to back up and try again. She'd learned how to avoid another vessel at the last minute and what to do if she couldn't. It was in mastering the paralyzing what-ifs that she had found the courage to take the helm, to face the open water. She knew that if the worst happened, she could handle it—most of the time.

A good fire is like an exorcism, a cleansing breath from the universe. In nature, fire clears away old and rotting vegetation, allowing for regeneration as new seeds take hold and grow. Without fire, trees can't reproduce—the litter keeps new seeds from growing. It's only the homes we build that are destroyed. But those can be rebuilt, too. In loss, there is renewal, the shedding of skin.

Maybe that was why Kate couldn't shed any tears, why she felt only a low-grade sadness. Maybe it was shock—maybe the breakdown would come later. The grief, the residual terror of running from a predator, swimming for safety, keeping Lulu from drowning—maybe it would all hit her when they were on solid ground. But for now, as she headed toward the mainland, all she could think was that if ever there was a place that needed an exorcism, it was Heart Island.

chapter thirty-seven

The world was a foggy, nebulous place for Emily. She had a mask over her mouth, and she lay in the back of an ambulance. Two uniformed police officers stood outside. The EMT had asked them to remove the handcuffs, and they'd agreed. Maybe they sensed her inertia, or that she had nowhere to go, no will to go there if she did. She listened to the sounds outside—purposeful footsteps, shouts, the occasional whoop or a short siren. She heard police radios hissing, spitting out staccato words and numbers. All of it was a swirl of activity, like a swarm of bees around her. But she was the still center, void and hollow.

The FBI agent Eliza Griffin had finally left after asking a million questions that Emily somehow managed to answer. The other woman, small and dark-haired, hiding behind thick glasses, seemed so different from anyone Emily had ever known. She was all purpose, all self-assurance. She had a gun at her hip, a shield around her neck. She talked like a man. *Run it down for me, Emily. Tell me everything, from the beginning.* Emily had the vague sense that she should ask for a lawyer. Somebody had said something about her having the right to call a lawyer. But wasn't that just something they said on television? Anyway, she wanted to tell the truth. So she did.

When she first saw him in the doorway, she thought it was Joe. She thought he'd come to tell her that the old woman had lied, that Emily was his daughter and always would be, and that starting now, he would take care of everything. She should get some sleep, and when she woke up, everything was going to be okay. But it wasn't her father. It was the man whose car they'd stolen. What was his name? She couldn't remember. It seemed like so long ago. Had it been only a few hours?

"How are you doing, Emily?" he asked.

"I'm okay," she said. "I'm so sorry. I'm so sorry for everything."

Her voice was muffled through the oxygen mask, so she wasn't sure he could understand her. Her words didn't even seem like words, more like incoherent mumbles, like those of a grown-up in a *Peanuts* cartoon.

"Emily," he said. He climbed into the ambulance and sat beside her. He was big and seemed cramped and uncomfortable in this small space. "You're the only one left to take the rap for this. The other two perpetrators are dead. You need to get a lawyer, okay? Don't say anything else to the FBI."

Why was he telling her this? Wasn't he a cop, too? Maybe it was some kind of trick. He was trying to get even with her for stealing his car. But no, he didn't seem like that kind of man. He was good; she could see that in him. She started thinking about Dean again, lying there in a pool of blood. Once upon a time, she'd believed he was a good man. Maybe somewhere inside, he was. She thought about their baby, how she'd betrayed and let down her child long before he ever knew the world. The tears came then. There was an endless river of them. She didn't think she would ever stop crying.

"You don't know me," the man said. "And I'm sure it's hard for you to know whom to trust right now. You've made some questionable moves, done some bad things, so you need to get a lawyer, someone whose job it is to help you navigate what comes next. When the agent comes back, tell her that you can't speak to her again without a lawyer."

She nodded because she couldn't find her voice or any words.

"Is there someone I can call for you?"

Was there? Dean was gone. Her mother would hate her forever. Joe Burke was not her father. For the flash of a second, she thought of Carol, whom she had betrayed and who was fighting for her life. Emily was almost crushed by the wave of regret and shame that followed. No, there was no one. She shook her head, and she saw that his eyes looked sad for her. She turned away from him.

He pressed something into her hand. "I don't know what I can do for you, Emily. But if you need some advice, give me a call."

She felt the vehicle buck as he exited. Someone outside said, "They're going to impound your vehicle for evidence, Jones. You'll have to ride back with me."

The card in her hand was plain white with black type: *Jones Cooper, Private Investigations*. There was a number and an e-mail. She tucked it into her shirt. She didn't know what anyone could do for her. But it gave her some comfort, however small.

Birdie heard the creaking of the dock and saw John Cross making his way down to her. She'd thought he was on the mainland, for some reason. He came to stand beside the boat and looked out across the water. The fire was contained, though the main house and many of the surrounding trees had been destroyed.

"What a nightmare." His voice was an awed whisper. "I'm so sorry, Birdie. What can I do?"

You can shut up. That's what she wanted to say. She didn't want his pity while he stood on the safety of his own island, his home and life perfectly intact. Of course, she couldn't say that. He'd pulled her daughter, her granddaughter, and the little trollop from the water. Not that they wouldn't have made it on their own. But she supposed she should offer some gratitude.

"I'm not sure there's anything we can do right now. But thank you. Thank you for helping my family." She thought it sounded sincere enough.

" 'My barn having burned to the ground,' " he said, " 'I can now see the moon.' "

Perfect. That's just what she needed. Haiku.

On a whim, she reached down and picked up the photo album. She opened it and removed the photograph. She handed it to John Cross; she couldn't say why. It was such a personal item, meaning so much to her. And she wasn't one to share. He stared at it a moment, then looked at Birdie. There was some kind of strange light in his eyes.

"Where did you get this?" he asked.

"That's my mother."

"With Richard Cameron?"

"Apparently."

John looked at the photograph for a long moment, then turned his eyes back to Birdie. "Why don't you come up to my house?" he asked.

The truth was that she was cold and so tired. There was nothing left to see, so she took the hand he offered and followed him up the path to his beautiful home. She sat on his couch while he made her some tea and then came to join her.

"I haven't been totally honest with you," he said.

"Oh?" She couldn't care less what he had to say. The sky out the window was so clear that it was impossible to imagine it had been raining at all earlier in the evening. It seemed that a glow emanated from the island, a kind of radiant heat. She would rebuild that house. She'd rebuild it her way.

"I'm Richard Cameron's great-nephew," he said. "He was my mother's uncle."

He delivered the information grimly, as though it should mean something to her. It didn't. No matter what he was to her mother, Richard Cameron was only a ghost to Birdie. She'd just recently learned his name. She looked over at John more closely. He bore no resemblance whatsoever to the man in the photographs, blond where Cameron was dark, big where Cameron was slim.

"The mystery of his death has been something of an obsession of mine," he said. "There were always rumors of an affair. But I've never heard a first-person account."

"Who told you there were rumors?"

"Roger Murphy," said John. "He used to work at the marina when he was young."

Birdie remembered, of course. He'd been so gorgeous; Caroline and she had always dissolved into giggles when he helped load the boat or pump the fuel. He was earthy and innocent. But that boy, those girls, were so long gone, it was as if they never existed.

Birdie found herself telling John Cross what she had seen that night so long ago. It was something she had always held on to, never shared with anyone, like some kind of secret shame. Tonight it seemed she couldn't stop from telling the story. It felt good to know that she was right after all. Even if it meant the destruction of everything she had believed about her parents.

"He wasn't a nice man," John said after Birdie had finished. "He battled clinical depression. He and his sister weren't close. In fact, she hated him."

"I understand that he was troubled."

"Do you know what happened to him?" He asked the question sheepishly, as if it embarrassed him to want to know.

"No," she said. "I don't know. My mother never confided this to me, obviously. I only recently learned of the affair, the truth of what I'd seen. I always thought it was a dream."

She wouldn't tell him. She wouldn't give it to him. It belonged to Kate now; it was her story to tell, passed down from Mother, to Caroline, and then to Kate. Even Birdie, as angry as she'd been, could see that Kate should be the one to tell it. She would do them all justice with her writer's heart.

"There's another rumor," said John. He wore a small smile. "That Kate has written a book. A thinly veiled fictional account of her grandmother's affair with a famous writer."

"Is that so?"

"I hear it's quite good."

"Of course it is," said Birdie. "She's Katherine Elizabeth Burke. Anything she chooses to do, she does well."

John offered a gracious nod, a lift of his teacup. But there was something dark in his expression. Birdie assumed it was jealousy. He was probably a failed writer, bitter and thinking everyone published was less talented than he. "You must be very proud."

Birdie was used to the pinched expression and tone of envy. It didn't bother her in the least. "I suppose I am."

chapter thirty-eight

The marina was a chaos of police vehicles, ambulances, and fire trucks. As her mother docked the boat in its slip, a news van was pulling down the rocky drive, gravel crunching loudly beneath the tires. She could hardly begin to process all the things that had happened, everything she'd learned. How could nothing be as you imagined it? It seemed to Chelsea that below the surface was another universe. Everyone wore one face, told one story of themselves, and then underneath was a whole other life, a rushing current of secret pains and buried shames, ugly truths. Was it so hard to just be what you were?

Chelsea stayed in her seat at the bow of the boat, even after her mother killed the engine and started tying off the lines. Once she set foot on land, Chelsea felt as if she were going to be swept away into chaos.

"Are you all right?" Kate asked. She came to sit beside Chelsea and wrap her in a tight embrace.

"I don't know."

"Fair enough," her mother replied. Only her mother told the truth, the whole truth of herself. There was nothing hidden in Kate; she wore it all out in the open. Chelsea could see that, and how much it hurt sometimes to be that way.

"Are *you* all right?" asked Chelsea.

"I am," Kate said. "I really am."

"How?"

"Because everyone I love is safe," she said. "And I really don't care about anything else."

"Not the house or the island?"

"The island was there before me, and it will be there after I'm gone. The house—well—we'll build a new one."

Kate then spoke about how new things couldn't grow until old things were destroyed. Even though Chelsea could understand how that might be so, it didn't offer any comfort. She remembered how her mother had bought her a snow globe of the city, a pretty skyline inside a big ball filled with glittering flakes. She'd loved it. But one day, while dusting, her mother had knocked it from the shelf, and it shattered on the desk. The shards went everywhere, the tiny sparkles flying onto the walls, the bed, and the pile of the carpet. Even though Chelsea had been too old to cry over such things, she had.

"I'm so sorry, sweetie," her mother had said. "I'll get you a new one."

"I don't want a new one," she said. "I want the one we picked out together."

She wanted the one that her mother had carried to the register and paid for, the one that had sat on her shelf for years, the one that she had picked up a thousand times and watched as the swirling pieces of silver rushed around the Statue of Liberty, the Empire State Building, the Chrysler Building, the little taxicabs. She wanted the one that was part of her room and all her memories of that room. She couldn't see how that thing could be replaced or how a replacement would do anything but remind her of the thing she had lost.

After her mother grew tired of her sulking about the snow globe, Kate had said, "It's just a thing. And things don't mean much, Chelsea. Only people matter."

Although she realized that was true, it didn't feel true. Even now sometimes she thought of that snow globe and how pretty it was and how much she had loved it. The finality of its being gone had never ceased to amaze and frustrate her. *It's silly to attach to objects, honey. We have to let go of everything eventually.* Why? Another of those questions that no one seemed able to answer.

On the air, she could smell smoke, the smell of the house burning. That was another thing that had been lost and would not be replaced. Everything on the island would be defined as before and after the fire. There was something eternal about loss, something endless. You could always lose the things you had, but you couldn't always get back the things you lost.

She found she couldn't say any of this to her mother, that she hardly had the words for all of it. It was just a mute and helpless feeling that she carried with her as they walked up the dock to find Lulu. When Chelsea saw her friend sitting small and alone in the back of an ambulance, she ran to her. They clung to each other. "I'm so sorry," Lulu kept saying.

Chelsea didn't know what Lulu was sorry about—all the awful things that had happened on the island, the fire, the lie she had told, the fight they'd had. It didn't matter. None of it mattered. Chelsea realized that her mother was right after all.

"Chelsea?" said Lulu.

"Yeah," said Chelsea.

"This was the worst vacation I ever had."

Somewhere deep inside, Chelsea wanted to laugh. But she couldn't; instead, she started to cry. Lulu did, too. Chelsea wondered how long it would be before she'd stop seeing that man coming after them, pushing through the door like some kind of horror-movie freak. Or when she would stop hearing Lulu scream as she beat at him with a shovel and he kept on coming. Or when she would stop feeling the pain that rocketed up her arms when she hit him in the face with that fire poker, and the sickening sound of iron on bone that followed the impact.

"We really kicked that guy's ass," said Lulu, still crying. "I had no idea you were such a killer."

"It runs in the family," said Chelsea. "On my mother's side."

Then they did laugh, in a way that was more like weeping, ragged and unhinged. But it felt good.

As Kate watched the girls embrace, she felt the first tide of real sadness, and a deep shudder moved through her body. She started shaking as if from a chill at her core. Then she saw Sean pull up and get out of the car. He looked frantically around the scene. Their eyes met, and he moved quickly toward her, past a police officer who tried to stop him. She watched him pulling away, pointing toward her, and finally, the officer let him pass.

"What happened? Where's Chelsea?" Sean said. He held her by the shoulders, then pulled her close.

"She's there," said Kate, pointing. "We're fine. Where's Brendan?"

"He's with my mother. What happened? Do I smell smoke?"

"I don't know where to begin," she said.

"Why don't you begin with me?" There was the young female FBI agent whom Kate had seen on the island. She introduced herself as Agent Eliza Griffin. "Are you up to answering a few questions about what happened out there?"

"Of course," said Kate.

"Come with me where it's warm," said the agent. She looked like a girl, maybe in her twenties. Somehow that happened. First you were the kid, no one taking you seriously. And then, all of a sudden, people much younger were in positions of authority, and you were supposed to listen to them. It was truly weird.

"I need to stay near my daughter," Kate said. It was impossibly cold. She felt like she would never be warm again.

"Do you need medical attention?" asked the agent.

Kate was about to refuse, but she did need medical attention— a blow to the head that had caused her to lose consciousness, a frantic swim through frigid cold water. She felt herself leaning against Sean.

"You're shaking," he said.

"I just want to tell it, what happened," she said. They moved to the back of an ambulance, and a paramedic wrapped her in a blanket. Sean was with her as she started to tell the story of what had happened that night. It was a rundown of events: the storm, the intruders, the stranded boat, watching one man kill another, running to Chelsea, getting knocked to the ground, getting the girls to safety. The federal agent asked questions that Kate answered to the best of her ability. But it was merely the surface, the events as they unfolded in chronological order. The meaning of everything was a current that flowed beneath it all. So much had happened here, not all of it tonight, that wouldn't mean anything to a young FBI agent looking to make a big arrest.

"Who were they to you?" asked Agent Griffin. "Why did they come to this place?"

Kate hesitated; it was private, wasn't it? Her mother had told her on the boat briefly that for some reason, the girl thought she was Joe's daughter. There was more to the story, she knew. She had some vague memory from her childhood. It lingered on the edge of her consciousness, though she couldn't access it. It was something Birdie would never want anyone to know. But the police had to know the truth. "The girl believed that my father, Joe Burke, was her biological father. I'm not clear on why. I think you'll have to ask my mother."

The news didn't seem to shock or surprise Agent Griffin; she wrote the information down in her book. Sean, on the other hand, was slack-jawed with shock. He looked like a caricature of surprise.

"So why would she come here?" asked Agent Griffin. "Did she think he was here?"

"I don't know. Apparently, the men she was with thought there was a safe."

Really, hadn't that girl come looking for the same thing everyone came here looking for, some feeling of family, a place where she belonged and was happy?

"Did you know Emily Burke?" asked Agent Griffin. "Did you ever have any contact with her before today?"

The girl had introduced herself as Anne, but Birdie had called her Emily. Kate hadn't realized they shared a last name, and something about that unsettled her. "No," she said. "Never."

The agent chewed on her pen, regarded Kate carefully. "Emily claims your mother pulled her from the burning house."

"If she did that," said Kate, "she had her reasons."

Kate suspected that it didn't have anything to do with altruism or compassion. Birdie probably wanted the girl to live to pay for her crimes. That would be just like Birdie, to risk her own safety to satisfy some rigid idea she had about justice. To her, death would be a way out.

"So you don't think they had a relationship?"

"My mother doesn't really have a relationship with anyone," Kate said. Then she started to laugh. She doubled over with it as the agent regarded her with a confused smile.

"Oh, boy," said Sean. Kate felt his hand on her back. She'd lost it like this a couple of times over the years. Once the floodgates opened, they were hard to close. "Kate, it's okay."

The laughing quickly turned to sobbing as all the pent-up terror, anger, and grief of the evening rushed up from within her.

"Kate," said Sean. She buried her face in his chest as the great sobs shook her. "It's all right. It's all going to be fine."

Even in the middle of the chaos, with the flashing lights of emergency vehicles and the smell of smoke thick in the air, even as she felt herself losing all of that in a field of white stars that had appeared before her eyes, she knew it was true.

chapter thirty-nine

After Birdie saw us, I knew things had to change. Jack and I had a terrible fight that night. We kept up appearances during the day, for the sake of the children, but while they slept, we walked to Lookout Rock. It was no less bitter for the fact that we had to keep our voices to whispers. He delivered an ultimatum for me to give up Richard or give up our family. During the summers, Jack would come and go from the island for work. Richard and I had our evenings after the children went to sleep. He'd wait for me near the trees on the north shore. There was no choice to be made, really. I told Richard the next night that we were through, and he seemed to accept my decision.

The letters he sent all through the following autumn were so desperate; I had to go to him. I told Jack that I needed to visit my sister because she was ill and none of us was sure how much time she had. That was true without being the whole truth. I spent a day and a night with my family, and on the way back to the city, I stopped at the marina and took the boat to Richard's island. It was cold, too cold by then to be up there. I didn't like it; it felt wrong to be there when the water was gray and the air was biting. Even as I headed out, there were flurries, a light coating of snow on the dock. It filled me with sadness. Heart Island was a summer dream. In my mind, it was never winter there.

We passed a day in the house. It was too cold otherwise—I couldn't stay in his tent, huddled by the fire. I've always hated the cold. I urged him to come back with me. I didn't want to leave him there, depressed and alone, slipping into that dark place he always tended toward. That was the problem with Richard, he always chose that sinking black-ness over life. It was why I chose to be with Jack. Poor Jack. He deserved so much better than me. He was such a good man, and I was a terrible wife.

Everything was fine until it was time for me to leave. That was when Richard told me that he couldn't let me go. He said he couldn't live without me. I told him that he had to learn to, that I could no longer betray us all every summer. Even though I knew it was the worst possible thing I could do, I told him I didn't love him anymore.

That is my deepest regret. What I should have done was played along and taken him home to his family. They were accustomed to getting him the help that he needed, helping him across those dark spaces, keeping him writing—which was the place he exorcised all his terrible demons. Honestly, I just didn't have it in me. Birdie had almost discovered us this summer. And the children all needed me a lot—Gene was struggling in school, Caroline was going through a very emotional stage, and Birdie, well, Birdie was just an angry little girl. She'd been angry since that night, as though she knew I'd lied and made a fool of her. Poor Birdie, she was always too old, too smart, for her years. She'd never even allowed herself to believe in Santa Claus. In her eyes, I saw all the judgment I deserved.

The irony there is that I have always suspected that Birdie might be Richard's child. She's so different from the other children, so hard and unyielding sometimes, so prone to anger and despair. Sometimes I see him in her long, thin fingers, her pale skin, and the line of her mouth.

Jack had been away a lot while I was at the lake with the children that summer. Richard and I were together almost every night while they slept. And Birdie by far has the greatest attachment to the island, as if she belongs to it and it to her. In a way, since she was conceived there, it's true. But this is not a thing that I dwell on too much. If Jack suspected, he never said. We were so good at that, turning away from the ugly and unpleasant and carrying on as if nothing were the matter. It wouldn't have done anybody any good to know the truth.

Heartbroken

Richard's death was an accident. Or maybe it was self-defense. There had been horrible rows before that one, before I even knew Jack. There was something about us, what we were together, that ignited this passion. What was lovemaking one moment could easily shift to violence. I wanted to leave, wanted him to come with me. But he grabbed my arm and begged me to stay. Then he became angry, claimed I never loved him. He told me that I was every whore and nightmare bitch who populated his novels. I'll never forget the things he said. He said: You've taken everything from me and left me empty, always yearning, always alone. I've had to face over the years that it was true.

I ran from him and he gave chase. I found myself climbing the rocks to Lookout Rock. Why didn't I run for the boat? I have asked myself this a hundred times. The rocks were slick in a way I wasn't used to, and I fell several times on the climb. And then when I was up there, I had no place to go.

"What now?" he asked at the top.

The water was black and still beneath us. Over us was a high white moon, thin wisps of dark gray clouds.

"Let me take you home," I said. "You need help."

Something about my words enraged him, and he was on me. Had it been just me, I'd have let him take me. But there were Jack, Caroline, Birdie, and Gene. They needed me, and I needed them. Richard was everything dark inside me, and they were everything good and light. I had to choose and I did. I fought for my life. In doing so, I caused Richard to lose his footing and fall from Lookout Rock into the water below. Should I have dived in after him, tried to find him in that cold black water? I should have, and I didn't.

I screamed for him, my voice a knife slicing the night with all sorrow. How long did I stay there? I don't know. But after a while, I heard a boat. And then Jack was there, miraculously. I told him. I told him everything. And then we left Heart Island, left Richard. We agreed to never speak of it, to forget it all. In the spring, they found his body. Poor Richard, everyone knew what a terrible wreck he was, how he wrestled the demons of alcoholism and depression. The end he found surprised no one.

If anyone saw us go to and return from the island that day, no one said so. Suspicion never once turned to us. And one might have thought the guilt would haunt us, but I have to be honest that it didn't. I can only speak for myself when I say that I felt as if I had been afflicted with a terrible illness in my love for Richard, and that night on Heart Island, I was cured. It's an awful way to feel, but that's the truth. I can't be honest anywhere else in my life, but I can be honest here. We'd met on the islands a lifetime earlier, when we were children. Our love for each other was born there. And it was only right that it should have died there, too.

"What is the difference between fiction and memoir, really? I mean, isn't there a bit of autobiography in every novel? And isn't there a bit of fiction in every memoir? Memory is elastic, and no two people have the same version of any given event. Our versions of our own lives are necessarily fictional to some degree, wouldn't you agree?"

The radio interviewer's face was partially obscured behind a huge gray microphone. The control panel beneath her hands was a light show of red and green, a million tiny levers and dials.

"Well," said Kate. She'd learned to take her time in answering questions. "I think the difference is in what you claim it is. How honest are you being with yourself, with others, about what you've written? Are you hiding behind a fictional account of a real event to avoid the consequences of telling your truth? Or are you claiming that an idealized version of your life is the truth? I think it's an important distinction."

The interviewer offered a thin smile. "So, then, your novel? Is it fiction based on truth? Or is it truth hiding in fiction?"

Kate breathed deeply. She'd answered this question so many times that the answer she was about to give felt scripted and practiced before she even opened her mouth.

"In reality, my grandmother had an affair with Richard Cameron. In her journals, and in the journals of my aunt, I learned about her version of what transpired between them. The story I tell was inspired by that affair and by those journals. But it is not a true account of what happened between Lana Heart and Richard Cameron. Nobody really knows that story."

This wasn't the whole truth. But it wasn't a lie, either. That was the thing about fiction: The real and the unreal worlds mingled to become something altogether different. It didn't stand against judgment in either place.

"The family of Richard Cameron thinks they do."

Now it was Kate's turn to offer a wry smile. "They're entitled to that. But with both parties long dead and no one living who was close enough to them to bear witness, I hold that it's impossible to know the truth now."

"And what about those journals?"

"Sadly, they were incinerated in the fire that destroyed the house on Heart Island, my family's vacation home. I'd brought those journals with me to share them finally with my mother. I never had the chance to give them to her."

The interviewer, a striking woman with alabaster skin and shockingly red hair, kept her sea-green eyes on Kate, and Kate held her gaze. So far, she'd been pretty impartial, though her questions were straight to the point.

"Some people find that to be a convenient coincidence."

"And I find it to be a personal tragedy."

The other woman looked down at her notes. "What do you think happened to Richard Cameron?" she said.

"I think he was a very unhappy man who struggled against the two-headed monster of depression and alcoholism, and that in losing my grandmother, he was overcome. He lost whatever war he was fighting within himself."

"You think he committed suicide."

In a sense, hadn't he? He'd attacked Lana, and she'd fought for her life. In the struggle, he'd fallen. Or at least that was Lana's account. One had to believe that if he wanted to overpower her physically, he could have done so easily. But in Kate's novel, the character who loosely represented Richard Cameron ended his own life. In the struggle at the highest point on the island, he realized what he was doing—hurting, trying to kill, the only woman he'd ever loved. In realizing what he'd become, he threw himself onto the rocks below. Kate's fiction had become a kind of truth for her. It was the only truth she had a right to tell. Both Lana and Caroline had, in a sense, confided in her. She wouldn't betray them by telling their stories. She could only tell her own.

"I *imagine* he did, one way or another," said Kate. "Either intentionally or by accident."

There was a moment of silence. Kate could see all the lights on the phone between them blinking furiously.

"The Cameron family holds that your grandmother and grandfather were seen visiting the island the winter before his body was discovered," said the interviewer. "They believe he was murdered and that your grandparents had something to do with that."

"There is absolutely no evidence to support that theory," said Kate. Again, it was a phrase she'd uttered so many times that it rolled off her tongue, some kind of boilerplate statement. "It's an unsubstantiated rumor."

"So it is. Well, Kate Burke, that's all the time we have today. Thank you for speaking to us about your new novel, *The Island*. I enjoyed it, and I know many other people are enjoying it as well. Ms. Burke will be signing tonight at Powell's here in Portland at eight P.M. Come on out and see her. This is KXL Radio's Beth Grayson, and this has been *Book Talk*."

———

A car waited for Kate as she exited the radio studio into a cold and rainy day. She felt a peculiar kind of exhaustion that came from being on the road too long. She remembered how Sebastian used to complain about a kind of brain fry that occurred after you'd talked about yourself and your creative output too much. You started to feel like a facsimile of yourself, something diminished in quality by too much reproduction.

Then there were the late nights, the endless flights, and the rich foods she would never eat at home. Luckily, on this leg, she had Sean with her; the kids were staying with Sean's mother. On the other stops, she'd been alone, and she'd felt like an astronaut on a line, floating out in space.

She hadn't expected any attention for the book, really. But the incident on the island, along with her relationship to Sebastian, had led to a bit of a media feeding frenzy. The book was climbing up the best-seller lists. She wondered what would have become of it if not for the factors that had nothing to do with her writing. She suspected not very much.

She hadn't expected to do so much talking about Lana and Jack. She had expected that it would be a matter known to no one except her own family. It was John Cross who turned the whole thing into the huge mess that it had become. He claimed that the photo Birdie inexplicably had shown him proved that Lana Heart at least had visited the island the winter Richard Cameron disappeared. But that photo, too, was missing. Kate had no idea what Birdie had done with it, and Birdie wasn't telling.

"What on earth possessed me to talk to that buffoon?" she'd railed after the media circus began.

"Maybe you just wanted to share it with someone," Kate had said, though she had wondered the same thing. Her mother, who gave nothing, who revealed nothing, had shared this critical piece of evidence with a virtual stranger. It mystified Kate, as so many things about Birdie mystified her.

"And you wonder why I hate people."

"I never wondered that, Mother."

"Well," said Birdie, "now you know, whether you wondered or not. Everybody is just out for himself."

The journals had, in fact, burned in the fire. Kate had brought them for Birdie, thinking that she deserved to see them. But now they were gone. It was just as well. She didn't want anyone to know what Lana and Caroline had written. It was so long ago, and everyone was gone. Her book was fiction, bearing little resemblance to actual events or people. It was her story, not theirs.

Back at the hotel, Sean was on the phone with his partner, Jane. He lifted a finger as Kate walked into the room, so she showered while he finished his call. She always had an urge to get into the shower after an interview, as if to scrub away her public persona. She didn't recognize this Kate. In her mind, she was a wife and mother, a closet writer; she was *justamom*. She liked that woman better. That woman knew what was real, what mattered. Kate the author thought about interviews and book signings, best-seller lists and book reviews (which had been mixed: some glowing, some not). It all seemed like an alternate universe, a place where it was impossible to ground and center oneself.

"You were great," said Sean when she emerged from the shower. "You're getting really good at this."

"Just in time for it to be over," she said.

She wondered what the event would be like tonight. Small or packed? The crowd sympathetic or accusing? Would the questions be about the actual book or about the fire, about Richard Cameron? Since Emily Burke's sentencing, there had been a lot of questions about that. How did Kate feel about her? What punishment did Kate feel Emily deserved?

The truth was that Kate felt nothing but compassion for the girl.

Emily had been victimized by Kate's father and by her own mother, Martha. She was told a lie that had corrupted her entire life. She'd fallen in with awful, murderous men who used her and coerced her into doing terrible things. She'd miscarried while in custody.

When Kate saw Emily on television or in the newspaper, she looked like a paper cutout of a girl, someone utterly defeated. She would serve time, they'd learned this week, a reduced sentence as an accomplice and an accessory to the crimes committed by Dean Freeman and Brad Campbell. To Kate, it didn't seem fair. This opinion infuriated Birdie.

"She's a grown woman," said Birdie. "She made choices, bad ones. You don't get a pass just because you had a less than perfect childhood."

Birdie was angry about Kate's compassion, saw it as a kind of weakness. Often, in the many lengthy discussions they'd had about that terrible night and everything that surrounded it—Joe's affair (which he flatly refused to discuss, calling it "none of Kate's goddamned business"), the love triangle among Lana, Jack, and Richard—Kate wondered if Birdie ever for a second suspected that Richard might have been her own father and, therefore, Kate's grandfather. Since the journals had burned, Kate never mentioned what Lana had written. What good would it do? She couldn't imagine what words she would use to broach that topic with her mother. Like so many things, it went unspoken between them.

Since hearing about Emily's sentence, Kate had been asking herself how much choice a girl like that really had. How could you make good choices if no one ever taught you how? How could you choose a good relationship if you didn't know what one looked like? Kate wondered whether she'd have chosen someone as wrong for her as Sebastian if she'd had a better childhood, if she hadn't confused control with love. In truth, it was only her desire to find a safe place for Chelsea that had allowed her to recognize the good in Sean. She chose right for them because she didn't choose from fear, or desperation, or all the myriad sad and lonely places from which we sometimes choose. When she thought about the baby whom Emily Burke lost, Kate felt irrationally sad.

But Kate couldn't afford to dwell in that place anymore. She'd spent too much time thinking and talking about Heart Island. She had one more book signing and then a life to get back to. Her children needed her. Over a year later, Chelsea was still having nightmares. On their return to the East Coast, she, Sean, and the kids would be moving into the house with which Sean had fallen in love. As a two-income family, they could easily afford it—without Kate's trust. And it felt like a time for new beginnings.

chapter forty

In the milky gray mornings, in the moments right after she opened her eyes, Emily could almost forget what she had allowed her life to become. For a second or maybe two, the morning dawned with its endless possibilities. She began each day with the slimmest ray of hope. And then the crushing weight of reality would settle on her, press down on her chest, constrict her breathing. The losses—of Dean, of her child, of herself—were almost too much to bear. She was buried beneath a drift of grief and sorrow. Each day, she waded through it, wondering if her life would ever be anything but this.

In her childhood room, there was the same pink cat with the ragged tail, the same torn Backstreet Boys poster, the white desk and chair covered in stickers. She thought of her little house, the house she'd lived in alone at first and then shared with Dean. She and her mother had sold all of the furniture on Craigslist, to help defray some of the costs of Emily's legal fees.

Her sentence was very lenient. The defense held that she'd been acting under emotional duress; the videotape of her being carried screaming from the Blue Hen, along with the testimony from Jones Cooper that she'd had a bruise on her face, had seemed to confirm that. But it wasn't the whole truth, and the jury apparently realized that. There were points, moments, when she might have altered the outcome of the situation, and she hadn't made the right choices. She would serve a year in the minimum-security division of a women's prison about an hour from where she lived.

Her lawyer had been optimistic about it. "You can use this time to get your head right, Emily," she said. "This is not hard time. I'm not saying it's going to be easy. But I'm saying that you can opt to see it as a new beginning."

Things could have gone a lot worse for her if it hadn't been for Carol, who'd pleaded for leniency. Carol had recovered from her injuries—almost completely. She walked with a slight limp, and there was a bit of a slur to her speech. She came to the sentencing hearing, though she'd never answered any of Emily's letters begging for her forgiveness.

"I could see that she was a girl who was in over her head. I don't think she had any idea what they were planning until that night, or how things might go," said Carol. "I think she was coerced into going along with them. And I believe that she thought she could help me by doing what they said. She was always a hard worker and a good person. She made a horrible mistake, but I don't think she should serve hard time."

On her way out of the courtroom, Carol offered Emily a sad smile. All Emily could do was weep at the table; the tide of shame and gratitude within her was so great that she thought it might take her away.

She'd enrolled in an inmate program where she would help train Seeing Eye dogs for the blind. It was part of the rehabilitation plan that would reduce her sentence. Honestly, the thought of it, that she could do something that might help people, was the only thing that pulled her from bed in the morning. It was a penance. When she came through, she might be cleansed.

She had another week before she had to turn herself in to custody. She kept thinking: *My life will begin again on that day.* She tried not to think of all the horror stories she'd already heard about even a minimum-security prison. *You will be used and abused, if you allow it,* her lawyer had told her. *The people in there will try to take what they can from you. They will try to hurt you. But if you stay strong, don't look for friends, keep your head down, and go to work, you might survive.*

Her mother had not judged her or lambasted her, as Emily thought she would. She had stood by Emily, helped her get a lawyer, had come every day to court. Joe's money, the sum that had been intended for her education, made it possible for her to hire a woman who specialized in cases like Emily's, someone who could help her get a reduced sentence as part of a special occupational therapy program. Joe hadn't reached out to her personally. At first she'd been hurt. Then it dawned on her fully that the man she thought of as Joe Burke was a fairy tale. He was not her father. The money he'd given for her education—she didn't even understand why he'd done that. He owed her nothing. She was nothing to him, only a little girl he was kind to once when he had loved her mother. The circumstances of his life had dictated his behavior, just as the circumstances of her life had dictated hers. Maybe it was his way of saying that he would have loved her if he could have. He might have been her father in all the ways that mattered, even if nothing linked them biologically. That was what she chose to believe, even if she had no reason to think it was true.

"Money is easy to give, if you have it," Martha had said. "The offering of it can masquerade as a good deed, even if you're just using it to keep people away from you, building a wall against reproach. You can use it to control people, to buy their distance."

Emily thought maybe it was simpler than that: Some people gave money instead of love because it was all they had to give. A full bank account and a life of good deeds achieved with money didn't mean a full heart or a giving soul—often just the opposite.

She showered and dressed and went downstairs, where her mother was making her breakfast. They hadn't spoken much since the sentencing. What was there to say? It was the end of a long journey and the beginning of another. She was shoring up her internal resources, and speech seemed like a waste of energy.

She sat at the table, and her mother brought her a cup of coffee, sat across from her. The kitchen was run-down, the appliances old, the linoleum floors so ancient that they'd never look clean no matter how much you scrubbed.

"I know this is my fault, Emily," said her mother. Emily looked up from her coffee and saw that her mother had her eyes cast toward the table. Emily could see the gray in her roots, the ragged condition of her cuticles, a stain on her blouse. "I want you to know that I'm sorry for all the ways I've failed you."

"Mom." Her instinct was to protest, to say that everything was okay, she would be okay. But wasn't that a big part of the problem with Emily, that she was always trying to make things okay for other people at her own expense, leaving her with a permanent emotional and spiritual deficit? That she was always looking for someone else to fill the emptiness in her, and that was why she was so vulnerable to people like Dean.

"I've made mistakes, terrible mistakes—for myself, for you," her mother said. "And I'm going to help you get through this."

Her mother, too, had made bad choices in the quest for love. Emily couldn't judge her, even though righteous anger would be so much easier. It was so much simpler to see other people's wrongs and make them pay. It was so much harder to have compassion, to see yourself in others and find forgiveness.

"I've made mistakes, too, Mom. And I'm going to do better."

In saying this, Emily felt something shift inside her chest. Something in her that had been closed since the night she helped Dean and Brad rob the Blue Hen. For the first time in a long time, she felt hope.

chapter forty-one

Birdie stood on the rocks at Heart Island and watched the first light of dawn crack the horizon. She wasn't going to swim today; her sciatica was dominating her life at the moment. Even though swimming was a suitable therapy for all kinds of pain, this morning she stayed on land.

She surveyed the skeletal structure of the new house she was having built. They had used the old foundation, but the house being erected was of her own design. She wanted to be sure she could see the dawn breaking from the master bedroom. Because while so many people seemed to cherish the sunset (including Joe), it was the dawn of a new day that Birdie prized. It was God's little reminder that no matter how dark the night, the sun always rises.

The workers would arrive by barge in a few hours, and then the whole island would be alive with the sounds of their hammers and saws, their loud music, their booming voices. They chased away the silence and the birds, but she didn't mind. It would be worth it to see this new house, the one that was exactly as she wanted it. For a little while longer, at least, there would be quiet.

She was alone with Heart Island. Kate and her family were taking a trip this year to someplace insane—was it Asia or Africa? Even though she and Kate were closer in some ways since the incidents of last summer and since the publication of Kate's book, there was more distance, too. Kate said no more often, visited less, and said that she'd be taking a year or maybe two off from Heart Island. If

Birdie thought about it too much, she felt things that were uncomfortable for her—sadness, regret, loneliness. So she simply didn't think about it. Theo made his weekly phone call but announced that he wouldn't be returning to Heart Island—ever. Though he said the reasons should be clear, she had no idea what he was talking about. It was something else she chose not to contemplate.

Joe would be staying in the city this summer, at her request. They were far beyond the point where divorce was seemly or financially advisable, but they would move in separate orbits for a good portion of the year. They would make the appropriate appearances, have dinner with friends. They could manage that much. This was best, wasn't it?

She climbed off the foundation, her sciatic nerve screeching in protest as she descended the steps. She walked stiffly around the house and up the path to Lookout Rock. It was here that she'd had a small gazebo erected, a place where she could sit and gaze out over the lake and the other islands, or back at the mainland.

From up here, she could see every point on the island not obscured by trees. She thought how much Caroline would have liked it, a place to sit and write. It was with her sister in mind that she'd had it built. It was an apology, in a way. It was too little and, of course, far too late. There was no making amends for a lifetime of catfights and angry words, misunderstandings, and grudges held for decades. Even now Birdie couldn't remember why they'd always fought. It was jealousy, she supposed, over who had what and who didn't— beauty, love, children, happiness, their mother's love and confidence, Heart Island. It seemed silly now, though it certainly hadn't then.

Sitting in the gazebo, Birdie remembered what it was like to be a child on Heart Island, before all the anger and bitterness between her and her siblings had erupted and then cooled and hardened. She remembered what it was like to play pretend or read, to nap in the hammock or gaze at the stars, to just *be* in this place that asked nothing but your presence. In a way, she'd spent her whole life trying to find her way back to her memory of it. But she wondered if that memory was, as Kate said, a fiction she had created, an idyllic dream of a place that never was. Maybe Heart Island was exactly what it was right now, and could never be what you wished it was or believed it had been once.

At the line of trees, she saw him. He was her companion in this place, always in the periphery, never coming into focus. If she marched toward him, as she often did, he'd disappear. She was not afraid of him anymore. He was not a destroyer, as she had once assumed of him. He was just a watcher here, as was she. He was someone who remembered—with passion, with regret, with love—something he would never have again.

Acknowledgments

So MUCH happens internally before words finally find their way onto the page that sitting down to write a novel often feels as if it's the last 5 percent of the process. Then, once the book is written, there are miles to go before it arrives on the shelves. Writing is a journey the author makes alone. But publishing is a team effort. Without the support of the following people, you wouldn't be holding this book in your hands.

My husband, Jeffrey, and daughter, Ocean Rae, are the rock-solid foundation of my life. Without them, I wouldn't be the person or the writer that I am. Every day, they fuel me with love, laughter, and light. In the chaos of our zany days, there is a special kind of peace, a place where I dwell and am at my happiest. Thanks, guys. You're everything, always.

The best editors understand that authors are a little nervous, a slightly crazy bunch, and do much better inside their own heads than without. These editors know how to get the best work out of their authors, usher them through the publishing process, and wait on the other side to cheer them on when the book hits the shelves. I have been so lucky in this respect. Shaye Areheart is a gifted and loving editor who has helped to shape my work, and she has become a dear and important friend. I can say the same about John Glusman, my in-house editor. I am indebted to them both—for their tremendous talent, their support, and their stellar friendship.

My agent, the brilliant and fabulous Elaine Markson, is my un-

Acknowledgments

flagging supporter, tireless champion, and wonderful friend. Her assistant, the incomparable Gary Johnson, keeps me sane, organized, and, most important, laughing. I really can't begin to list everything they do for me, day after day, or to express my endless gratitude. I hope they know how much I appreciate them.

I also offer my humble thanks to the excellent team at Crown, including but not limited to Maya Mavjee, Molly Stern, Zachary Wagman, Jill Flaxman, Jay Sones, David Drake, Annsley Rosner, Sarah Breivogel, Linda Kaplan, Karin Schulze, Marysarah Quinn, Nupoor Gordon, Cindy Berman, Domenica Alioto, Christine Kopprasch, Jacqui Lebow, Christine Edwards, Andy Augusto, and Kristen Fleming. And I can never heap enough praise on the amazing, top-notch sales force. The reps are on the front lines of an ultra-competitive, ever-changing business. I know that my books find their way into the hands of readers largely through their tireless efforts on my behalf.

My family and friends continue to cheer me through the good days and drag me through the challenging ones. Thanks to my parents, Joe and Virginia Miscione, and to my brother and his wife, Joe and Tara, for their love, support, and for endlessly spreading the word. I haven't published a thing that the dear, funny, and talented Heather Mikesell hasn't read first. Marion Chartoff and Tara Popick, my two oldest friends, have been with me on this journey every step of the way.

About the Author

LISA UNGER is an award-winning *New York Times* and international best-selling author. Her novels have sold over one million copies in the United States and have been translated into twenty-six different languages.

She was born in New Haven, Connecticut, but grew up in the Netherlands, England, New Jersey, and New York, where she graduated from the New School for Social Research. Lisa now divides her time, along with her husband and daughter, between Florida and New York City.